THE PICK,
THE SPADE
AND THE CROW

ALSO BY BILL ROGERS

BILL ROGERS

THE PICK, THE SPADE AND THE CROW

THOMAS & MERCER

Text copyright © 2016 Bill Rogers

Published by Thomas & Mercer, Seattle

www.apub.com

Amazon, the Amazon logo, and Thomas & Mercer are trademarks of Amazon.com, Inc., or its affiliates.

ISBN-13: 9781503938304
ISBN-10: 1503938301

Cover design by Stuart Bache

Printed in the United States of America

This book is NOT dedicated to the literary agent who told me, in front of a packed room of aspiring Third Age writers at the Theakstons Old Peculier Crime Writing Festival, that anyone over fifty-five was too old.

Instead, it is dedicated to Amazon Publishing, who prefer to let you, the reader, decide.

Chapter 1

He was going to die. He had sensed it from the moment that he was taken. Now he was certain. One question gnawed his brain, like the rat he had heard scuttling across the cold concrete floor.

Why?

The longer he tormented himself, the more torturous it became. What little time remained should have been spent remembering everyone who had ever loved him, arriving at a gradual resignation born of the knowledge that he was loved, had made his mark and left a legacy. Instead, he was forced to rummage through the murky corners of his mind to which he had consigned his dirty little secrets.

In this dark, confined space it was easy to imagine himself behind the grill, a fug of stale tobacco on an unwashed habit, heavy breathing, and a hint of communion wine. Seven years old, his First Confession, stumbling through the litany.

'. . . *In my thoughts and in my words, in what I have done, and in what I have failed to do . . .*'

And yet, in the grand scheme of things, nothing he had ever done, or failed to do, had been more than a minor transgression. Not one of them a capital offence. Not even close. And so he shifted focus from why he deserved to die, to what it was that he had to lose.

His most precious possessions were his wife and the modest four-bedroom detached in parkland on the outskirts of a market town. Most recent valuation, three hundred and ninety thousand pounds. That would go to Harriet, free of mortgage. There was his life insurance. A company car. Three ISAs for a rainy day.

The screech of metal on metal set his teeth on edge. He curled into a ball in the corner, knees tucked to his chest, arms protecting his head. The door swung back on its hinges, and clanged against the wall. He winced, and waited for a blow, a boot, something, anything. Anything but silence.

A hand grabbed his hair, another the ties that bound his wrists. He was hauled to his feet. He tried to speak, to plead. The gag, dry as leather, scraped against parched lips. The sound he made bore no resemblance to the words that had formed in his brain. He lost his footing, and was dragged backwards into the cool night air.

His feet, loosely bound, grazed against a hard slippery surface. He winced in pain as his back rammed into a metal object. His legs were raised, his feet gripped. He was propelled backwards. His head slammed against an immovable object.

There was a moment of surreal calm before his senses tuned in. The crown of his head throbbed. A dull ache pulsed across his temples. His wrists burned. The pain in his spine was unendurable. He forced himself to concentrate beyond his body.

He could hear the low growl of an engine, and the hum of the road surface, every pothole, deceleration and sudden turn, a jolt of electricity. The floorpan beneath him was wet. There was a familiar musty smell. He had voided what little had been left in his bladder. He listened in vain for the sound of other vehicles.

Close to delirium, his mind wandered to their first holiday, just him and Harriet. They had set off at midnight, travelling through the night to avoid the traffic. He had stopped in a lay-by north of Torquay to watch the sun rise above the seven hills. Beside him, his wife slept soundly. A shaft of light had crept up the side of the valley, and bathed them in a golden glow. It had been a moment of wonder, of fulfilment, and of searing love. He began to weep.

The engine cut out. The vehicle rolled slowly forward, and came to a gentle stop. There was a muted curse. A man's voice, he thought. The engine started up again, and they set off.

Perhaps ten minutes had passed when he was flung against the side of the vehicle and then back to the centre. The surface beneath the wheels felt rough and slippery. As the vehicle lurched from side to side, the gag choked off his screams of pain.

The vehicle stopped. There was a scuffling noise, the sound of metal on metal, and then silence. Time passed.

He heard the rear doors open. His legs were grasped in a vice-like grip. His body was pulled forward, and then lowered to the floor. The ground was cold against his head. He heard the crunch of feet on leaves as he was dragged, his head bouncing helplessly. His back struck something hard. Pain erupted in his spine. They stopped. Now he was suspended in mid-air as though in a hammock. He was carried forward. Now he was being lowered. Lower. And lower. And lower. Finally, he came to rest.

His body began to shake uncontrollably. The gag caused his jaw to dislocate. He felt the tarpaulin on which he had lain dragged from beneath him. Something cold and hard hooked beneath his blindfold, and ripped it from his eyes. It was dark. Gradually his eyes began to focus.

He could see the black skeletal shape of naked branches against a steel-grey curtain of sky. Scudding clouds obscured the stars. Now there was a figure, a sinister shadow, bending over the side of the pit. A hard rain began to fall, splattering his face and body. Covering his mouth and eyes. Blotting out the sky. Erasing his life.

Chapter 2

'DI Stuart, it's good to see you again.'

Barbara Bryce gestured towards one of three casual chairs in an otherwise minimally furnished office. Jo sat down. The Deputy Director smiled.

'You look bemused.' Her penetrating grey eyes scanned Jo's face. 'Let me guess. You're wondering why the National Crime Agency approached GMP to see if they were prepared to offer you a secondment. Am I right?'

Jo nodded.

'Well, yes, I am.'

'That's easy. It's because you're a bloody good detective, you have the experience and the skill set we're looking for and – although if you repeat this, I'll deny I ever said it – because you're a woman.'

Jo frowned.

'And you needn't look so shocked,' said Bryce. 'The Agency is man-heavy. We inherited most of our staff from the Serious and Organised Crime Agency, and the bulk of them, no pun intended, came from the Met. Neither they, nor the Border Agency and Her Majesty's Customs and Excise, where the rest have come from, have a brilliant track record for gender balance in senior roles.'

The Deputy Director leaned back in her orange executive chair.

'You needn't worry. Your secondment is in line with our diversity and equality policy. When we have several candidates meeting the person specification, we will always appoint the candidate from the least represented category of employees. But in this case your gender was never the deciding factor. As far as the job is concerned, you've been there and done it. Furthermore, we take our recruitment very seriously, particularly where the post involves especially sensitive or stressful work.'

She rocked gently in her chair as she considered how best to proceed. She sat upright, and placed her hands on the arms of her chair.

'Okay,' she said. 'Let's talk about the elephant in the room, the undercover operation that went wrong. Not your fault, but it very nearly cost you your life.'

'It was nobody's fault,' said Jo. 'Other than the perpetrator.'

'Be that as it may, you were still seconds away from becoming his next victim.'

'But I didn't. And I don't regard myself as having been a victim in any way.'

Bryce nodded.

'I know. And I also know that you haven't allowed that experience to affect your operational ability. Which is another reason why we were eager to have you join us.'

Jo felt herself beginning to blush. Not with embarrassment, but with irritation bordering on anger.

'So because I was abducted, restrained, and assaulted by a serial killer, that makes me an ideal candidate for what exactly? Criminal Profiling?'

'Our Behavioural Sciences Unit,' the Deputy Director replied. 'The BSU. We don't like the term criminal profiling for reasons that I hope will become clear.'

'Good,' Jo retorted. 'Because I'm a detective, not a psychologist. It's what I do, and it's what I enjoy doing.'

Bryce nodded.

'Just as well, because that's what we wanted you for. What we *need* you for. We have crime analysts, and behavioural profilers. What we need are investigators capable of working with, and liaising between, our Serious Crime Analysis Section, of which the BSU is a part, and senior investigating officers in all other UK forces.'

Jo felt her anger beginning to subside.

'So it isn't because you thought that what I experienced made me better able to get inside the perpetrator's mind?'

The Deputy Director smiled broadly.

'Whatever made you think that? We want you despite what happened, not because of it. We just had to be sure that you were fully recovered. For your sake as much as ours.'

'I'm sorry,' Jo began. 'I thought . . .'

Barbara Bryce raised her hand again.

'You've nothing to be sorry about. In your shoes I'd probably have felt the same.'

She leaned forward and pressed the intercom on her desk.

'We'll have those drinks now, please.' She turned to Jo. 'Coffee, tea, or something else?'

'Coffee's fine. A splash of milk.'

'That's two Americanos, one with a dash of milk, and two glasses of water.'

She settled back, hands clasped in her lap.

'Just remind me,' she said, 'of the path your career has taken up to this point.'

Jo was surprised. Bryce had clearly checked her record before approaching GMP, so where was this heading? There was no point in trying to second-guess her. She gave a mental shrug, and began.

'After I passed out from the National Police Training Centre at Bruche, I did two years on the beat. By then I knew that what I really wanted to do was become a detective. I applied for the Professionalising Investigation Programme, and took the sexual offences option.'

She paused to check that she wasn't giving too much or too little detail. The Deputy Director's demeanour reassured her.

'I joined the North Manchester CID on Division for four years, everything from shoplifting and muggings, to robbery and indecent assault. Sometimes I worked on eight different cases at the same time.'

'You worked Vice at some point?'

'Two years of it. Not my favourite posting. But I did get experience in undercover work.'

She paused. But for that, she would never have placed herself at the mercy of a killer. The door opened. Jo waited until she had been handed her coffee, took a sip, put the cup back down, and carried on.

'I took my Sergeants' exam, and then had to wait two years for a substantive post. My lucky break. It was with the Force Major Incident Team. DCI Caton's team.'

Her eyes shone with remembered excitement.

'We only covered cases like murder, serial murder, abduction, serial rape too, before they set up the Serious Sexual Offences Unit. DCI Caton encouraged me to take my remaining PIPs courses and OSPRE exams, and go before the Inspectors Board. That's it.'

The Deputy Director smiled, and nodded.

'A meteoric rise, and one that explains why you're a perfect fit. Specialisation is the key, Stuart. Crime and criminals are changing along with the technology. We have to be ahead of the game, not behind it. The skills needed to catch a serial killer, a paedophile, or a serial rapist are very different from those needed to catch a fraudster

7

or an armed robber. Especially when it comes to dealing with the victims. We have brought together some of the best, and by that I mean most intelligent, skilful and experienced officers, in all areas of serious and organised crime.'

She rubbed the knees of her trousers distractedly as though scratching an itch.

'I won't pretend that we have enough resources but we still have some of the most up-to-date technology and data gathering systems at our disposal. But it's still the human resource that remains paramount. The BSU is a small unit consisting of two identically staffed teams. Each has a civilian psychologist with a doctorate in criminal forensic psychology, a senior intelligence officer, and experienced senior investigators, plus appropriate administrative staff. The unit has been based at the College of Policing, at Bramshill House. You may have heard that it's just been sold?'

'A lot of people will miss it,' Jo said.

'The College of Policing has moved to Ascot, and the European Police College is off to Budapest.'

'And the BSU?' asked Jo, wondering how she would break it to Abbie that this meant a move to Berkshire. It would mean an end to the secondment.

'Team A has moved to Sunningdale. Team B, your team, is on its way . . .' she paused dramatically, her eyes full of mischief, '. . . to your neck of the woods. Salford Quays, to be precise.'

Jo smiled with relief.

'I thought that would cheer you up,' said the Deputy Director. 'If you hurry, you'll be in time to help them settle in.'

She stood, and came out from behind her desk.

'I'll introduce you to our Head of Human Resources. Just a couple of forms to sign, some i's to dot and t's to cross. Your car will be delivered tomorrow morning.'

She held out her hand.

'Welcome aboard, Senior Investigating Officer Stuart,' she said. 'I don't think you'll regret it.'

Chapter 3

It was seven in the evening when Jo arrived at the secure communal entrance to the apartment building. At the centre of the bohemian Northern Quarter, it housed sixty loft apartments above a score of retail businesses, including creative art-and-design enterprises, bars and an eclectic mix of restaurants. She and Abbie had only moved into their apartment a month ago. Abbie had argued that this was exactly what they needed. A place that would suit their urban lifestyle, give them more space and time for each other, and to start a family. Jo had bought into all of that. Now, a month shy of her thirty-third birthday, she was beginning to ask herself why.

She stepped into the airy foyer, placed her bag and document case beside one of the ornate iron pillars, and sat down on the edge of a wooden trough. She looked up at the trunk of the three-metre-tall ornamental tree to where it reached up past the mezzanine that housed their apartment, and into the glass and steel vaulted roof space. She knew from their text exchanges that Abbie had finished her shift, and would be up there waiting for her. She would have to wait a little longer for Jo to gather her thoughts.

When Jo had broken the news that she had been invited to join the NCA, Abbie had pretended to be pleased because she could tell that Jo was both flattered and excited by the prospect, but it was obvious that she had reservations. Uppermost was her concern that this would set back their plans to become a family. Jo shook her head. Who am I kidding, she thought? Not our plans, *her* plans.

For several years she and Abbie had skirted around the issue. Early in their relationship they had agreed that being a parent at some stage was on the agenda for both of them. But Abbie's maternal instinct was by far the stronger of the two. For her, the clock was ticking.

They had talked interminably about the alternatives, such as fostering, adoption, AID by donor, with or without a surrogate mother. In the end, Abbie had told her that she needed to experience the joy of carrying and delivering her own child. She had found a donor, she said. A friend from university who was also gay.

'Think about it, Jo,' she'd said. 'We will know the father. James is healthy, he rowed for London Uni, and he got a double first in Economics. He's got a lovely personality. Just wait till you meet him.'

In the end, Jo gave in. She suspected that for Abbie there would always be a void that nothing could fill. The very least she could do was be as supportive as possible. Her reservations were complicated. It wasn't that she didn't want to be a parent – just that she had no idea how she could do justice to that and still pursue her career. Raising a child was an awesome responsibility.

Jo had seen far too many examples of children starved of love and affection, denied the real attention and active listening that enabled them to grow with confidence, and develop self-esteem. Lonely, lost and angry children with self-centred parents or broken homes, who became self-harmers, fell into bad company, and emerged either as victim or perpetrator. For God's sake, she had come perilously close to that herself. She had to shake her head to chase the memories away.

The front door of an apartment slammed shut, the thud echoing around the mezzanine. There were footsteps immediately above her, followed by the sound of clacking heels on bare wooden treads as someone descended the floating stairway. Jo sighed, and stood up. It was time to face the music.

Abbie stood waiting in the open-plan lounge. Despite her broad smile and open arms, in the shadows from the downlights she looked tired and apprehensive.

'You must be knackered,' Abbie said, hugging her a little tighter and a little longer than normal. 'I'm putting the final touches to dinner. Why don't you go and freshen up, and slip into something comfortable? I'll have a drink ready for you.'

'Aren't you going to ask me if I took it?' said Jo warily.

Abbie was already walking away towards the galley kitchen.

'Of course you did,' she said in a tone that was impossible to decipher. 'You can tell me all about it when you've changed.'

Jo picked up her bags, and went into the bedroom. She dropped them on the floor, kicked off her shoes, and flopped down on the bed. The confrontation would have to wait. Abbie was the one who hated fierce conversations, which was surprising given her job. A staff nurse must have to deal with all sorts of stressful situations – tardy staff, demanding patients, arrogant consultants, and hard-pressed managers.

Jo's gaze moved from the exposed brickwork to the wooden beams. Hard unyielding surfaces, softened only by the green and purple blinds, and matching duvet. She sighed, and swung her legs off the bed. No point in prevaricating, it only made it worse. Hopefully everything would feel different after a shower and stiff drink.

The table was set with their best place mats, napkins and wine glasses. Floating candles vied with flower petals in a glass bowl. Abbie came towards her carrying two glasses of what looked suspiciously like champagne.

'A double celebration,' said Abbie, handing her a glass.

'Double?'

Abbie took her arm and led her to the sofa.

'I think you'd better sit down.'

'Now you've got me worried,' said Jo.

They sat side by side, their glasses suspended in mid-air, the pale liquid untouched, bubbles popping gently. Abbie raised her glass.

'Like I said, a double celebration. To your new job, and to mine.'

Jo sipped the champagne, and placed her glass on the coffee table.

'You've kept that quiet.'

Abbie twirled her glass by its stem, and relaxed back on the sofa.

'I didn't want to say anything. I didn't want to do anything that might influence you one way or the other. Besides, I wasn't sure I'd get it.'

'Have you been promoted? It's about time.'

'Something completely different.' Her sip was hesitant. 'With a drug company.'

'Abbie!' Jo began.

'And before you say anything, hear me out. I know what you're thinking. That I've crossed to the dark side. Betrayed everything I believed in. Well, you're wrong. Okay, I admit I've become increasingly frustrated with the cuts, the staff shortages, the mindless targets, the management threats and snap inspections. But that's not the real reason.'

She reached across, relieved Jo of her glass, placed it beside her own, held Jo's hand and stared straight into her eyes.

'I know our starting a family isn't as high on your agenda,' she said, squeezing Jo's hand to prevent her from interrupting. 'But I also know that's only because you're scared about how we'll make it work. Well, I've found a way. This job is based in Manchester. I can work from home and, providing I put the hours in, it's up to me how I organise them. Virtually all of the team meetings, and most of the training, will be by video conferencing. That means I'll be able to drop the children off at school and pick them up. When the schools are on holiday, I'll be around far more than most parents. And I can do my paperwork in the evenings and at weekends when you'll want to be having some quality time with them.'

It had all come out in a rush. She took a deep breath.

'What d'you think, Jo? I can always tell them I've changed my mind.'

Her eyes searched Jo's face for the slightest clue. Jo placed her other hand over Abbie's, and squeezed.

'Of course you must take it,' she said. 'It sounds like a great opportunity.'

She put her glass down and stood up.

'Where are you going?' asked Abbie.

'To the loo,' said Jo. 'Must be the champagne.'

Jo splashed her face with cold water, mopped it dry, and replaced the towel on the heated rail. She turned, gripped the marble sink surround, and stared into the mirror at a face full of angst.

'*Children*?' she muttered. 'How many does she have in mind?'

Chapter 4

Jo stared into a glass bubble above the large green button, and spoke her name. Beyond the barrier three blue and yellow striped retractable posts disappeared into the tarmac. The barrier rose silently. She drove in hesitantly, expecting one of the posts to appear at any moment through the floor of her brand-new Audi A4 hatchback.

The northern hub of the NCA's Behavioural Sciences Unit was on the fourth floor of ten in one of the many anonymous glass and steel buildings lining the edge of the Salford Dock basin of the Manchester Ship Canal.

Three males cloned from an ex-military template manned the reception area. Early fifties, identical navy sports jackets and grey flannels, stocky build, erect bearing, hard, suspicious gaze. Two were seated at the desk, one stood beside revolving doors set into a toughened glass screen that appeared to be the only access to the lifts and stairs beyond. There was an almost imperceptible raise of the concierge's eyebrows as he checked Jo's ID on the computer. He grunted, and handed her a form.

'Write your car registration on here, please, Ma'am,' he said. 'Then sign at the bottom.'

He handed her a temporary security pass on a chain.

'Till you get your own, Miss Stuart.' He held out a brown fools-cap envelope in his other hand. 'And this arrived for you.'

She placed it in her document bag, pulled the chain over her head and walked to the revolving doors.

Male number three stepped forward.

'I'm sorry, Ma'am, but I'll need your pass.'

It was swiped against a panel attached to the door frame. He handed it back.

'Go ahead, Ma'am,' he said. 'You're on the Fourth Floor, Sector A. Lifts three through six.'

She had no option but to turn right out of the lift. Sector A was immediately ahead of her. There was a speakerphone, and another electronic swipe pad. She tried her visitors' pass, and was greeted with a red light. She pressed the buzzer for the phone. There was no response.

While she waited, Jo took the brown envelope from her bag and opened it. Inside were several forms from Human Resources, and a shiny new security pass with her photo on it. It must have been couriered overnight. She tried the pass against the pad, and was rewarded with a green light, followed by a buzz and a click. She pushed the door open with her shoulder as she bent to retrieve her bag, then stepped through the doorway and into the corridor.

Fifteen metres ahead of her, a man rounded the corner. In his late twenties she guessed, British Asian, good-looking enough to have stepped out of a Bollywood film set. He looked flustered, but pleased to see her.

'You must be Stuart,' he said. 'I'm Shah. Ram Shah. Welcome to the Mad House.'

'I wouldn't know about mad,' she replied. 'But it's certainly secure.'

He grinned.

'I don't know who else is resident here but they must have a hell of a lot of secrets to hide,' he said.

She followed him around the corner, down another corridor, and into a room three metres wide by ten long, with windows along two of the sides. Empty crates were stacked along the walls. Bubble wrap and polystyrene packing was strewn across the floor. Unopened crates stood on desks alongside monitor screens and desk tidies. Cables snaked in untidy jumbles. She counted three men in blue overalls beavering away on or under desks, with two other men in jeans and T-shirts anxiously supervising.

'I've come at a bad time,' she said. 'Why don't I come back later?'

Shah laughed.

'Nice try. We need all the help we can get, and if you're not careful you'll end up with the desk next to the Xerox machine.'

He clapped his hands, and shouted to get their attention.

'Guys! This is SI Stuart.'

'Jo,' she told him.

'Correction,' he said. 'It's Jo. Another pair of hands.'

One of the T-shirted men turned, straightened up, and nodded. He looked harassed, but managed a smile and a nod of acknowledgement before turning back to talk to the technician kneeling by his side. The other one was even more preoccupied and ignored them completely.

'Max!' shouted Shah. 'This is Jo, our new colleague.'

Without looking up, the man named Max pointed across the room. 'Over there,' he muttered. 'Her desk is over there.'

'I'm sorry about that,' said Shah. 'It's been a bit fraught. Some of our most sensitive stuff hasn't arrived.'

'Don't worry,' Jo told him. 'Just show me what you want me to do.'

Three hours later, some semblance of order had been achieved. Five of the desks had their own workstations up and running. The majority of the cables had disappeared mysteriously beneath the floor panels. Jo's three colleagues were busily checking that the data on their computers had come through the move unscathed. Apart from visits to the newly installed water dispenser, none of them had had anything to eat or drink all morning. Jo stood up, and stretched.

'I don't know about you guys,' she said. 'But I could do with a break. Does anyone fancy a coffee and a bite to eat?'

'Brilliant idea!' Shah exclaimed. 'What about you, Andy?'

The man sitting immediately opposite Ram appeared not to have heard.

'Andy!' said Ram.

The man looked up. He had short brown curly hair, intelligent hazel eyes, and smile lines around his mouth. Jo placed him in his mid-forties. He wore brown cargo pants, trainers and a T-shirt on which was printed an image of what looked like the top half of a scooter, below the logo LIFE BEHIND BARS.

'No need to shout,' he said. 'It'll be a chance to get to know our colleague a little better under less stressful conditions.'

He stood up, arm outstretched, and crossed to Jo's desk.

'Andy Swift,' he said. 'Good to have you on board, Jo.'

He was around five foot nine, a couple of inches taller than her. His grip firm but friendly.

'Thanks,' she replied. 'I'm looking forward to working with you all . . . I think.'

His smile broadened. He bent and stage-whispered in her ear.

'I don't blame you for being cautious. We're all a bit weird, but it's not always like this.'

'No, it's usually far worse,' Ram Shah confided. 'What about you, Max? Are you going to join us, or are you afraid to unplug your umbilical cord?'

The man snorted, clicked his touchpad and scooted his seat away from the desk.

'I've just had a heads-up on a possible job,' he said. 'I had to respond or it would look like we didn't care.'

'Or maybe that we were in the middle of moving offices?' said Shah.

Max used the arms of his chair to lever himself up. For the first time she realised how much bigger than the others he was. Six foot three, pushing fourteen and a half stone, broad-shouldered, with just a little thickening at the waist. Like a rugby player who had begun to neglect his fitness. His mid-blond hair, curling up on the nape of his neck, was due a cut. A day's stubble on his chin and dark shadows beneath his eyes made her wonder if he had had a sleepless night. He walked across to join them.

'Max Nailor,' he said, towering over her. He offered her a hand the size of a bear's paw. She shook it, and was surprised at his listless grip.

'I'm Jo,' she said.

'I gathered.' He had a Home Counties accent with just a trace of the East End. 'I hope you know what you're doing. It's not exactly the cut and thrust you'll have been used to.'

He turned to Shah.

'This had better not be another bloody vegetarian.'

'For the last time,' Shah replied. 'I'm not a vegetarian. But neither am I, unlike some, prepared to stuff myself with meat of indeterminate origin coated in fried fat of equally dubious heritage.'

'Get over yourself,' said Max. 'Where are we going?'

'I don't know,' said Shah. 'Like you, I'm a stranger to these parts. I thought we'd ask a native.'

The three of them stared at Joanne Stuart. She was momentarily disconcerted by their combined gaze.

'Only we were led to believe you actually live round here?' said Andy Swift.

'I do, sort of,' she said. 'And you're in luck. There must be at least a dozen or so bars and restaurants within four minutes of here. Italian, Chinese, Asian fusion, traditional British pub grub, there's even a branch of The Pie Factory in Media City.'

'I only want a coffee,' said Andy Swift, 'a sandwich, so long as it's vegan, and a walk in the fresh air.'

'Me too,' said Shah. 'What about you, Max?'

Nailor shoved his hands in his trouser pockets and shrugged.

'Penelope's Kitchen is as good as anywhere,' Jo told them. 'We shouldn't need to queue unless there's a film crew in. We can walk along the side of the quay. Four minutes at most.'

'Sounds perfect,' said Swift. '"Lay on, Macduff, and damned be him that first cries 'Hold, enough!'"'

'It's not Macduff. It's Stuart,' quipped Shah as he headed for the door.

Chapter 5

They strolled along beside the North Quay in unseasonably warm November sunshine. On the opposite bank, the sun's rays lit up the glass and steel of the Lowry Theatre. They stopped to watch a pair of swans dip their heads in the water.

Andy Swift had removed a camera from his backpack, and was snapping away. When they set off again, Nailor was twenty paces ahead of them.

'Looks like Max had a rough night?' said Jo.

'Rough year,' said Shah.

Andy Swift held up his camera. 'Got some amazing shots.'

'Do you do a lot of photography?' Jo asked. But he bounded ahead and began photographing the Lowry Theatre on the opposite bank.

'It's one of his little obsessions,' said Shah, leaving Jo to wonder what the others might be.

They had reached the end of the basin. Nailor was standing by the foot of the bridge staring across the piazza at the television studios.

'We're over here,' said Jo, pointing to the right.

She led them between the University of Salford Media Studies building, and a large long single-storey construction that was The Pie Factory. Hidden away at the rear was Penelope's Kitchen. Several dozen people were seated outside the red-brick cafe in deck-chairs, and at picnic tables on wooden decking. Inside the cafe, long wooden communal tables, the low ceiling and long counters gave the feel of a student refectory. They found four spaces at the end of one of the tables.

'Who are all these people?' asked Andy Swift.

'TV crew, cast members, media students, and residents of the quay, people who've done their shopping at Booths supermarket next door. Welcome to the Northern Powerhouse.'

Shah chose the Kickin Chicken, Jo a halloumi salad, and Andy Swift the vegan falafel and vegetable kebab.

'What about you, Max?' asked Shah.

Nailor seemed listless and preoccupied. Shah nudged him gently with his elbow, and pointed to the menu.

'If you like meat, I can recommend the Kevin Bacon double burger with fries,' said Jo.

'Okay,' he said. 'And a coffee.'

'Wow!' said Shah. 'Would you look at that. A heart attack on a plate.'

Nailor ignored him. He was far too busy. His golden brioche with its stack of succulent burgers, smothered in American cheese, fragrant onions and crispy bacon was disappearing at a rate of knots, not to mention his side order of fries.

By the time they had finished eating, the crowd had diminished considerably but they still had too many close neighbours for easy conversation. At the far end of the room, a couple of sofas with a coffee table between them had just been vacated. They took their refills there.

'Where are you all staying?' Jo asked.

'Max and I are next door in the Holiday Inn,' said Ram. 'We're both looking for somewhere to rent to start with.'

'Together?'

He chuckled.

'You must be joking. We'd probably kill each other.'

'That's the truth,' muttered Nailor.

'You won't be stuck for choice,' she told them. 'There are hundreds and hundreds of apartments within walking distance of the office, thousands within a couple of stops on the Metro.'

'My family and I are staying at the serviced apartments on the other side of the BBC Studios,' Andy Swift told her.

'You have children?'

'Holly and Oliver. She's nine, and he's seven. Rachel, my wife, has just secured the post of Deputy Director of Student Support at a local high school. The children have got places at one of the feeder primaries. Now all we have to do is find a house.'

'Your wife's a teacher?'

'A counsellor. That's how we met. We were both studying Psychology at Surrey University.'

'I worked as a clinical psychologist for ten years,' Swift continued. 'Then I studied for a Masters in Investigative Psychology. When I completed my PhD, I joined the faculty at the International Research Centre in Investigative Psychology.'

'I can see why the National Crime Agency wanted to poach you,' Jo said.

His phone rang. He glanced at the screen.

'I'd better answer this,' he said. 'It's Harry.'

'Harry Stone,' Shah confided. 'Deputy Director of Specialist Services. Our boss.'

'Yep, Boss,' said Swift. 'We're just a few minutes away in Media City, having a coffee.'

He glanced across at Joanne Stuart.

'She's here with us. Helped us move in. Worked her socks off. We all did. That's why we reckoned we'd earned . . .'

He glanced at Nailor.

'Yes, he did mention something about . . . Oh, right. We're on our way. Be with you in five.'

He ended the call, put the phone in his pocket and stood up.

'Time to go. Harry's waiting for us to let him into the office.'

'Story of our lives,' complained Shah. 'It's either feast or famine.'

Jo liked the sound of that.

Chapter 6

'Tell me about Harry,' she said as they hurried down Broadway.

'He's a good bloke,' said Shah. 'A great boss. Late fifties . . .'

'Fifty-five.'

'He was a Chief Superintendent in the Met,' Shah continued. 'Then he joined the Serious and Organised Crime Agency. When it changed into the NCA, he was a shoo-in for Deputy Director Specialist Services.'

'He's trying hard to build bridges between the Regional Forces, us, and our Missing Persons and Child Exploitation and Online Protection teams,' said Swift. 'He's very protective of his staff.'

'He still lives in London so he has to come up to the regional headquarters in Risley every week. Stays over sometimes, but more often than not he commutes.'

'Must be difficult for his family?' said Jo.

Shah slowed down until Swift and Nailor were well ahead of them, and then lowered his voice.

'He lost his wife to breast cancer a couple of years ago. One way or another, his elderly mother and his daughter are giving him hell. You're better not asking about his family. He's stressed out at work, and at home, and he's lonely. To tell the truth, we're all worried about him. Well, Andy and I are. Max is too bound up in his own problems.'

He pushed open the doors to their building, and waited for Jo to enter.

'There he is now.'

Stone had his back to them, and was talking to Swift and Nailor. He reminded Jo of Gordon Holmes from her old team. Medium height for a man, built like a tank. His hair was turning salt and pepper with a broad black badger streak. He turned around.

'Harry Stone,' he said, holding out a hand only marginally smaller than Nailor's. 'Sorry I missed you in London, I was called away.'

It was a North London accent, resonant with natural authority.

'Good to meet you, Guv,' she said.

He smiled at her use of the term.

'This lot call me Boss – among other things. You can do the same, Jo. Guv reminds me too much of the Met.'

His eyes were sharp and bright, not yet clouded by age or bitter experience, but worry lines were scored around his eyes, mouth and across his forehead. She instinctively felt sorry for him.

'Come on,' Stone said. 'Take me upstairs and show me what you've been doing all morning, then I'll give you the good news.'

———

They were in a small corner room, around an oval table. Stone handed each of them a brown folder.

'This is it,' he said. 'One extra for our new Senior Investigator.'

The title page was succinct.

Operation Hound
Murder Investigation
Victim – Charles Deighton

Jo turned the page and stared at the headshot of a man, presumably a passport photo, looking directly into camera. It was the sort of image that might have been chosen to represent the average middle-aged Caucasian male.

Charles Deighton was fifty-seven years of age when he died. Married with no children. A civil servant with thirty-seven years behind him as a higher executive officer with Her Majesty's Revenue and Customs. If she remembered rightly that was where most fast-stream graduates started. Either he had reached his competency ceiling early on, or he had lacked ambition. His body had been found in Birkacre Woods, Chorley, a Lancashire market town twenty miles or so to the west of Manchester.

The next photograph showed the corpse in situ. All but skel-etonised, the victim lay on his back, empty eye sockets staring back at her. The jaws were open and distorted, as though he had been trying to scream. A fibrous mass filled the hole behind his teeth. Both hands lay across the lower part of the ribcage, still held together by what looked like a cable tie.

'Might never have been found,' said Stone, 'had the dog not chased something into the woods. And even then it might not have flagged up as suspicious if his owner hadn't been a former police dog handler. What are the odds of that?'

'Was it a retired police dog?' Nailor wondered.

'No. It was a sheep dog he got to keep him company. He'd trained it though.'

'What flagged it up as suspicious?' asked Shah, who seemed happy to hear the story first and read it for himself later.

Jo was reading intently. 'A depression in the ground that didn't look right,' she told him. 'That and the fact that the dog had started digging. Fortunately, he had the good sense to pull the dog away, mark the spot, and contact his former boss.'

'I doubt they'd have followed up on it if he'd been Joe Public,' said Stone. 'As it was, they could easily have missed the victim. When the body dog the Division sent got excited, they started a proper forensic search, only to discover the skeletal remains of a cat half a metre down.'

'A cat? In a wood?' said Nailor.

'From the size of the original depression,' Stone continued. 'They'd been expecting at worst to find a child. Maybe a baby, still-born or aborted. When they found the cat, I bet they didn't know whether to be relieved or pissed off that they'd wasted their time.'

'What made them keep digging?' asked Shah.

'The dog was still antsy. The handler insisted that he was marking something other than the cat. They dug down two more feet, and uncovered two planks. The victim's remains were a foot below the planks.'

'Why go to all that trouble?' said Swift.

'You're the psychologist,' said Shah, 'you tell us.'

'Well,' he replied, 'take the cat. It could either be a distractor, in the sense that if the grave was disturbed, say by an animal, anyone finding the cat's remains would simply ignore it, or fill it in again.'

'Or?' said Ram Shah.

'Or it could have a particular meaning for the perpetrator. A lot of serial murderers cut their teeth on cats. Killing and skinning them when they were teenagers, or even younger.'

'I've never come across one being buried with a corpse though,' said Shah. 'Not unless it was an old lady's last request.'

'I bet it was a distractor,' said Jo. 'We know that as a result of decomposition a body buried directly into the ground always leaves a shallow depression on the surface. If that was spotted, as it was by our retired police dog handler, finding the cat might have had the result that Andy hypothesised, except that it probably wouldn't have done without the planks.'

'Go on,' said Stone.

'According to the crime scene report, the two planks together were longer and wider than the victim's body. By placing them above the body, our unidentified subject ensured that there would not be any additional surface depression resulting from the decomposition of the corpse. Even though a void would have formed under the planks, the foot of soil on top of them would have remained level. No one would suspect there was another corpse beneath the cat.'

Stone nodded thoughtfully. 'This is a highly organised perpetrator.'

'I can't see anyone bringing planks with them to a dump site,' said Shah.

'The local team think they were probably taken from a building site close to the crime scene,' she told him.

'*Think*, and *probably*, doesn't suggest a very thorough investigation,' observed Nailor.

'The body had been in the ground for more than ten years,' Harry Stone pointed out. 'Finding out if a couple of planks had gone missing from a building site after all that time would be a big call, even assuming the firm was still in business.'

'Even so, it suggests someone thinking on their feet,' said Jo.

'Indeterminate cause of death,' Nailor pointed out. 'Not surprising, given the length of time he's been in the ground. No signs of physical injury, such as blunt trauma to the skull, no evidence of bone damage associated with stabbing or shooting.'

'He could have been poisoned,' suggested Shah.

'No trace of that in the hair samples they took,' said Jo. 'And he wasn't strangled because the hyoid bone was intact.'

The room went quiet for a moment as they read on. His jaw had been dislocated. Possibly by the effort of fighting to expel the monkey gag – expertly knotted from one-centimetre-diameter rope – that had been forced into his mouth. Cable ties were still around his wrists, and rope remains looped loosely around the ankle bones. There was severe damage to the bones of both hands. The middle phalanx had been fractured, and the distal and proximal interphalangeal joints had been dislocated. There were abrasions to the distal phalanges, the tips of the fingers. These were not consistent with the fingers having been stretched, or smashed as you might expect from torture or punishment. The pathologist's conclusion was far more horrific.

'Buried alive,' said Shah. 'The poor beggar was scrabbling with his hands to claw his way out.'

'Or to create a pocket of air to breathe in,' said Nailor.

Jo shook her head.

'All the time knowing that he didn't have a hope in hell.'

'What kind of sick bastard buries someone alive, and sticks a dead cat on top for good measure?' wondered Shah.

'That's what the local force are hoping we can tell them,' said Harry Stone.

'Without a motive or any suspects it won't be easy,' Shah reflected.

'Which is precisely why it landed on our desks.'

Stone looked at his watch.

'I'm afraid I'm going to have to go. I have to get back to Risley, and then catch the last train from Manchester back to Euston. I wanted to bring this investigation over in person so I could welcome you to the team, SI Stuart, and see how you're settling in. From what I've seen, you'll manage fine without me. At this stage, your role is to advise and support. Above all, remember that you're representing the National Crime Agency. Most of the Senior Investigating Officers in the regional police forces you're going to be working with won't have the faintest idea what we're about. They won't thank you for muscling in on their case, especially since the fact that you're involved at all implies that they've failed in some way. You're going to have to be tactful, modest and above all bloody well prepared.'

He waved a hand in the direction of Ram Shah and Andy Swift.

'That's where these two come in. Max too, of course, although he has an investigation of his own that he's working on at the moment. What is it they say? The sum—'

'Is greater than the parts!' said Shah on cue.

It was obvious from the expressions on the faces of the other two that as a rallying call it was something of a spent force. Stone didn't seem to notice. He pushed back his chair and stood.

'Right,' he said, 'I'll leave you to it.'

Chapter 7

Shah placed a folder on her desk.

'It's not a lot to go on.'

'It's alright,' Jo replied. 'I didn't expect much to be honest.'

He shrugged.

'Garbage in, garbage out.'

She held up the five sheets of paper inside the folder.

'It's a start.'

'Don't worry,' he said, 'I'll keep digging. No pun intended.'

He reminded Jo of Detective Constable Hulme, and suddenly she was missing her former colleagues in the Force Major Incident Team, and realising how much lonelier this job felt. *Get a grip*, she told herself. *This is an amazing opportunity.* She sat back, and began to read.

The first report was dated two days ago. It detailed the recovery in America of the bodies of seven females, in separate locations. They had been buried in damp ground. The suspect was a man already in jail for serial murder. There was no mention either way as to whether or not the women had been buried alive.

The second was even less helpful. In Illinois in 1987, a thirty-year-old man and his twenty-six-year-old girlfriend had kidnapped the heir to a media empire with the intention of holding him to ransom. They put him in a wooden box, three feet underground with water and some light and air via tubes to the surface. Unfortunately, they had buried him in sandy soil, which seeped into the makeshift box and suffocated him. The couple were currently twenty-eight years into a fifty-five-year sentence.

There followed a series of accounts of murders in the UK carried out as gangland hits, or reprisals. In several cases, there were witness accounts that the burials had taken place while the victim was still alive. None of these had been forensically substantiated. Shah had added a note in which he stated that in the majority of gangland killings the body was disposed of by burning, either in a car or on open ground, to destroy forensic evidence while leaving a message to others thinking of falling foul of the perpetrators.

The remaining pages listed all the different forms of immurement through history, including those in which people had been bricked up or entombed, above the surface or below ground. Fascinating as these were, she could see no connection with the case of Charles Deighton. But she knew better than to discount any of it. Who was to know what was in the mind of the killer. She decided to consult their resident psychologist.

Swift swivelled in his chair, and dragged another across for her to sit on.

'How are you doing?' he asked.

She handed him Shah's analysis.

'See for yourself. There's nothing on the system. The only recent live burials are definitely unrelated, if only because the perpetrators are still in prison. There aren't even enough similarities to explain it as a copycat killing. Everything else is ancient history.'

He skimmed through them, and handed them back.

'In which case,' he said, 'we move to phase two.'

'Which is?'

'The mind of the killer.'

'That sounds like the title of a book, or a film?'

'Add a word, and swap a determiner for a pronoun, and it's both. And a YouTube video.'

She thought about it.

'*Inside* the mind of *a* killer?'

'There you go,' he said. 'The phrase has been used by journalists, neurologists, and psychologists, but never a police officer as far as I'm aware.'

'There's Professor Canter's book,' she said. '*Criminal Shadows: Inside The Mind of the Serial Killer*. I've got it at home. Only I always think of it as just *Criminal Shadows*.'

'That's how everyone refers to it,' he said. 'We can never really get inside the mind of a serial killer, but every such crime casts a shadow that gives us pointers to the narrative the perpetrator has in his head. The story he tells himself that causes him to behave as he does. More often than not it also provides the perpetrator with a justification for his or her actions.'

'So what is the story here?' said Jo, picking up the Operation Hound file. 'What narrative would lead someone to take an inoffensive middle-aged man off the street, drive him to a secluded wood, and bury him alive?'

'Not so secluded,' Swift reminded her. 'A matter of yards from a lane, and less than two hundred from a housing estate.'

'With the presence of mind to cover the body with a compacted layer of soil, put those planks on top, and then place a cat in there as a distractor?'

'What makes you think the cat was placed?'

She leafed through the file until she found the relevant photographs.

'See for yourself.'

The first of the photographs showed the skeleton of the cat lying on its side, curled up with its paws tucked in, as though sleeping. The second was a negative of the same cat overlaid on one of the photos of the remains of Charles Deighton. Notes and arrows on the surface of the composite photo drew attention to the fact that the cat appeared to be lying directly over Deighton's skull.

'The SIO didn't think that was a coincidence,' she said.

Swift nodded.

'Which raises a host of questions.'

'Like what significance did it have for the unsub?'

'And what was he trying to tell us?'

'Surely,' she said, 'the whole point of the planks and the compact soil beneath them, was that whoever found the cat wouldn't bother to dig any further. So the position of the cat relative to the body would never have arisen except in the unsub's mind?'

'Unless the unsub was allowing for the possibility, however remote, that the body beneath *would* be found. And by someone with the presence of mind to take photographs along the way.'

'That's Byzantine thinking.'

'Compatible with a killer with higher-order thinking skills, Jo, which a significant percentage of serial killers possess.'

'So what was he trying to do? Blot out the victim's face? Disrespect him even in death? Recreate something from his childhood? Maybe he had a cat that used to curl up on his head when he was in bed? I had a friend whose cat used to do that.'

Swift was sceptical.

'That suggests a compassionate gesture. It's hardly in keeping with having killed the cat, and buried the victim alive.'

'It would help if we knew whether or not he brought the cat with him, or found it nearby. The same with the planks.'

'That's true. If he came prepared, that would suggest that the cat was integral to the narrative, rather than something improvised.'

'There's nothing in the report,' said Jo. 'But it would be worth asking the senior investigating officer. They must have asked about missing cats in their house-to-house enquiries.'

Andy Swift pointed to the folder. 'Is there anything in there about the position of the body?'

Jo flicked through the photographs and diagrams until she found one with a compass superimposed.

'Here we are,' she said, laying it between them on the table. 'The body is supine, which suggests that he was either dropped or lowered on to his back. Given that he was alive at the time, he might just as easily have landed on his front, and turned over as the earth showered down.'

'That's unlikely,' Swift said. 'The natural response in that position is to rise on all fours, and then stand up. They wanted him to see the sky closing in on him. Didn't it say they found the remains of what they thought was a blindfold?'

Jo nodded.

'He was fully clothed when he was buried. Most of the material had rotted, but there was a blindfold beside the body. There was also a wide strip of blue plastic under his head that trailed out to the left of his skull. Forensics reckoned it was torn from a piece of plastic sheeting.'

Swift leaned back in his chair, and steepled his fingers on his chest.

'So, he's lying on his back, mouth gagged, eyes open, and he can't stand up because the grave isn't wide enough for him to roll over, and in any case his feet are bound, and his hands are tied in front of him. His killer wants to watch as his victim slowly suffocates as the earth piles in.'

Jo placed a second photo beside the first. It showed two skeletal hands, bound at the wrist by a white cable tie, poking through a layer of soil.

'And, because of this, we know that the victim was trying desperately to claw his way out as the soil rained down. As the scenes of crime team excavated all the soil around the hands, and finally reached the torso, the arms must have collapsed into the position shown in the first photo.'

'Do you know anything about body placement for burial?' asked the psychologist.

'Not really. Is it relevant?'

'It is in most cultures,' he told her. 'In Peru, for example, members of the royalty were buried standing upright, as were warriors in some Eastern cultures. In ancient Persia, rulers were buried in a sleeping pose but their servants were buried with them in a crouching position ready to provide service in the afterlife. In Islam, the body is laid on its back, hands by its sides, and with the head turned to face the Kaaba in Mecca, a direction known as the Qibla. In many societies, the body is placed in a foetal position with the knees tucked under the chin.'

'What if a body is face down?' she asked.

'More often than not that is done as a deliberate mark of disrespect. Then there's the direction in which the body is pointing. Some Christian traditions had their priests buried facing the other way so that come the Resurrection they would rise facing their flock, ready to preach to them.'

'I don't see how any of that helps us in relation to Charles Deighton,' she said.

'Neither do I,' he admitted. 'But the first rule of forensic psychology is, "*rule nothing out*".'

He pointed to a photograph on which the compass had been overlaid.

'Looking at this, I very much doubt that the orientation of the body was deliberate. South south-west has never appeared in the lexicon of inhumation rituals as far as I'm aware. It's more likely that the unsub was trying to avoid the roots of the nearby trees.'

He grinned, and Jo wondered if he had been pulling her leg all along.

'Are you winding me up?' she asked.

He raised his eyebrows.

'No, I'm deadly serious. I found a lot of this stuff fanciful too, until I listen to the stories serial killers told after they'd been incarcerated.'

Jo shuffled the papers together, placed them back in the folder, and then turned to face him.

'If serial killers are by definition both self-deluding *and* master storytellers, how do you know when they're telling the truth?'

'Sometimes you can't,' he told her. 'But that's when it's important to weigh what they say against what they do. That's why we're called the *Behavioural* Sciences Unit. A lot of these killers possess a tremendous sense of invincibility. They're supremely arrogant, and proud of their achievements. They have no sense of remorse – indeed, they're the epitome of self-righteousness. They want to tell you why they did what they did, and delight in telling you how they did it, and how they got away with it for so long.'

'Have they never been known to show remorse?' she asked.

'Good question,' he replied. 'It isn't true that all serial killers and rapists are devoid of empathy. In the case of those with a narcissistic personality disorder, empathy tends to be reserved for themselves, not their victims.'

He shook his head as though trying to clear it, stretched out his arms, and loosened his shoulders.

'Almost universally these perpetrators lead a double existence, Jo – you know that. They're capable of displaying entirely different feelings and behaviours in each of their lives. It's what makes them so difficult to detect. Even their nearest and dearest can be shocked and devastated when they discover the other side of the person with whom they share their beds.'

He saw the look on her face.

'Oh God, I'm sorry,' he said. 'Here am I telling you.'

Chapter 8

It felt as though she had been punched in the solar plexus. She struggled to take a breath. This was the first indication that any of them knew about her abduction. Of course they would have wanted to find out about the new member of their team. And who better placed to research her? It had been naive to think otherwise.

'It's alright,' she said at last. 'I wasn't remotely close to him, quite the reverse. But from what contact we had previously, you would never have guessed that he was capable of doing what he did.'

'Including what he tried to do to you?'

Now she was annoyed. It felt like he was fishing for information. Dredging up something with which she believed she had come to terms.

'Look, Andy,' she said. 'I need to state my position on this. Otherwise there'll always be an elephant in the room about which everyone else in the team has made ill-founded assumptions. I had enough of that from colleagues in Manchester until my DCI put them straight.'

He looked suitably chastened.

'Fair enough,' he said. 'Go ahead.'

Jo took a deep breath and exhaled slowly.

'I was working undercover on an investigation into a series of murders, exclusively of women, all of whom had direct contact with the suspect.'

She paused to check how much of this was news to him. He nodded.

'That much I know, Jo, as do the others. That and the fact that he abducted you, but your colleagues found you and pursued him. He drowned trying to escape.'

'And that's all you know?'

'That's it,' he said. 'When we found out that we had a new colleague, Shah couldn't resist looking you up, just media accounts. There was never any question of breaching data protection, or invading your privacy.'

She placed her hands on the table palms down, mirroring his. Then she clasped them together, tightly entwining her fingers, unconsciously grounding herself. Slowly she raised her head, and made eye contact. Her gaze was unwavering, her voice strong and steady.

'I volunteered for the role. My one mistake was to underestimate the unsub. We all did. He had a partner in crime of whom we were unaware. That man used an agricultural Taser to incapacitate me. He dragged me inside a four-by-four, my hands and feet bound with cable, and drove me away in full view of our watchers. I was driven into a forest, and tied to a tree. The dominant perpetrator arrived. He told me he was going to rape me, strangle me, and then dispose of my body. He ripped off my blouse. But when he reached around to unclasp my bra he found the wiretap transmitter. I managed to delay him long enough. He heard the helicopter coming, and my Boss shouting as he ran towards us. Both of the perpetrators fled. One was caught. The dominant one ran towards the mere. They found blood on a branch by the margin. The helicopter suddenly lost thermal images. Our divers never recovered his body. He was presumed drowned.'

Swift moved a hand towards her. She moved hers away.

'Don't!' she said. 'And please don't say anything.'

He moved his hand back.

'Sorry,' he said.

'Especially not that,' she told him. 'I don't need sympathy. Sympathy casts you as a victim. I was not one of his victims. In the end he was *my* victim. I was the one who got him to confess. I was the one who was responsible for cracking the case.'

Swift was about to comment, but thought better of it.

'I had seven sessions of counselling, primarily for post-traumatic stress. Not because of what he did, but because of the times I woke up in a sweat imagining what he had been about to do.'

She pushed herself back, and folded her arms.

'The upshot is that I'm fine now. If anything, I came out of it stronger, wiser, and more determined than ever to catch bastards like the one that killed Charles Deighton.'

When it was clear that she had finished, Swift said, 'We're very lucky to have you as a colleague, Jo.'

'Thank you,' she replied. 'You'll tell the others?'

'Of course.'

'Tell us what?'

Max Nailor had emerged from his workstation and was walking towards them. He was shrugging his arms into his jacket.

'It'll keep,' said Swift. 'Are you off somewhere?'

'That case Stone assigned me? I've arranged an initial meeting with the Senior Investigating Officer. To get a feel for it, and to clarify the terms of engagement.'

'I realise you're the lead investigator,' said Swift, 'but that doesn't mean you have to do it all on your own. Would you like Jo to go with you?'

Nailor frowned.

'Thanks, but no thanks. No offence, Jo, but I'm on top of this. If I need a hand I'll let you know.'

He headed for the door.

'No offence taken,' she called after him, cheerily hiding her disappointment. 'In any case, I need to get on with making an appointment with Lancashire Police to get things moving with my double murder.'

Nailor stopped and turned.

'Double?'

'Charles Deighton and an anonymous cat.'

He shook his head and left the room.

'Not noted for his humour, our Max,' said Stone, 'but don't let that stop you from trying.'

Jo had extensive and wearisome experience of having to win over male colleagues. Especially the ones that had come on to her assuming that she was available, and then felt rebuffed when she put them straight. There was nothing worse to deal with than hurt male pride. Max, she had already decided, would be far less of a challenge. It would just take time. She placed a hand over the file.

'Why do I have a feeling that I may be turning up empty-handed?' she said. 'Not a good way to start.'

'You're underestimating what you have to offer,' Swift assured her. 'Let alone what *we* have to offer. Never discount the value of a fresh pair of eyes. You have the whole team behind you. What are you going to tell the SIO? What was his name?'

'Renton. Martin Renton. That we've searched the databases for previous cases of live interment, burial with an animal, attempts to disguise burial direct into the soil, and male abduction resulting in burial. I'll have to tell him that unfortunately none of that has recorded any hits that take us forward at this stage, but some of the feedback may illuminate the investigation further down the line.'

'Is that strictly true?'

'Which part? The hits not taking us forward, or them potentially helping us in the future?'

'Them not taking us forward.' He opened the file and searched for the digest Ram had provided. 'These gang-related killings,' he said. 'What motive would you attribute to them?'

'Well, I'd have to know more about each of them to be certain, but as a general rule they would appear to be executions.'

'So, essentially a punishment.'

'Yes.'

'For what?'

Jo started to count them off on her fingers.

'Breaking a gang rule, such as the code of silence. Acting as a police informer. Attempting to rip off the rest of the gang by taking a larger share. A competitor trying to move into the gang's territory, or to remove an obstacle to the gang's operations. Of course there could be a personal motive unconnected with the gang itself.'

'Such as getting rid of your mistress's husband?'

'It's been known to happen.'

'Indeed it has. But something as cruel as burying someone alive, and wanting to watch them, and have them watching you watching, doesn't that sound more in keeping with all of the other reasons you listed? Doesn't that suit a motive such as revenge for betrayal, or vengeance for another kind of perceived wrong?'

'Of course,' she said. 'But I'm not sure what point you're making?'

'What do you know about the psychology of retribution?'

She shrugged.

'I've never heard of it.'

'No reason you should have, although if I had my way it would be part of the training for every detective. The key point is that revenge is not as sweet as we think it will be. On the contrary, there is something called the "revenge paradox". In essence that means that when we take revenge on another person, we end up feeling worse than we did before. Not merely worse, but even more angry.'

'Because we feel guilty that we've behaved out of character?'

'Surprisingly, no. It's because having taken revenge we continue to think more and more about the original hurt that was done to us. Taking revenge has somehow magnified the importance of the original act. Taking revenge doesn't provide closure, it's like picking the top off a scab and revealing the wound beneath.'

Jo frowned.

'That sounds counter-intuitive.'

'But it would explain why people who forgive are much more likely to find peace of mind than those who seek revenge.'

Jo had to agree. It was after all one of the first things that her counsellor had put to her. And now she thought about it, it was what she had done. She had rationalised her tormentor's behaviour based on what he had told her about his motivations. And it had worked. In a strange way she had ended up feeling sorry for him, and regretting that he had died as he had. And she had found peace. Most importantly, she had been able to move on.

'I understand that,' she said. 'But what bearing does it have on Operation Hound?'

'If this was about revenge,' he said, 'then it may well have left the perpetrator even more angry. That anger may have been apparent to those around him. He may have had to find outlets for it.'

'But revenge makes it less likely that he's a serial killer?'

Swift shook his head.

'That depends on how many people were involved in the act for which he was seeking revenge.'

'My head is beginning to hurt,' she said.

He eased his chair back and stood up.

'In that case, Jo, it's time you got out of the office. I suggest you make that call.'

45

Chapter 9

It had taken just under three-quarters of an hour to get to the Lancashire Force Headquarters in Hutton, near Preston. DI Renton, she was informed, was in a meeting.

Two male officers, close to retirement, stood waiting by the lifts. They were staring in her direction, brazenly giving her the elevator eyes treatment. She wasn't surprised – experience had taught her that it was more often than not the senior uniformed officers who had yet to come to terms with the meaning of sexual harassment. The lifts pinged, the doors opened, and the officers stepped in. They stood facing her. She gave them a forensic stare of her own. One of them shifted nervously, the other looked down at his feet. The doors closed.

'You must be Agent Stuart?'

He was a similar age to her, tall and slim. He appeared anxious and twitchy, as though under pressure.

Jo stood up, and held out her hand.

'Joanne Stuart, NCA Senior Investigator,' she told him. 'We don't have agents.'

'Bit of a misnomer then, Agency?'

He smiled, and shook her hand.

'DI Renton, Senior Investigating Officer. Sorry to keep you waiting.'

'That's okay. It's been interesting.'

He looked around the foyer.

'If you call this interesting, you need to get out more.'

'People-watching is our stock-in-trade,' she said.

He glanced at his watch.

'We'll have to be quick, I'm afraid. I'm on a tight schedule. Stairs alright?'

'Fine by me,' she told him. 'All I've done so far today is sit on my backside.'

Renton set off at a brisk pace leaving her several strides behind. By the time they reached the second landing, he had doubled that distance and she had to hurry to keep up. He led her down a corridor and into a small meeting room. They pulled up their chairs, and sat down.

'Look, I'm sorry if I seemed a bit brusque,' he said. 'But it's manic right now. We've had two murders and a child abduction turn up within two days of each other.' He took a handkerchief out of his pocket and wiped beads of sweat from his brow. 'You should be talking to the detective superintendent who was the original SIO on this one, but he's just taken enforced retirement. We've lost two supers, seven DIs and fifteen detective constables in the past two years, and now we're facing another two years of cuts.'

'I've been there,' she said.

'Of course you have. You were with GMP's Major Incident Team?'

'Until last Friday.'

'At least they've sent someone who knows what she's doing, though I'll be surprised if you've turned up anything new. As far as I can tell we did a decent enough job first time around, and still drew a blank. There was bugger all to go on.'

'I can't disagree with that,' Jo told him.

'Between you and me,' he said. 'My lot are not happy about the decision to call your lot in after the last Major Case Review.'

'I'm not surprised. I'd feel exactly the same. But I'm not here to take over, or to show you up. Just another pair of eyes, with some specialist backup.'

'Suits me,' he said. 'I've just been told I have to support the team working on that child abduction.'

'So who am I going to be working with?'

'I've got a woman DS who'll bring you up to speed, and you'll always be able to contact me if you need to.'

Renton glanced at his watch again, and then pointed at Jo's briefcase.

'Why don't you tell me what you've got?'

Jo began to unclip the case.

'I wouldn't hold your breath,' she said.

Fifteen minutes later she had told him what the BSU had been doing. About the searches that Ram Shah had made, the criminal behaviours Andy Swift had noted from the crime scene evidence, and the questions that had arisen. The DI's frown matched the disappointment in his voice.

'So that's it, is it?'

'I did warn you.'

He sighed, and nodded.

'And to be fair, I did say we weren't expecting much.'

She slid a sheet of paper across the table. 'What about the questions we raised?'

Renton dragged it towards him with one finger, and scanned swiftly down the sheet. Then he checked his watch, and looked up.

'I'll make this quick,' he said. 'All of his family, friends and colleagues came up clean. And that was after extensive enquiries. There were only two exceptions.'

'His wife Harriet, and his best friend, Raymond Carter?'

'That's right. Although, as I understand it, neither of them merited any special attention from us at the outset. Charles and Harriet Deighton's marriage was by all accounts a stable one. Neighbours and friends never reported any bickering, let alone serious arguments, and there had never been any question of domestic violence. Carter was a fellow Mason who belonged to the same Lodge as Deighton. He knew Mrs Deighton solely through Ladies' Evenings and other social events at the Lodge.'

'So why did they become suspects?'

'Because within six months of his disappearance they became a bit of an item, and two years later they were shacked up together.'

'Those timescales don't seem that unreasonable,' Jo said. 'A woman who feels abandoned at best, and bereaved at worst, consoled by her husband's best friend?'

He raised his eyebrows.

'Married woman, and no body? Thing is, he had cast-iron alibis for the time when Deighton was believed to have been abducted. And she's unlikely to have been able to do it on her own.'

'You looked at other contacts they may have had? Someone either or both of them could have paid to kill the husband?'

'What you've got to remember,' he said, 'is that the original investigation was a Missing Persons enquiry. A middle-aged man, with no known enemies, had disappeared. There was no evidence that he had been assaulted. No evidence that he had been abducted.'

'Did they actually look for any evidence?'

'Not as far as I can tell. You know how it is. Is he vulnerable? No, he isn't. There's no known medical condition, he's not alcoholic or drug dependent, and he has no mental illness. Ergo, he's not a priority. Over two hundred and seventy-five thousand people go missing every year. And they're the ones we know of. That's an entire city the size of Plymouth. Okay, most are children and young persons, and most of those are teenage girls. The majority turn up after a few days. But over seventy per cent of those over twenty-four years of age are males. What's more, only twenty per cent of those who are traced decide to go back to the place they left. They were depressed and no one knew, they got bored, they felt hemmed in, life was passing them by, work got too much for them, they were sick of being nagged, or they'd cocked up and couldn't face the consequences.'

He paused for a moment, and shook his head.

'There are more than twenty thousand people who have been missing for over a year. Even if we had the resources, which we don't, we'd never be able to track them all down. Not if they don't want us to.'

Jo knew he was right. It was ironic that in an age where more people were connected by social media than ever before, where over thirteen million cameras kept watch on the streets and other public places, more people simply slipped out of sight. All they had to do was use a different name, find jobs that paid them cash in hand, stay in hostels, squats or short-term lets, and so long as they stayed out of trouble they'd never be found.

'So without a body, or an apparent motive, nobody would have thought to check the wife and boyfriend's mobile phones?'

He shook his head.

'No reasonable cause.'

'I was wondering how you'd feel about my talking to them,' she said. 'Starting with Mrs Deighton. Only I don't want to tread on your toes.'

The door opened, and a young man peered round.

'There you are, Boss,' he said. 'Sorry to interrupt but we're moving out?'

'Tell them I'm coming,' Renton replied. 'You can leave the door open.'

He turned back to face Jo.

'Do what you like,' he said. 'Don't mind us.'

He pushed back his chair and stood up.

Jo took it as her cue to stand. She began to gather up her papers.

'I'm sorry,' he said, 'it's the abduction case. A six-year-old girl.'

'I'm sorry,' she told him. 'Bad timing.'

'You'll want to see the crime scene first,' he said, as he walked towards the doorway. 'I know I would. Detective Sergeant Charnock is expecting you at Chorley nick. Ask at reception, they'll give you the GPS location.'

He was gone before she had time to respond.

'Nice to meet you too,' she said to the empty room.

Chapter 10

Detective Sergeant Jean Charnock wasn't at all put out that Jo had been parachuted into Operation Hound. In her early to mid-fifties, she was even closer to retirement than her Boss, Renton, and surprisingly cheerful.

'Don't worry,' she confided. 'Some of the others may be bothered that you've been sent to give us a hand, but I'm glad of a bit of female company.'

'I'm hoping I'll bring a bit more than that,' Jo began.

'Hold up, Ma'am,' said Charnock. 'I wasn't implying that was *all* I was expecting. It's not as though *we've* a lot to show for six months' work.'

'Fair enough,' said Jo.

'I guess you'll want to see the crime scene – what's left of it, anyway?' said the Detective Sergeant.

'That would be good. We can talk on the way.'

'You'll have to speak fast then,' quipped Charnock. 'It's only a mile and a half.'

Their route skirted the pedestrianised centre of this pretty market town, past Booths supermarket and the railway station, and out on to the A6. As they approached a large roundabout on the outskirts of the town, the Detective Sergeant chuckled, and nodded towards a sign for the hospital, and Charnock Richard.

'See, we Charnocks even have a place named after us.'

'Any connection?'

'Possibly, but I'm not one for ancestry so I wouldn't know.'

She took the first exit at the roundabout, and drove uphill with woods on either side, before turning right on to a road with woods on one side and large detached houses set high up off the road, soon replaced by more trees.

'Nearly there,' said Charnock, her tone now serious and her manner formal.

'What's on the other side of all these trees?' Jo asked.

'This is a single modern housing estate, divided by this access road. Big houses down this end, mainly detached. More semis down the far end where we're heading. A lot more trees and green space than most. It was one of the stipulations made by the planning department because it's eaten into the green belt. Most of it was already finished when our victim was buried.'

'In 2005 then?'

'That's what the pathologists reckoned.'

'You think otherwise?'

'Not really. It's just that when it comes to rates of decomposition, spores, biological deposits, and insect activity, we just have to take their word for it, don't we?'

Jo had to hang on to her seat belt and press the other hand against the fascia as the car turned sharply to the left, and stopped at the kerb. Charnock pulled on the handbrake, and switched off the engine.

'Here we are,' she said.

Climbing out, Jo removed her tablet from her bag. Selecting the video option, she turned slowly through three hundred and sixty degrees, capturing two groups of houses on either side of a narrow metalled road that stretched towards farmland in the distance, then the wider road up which they had come, and that continued to the left with trees on either side. Behind her stood a padlocked wooden five-barred gate, with a smaller gate for pedestrians beside it, beyond which a sandy footpath disappeared into the woods.

'It wasn't like this when the body was buried,' Charnock told her. 'These houses behind us hadn't even been started. It was the builders' compound where all the materials and some of the machinery was kept.'

'So that was where they thought the planks may have come from?'

'It was a reasonable assumption. I mean, who's going to go to all the trouble of lugging two bloody great planks, as well as a body, into the woods?'

'Someone who has a good reason for needing them?'

Charnock thought about it.

'I suppose so. They'd need a big van or a pickup though. Be a bit conspicuous strapping them to a roof rack.'

'But nobody checked with the builders at the time?'

'I know it was actioned. I think the DS put one of the DCs on to it. I'm pretty sure he drew a blank. Builders had moved on, you see. And I doubt a couple of planks going missing would have been something they'd remember after all that time.'

So much for 'check everything', Jo reflected.

'What about the cat?' she asked.

Charnock was surprised by the change of tack.

'What about it?'

'Was there any evidence that it had belonged to someone round here? There was nothing in the case notes.'

'Same problem. Ten years gone by. I know it was on the list of house-to-house questions because I put it there.' Her eyes lit up.

'Come to think of it, so were the planks. Just in case someone had been building an extension, putting a patio down, that sort of thing.'

'Had they?'

She shook her head.

'No. Nor did anyone report their cat missing.'

In which case, Jo reflected, it suggested a highly organised killer for whom the cat had always been a part of the plan. She pointed to the gate.

'Is this where the killer entered the wood?'

Charnock shrugged.

'It's highly likely. There are several other ways in, but they're all problematic. Either near impossible to negotiate lugging a body let alone a couple of planks, or easily visible from the road. I'll show you later.'

'Okay,' said Jo. 'Lead on.'

The DS pushed open the smaller gate and set off. Jo followed five metres behind holding her iPad.

The wide sandy path had a broad grass strip on either side, and was flanked by a range of small deciduous trees.

'Were these trees here ten years ago?'

Charnock carried on walking as she replied. The wind had picked up and Jo had to strain to catch every word against the creaking of the naked branches.

'Aye, they were. As long as I can remember. But the paths were little more than tracks that walkers trod in over the years. Over the centuries, even.'

She stopped for a moment.

'When the houses were built, the paths were tarted up, gates put in, and this part became little more than a fancy hedge. But it turns into a proper wood the further on you go. You'll see.'

After sixty metres the path split. Charnock took the left fork that led them east into a wood that was populated with much larger trees. Oak, beech and sycamore crowded in, their canopy all but blotting out the sky. Ninety metres later, they reached a clearing where a wider green swathe cut across their path horizontally from north to south. Overhead, three rows of telephone wires were strung from poles set fifty metres apart. Charnock turned left, and set off through the damp ankle-high grass and weeds.

'Sorry about this,' she called over her shoulder. 'I should have warned you.'

Yes, you should, thought Jo. *But then I should have had the sense to come in my own car, and I'd have been able to change into the boots I keep in the back.* It was becoming difficult to hold the tablet steady, as well as check her foot placement. Several times she stumbled, and was relieved when after a hundred metres or so Charnock came to a stop.

'This is it,' she said, pointing to her left. 'In here, twenty metres, that's all.'

It was evident that some of the bushes at the edge of the wood had been cut back or trampled during the investigation. Nature was now reclaiming it for herself. A tangle of blackberry bushes had formed, and wilted foxglove spikes thrust out of the sandy soil.

Jo followed her, cursing when she had to stop to free her trousered ankle from the clutches of a determined tentacle. There was a significant gap at this point between the trees, and the going was easier underfoot on a soft layer of springy leaf mould. Within seconds she had caught up with a stationary DS Charnock.

They were standing in a small clearing, some three metres in diameter, surrounded by the trunks of some impressive trees. There was nothing to suggest that this had once been a crime scene. No scraps of yellow police tape caught on the lower branches. No flattened approach route. One autumn's worth of leaves covered the ground. A patch of heart-shaped wild violet leaves poked bravely between the gnarled trunks of the trees. Somewhere deeper into the wood a magpie chattered a warning.

'You can see why he chose this place,' said Charnock. 'Far enough from the main path, well out of sight of the houses, not somewhere people would normally be walking.'

'You say you walked these woods as a child,' said Jo. 'Did you ever come across this clearing?'

'Not just as a child,' she replied, 'as a teenager and an adult too. We used to regularly bring our kids to Duxbury Woods, and Birkacre. Never been here, though. Why would we? Not when there's plenty of better places, ones that take you from somewhere to somewhere.'

'To pick the blackberries?' Jo suggested.

'They weren't here when the body was discovered. We probably tramped a broken stem in when we arrived. You know how easily they take root.'

Jo took her word for it.

'Besides,' she continued. 'There's loads of places, a bloody sight more accessible, with banks full of blackberries.'

'Then how come the guy who discovered the grave stumbled across it?'

'That's easy. He was using the track beneath the telegraph wires as a short cut to get out on to the main road. Just happens he has an inquisitive dog. Probably chased a rabbit or a bird into the wood. One in a million chance.'

Jo scanned the clearing again.

'Wasn't there something in the case notes about a carving on one of these trees?'

Charnock nodded.

'That's right.'

She stared at two oak trees five metres apart on the edge of the clearing, and then walked towards the nearer of the two.

'It was this one over here.'

She peered at the trunk. And then rubbed at it with her fingers.

'Gotcha!' she said, pointing to a five-centimetre-square patch of the trunk level with her shoulders. The bark had been peeled away, and some kind of moss or lichen had grown over it. The detective sergeant had cleared enough of this to reveal a shape neatly carved into the smooth wood beneath. A horizontal line with an identical vertical line where it ended on the right-hand side. Was this, Jo wondered, supposed to be two sides of a square? Or was it unfinished?

'We were lucky to find it,' said Charnock. 'An eagle-eyed member of the scenes of crime team happened to be an amateur botanist. Apparently he could tell it wasn't a natural phenomenon, so he scrubbed it like I did, and revealed this.'

'Do we know if it was definitely carved at the same time that the body was buried?'

'Not for definite, but then or thereabouts. All to do with the time it takes for the moss to seed and grow to the stage it was when he spotted it.'

'Not likely to have been a star-crossed lover,' observed Jo. 'The patch would have been bigger, and the carving more identifiable.'

'That was the conclusion we reached. Not a graffiti tag either, for the same reason. It's a mystery.'

Jo switched off the video recorder, and took a photo of the carving.

She turned to look back in the direction they had come.

'Two hundred and thirty metres,' she said. 'It's a hell of a long way to carry a body, let alone two planks. It must have taken at least two people. Maybe even two trips.'

'That's what we concluded. And whoever it was went to a lot of trouble to make sure the body wasn't discovered. Otherwise they would have dumped it nearer the road.' She checked her watch.

'Have you seen enough, Ma'am? Only I should have finished half an hour ago, and my hubby will be wondering where I am.'

'No, that's fine,' said Jo, as they started to walk back to the car. 'I'm running late myself. About tomorrow, I had a word with DI Renton and he's okayed me to re-interview Mrs Deighton, and some of the other witnesses. I was wondering if you wanted to come with me?'

Charnock laughed.

'No way! I've seen enough of that lot, and they've certainly seen enough of me. Besides, the Boss wants me to hold the fort while he's working on this missing girl. If they don't find her soon, we'll all be pulled in on that. You're welcome to talk to whomever you want, Ma'am. Though I can't think what good it'll do you.'

Chapter 11

On the journey home, Jo selected BBC Radio Manchester. She wanted to stay in touch with what was going on, after all it was still home even if it was no longer her patch. No, that wasn't strictly true, she realised. The whole of the north-west was part of her patch now.

She had missed the news and so, as she passed the Macron Stadium at Middlebrook, she switched to Smooth FM in anticipation of the big slowdown as the rush hour traffic began its tortuous crawl towards the city centre.

They were playing Stevie Wonder's version of the Beatles' hit 'We Can Work It Out'. *If only*, she thought.

The visit to the crime scene had resolved nothing beyond the fact that they were almost certainly looking for more than one person, and the killers had gone to exceptional lengths to hide the body. On the other hand, why not burn it, or dismember it and scatter the remains far and wide? Or dissolve it in acid, as John George Haigh had done. Andy Swift was right. There was a compulsion of some kind to punish the victim in this particular way, and still avoid detection.

Before she left, she had persuaded DS Charnock to have one more go at finding out about those planks, and the cat. It was a long shot, and Charnock had not been overly impressed by her explanation that these were part of the shadows the criminals had cast, the psychological traces they left behind.

Tomorrow would be about visiting the widow, and the best friend who couldn't wait to slither into her bed. She was looking forward to that.

She tried to reach the office on her hands-free, but it went to voicemail. She decided not to bother them on their mobile phones. What was the protocol, she wondered, for keeping her colleagues up to date? And how was she supposed to report to Harry Stone? She realised that she was missing the easy camaraderie of Tom Caton, Gordon Holmes, and DS Carter, and the knowledge that you had support and advice on tap. Not the deadlines, and the crazy workload though, she didn't really miss those. Or did she?

Her phone rang. It was Abbie.

'Where are you, Jo?'

'On the M61, crawling towards the Kearsley spur. Should be with you in about forty minutes.'

'You should have left earlier – would've only taken you fifteen minutes from there.'

'I know, but it was difficult. I did send you a text.'

'Well, you'd better hope the traffic clears because I'm on a seven pm to seven am, starting today.'

She sounded resigned, but Jo sensed she wasn't happy.

'Nights? For how long?' she asked.

'It's only four days, and then I've got three off. I couldn't really say no, given that I've handed in my resignation.'

'That means we'll see hardly anything of each other this side of next weekend.'

'Unless you start coming home at a reasonable time.'

Jo knew she was right. Being able to work a little bit more flexibly was one of the supposed pulls of this job.

'I will, I promise,' she said, hoping it was true.

'If you miss me, you'll find a vegetable lasagne in the fridge. I made it this morning. All you have to do is pop it in the microwave. Three and a half minutes on maximum. Mind you don't burn your tongue. Oh, and there's that half a bottle of red left over from Sunday.'

Jo didn't know whether to smile at the wine, or frown at the lasagne. Two veggie meals in one day. And to think she'd passed up on the offer of a pasty.

'You spoil me,' she said.

'It won't last if you keep coming home late.'

'I know. Hopefully I'll be home before you go.'

'Laters then. Love you.'

'Love you too.'

The traffic came to a halt again. She switched over to Manchester Radio just in time for the traffic news. There was congestion on both the clockwise and anti-clockwise carriageways of the M60, courtesy of the ongoing Super Highway roadworks. Furthermore, a lorry had spilled its load on the M602 near the Hope Hospital turnoff. Long delays were expected.

It was ten to seven when she finally pushed open the door to the apartment. Abbie was long gone. The vegetable lasagne sat on the kitchen table in a microwaveable bowl with a pop-up fly net over the top. A half-empty bottle of Merlot stood beside it. A hastily written note accompanied them.

Told you so! There are some pineapple chunks and a tub of yoghurt in the fridge. Enjoy. XXX

Jo sighed, dumped her document case on one of the chairs, and took her jacket into the bedroom. She sat on the bed, and kicked off her shoes. There was an episode of *Corrie* to watch while she had her dinner. After that, if memory served her right, there was *George*

Gently on one side, and *Vera* on the other, but she'd developed an aversion to TV detectives. She examined the bottoms of her trousers. There were brown and green stains, and one of them had been badly snagged by that damn blackberry bush. She shrugged them off, and tossed them in the corner where they were rapidly joined by socks, blouse and underwear. She slipped on a fresh bra and pants, opened a drawer and took out her favourite trackies and matching T-shirt. The '*Come to the Dark Side*' ones with the Cookie Monster on, that Abbie had bought her last Christmas.

She gathered up her discarded clothes, padded through to the bathroom, and tossed them in the Ali Baba laundry basket. Back in the kitchen, she picked up her document case, had second thoughts and put it down again. There would be plenty of time to prepare her questions for the following morning. A long, lonely night stretched out ahead of her, and an early start in the morning.

Chapter 12

It made no sense. The body had been dumped on the outskirts of Chorley. At the time of his abduction, Charles Deighton had been living in the hamlet of Ringley, eleven miles away as the crow flies. It was nearer to fifteen by car.

Jo had done as Caton, her mentor, had taught her, and allowed time before her appointment to get a feel for the place. She was standing with her back to the La Roma restaurant, housed in what looked like a former traditional black and white inn, on a bend in the River Irwell. Immediately ahead of her was an ancient stone bridge, blocked off to all but pedestrians by five sturdy iron posts. On the far side of the bridge rose the isolated sandstone clock tower of the former St Saviour Church, whose more recent incarnation was just visible some way behind it. The only sounds she could hear were the hum of cars on the nearby A667, and the gentle murmur of the river.

According to the case notes, Charlie Deighton had spent the evening in The Grapes, three-quarters of a mile away in Stoneclough. He had left at around 11.20pm, and was seen walking back home along Ringley Road. He had called in at Holts Riverside for a bag of chips. From there, it would normally have taken him no more than ten minutes to reach his house in Ringley. Jo had driven the route on her way there this morning. It was a straightforward journey, with houses crowding the road for the entire journey on at least one side, and most often on both sides. There were two exceptions.

Shortly before the road divided where a bridge carried the A road north-east towards Kearsley, the leafless branches of overhanging trees and high walls on both sides masked the road from the houses and flats set back behind them. The other was on Kearsley Hall Road itself, less than two hundred yards from the Deighton residence. Bushes and trees bordered the river. On the opposite side, two huge sycamores masked the road from the houses. There was a side road here, little more than a lane, where it would have been possible to park up unobserved, and wait until Deighton passed.

Either of those places would have supported a quick and silent abduction. The presence of a half-eaten packet of chips in the gutter, or some cigarettes stubs, would have helped the police to pinpoint the very place. As far as Jo could tell no one had bothered to look. She got back in her car and drove the short distance to the address she had been given.

The Deightons' house was a 1990s semi-detached, with a side extension that made it stand out from its neighbours. The garden was neat, with flowerbeds around a lawn with a small magnolia in the centre. On the brick-paved drive stood a red Audi TT with a soft top, and a 2013 number plate. Jo did the maths. It had been brand new seven and a half years after Charles Deighton had walked out. That would have been six months after her husband had been officially declared dead. No sightings, no phone calls or texts, bank balances untouched, credit cards unused, passport still in the drawer where he kept it. It hardly counted as indecent haste. The same couldn't be said for the speed with which his best friend had moved in.

In the front room there was a fleeting movement in the shadows. Jo opened the gate. The front door opened, and a woman stood, arms folded, waiting for her to walk up the drive. Jo took her time. First appearances weren't everything, but it was surprising what you could learn from them.

Harriet Deighton had made an effort. She wore a fitted red blouse tucked into a navy-blue pencil skirt. Her hair looked as though it had recently been coloured jet black, and then cut into a severe bob. It aged her. Having said that, she still looked younger than her husband had been when he went missing ten years ago.

'I've been expecting you,' she said, as she led the way into an open-plan lounge and diner. She made it sound like a rebuke. Jo checked her watch. She was several minutes early.

'Please, take a seat.'

Jo placed her document case on the floor beside the nearest of the sofas, and sat down.

Harriet Deighton hovered. 'I've made some scones. Would you like tea or coffee?'

'Coffee would be fine,' Jo told her. 'But no scone, I'm afraid, I've only just had breakfast.'

The room was quaintly furnished with floral lattice wallpaper, art nouveau tiles around the fireplace, and a heavy patterned fabric on the chairs and sofas that would not have been out of place in the late Victorian period. Wall-mounted racks held a bewildering array of decorative plates. Bookshelves, coffee tables, and the bay windowsills were crowded with Crown Derby paperweights and figurines.

On the shelf were three photographs in identical silver frames. One, Jo assumed, was of Harriet Deighton's parents, taken on a cruise. Another was of her and her husband, Charles, on their wedding day. The third was a much more recent photo of her with a different man at some kind of formal event. She wore a scarlet full-length dress, while her partner sported a dinner suit with a matching red bow tie. Jo stood up to take a closer look.

The wedding photo confirmed the age gap between the Deightons. Harriet could almost have been Charles's daughter. Jo picked up the third photo to scrutinise it more closely. The man in the other photo was much nearer her age. If this was Raymond Carter, they appeared to make a much better match. It wasn't just about the ages either, they seemed far more at ease with each other than did Harriet and Charles. Carter was also quite good-looking. Broad-shouldered, square-jawed, a full head of curly blond hair, and he towered over Harriet Deighton.

'Before you ask, that's Ray.'

Harriet Deighton stood behind her holding a tray with two mugs, a jug of milk, and a bowl of sugar. She placed it on the coffee table.

'It was taken at last year's Ladies' Evening.'

Jo replaced the photo, and sat back down on the sofa. Mrs Deighton sat on a chair at an angle to her.

'He lives with me,' she said. 'We're partners.'

It sounded as though she was expecting criticism, and trying to head it off.

'I was aware of that, Mrs Deighton,' Jo told her.

Mrs Deighton took a sip, put the mug down and folded her arms.

'The National Crime Agency,' she said. 'So they've brought in the big guns.'

'The Lancashire Force has asked for our help,' said Jo. 'Another pair of eyes.' It was becoming a stock phrase.

Harriet Deighton observed her coolly.

'You didn't say why you wanted to see me. I can't imagine there's anything I can tell you that I haven't already told them.'

'I do understand, Mrs Deighton, but sometimes there are things we forget, or that our subconscious may have blotted out, that come back to us when we recall past events with a different person.'

'Blotted out? It's not as though I've been suffering from post-traumatic stress.' She paused. 'What am I supposed to call you, by the way?'

It was a great question. How were people supposed to refer to her? They couldn't call her Agent or Detective Inspector, and Senior Investigating Officer felt far too clumsy, not to mention self-important. Ms Stuart was definitely out of the question.

'SI Stuart,' she said, 'or Officer. Whichever you prefer.'

Jo took a mouthful of coffee from her mug, then picked up her tablet.

'Do you mind if I record our conversation?'

Mrs Deighton frowned.

'This is on the record then? Like an interview?'

'Not in the sense of a formal interview, under caution,' Jo told her. 'It's more of an aide-memoire, for both of us. I can send you a copy if you like, but I won't be asking you to sign anything. It's just that it saves me taking notes. This should make it easier and quicker for both of us.'

'I suppose so,' she replied.

Jo selected *Record*, and placed the iPad between them on the coffee table.

Chapter 13

'The evening that your husband went missing, you were waiting for him to return from the pub?'

'No, I'd retired early. I was in bed watching TV.'

'You didn't hear your husband's car being driven away?'

'We have excellent double-glazing, and I like the sound turned up when I'm watching a movie.'

'How long was it before you started to worry that he was late?'

'When the film ended.'

'Which was?'

'Midnight.'

'So you rang The Grapes?'

'Yes.'

'And?'

'They told me he had left well over an hour before.'

'What did you do then?'

'Look, is this really necessary? I told you, I've been through all this dozens of times with the police. Not to mention two inquests.'

'I do understand, Mrs Deighton, but if you could bear with me, hopefully this will be the last time.'

'If you say so.'

'Would you like me to repeat the question?'

'No, thank you.'

Mrs Deighton picked up her cup and pretended to take a sip. She put it down, and crossed her legs.

'I went to sleep.'

'You weren't worried that he might have come to harm?'

She sniffed in disapproval.

'I certainly didn't expect him to be abducted.'

'I meant knocked over by a hit-and-run driver, for instance, or mugged.'

This was met with a raised eyebrow.

'My, what a vivid imagination you have.'

'It happens far more often than you might think, Mrs Deighton.'

'Well, I didn't think any such thing. Besides, had that been the case, I'm sure I would have found out fairly quickly without having to get dressed again, and set off in search of him.'

'So you went to sleep.'

'I've already told you that I did.'

'And you woke up at around seven thirty am.'

Mrs Deighton's eyes lit up.

'So you *have* read my statements. And this is just what? An attempt to catch me out?'

'No, to clarify things in my mind.'

'Must be full of cotton wool.'

'Sorry?'

'Your mind. Full of cotton wool.'

Jo ignored it. She had dealt with witnesses far more annoying than Harriet Deighton.

'When you woke up and found that he still hadn't returned, what then? Did you ring the police?'

'As you well know, I rang Ray.'

'Raymond Carter, your husband's best friend?'

This time she actually clapped.

'Well done.'

Jo gritted her teeth.

'You rang him because?'

'He was his best friend.'

'Had they been drinking together in The Grapes?'

'No.'

'Did your husband often go back to Mr Carter's house on a sudden impulse, and stay the night?'

'No.'

'Did he ever go back there that late at night without letting you know?'

'No.'

'So why did you decide to ring Mr Carter first?'

'Because he was his . . .'

'Best friend!' said Jo, finishing the sentence for her. 'But that doesn't explain why you rang him.'

Harriet Deighton leaned forward and spoke very slowly, as though talking to a child.

'Raymond . . . knew . . . Charles . . . better . . . than . . . anybody else. Me . . . included.'

Then she tired of the game, sighed, sat back, and continued at a normal pace.

'I thought he might have some idea where Charles was. What he was playing at. If he'd had a midlife crisis, for example? If he was playing away?'

'And was he?'

She threw her head back in a theatrical gesture, and laughed.

Jo waited for her to explain, but she merely sat there smiling, and shaking her head as if enjoying a secret joke.

'And that's funny because?' said Jo.

'For so many reasons,' came the scornful reply. 'Charles was far too proper to do anything so sordid. He regarded himself as a gentleman, which really meant that he never said what he really thought. He never committed himself. And I'd be surprised if he was up to it. We hadn't made love in over five years.'

She made sure that she had Jo's attention.

'He couldn't get it up, you see. And he was too proud to do anything about it. Wouldn't see the doctor. Wouldn't try Viagra or any of those other remedies. I even kitted myself out at Ann Summers. That was when he started sleeping in a separate room.' She glanced across at the photo of her and Carter, and smiled. 'Wasn't a complete waste of time and money though. They've come in handy since.'

'There was no mention of any of this in your previous statements,' said Jo. 'In particular, your husband's impotence.'

'That's because this is the first time I've been interviewed by a female officer. There's a limit to what you can tell a man. And I didn't know that he was dead until earlier this year. I didn't think it was fair to share his sad secret in case he might turn up.'

'But I understood that Detective Sergeant Charnock had interviewed you several times.'

'Never on her own though. Always with her boss, or that other guy with the miserable face.'

Jo had no idea who she was referring to, not that it was relevant. She simply didn't believe Harriet Deighton's excuses for not revealing it before.

'Did your husband ever mention any problems he was having at work?'

Harriet Deighton sat up straight.

'Problems? What problems? It's news to me.'

'I'm not saying there were any. I'm merely asking if he ever mentioned any?'

'No, he didn't. Okay, he was frustrated at times by managers above him who couldn't hold a candle to him . . . his words, you understand . . . and underlings who couldn't follow simple instructions, and couldn't even spell. But no problems. And before you ask, no enemies either.'

'Outside of work then?'

She shook her head. Not in reply, but as an expression of frustration.

'You simply don't understand, Detective. Charles was the most mild, meek, inoffensive little man you could ever meet. He could be bumptious at times. He had an exaggerated opinion of himself. But he wouldn't say boo to a goose . . .'

And certainly not to you I bet, thought Jo. And why, if you had such a low opinion of him, did you marry him in the first place?

'. . . nor would he dream of doing anything dangerous, risky, or the least bit dishonest. He was basically a good person. He was not enemy material. More of a victim, I suppose. Which is what he became. Though God knows why.'

'What about his social life and outside interests? There is very little in the case file about those.'

'That's because he didn't have much of a social life outside of the Masons, and his only other interests were the garden, and Friday-night sessions at The Grapes. He played cribbage and dominoes. I can't see him piling up gambling debts with those, can you, SI Stuart? Leastways not ones that would get him killed.'

'The Masons,' said Jo. 'As in the Freemasons?'

'It was like a family for him.' She smiled ruefully. 'More so than me. It made him feel important, mixing with influential people. Doing charitable work. And he loved the pseudo-secrecy, the air of mystique and the rituals.'

Jo turned and pointed to the photo of Harriet Deighton and Raymond Carter.

'Ladies' Evening?'

'That's right. At the Lodge. It's where Charles and Ray first met.'

'The Lodge?'

'The Masonic Lodge. Ray is WM this year.'

'WM?'

'Worshipful Master. Charles never made it past Junior Deacon.'

'How many years had your husband been a member?'

'Seventeen.'

'And how often he did attend meetings?'

'The Lodge meetings are the second Tuesday of every month from September through to May. Charles never missed a single one. Then there are social events like Ladies' Evenings and so on. All of the installations of officers generally take place on Saturdays.'

'It was a significant part of his life then?' said Jo, wondering why there was so little mention of it in the case notes.

'It lit up his otherwise pointless existence.' It was said with a fraction more pity than resentment. 'And before you ask, he had no enemies there either. Quite the reverse. The Brethren loved him, in the same way that some people love their lapdogs.'

It was a cruel thing to say, and said without emotion. Jo recalled what Renton had said about it being a stable marriage. No mention of the word happy. No surprise then that people thought he had simply walked away from this loveless relationship.

'What did you really think had happened, when you realised that the car had gone?'

'I told you. That he'd had a mid-life crisis, or a brainstorm. I don't know.'

'Had he been at all depressed?'

'He was always mildly depressed, unless he was in the garden, or off to his precious Masons.'

Whenever he was away from you then, Jo reflected. She decided that it was time to touch a nerve, and see how Harriet responded.

'When did you first start seeing Mr Carter? Before or after your husband disappeared?'

Harriet Deighton clapped for the second time.

'Well done, detective,' she said. 'You finally got there. Took you longer than I expected, but nevertheless you made it. I'm disappointed with the "seeing" bit though. I'd have thought you might have managed something a little more colourful.'

'I'm glad you've clarified that,' Jo responded. 'So, was it before or after your husband disappeared that you began your affair with Mr Carter?'

Deighton stood up.

'I'm tired of repeating this. Let me say it one last time. Our relationship developed *after* my husband went missing. Not that it would make a blind bit of difference if we'd been at it for years. Neither of us had anything to do with my husband's disappearance, or his death. Now, if you don't mind, I'd like to get on.'

She piled the cups and saucers on to the tray, and carried it out of the room. Jo selected the *Stop* button, switched off her iPad and placed it back in the document case. She stood up as Mrs Deighton appeared in the doorway.

'So, Detective,' she said. 'No astounding revelations, no traumatic events brought back to mind. Like I told you: a complete waste of your time, and mine.'

'I'm sorry you think so,' said Jo, walking past her and into the hallway. She opened the door herself, and stepped on to the driveway.

Harriet Deighton stood with one hand on the door and the other on her hip.

'I'm surprised you didn't ask me about the life insurance?' she said.

'No need,' Jo told her. 'I was already aware that they didn't pay out for seven years, and even then it barely paid off the mortgage. There was one thing I wanted to ask you though.'

'Go on.'

'Did you have a cat?'

'A cat?'

'That's right.'

'No, we didn't. They were always peeing on Charles's geraniums. He hated them.'

'Now that *is* interesting,' said Jo. She turned and walked down the drive, leaving Harriet Deighton with a puzzled expression on her face.

Chapter 14

'Not here,' said Raymond Carter under his breath as he hurried her past the bank's meet-and-greet staff, hugging their tablets as though they expected them to be snatched at any moment.

'We could always sit in my car,' Jo suggested when they reached the pavement.

'Definitely not.' He looked left, then right and finally made up his mind. 'The Saucy Butty is usually quiet about now.'

She kept pace as he strode along the street.

'I assumed that as the manager of the bank you'd have your own office?'

'I do. But putting a Do Not Disturb notice on the door raises eyebrows.'

'I could have been a customer for all your staff would have known?'

'Ordinarily, I would agree. But since whoever made the appointment on your behalf mentioned that you were from the National Crime Agency, that would take some explaining.'

'Ah,' she said. 'That was me. But I could have been investigating fraud, money laundering, the hacking of customers' accounts?'

'And that would be better how exactly?'

He had a point. On the other hand, scurrying out of the office with her in tow seemed like the worst option of all. They had reached a busy junction, and the pelican lights brought him to a halt. He turned and stared down at her from a commanding six foot three.

'I've already been over this time and again with Lancashire Police.'

'Then it was a missing person enquiry. Now it's a murder investigation. The Police will not rest until the perpetrator is brought to trial.'

'Is that supposed to reassure me?'

'Catching the man who murdered your friend? Yes, I would have thought so.'

'Fat chance of that happening,' he mumbled.

The little green man began to flash, and he set off. She caught up with him on the far side.

'What is that supposed to mean, Mr Carter?'

'That I don't see how you're going to catch anyone when it's a motiveless crime.'

'There is always a motive.'

Carter stopped suddenly on the corner of a small row of terraced shops. There was a pharmacist, a boutique, and the Saucy Butty cafe. He opened the door, and disappeared inside. She followed him in and joined him at the back of the cafe. A waitress hovered.

'A latte and an Eccles cake for me,' he said. 'You get what you want, but I have to be back in half an hour. I've got an appointment.'

'Do you have Earl Grey?' Jo asked.

'Earl Grey *and* Lady Grey.' The waitress replied.

'An Earl Grey would be fine.'

'Nothing else?'

'No, thanks.'

The waitress retreated to the servery.

'Keep you on a tight rein then,' Carter observed.

'Sorry?'

'The NCA. Expenses don't run to an Eccles cake?'

'I'm not hungry,' she said. 'And given you're in a hurry, I thought you'd prefer that we got straight down to it.'

'Fine by me.'

He leaned back at an angle against the wall, and folded his arms. She had already taken a dislike to him, but that could easily have been because of his association with Harriet Deighton. Anyone who could love her, Jo had decided, needed his head testing.

She found the file on her iPad, and brought up the list of questions she had prepared. She began by following his lead.

'What did you mean,' she said, 'about finding a motive in this case?'

'Let's go through them,' he said. 'Greed? Charlie earned a relative pittance, had no savings, and didn't even have a decent life insurance policy. Jealousy? No one could possibly be jealous of Charlie, not even Quasimodo. Don't get me wrong, he was personable enough, but he lacked charm, gumption and testosterone. The same goes for lust – he didn't have it in him. Then of course, there's revenge.' He shook his head. 'For what? In any case, Charlie was incapable of hurting anyone.'

He paused while the waitress placed his coffee and pastry on the table in front of him.

'The Earl Grey's brewing,' she said. 'Only be a minute.'

Carter watched her depart, leaned forward, and lowered his voice.

'Unless you think he messed up someone's Pay As You Earn calculation?' He gulped his coffee, then picked up the cake and took a bite. 'I can't see him having stumbled across some dangerous dark secret can you?'

Crumbs of flaky pastry sprayed across the table. Several landed on the screen of Jo's tablet. She brushed them off with her sleeve.

'That was an interesting perspective of yours on jealousy,' she said. 'After all, Mrs Deighton is an attractive woman. Surely it was possible that someone might have been jealous that he was married to her. Might have lusted after her? Might have wanted to possess her?'

He had another drink. Put the cup down. Raised his eyebrows.

'Like me, for example?'

The waitress arrived with Jo's tea. She took a careful sip, then put the cup down and looked at Carter. 'If you say so.'

He leaned forward again. His voice had a harder edge. It made her wonder what he'd be like when he was really angry.

'Point one: I don't possess Harriet, we love one another. Point two: I never lusted after her, I admired her. Not least for putting up with Charlie with such equanimity. Point three: I was Charlie's best friend. His only *real* friend come to that. Point four: I have a cast-iron alibi for the night that Charlie went missing. It's in the file. Check it if you don't believe me!'

'I already have,' she said. 'You were in Birmingham on a two-day course on Ethical Banking in the Twenty-First Century. But I wasn't talking about you. I wondered if there was anyone else that might have been taking an interest in Mrs Deighton?'

He visibly relaxed.

'No, there wasn't. If there was, I would know.'

'There is one thing that puzzles me,' she said.

He picked up the Eccles cake and took another bite.

'What's that?'

'If Mr Deighton was your best friend, how come you had such a low opinion of him?'

He shook his head, and waited until he had finished dislodging a currant from between his teeth with his tongue.

'I didn't say he was *my* best friend, I said I was *his* best friend. His only friend.'

'The distinction being?'

'That he latched on to me at the Lodge meetings. I was the only one really prepared to take him on.'

'Why did you?'

'Because I felt sorry for him.'

'And because of his wife?'

He shrugged.

'Well, that was part of it, I suppose. My wife took to Harriet. She invited her and Charlie to sit with us at a Ladies' Evening. That sort of cemented our friendship.'

'Yours and Mr Deighton's, or yours and Harriet's?'

'Very clever,' he said. 'Both, as it happens.'

'Your friend's disappearance did suit you though,' she observed. 'It brought you and his wife closer together.'

He pushed the plate away, and locked eyes with hers.

'*Post hoc*,' he said. 'It means . . .'

'. . . *ergo propter hoc*,' she said. 'I know what it means. Because an event has occurred following another event, it does not follow that there is a causal relationship between them. On the other hand, it does not rule out the possibility that there is such a relationship.' She smiled. 'Rigging the Libor rate, and bankers receiving eye-watering bonuses, would be one example of an exception to the rule.'

His right eye twitched and his pupils contracted. He sat back and folded his arms again.

'Let me be very clear,' he said. 'I was saddened when Charlie went missing. I was sickened when I heard that he had been murdered, and especially how he was killed. Yes, it brought Harriet and me together. I have no regrets about that and no reason to feel guilty, other than how the divorce affected my wife and daughters. I was eighty miles away when Charlie disappeared. The hotel CCTV established that I never left the hotel, and my car remained in the car park for the entire duration of my stay.'

He pushed back the sleeve of his suit jacket, looked at his watch, then turned his wrist so that she could see the dial, and tapped it.

'Time's up, I'm afraid.' He lifted the sugar dispenser, slid out the bill tucked beneath it, and pushed it towards her. 'I assume you'll be putting this on your expenses?'

He stood up.

'I'm going now.'

Jo stood too. She positioned herself so that it was impossible for him to squeeze past.

'Just one thing,' she said. 'I understand that you are the Worshipful Master at the Lodge that you and Charles Deighton attended.'

He looked surprised.

'I don't see . . .'

'Only I wondered if you could arrange for someone to show me around?'

'Of course, I can do that, but I don't see . . .'

'It seems to me that the Masons were a central part of your friend's life,' she said. 'I need to know more about that life, and about him. Your Lodge would be a good place to start.'

He looked as though he was about to object, then he glanced at his watch.

'For God's sake!' he said. 'Look, you can't attend the Lodge, because you're not a member. But I can arrange for you to visit the Masonic Hall where the Lodge meets. Will that do?'

She nodded.

He reached inside his jacket pocket, and took out his phone. He had the number on speed dial. It was answered almost immediately.

'It's me,' he said. 'Can you hang on a moment?'

He put his hand over the phone, and turned to her.

'Perhaps you could pay while I sort this?'

It didn't sound like an option.

Chapter 15

The building came as a surprise. The few Masonic Halls that she had come across before were all suitably imposing Art Deco structures, like the Freemasons' Hall in London, the Salford Central one on the Crescent, and the Central Manchester one near the Crown Courts.

This Hall was of modern construction, late '60s she guessed, with a much more recent extension. Of red brick, with grey-tiled apex roof, double glass doors, and two windows on the upper storey, it could easily have been mistaken for a large church hall, community centre or even a sports centre.

A large silvery compass and set square on the wall was mirrored below by a row of smaller gold images on the double glass doors. A free-standing sign declared that the building was available for hire for conferences, weddings, birthdays, christenings, dinners, dances, and any other special occasion. Jo rang the doorbell.

A short, dumpy, cheerful-looking woman in a brown trouser suit appeared, and opened the doors.

'You're Detective Stuart,' she declared with a broad smile. 'Come on in.'

Jo wondered how Carter must have described her to merit immediate recognition. She put her case on the floor and reached in her pocket for her ID.

'No need for that, love,' the woman stated. 'I'm Dorothy Hunt, by the way. I'm the Stewardess. You can call me Dotty.'

'Stewardess?' asked Jo, as she followed her down a corridor. 'I thought the Freemasons were male only.'

'Not in France they're not. Didn't used to be here either. Some of the high-up suffragettes were women Masons. Not any more, and I wouldn't hold your breath if you're hoping that'll change on this side of the Channel any time soon.'

She opened a door and stepped aside, to allow Jo to enter first. They were in a large hall, with a bar along the length of one wall. It had been set out with circular tables, and chairs whose upholstery matched the plush blue carpet, one section of which had been wood-panelled to create a dance floor.

'I'm not a Mason. I'm a profane like you.'

'Profane?'

Dotty laughed.

'Doesn't mean what you think, love. It literally means "someone who stands outside". In this case, outside of Freemasonry. I'm just responsible for the hire and running of the premises. Including the bar, the kitchens, and the function and meeting rooms. It's a full-time business, believe you me.'

'How many rooms do you have?'

'Well, we've got this hall that seats a hundred and sixty set out like this, and two hundred and fifty in rows. There are three more about half this size, and another four rooms that'll take about twenty each. Then there's the Temple, but I'm only responsible for making sure it's cleaned properly.'

'This is a really big Lodge then,' said Jo. 'I had no idea that Freemasonry was still this popular?'

'It's not that, love. There are six Lodges that meet here, plus three Chapters. It'd be far too big for just one Lodge. Mind, they do have a recruitment drive at the moment to try to get some younger members, and not before time. We have more wakes than we do installations.'

A door opened at the far end of the hall. A man entered.

'Here's Mr Wakeman,' she said. 'He's the Tyler for the Home Lodge.'

'Tyler?'

'I'll let him explain. I've got to chase up a replacement sous chef – ours has gone down with man flu.'

She headed for a door beside the bar, smiling and nodding to Wakeman as she passed by. He was in his sixties, Jo guessed, of medium height, slim, bald, and of South East Asian heritage. He smiled as he neared her. It was a knowing smile that made her feel uncomfortable. He held out his hand.

'Officer,' he said. 'Raymond has told me all about you.'

His hand was freezing cold, so much so that she swiftly withdrew her own. He laughed.

'I'm sorry, I should have warned you. We've just taken a delivery of ice for the bar and kitchens. I dealt with it because Dotty was busy.'

'That's a relief,' she replied. 'Much better than any alternative explanations I can think of.'

'Like I'm a ghost? Walking dead? Or maybe someone they keep in the deep freeze, and only let out on high days and holidays?'

He laughed again. It was an irritating laugh, half snort, and half chuckle, wholly self-congratulatory.

'This is your lucky day. I only came in this morning because I had no appointments.'

'What is it you do?'

'I'm a financial adviser.'

'Actually, I meant as Tyler of the Home Lodge?'

His surprise was fleeting.

'Of course, Dotty will have told you. It's rather an important role, really.'

Jo had a feeling that he was trying to convince himself as much as her.

'I am charged,' he continued, 'with examining the credentials of any person seeking to enter the Lodge, to make sure that they are in fact accredited Masons. There was a time in our history when all sorts of people attempted to infiltrate Masonic meetings for all manner of nefarious purposes. Traditionally, one would sit in the anteroom of the Temple, or meeting room, with a drawn sword. However, as a long-serving member of the Lodge, and a Past Master, I am permitted to "tyle from within". I still have my sword, of course.'

'Of course,' she said, keeping her face straight. 'Must be really important, with it being a secret society.'

She watched him wonder if she was being serious, and then deciding to give her the benefit of the doubt.

'Well, it is more ceremonial now because, contrary to popular belief, we are no longer a secret society. Quite the reverse. Ahead of our three-hundredth centenary in 2017, the United Grand Lodge is determined to dispel the myths that surround us and show us for what we are – a modern, open and welcoming organisation.'

You might have to put that sword away then, she was tempted to tell him.

'Now, how would you like to proceed?' he asked. 'With a tour of the building? I can answer along the way any questions you may have about Freemasonry, or poor Charlie Deighton.'

For such a short conversation, she reflected, Raymond Carter's briefing must have been pretty comprehensive. Unless, of course, he had rung Wakeman again after she had left. She wondered what else they had discussed.

'That would be very helpful,' she said.

'I assume Dotty explained about this room?' he said.

'Yes, and about there being another seven rooms, and the Temple serving six Lodges and three Chapters. As well, I assume, as being rented out for the various functions displayed on the board outside?'

His eyes widened with affected surprise.

'Well remembered,' he said. 'And all without the aid of notes.'

Jo had been patronised by sharper knives in the block.

'Home Lodge,' she said. 'Is that the Lodge to which Mr Deighton belonged?'

'Er . . . yes,' he replied, surprised by the sudden formality in her tone.

'And how long have you been a member of Home Lodge, Mr Wakeman?'

'Thirty-five years, but I don't see . . .'

'So you will have known Mr Deighton extremely well, especially with you having been Tyler?'

'Yes, I suppose I did.'

'And all of the other members of the Lodge?'

'Of course, but . . .'

'And I assume you'll also know all of the members of the other Lodges and Chapters by sight, with you being Tyler?'

'Well . . .'

'And you'd also have been aware of any profanes who attempted to gain unauthorised access to the meetings?'

'Yes, but . . .'

'Good,' she said cheerfully. 'I can tell that you're going to be a great help, Mr Wakeman.' She paused, enjoying his discomfort. 'Now,' she said, 'that tour of the building?'

It took ten minutes to visit the kitchens, the smaller halls, and the seminar rooms. They passed several offices on the way. She had not asked any questions, content to let him explain the workings of the building. Now they were standing on the first-floor landing outside two impressive wooden doors emblazoned with the red rose of Lancashire. At the far end of the landing, propped up against the banister, was a set of six brightly coloured hobbyhorses. He pushed the door open, and stood back to allow her to enter.

The first thing that struck her was that it was far less ornate than she had expected. The second, was that the central expanse of the floor was covered in a carpet displaying the black and white tiles of a chequerboard. At their centre was a circle containing two five-pointed stars, one superimposed over the other. He saw her staring at it.

'The mosaic pavement,' he said. 'One of our most important symbols, drawn from the tracing board used by the ancient Greek architects. It represents the duality of human consciousness. Good and evil. It also represents the aspiration for balance in a Mason's life.'

'Ying and Yang?'

'Exactly.'

On the two longest sides of the room were double rows of chairs. Several of them were larger than the others, and cushioned. At the far end was a raised platform, with a table at the front. Behind it were three chairs, the central of which was the most impressive. There were two more chairs, each with a small table in front, one in the left corner, the other in the right. Above the central chair hung a large painting full of Masonic symbolism. She recognised an all-seeing eye, the sun, and a crescent moon, each of them atop a pillar. There was also the ubiquitous compass and setsquare. Above them all hovered a gilt triangle emitting golden rays. The remaining three walls were also hung with smaller paintings. One she suspected was the head of St John the Baptist on a silver plate. Most of the others showed symbols that meant nothing to her, beyond the fact that they looked like tools of some kind. A banner above the door declared *Truth, Honour, Virtue.*

Wakeman walked into the centre of the room, and turned to face her.

'Behind you,' he said, 'is the Tyler's chair, and also the Inner Guard, the Junior Deacon and the Senior Warden. Here, on the left, sit the Warden and the Junior Stewards.'

He beckoned her to join him, and then turned so that they were facing the far end of the room.

'In the centre sits the Worshipful Master, to his right the Immediate Past Master and the Senior Deacon, which was where Charles Deighton sat. To the Worshipful Master's left are the Chaplain and the Director of Ceremonies.'

'And the ones in the two corners?' she asked.

'The Secretary and the Treasurer.'

'That's a lot of roles,' she observed.

'It reflects a time,' he said, 'when the average Lodge had close to a hundred members.'

'And now?'

'My own Home Lodge has fifty-seven members. There is one Lodge that meets here, however, that has barely enough to fill all of the potential roles. Unless they can recruit another dozen or so brothers, I fear they will have to merge with another Lodge or fold altogether.'

'What's behind that door?' she asked.

He strode over, and unlocked it.

'See for yourself,' he said. 'This is where we store some of the regalia we use for our rituals.'

Two rows of shelves held a stone mallet, trowels, setsquares, plumb lines and various other implements she was unable to identify. A large smooth stone cube hung from the apex of a brass tripod that stood in the centre of the room. In one glass case she glimpsed a rope noose, a silver dagger, and a black blindfold. A wooden case contained a human skull, and several bones. A ceremonial sword stood on its own in one corner, a wooden coffin was propped up in another.

'I can see why you keep this room locked,' she said.

'I shouldn't actually have let you see all this,' he confided as he followed her out, and locked the door behind them. 'Please don't tell anyone else.'

'Why?' she joked. 'Will you end up in the coffin?'

He was not amused.

'We take our rituals very seriously. They are redolent with symbolism, and are intended to reinforce the values by which we try to lead our lives. There are two reasons why we wish to keep some of them secret: firstly, for reasons of tradition; secondly, because for those who do not understand their import, they too easily become a focus for ridicule.'

'I'm sorry,' she said as he walked briskly towards the doors through which they had entered. 'I didn't mean to offend you. I really appreciate you taking the trouble to show me all of this.'

She waited while he locked the doors behind them.

'There was one thing though,' she said. 'In fact, I'm not sure how to ask you this.'

'Go on,' he said.

'These hobbyhorses. What do you use them for?'

He surprised her with a burst of laughter.

'Last night,' he said, between snorts and chuckles, 'we had an event in the hall downstairs to raise money for a local hospice. Nothing to do with our ceremonies – it was a Race Night!'

Chapter 16

'It must engender a real sense of camaraderie,' said Jo, 'all of these rituals, the secrecy, the shared sense of values, the charitable donations?'

'It does,' he said. 'It's why I've been a member all this time.'

Dorothy Hunt had lent them her office. She had even brought them a cup of tea each and two scones. Wakeman seemed more relaxed, thanks to Jo's apparent empathy for his organisation.

'How did Mr Deighton get on with his fellow Masons?' she asked.

Wakeman had to think about it.

'Well enough, I suppose. He wasn't exactly the life and soul of the party so to speak. But he was respected. He certainly took it all very seriously. He was more committed than most.'

'In what way?'

'Well, for a start, he never missed a meeting.'

'But he never progressed further than Senior Deacon?'

'That's right. All of the officers up to Senior Deacon are appointed. Beyond that, they have to be elected. I'm afraid that although Charles did stand for election on numerous occasions, he was never successful.'

'Despite the fact that he was respected?'

'Respected is one thing, it's not the same as popular. And to be frank, sometimes it takes more than commitment. You have to be up to the job.'

'Did you like Mr Deighton?' she asked.

Wakeman didn't seem sure how to answer. He reached for his cup. She could tell that he was playing for time. He took a sip, put his cup down and finally made up his mind.

'*Like* isn't a word I would use. Charlie wasn't someone you could really like. He was just a bit too needy, if you follow me. Desperate to be part of whatever was going on, but not really sure how to connect. Like I say, I respected his enthusiasm and commitment. But I could never have been his friend.'

It came across as an honest response. It also fitted with the picture she was beginning to build of the victim. Someone emasculated by his wife, and never quite making it at work or in the Masons. It was hardly surprising that he found it difficult to connect.

'What was the general response when he went missing?'

'Bewilderment, I'd say. Yes, bewilderment. He didn't seem to have been having any major problems. Not that there was anyone he would have confided in if he had.'

'There must have been some theories though? There usually are in such a tightknit organisation?'

Wakeman frowned.

'Well actually, no, there weren't, not really. Okay, there were a few half-hearted jokes about him having misdirected tax rebates into his own private account, or having finally decided to cut the apron strings.'

'What did they mean by that?'

He raised his eyebrows.

'You must have met Mrs Deighton?'

'Yes.'

'Well, there you are then,' he grinned. 'You must know what I mean?'

Jo did, but she wasn't going to let him off that lightly.

'Enlighten me.'

He took another sip.

'Let's just agree that she's dominant, shall we? Dominant and demanding, in more ways than one, apparently. She spent more than either she or Charlie earned. I wouldn't be surprised if the life insurance came in handy to pay off all their debts.'

'And you know this how exactly?'

'It was common knowledge. About her spending that is. We could see it with our own eyes. When there were Ladies' Evenings, or other such social events, she would always turn up in designer clothes. Not just the dresses either, the shoes, handbags and the jewellery.'

Jo didn't recall reading about any of this in the case file.

'Mr Carter must have known about all of this?'

'Oh yes. We all did.'

'And yet he began a relationship with her shortly after Mr Deighton went missing?'

'I don't know about after,' he said. 'In any case, Ray is a totally different kettle of fish. He has the means, the authority, and the stamina that poor old Charlie lacked.'

'What did you mean about it not being *after?*'

Wakeman pretended to look puzzled.

'After?'

'When I said that Mr Carter began his relationship with Mrs Deighton after her husband went missing, you said, "*I don't know about after.*" What did you mean by that?'

'Ah,' he said, 'just a slip of the tongue.'

'I don't think so, Mr Wakeman,' said Jo, in her most authoritative tone. 'You were implying that the relationship began *before* Mr Deighton went missing. How long before?'

He squirmed in his seat.

'Now, I don't know that for a fact. It was just a rumour at the time.'

'Based on what?'

'Mainly on the way they acted when they were together at functions.'

'Which was?'

'Friendly.'

'How friendly?'

'This is very difficult,' he said. 'Raymond is a friend.'

'I can keep secrets too, Mr Wakeman,' she said. 'How friendly?'

'Well, just a bit more intimate than you might expect of someone with the wife of a friend.'

'Mainly?'

'I don't know what you mean?'

'You said "*Mainly.*" What were the subsidiary clues that the two of them were close?'

'Ah,' he said. 'You mean them having been seen together?'

'If you say so. Where, when, and by whom were they seen, Mr Wakeman?'

He paled slightly.

'This won't go any further?'

'I can't promise that,' she told him. 'But I can promise not to reveal my source.'

Ordinarily it was not a promise she would make lightly, but assuming he was going to provide her with other sources she could pursue them instead. Fortunately, she was right.

'One of the Brethren saw them together at Chester Races about six months before Charles disappeared. They were drinking champagne. Joined at the hip. Having a great time.'

'His name? This member of the Brethren.'

'You won't tell him it was me that told you?'

'How many of the Brethren did he share this little bit of gossip with, would you say?'

The hint of a smile appeared on his face.

'Lots of them,' he said.

'There you go then.'

So he told her.

Chapter 17

Jo was climbing back into the Audi when her phone rang. It was Harry Stone.

'Where are you?' he asked.

'I'm just leaving the victim's Masonic Hall,' she told him. 'I'm sorry, Boss, I should have let you know what I was doing.'

'That's not why I rang. I just wondered how you were getting on.'

She closed the car door, and brought him up to speed.

'So,' he said, 'we've got a carving on a tree that may or may not be connected, and wasn't really followed up on in the original investigation. Also, if I've understood you right, you're convinced that we're looking for more than one person because it would have been impossible for someone to do it on their own. Then there's a domineering, high-spending wife having an affair with the victim's best friend before he went missing, that nobody mentioned at the time. And, finally, you've confirmed that there's no evidence that anyone else had it in for him.'

'I know,' she said. 'It's not much to show for two day's work.'

'It wasn't a criticism. On the contrary. Little acorns, Jo.'

She couldn't help smiling. He sounded just like her father when she was growing up. *'Little acorns, Jo; mighty oaks from acorns grow.'* It was a bittersweet memory.

He misinterpreted her silence.

'Are you still there?'

'Yes, Boss. I was just thinking.'

'Good. That's what you're paid for.'

'I need to get back to the office,' she said, 'and dig a bit further into the wife and the boyfriend. And I'm hoping that Ram can do some research for me into missing persons, and that carving.'

'Good idea,' he said. 'I'll put the kettle on.'

'I thought you were back in London, Boss?'

'Something came up.'

He didn't sound very happy about it.

⏋

'It's Max,' Ram told her. 'Seems he got up the nose of the senior investigator on Operation Gannet. The Boss has had to pour oil on stormy waters.'

'I see.'

He grinned.

'That's his name, the SIO. DI Waters.'

Jo was beginning to warm to his humour, just as she had with DC Hulme.

'I've got something I hoped you could help me with?' she said.

He grinned again.

'That's what I'm here for.'

'The way I see it,' she said, 'there are two possible lines of enquiry. The first involves the wife and her partner, supposedly the victim's best friend. It's looking like they were lovers before Deighton went missing.'

'There was no inkling of that in the murder file?'

'No, there wasn't. And as yet it's word of mouth. I've still got to interview the source of the gossip. But assuming it is true, I'm still left with the fact that the best friend had a watertight alibi.'

'So you'll need to find out if either of them had mutual friends who could have helped carry out the abduction?'

'Or paid someone to do it?'

'Their phone records, and bank statements would be a good place to start,' he said. 'Mind you, it was ten years ago. That's going to take some doing. I'd have thought that was something the original investigation would have done.'

She shook her head.

'It was only a MisPer at the time. Carter had a cast-iron alibi, and the wife couldn't have done it alone. Not only that, the original enquiry had no evidence that the two of them were at it together before he went missing.'

'You said there were two lines of enquiry?'

'The other one is that it had something to do with him being in the Masons.'

Shah frowned.

'I know,' she said. 'It's a long shot. I just have this feeling. Call it intuition.'

'So what have you got for a motive?' he said. 'The guy's given away Masonic secrets? Aren't they supposed to keep them on pain of death?' He grinned. 'Only joking. On the other hand, perhaps he'd uncovered some kind of corruption. Cronyism that could have cost them their jobs, or even had them sent down for a stretch. Now that is a real possibility.'

'Good point,' she said. 'Except . . .'

'Go on.'

'If Andy is right, this has all the hallmarks of a possible serial killer, not a one-off revenge killing.'

'You think someone might have targeted him because he was a Mason?' He sounded far from convinced.

'I don't,' she admitted. 'But it's either that, or personal.' She sighed. 'I suppose the burial alive could have been revenge for betrayal. I just don't know.'

'In that case,' he said, 'how d'you want me to proceed?'

'Go ahead with the wife and boyfriend. At the same time, ask Missing Persons for a targeted search of their database covering the last fifteen years, with the following identifiers: male, aged twenty-five to sixty-five, Freemasons, went missing on foot, or own car abandoned, still missing.'

'Why don't I ask them for two lists?' he suggested. 'One with, and one without, Freemasonry as an identifier? That way you might pick up ones that were Masons but never identified as such, given they don't always disclose their membership.'

'That would brilliant,' she told him.

'You'll have to join the queue,' he said. 'But I should have something for you on the MisPers analysis by tomorrow afternoon. I can't promise how long the other one will take.'

'Don't worry,' she said. 'Just do your best.'

He pretended to be offended.

'I always do. By the way, the Boss said to tell you to go straight in when you arrive. He's in the corner meeting room.'

Max Nailor passed her as she stepped out into the corridor. Her fellow investigator looked preoccupied.

'Hi,' she said. 'How's it going?'

He raised his right hand to show that he had heard her, but carried on walking. Then he was through the door, and gone. She shook her head and knocked on the meeting-room door.

'Come!'

She turned the handle, and stepped apprehensively into the room. Stone had his back to her, and was staring out across the waters of the Huron Basin.

'You wanted to see me, Boss?'

His shoulders visibly relaxed. He turned and smiled at her. He looked even wearier than he had the previous day.

'Jo, come on in and sit down,' he said, pulling out a chair for himself. 'I'm sorry I bellowed, by the way. It's been a rough day.'

'No worries, Boss.'

She placed her document case on the table.

'How did you get on with the Lancashire SIO?' he asked.

'Okay, I think. He's tied up with a child abduction, so he asked his number two to show me around the deposition site. He seemed reasonably happy that we were involved.'

'Thank God for that.'

'If I had to guess, Boss, I'd say not only did they come up against a brick wall, but he's also massively stretched resource-wise.'

'Aren't we all? If the dynamic duo have their way, it's going to get even worse.'

'The dynamic duo?'

'The Home Secretary and the Justice Minister.'

'They're already vying with each other to see who can make the deepest efficiency cuts. Once the Human Rights Act has disappeared up the Swanee, sixty per cent of what we do has been privatised, all of the agencies are on payment-by-results, and local community justice groups have been issued with ducking stools, where do you think that'll leave us?'

'Investigating *thought crime*?'

'Very good,' he said. 'George Orwell was only out by three decades.'

He examined his hand, and gave it a good rub.

'Where were we?'

'Operation Hound? The Charles Deighton murder?'

'Oh, yes. You wanted Shah to do some digging?'

She summarised her discussion with Ram, and the actions he had agreed to take.

'Makes sense,' he said. 'You've done a good job winkling out the fact that they were lovers prior to his disappearance.'

'I still have to verify that. Fortunately, the source works here in Manchester. He's an estate agent. I'm hoping to catch him before he finishes work.'

'You mentioned something about a carving on the tree?' he said.

Jo found the photo folder on her iPad and brought up the ones she had taken at the scene. She angled it so that he could see, and slowly flicked through them.

'Let me see that third one again,' he said. 'The close up.'

He used his thumb and forefinger to zoom in, then sat back and folded his arms. It was not a defensive gesture she realised, it was what he did when he was thinking hard. Like DCI Caton leaning back with his hands behind his head, or Gordon Holmes rubbing his chin. She wondered what people thought her own mental prop was.

'And you're sure it was carved at the same time that Deighton was buried?' he said.

'"*There, or thereabouts*", according to their expert.'

He nodded.

'I think I know what it is. And if I'm right, it strengthens your theory about it having something to do with his having been a Mason.'

She felt a tingle of excitement.

'I used to be a Mason, Jo,' he said, taking her completely by surprise. 'Not a lot of people know that. No reason they should, given that I resigned a long time ago. Long before serving officers were asked to state whether or not they were Freemasons. There

101

were several reasons why I resigned. The first was that I joined for all the wrong reasons. I thought you had to join if you wanted to get on in the Met.'

He shook his head.

'I'm not proud of that. My only excuse is that I was young and impressionable, and my first DI told me I'd be a fool not to. The second reason is that I didn't really take to it. I'm not going into all that, I just didn't. And finally, I couldn't afford the time. I had a wife and young daughter who deserved to see more of me, and my passion was playing for the Met soccer team. I couldn't divide myself four ways: work, home, soccer, Lodge. So I resigned.'

'That must have been difficult?'

'It was. I got a lot of stick to start with, but I survived.'

He grinned.

'They didn't bury me alive. Which brings me neatly to your carving. I think it might belong to a Masonic cipher.'

'A cipher?'

'A code in the form of a cryptograph. One that uses signs or symbols that would only be understood by those who know how to crack the code.'

'A sort of Masonic Enigma Code?'

'Exactly, except that Freemasonry has more than one. Look, I'll show you.'

He typed, *Masonic ciphers*, into the search bar, and pressed return. The second offering was *Images for Masonic ciphers*. He clicked on it. The screen was immediately filled with row after row of screen shots of all manner of alphabetic, numeric, and symbolic codes.

'So many?' she said. 'It's bewildering. How on earth could anyone remember all of these?'

'They don't have to. Different Orders and Degrees of Masonry have their own particular ciphers. I'll need to do a bit of research on this, but I can't do it now, I'm afraid. I have to get back to London.'

He pushed back his chair, and stood up.

'I wouldn't get carried away just yet. I'd wait and see what Shah's MisPers analysis turns up. In the meantime, don't you think you should bring DI Renton up to speed? We wouldn't like him to think you were going it alone.'

'I will,' she assured him, 'as soon as I've spoken to this source. Hopefully he'll confirm Wakeman's story, and I'll look like less of a chancer.'

'I doubt you'll ever be mistaken for that,' he said. 'Now if you'll excuse me, I've got a train to catch.'

Chapter 18

Karl Kantrell was nervous. It showed in the manner in which he stood as Jo entered the room, the way in which he adjusted his tie, and in the contradiction between his overconfident smile and the tremor in his voice. He held out his hand.

'How do you do?' he said.

His hand was clammy, but then he was on the large side – at least sixteen stone she estimated, which was a lot for someone only five feet five inches tall. There was no hint of a special grasp, no unnatural pressure of the thumb. Not that as a mere woman, and a profane, she had been expecting one.

'I'm fine, Mr Kantrell,' she said. 'How are you?'

'Oh . . . fine,' he said. '*Really* fine, as it happens. Please, sit down.'

She placed her document case on the floor beside her.

'Have you landed a big one then?'

He looked confused.

'Made a big sale? A whole apartment block perhaps?'

Relief flooded his face. The laugh when it came was forced.

'Not a whole apartment block. Never happens. Not unless it's a company moving their head office. Now that would be a coup. But yes, we have had a number of gratifying sales this week.' He made a point of looking at his watch. 'Actually, we were hoping to have a bit of a celebratory drink, my staff and I.'

'Don't worry,' she said. 'I'm sure we'll have this sorted in no time.'

He tried to smile, but it only made him look even more anxious. 'Sorted?'

'Resolved,' she said. She reached down, then placed her iPad on the table between them.

'Do you mind if I record this conversation, Mr Kantrell? It's so much easier than having to take notes.'

As she switched the tablet on, he gawped at it with the panicky stare normally reserved for venomous reptiles.

'Record?'

'That's right. You don't mind, do you? It's not as though you're under caution, is it?'

That didn't seem to help matters.

'Look . . . Ms . . . excuse me,' he stuttered, 'But what do I call you?'

'SI Stuart, or Officer,' she said calmly.

'You mentioned on the phone, SI Stuart, that this was about poor Charlie Deighton. I'm not sure that I'll be able to help you much. I barely knew him.'

Jo selected *Record*.

'Mr Kantrell and Senior Investigator Stuart,' she intoned. 'Sixteen forty-six hours, on the fifth of June 2015. Kantrell's Premier Properties, Manchester.' Then she sat back in her chair, and made sure they had eye contact.

'Mr Kantrell,' she said. 'How did you come to know the deceased, Charles Deighton?'

He loosened his tie, and sat back as though trying to mirror her.

'We were members of the same Lodge. That's where I first met him. I was already a member of long standing when he was admitted.'

'And how long were you members of the same Lodge before he disappeared?'

He had to think about it. There were small beads of sweat on his forehead, and along the collar line of his shirt.

'Six years, maybe seven.'

'So you were brothers in the same Lodge for at least six years, and yet a few minutes ago you claimed that you barely knew him?'

He took a handkerchief from his suit breast pocket, and ran it along the inside of his collar.

'It's a large Lodge, and I never really got to know Charlie very well.' He crumpled the handkerchief in his hand, and closed his fist over it. 'And, to be honest, it doesn't feel right to be talking about one of my brethren behind his back so to speak, especially since he's dead.'

'Isn't that the point, Mr Kantrell? That he's dead? And the manner of his death?' She shook her head as one might with a naughty child. 'You weren't exactly scrupulous about not talking behind his back when he was alive, were you?'

'I don't know what you mean?'

His eyes were all over the place. Jo was beginning to wonder if he had St Vitus's Dance.

'I'm referring to a rumour that circulated about your having seen Mrs Deighton behaving in an intimate manner at Cheshire Races with Raymond Carter, another member of your Lodge.'

He looked embarrassed.

'Oh, that.'

She decided to let him squirm. Which he did so effectively that the leather seat beneath his ample behind positively squealed. It made her think of Sir Alex Ferguson's famous expression, '. . . *it's squeaky bum time.*' She had to fight hard not to smile.

'It wasn't a rumour,' he said with as much gravitas as he could muster. 'It was a fact. Yes, I saw them. And yes, I may have told someone at the Lodge. I was concerned.'

'Concerned?'

'For all three of them,' he said. 'And for the reputation of the Lodge.'

'Of course,' she said. 'That was very brotherly of you.'

Jo let him squirm a little longer. By which time he was ready to tell her whatever she wanted to know, so long as he could lock up and hurry after the rest of his staff, who would already be wondering what he had done to attract the attentions of the National Crime Agency.

Kantrell glanced up to the left without moving his head, and then down at the desk. Finally, he looked up, but was unable to maintain eye contact with her.

'Look,' he said, 'shortly after I joined the Lodge to which Charles Deighton and Raymond Carter belonged, I became a member of a Royal Arch Mason Chapter. Consequently, I spent very little time in their Lodge. And I never socialised with either of them.'

'But you knew both Raymond Carter and Harriet Deighton well enough to recognise them at the races.'

His hand went to his mouth as he muttered a reply.

'I'm sorry,' she said, 'could you repeat that?'

'You've met them both,' he said. 'So you'll know they aren't the sort of people who merge into the background.'

He pushed his chair back.

'Now, can I go, please? My staff are waiting for me.'

He was wrong. The main office was empty. They had decided to go ahead. Jo waited for him to lock up and then watched Kantrell as he waddled across Watson Street, and into the Hilton Hotel. Now he would have to wait on his own in the queue for the lifts to the Cloud Bar. It served him right for dithering.

On her way back to the Great Northern car park, she reflected on the interview. She felt sure that he'd been telling the truth about seeing the two of them in Chester. But he had definitely lied about how well he had known Carter and Deighton. There had been no clock high up on the wall behind her. Every time he looked up there, he had been creating a false narrative. Then there was that hand over his mouth. And throughout the interview he had been way beyond nervous. There was something that Mr Kantrell was desperate to hide. First things first, she needed to bring DI Renton up to date.

Chapter 19

'You'll have to make this quick,' Renton told her. 'That abduction turned out to be a runaway grooming case.'

'You found her then?' said Jo.

'Thank God. But it looks like it's connected to a child sex ring. Can you imagine how much work that's generating? The Chief Constable is throwing everything at it bar the kitchen sink. He doesn't want a scandal like the one in Rochdale on his watch. So, Operation Hound. What have you got for me?'

She told him her theory that there was more than one person involved in the disposal of the victim, that there was new evidence that Raymond Carter and Harriet Deighton had been cheating on the victim prior to his disappearance, and the possibility that the carved symbol on the tree belonged to a Masonic cipher.

'More than one person, I'll go along with,' he said. 'And the best friend banging his wife, I grant you that should have been picked up from the outset. But it doesn't change the fact that Carter had a cast-iron alibi. As for the murder being part of some secret Masonic ritual, I reckon you've been reading too much Dan Brown.'

'I did say it was all a bit tentative.'

He grunted.

'Well, if you turn up something more substantial, let me know. Better still, let DS Charnock know. She can tell me, and if it's a goer you can come up and see me again. Till then, good luck.'

'So you're happy for me to . . .'

'Sure,' he said. 'Bye now.'

He ended the call before she had time to respond.

In light of what had happened with Max Nailor, Renton's response left Jo feeling exposed. It was all very well giving her carte blanche to get on with it, but without a witness to the fact, it was his word against hers. Not worth a bean if it all went belly-up. She was wondering if she should check with Harry Stone when her phone rang. It was DS Charnock.

'I was about to ring you,' Jo told her. 'I've just finished speaking with your Boss.'

'How is he? I haven't seen or heard from him since the day before yesterday.'

'Busy.'

'He's always busy. You should see the workload he's left me with.'

'Thanks for finding the time to ring me.'

'It's not me you want to thank, it's the keen young Detective Constable I put on to the mystery of the disappearing cat and the planks that went walkabout you should be thanking.'

'You mean . . .'

'It turns out there was a little old lady lived in the farm down that lane at the end of the estate. You know, the one beside where we parked. She moved a couple of years ago into a care home in Adlington. Wasn't there when we did the initial house-to-house enquiries. Being young and keen, my lad decided to pay her a visit.'

'It was her cat?'

'We'll never know,' Charnock replied. 'Not without doing a DNA on the offspring, and that's probably a nonstarter because I'm not sure we've still got the cat's remains. But she does remember a cat going missing about the time we know that Deighton was buried. That's a miracle in itself because she can barely remember what happened yesterday. It was a farm cat, virtually feral, and it was her best ratter. She was gutted when it disappeared. Couldn't believe it really, because it knew how to look after itself.'

'And the planks?'

'My DC excelled himself there. The firm went bust early in 2009. He tracked down one of the Directors and got hold of his staff records. Not complete, obviously, because he had a shedload of casual labour. But among the full-time staff was the name of the site manager. He tracked him down through his National Insurance number, and found him managing the erection of a large office block in Leeds. Long story short – yes, some planks did go missing about then, together with two sets of tools, and a cement mixer. Set them back a day and half, and time is money.'

'So neither the cat nor the planks were part of the original plan,' Jo reflected. 'The killer was simply thinking on his feet.'

'Or *her* feet?' said Charnock.

'Or *their* feet.'

'At least we know it wasn't part of some dark satanic ritual,' said the Detective Sergeant, 'involving a black cat, and planks to prevent the victim from returning as a zombie.'

'Voodoo,' said Jo.

'Voodoo?'

'You're mixing your metaphors. Black cat is satanic rites, but zombies are voodoo.'

Charnock laughed.

'I'll take your word for it. My only reference point is the Pendle Witches. I'm always up for that on a Friday night.'

'I don't follow?'

'Pendle Witches. It's a beer named after the eight women and two men who were hanged as witches at Lancaster Castle in 1612.

Lovely English Pale Golden Ale. Moorhouse's Brewery, up our way, in the Trough of Bowland. Coincidentally, they do one called Black Cat as well. You should try it.'

'When we've cracked this case, we should have a pint together,' said Jo.

'*When* we crack it? Does that mean you've made some progress?'

Jo repeated what she had told DI Renton. Charnock listened without interruption.

'What did my Boss say?' she asked.

Jo told her.

'No surprises there,' Charnock said. 'He's not known for his imagination. He was right about our having missed the star-crossed lovers though. I'll look forward to seeing what you come up with in relation to their finances.'

'Me too,' said Jo.

She paused while she decided how to phrase the next question. She didn't want to appear presumptuous, however friendly and reasonable Jean Charnock was coming across. After all, the DS was still nominally heading up the investigation.

'Look,' she said. 'I should really have cleared it with you or your Boss before I set our Intelligence Analyst off running. Are you okay with this, or would you prefer to have your people work on the searches?'

'You must be joking,' Charnock replied. 'I bet you can do in a day what would take us a fortnight, always assuming I could get it moved up the waiting list. You carry on, Ma'am. That's what Renton told you, and if he hadn't I would have. We can't afford to look a gift horse in the mouth right now. You go for it.'

Jo stopped at the lights at the end of Regent Road and applied her handbrake. Another fifteen minutes she estimated, and she would be back at the apartment. She reflected on Charnock's parting comment, and smiled. She had never been compared to a gift horse before. In her experience, you rarely got something for nothing, and if you did there was a good chance that it had something wrong with it. DS Charnock was very fond of her metaphors. The one that sprang to Jo's mind was *'falling at the first fence'*.

Chapter 20

'I'm glad you texted,' said Abbie, 'otherwise I would have started without you. Did you bring the elderflower pressé?'

Jo placed the bottle on the table, and gave her a hug. There was something half-hearted about the way in which Abbie responded. Jo assumed it was because she was busy cooking.

'What are we having?' Jo asked.

'Seafood risotto with prawns and shrimp.' Abbie picked up the bottle. 'This is for me. I'm on duty in an hour and a half. There's some Chablis left in the fridge if you fancy it?'

'You bet,' said Jo. 'Can I help?'

Abbie wiped her free hand on her apron.

'No, you're fine. Another ladle of stock, a couple of quick stirs and we're good. You get changed and it'll be on the table when you come through.'

'This risotto is seriously good,' said Jo, raising her glass. 'Cheers.'

'There's nothing to it,' said Abbie. 'Once you've done one risotto, you've done them all. It's just a matter of varying the wine and the type of stock according to the main ingredients. You should give it a try.'

'I might just do that.'

'On the other hand, when we have a place with a garden you could concentrate on that, and let me do the cooking.'

'A place with a garden?' said Jo. 'That's going to be a long way off. We've only just moved in here.'

Abbie put her fork down, and adopted a serious expression.

'Sooner rather than later,' she said. 'After all, there will come a point when we've outgrown this apartment. And let's face it, while it's great for us, single and fancy-free, when we have a family it'll be far from ideal. City centre, top floor, no garden?'

Jo wanted to tell her that she should have thought of that before she agreed to let her buy this place. Somehow she managed to smile.

'Still a good few years off,' she said. 'After all, we haven't reached square one yet.'

Abbie reached across the table and laid her hand over Jo's.

'You haven't forgotten, have you?'

Jo looked up.

'Forgotten?'

'The meeting with James on Saturday morning, please tell me that you haven't forgotten. That you're not working?'

'Of course I haven't forgotten,' said Jo, placing her other hand over Abbie's. 'It's on the calendar in red, it's on that note you put on the fridge door, it's on the calendars in my phone and iPad, and you've texted me two reminders. I'm surprised it isn't on Facebook.'

Abbie's laugh was forced.

'Sorry.' She eased her hand away. 'I know I've been obsessing about it, but it's a really big deal.'

'It's only a meeting,' Jo reminded her. 'There's a hell of a long way to go.'

Abbie speared a prawn.

'I want you to like him,' she said. 'I want you to like each other.'

'Stop worrying,' Jo replied. 'You picked me after all, so your taste can't be that bad.'

'I should have asked,' said Abbie. 'How's your new job going?'

Jo took a sip of her wine. It was pleasantly crisp and cool.

'It's weird. I haven't yet worked out the boundaries.'

'Boundaries?'

'How far I'm supposed to be working on my own, and how far I'm supposed to be checking everything with the rest of the team. I'm not even sure if I have a boss when Harry Stone is in London. I mean, I can hardly keep ringing him up, he'll think I'm not up to it. On the other hand, if I don't keep him up to speed . . .'

Abbie nodded thoughtfully.

'Damned if you do, damned if you don't.'

'Exactly.'

'Err on the side of caution is my advice,' said Abbie. 'He'll soon tell you if you've got the balance wrong. You're still writing everything up, like you had to with GMP?'

'God, yes!'

'Then why don't you create a shared folder, so he can have a look at what you've been doing whenever it suits him?'

'That's a great idea,' said Jo. 'Why has nobody thought about that?'

'Maybe they already have. Maybe no one thought to tell you that's the way they do it. Sometimes it's just about asking the right questions.' Abbie scooped up a forkful of the rice. 'That's something I'll have to do when I start *my* new job.'

Once Abbie had picked up her bag and left for work, Jo stacked the dishwasher, then settled down to catch up on two episodes of *Corrie*, followed by *Downton Abbey*. She found it impossible to shake off Operation Hound, and mentally sifted through the interviews with Harriet Deighton, Carter and Kantrell.

Lying in bed, attempting to read, Jo's mind drifted back to the artefacts room in Deighton's Masonic Hall, the noose, the dagger and the blindfold, the human skull and the coffin. Then she recalled the crime scene in Birkacre Woods. The ropes, the blindfold, the grave and the skeletal remains. There were so many similarities. Too many echoes.

That night she dreamt of dark satanic rituals that threatened to surface painful memories, and push her towards the yawning chasm of her greatest fear.

Chapter 21

Jo woke early, bathed in sweat, her nerves on edge, and set off immediately for the gym. It was 6.30am when she arrived. This morning's session would be a one-to-one with Grant, her personal instructor. It was eighteen months since she had begun to practise Krav Maga, the Israeli military self-defence programme.

It had started as part of the healing process following her abduction, but was now an essential part of her life. She was determined never to feel as vulnerable again.

From day one of the *Stay Away* women's self-defence programme, she had realised that this was exactly what she needed. It provided a much-needed boost to her self-esteem, renewed her confidence, taught her skills way beyond those her initial police training had provided, and was the perfect way to keep fit. As she changed into her kit, Jo recalled that first group session.

'Forget James Bond, Matt Damon, Jackie Chan,' Grant had begun. 'Forget every fight sequence you've ever seen. They're all bullshit. Real fights last seconds. If you haven't finished it within three seconds or less, you're going to lose.'

He had pointed to Jo.

'You're a cop. How many street brawls have you been called to where a single punch has killed someone? Worse still, turned them into a vegetable?'

'More than I care to remember,' she'd admitted.

'Exactly! You don't want to get in a fight, ever. Especially if there's a knife involved.'

He turned to the guy next to her.

'You say you've done jujitsu. What d'you do if someone comes at you with a knife?'

The guy turned sideways, and began to raise his left arm in a blocking motion.

'Wrong!' said the instructor. 'You run!'

Mr Jujitsu had the temerity to raise his hand.

'What if you can't run?' he asked. 'What if you're in an alley that's a dead end?'

The instructor shook his head despairingly.

'If you're in an alley with a dead end, then you're a bloody idiot for having gone in there in the first place. However, it's a good question. If you can't run, you disable the bastard, and *then* you run. But what you *don't* do, is try to disarm your attacker.'

He stepped back. As he spoke, he scanned the entire group, making sure that he had eye contact with each of them in turn.

'You never, ever attempt to disarm an attacker. What do you never, ever try to do?'

'Disarm an attacker!' they chorused.

'What *do* you do?'

About half of them managed to remember.

'Disable him!'

He nodded his head.

'We're getting there.'

He paced up and down a few times to make sure he had their full attention. Then he stopped.

'Time to recapitulate.' He counted off on the fingers of his left hand. 'Rule one, avoid violence at all costs. Rule two, be prepared to do whatever it takes to stay alive. Rule three, you will never, ever win a defensive fight. Rule four, get in first and finish it fast.'

He had smiled grimly.

'Now, are you ready?'

Jo placed her kit bag in the locker and entered the code.

Everything Jo had learned in her police self-defence training, other than techniques to defuse situations, had been focused on restraint. The result was that officers neglected to develop their skills in contact combat, relying on the fact that they were equipped with batons and Tasers. Fine if you had time to draw them. She had not. Whether experience of Krav Maga would have prevented her own takedown was something she no longer wondered about. What she did know was that if someone ever came for her again, they would find her prepared. Alert to the warning signs, senses heightened, physical skills honed to perfection. Prepared to do whatever it took. Prepared to kill.

She checked that her car keys, and warrant card were in the slim security pouch, and attached it to her belt so that it sat at the base of her spine. Anyone could break into a locker in a matter of seconds, lock or no lock. Besides, keys were one of the weapons she was now trained to use.

Grant was already in the gym. He was manoeuvring into place a heavy standing bag, on a circular weighted base.

'Meet Bob,' he said.

There were twelve black cylindrical bags of varying weights suspended from a steel rack bolted to the ceiling, but this one was unlike any training bag she had ever used before. It consisted of the top two thirds of a flesh-pink male dummy, with the ripped torso of a heavyweight boxer.

'Bob's skin is Plastisol,' said Grant. 'And he's filled with urethane foam. This is as lifelike as you're going to get without a human training buddy. Go ahead, Jo, feel him.'

She ran her hand over Bob's abs and up across his pecs.

'It's uncanny,' she said. 'Does Ann Summers know about him?'

He laughed.

'If she does, I doubt she'd expect him to be used quite the way we're going to use him. And how neat is this?'

He placed his hands under the base of the dummy just where the shorts ended, and lifted the whole of the torso until it was at the height he wanted.

'You can practise on a guy who is shorter than you, the same height, or even so tall you'd have to jump up to thunderclap him. But before I let you loose on Bob, it's warm-up time.'

Three sets each of thirty press-ups, star jumps, and burpees later, Jo wiped the sweat from her face and hands on a towel and turned to face the dummy.

'Okay,' said Grant. 'Today you're doing head strikes, jabs, elbows, straight punches, angle shots, hooks and uppercuts, and we'll finish with a series of knee strikes to the groin. Ready?'

Jo nodded.

'Assume the position.'

Jo stood with her left foot forward, her knees bent slightly, and both hands raised as though preparing to defuse a situation. Failing that, it would confuse the aggressor, and leave her ready to strike.

'Sequence one,' said Grant. 'Nose strike, thunderclap, elbow strike.'

Jo counted silently to three, then yelled and simultaneously launched a devastating attack. The heel of her left hand struck the base of Bob's nose. As his head flew backwards, her cupped right hand slapped hard against his left ear. As his head jerked sideways

121

her left elbow smashed against his right cheekbone. She quickly stepped four paces back, and assumed the position once more.

Had Bob been a real person he would have had a broken nose, ruptured eardrums, and a fractured cheekbone. More importantly, she would have been long gone before he had realised what had happened.

'Not bad,' Grant declared. 'Let's try it again, shall we? A little faster this time.'

Chapter 22

Andy Swift was at the barrier talking to the security guy when Jo arrived. He wore a helmet, a cycle vest over a long sleeved T-shirt, and padded knee and elbow protectors. He had one foot on what looked like a cross between a child's scooter and a moped. It was fluorescent green. A long head post, supporting twin lights between the handlebars, gave the impression of an *E.T.* alien. Jo lowered her window and pipped her horn.

He turned and grinned at her.

'Meet Charly,' he said.

'Charlie?'

'Charly MZ.' He spelt it out. 'The only legal motorised urban scooter in the UK. The Quays are perfect for this little beauty.'

The barrier rose. Andy adjusted his backpack, and sped away with a regal wave of his hand.

'Breath of fresh air, he is,' offered the security guard. 'Nutty as a fruitcake, but I'd have him over the rest of them that park here. Excepting you, of course. They think themselves better than they are, most of them. Not Mr Swift.'

The minute that Jo entered the incident room, Ram Shah was on his feet waving to her.

'Jo!' he called. 'You've got to see this.'

She shrugged off her jacket as she walked, draped it over the chair he'd pulled up beside him and sat down. His dark brown eyes were alive with excitement.

'Is it the wife, the boyfriend, or Missing Persons?' she asked.

'I'm still waiting on the phone records and the bank statements,' he told her. 'Mind you, with our powers, I should have them soon. It would have taken you five times as long with GMP.'

She didn't doubt it. With what little they had so far, she doubted that any regional force would have been granted any access at all.

'It's Missing Persons,' he said.

'You've got a match already?'

'*A* match?' he laughed. 'I've got seventeen of them.' He pointed to the screen.

She craned forward. All of them were Masons at the time at which they were reported missing. The youngest was twenty-seven years old when he disappeared, the eldest seventy-one.

'When I saw how many there were, I decided to widen the parameters,' he explained. 'I went from twenty years of age up to eighty. That pulled in just the extra one.'

Jo was already processing the rest of the table. Fourteen of the men were assumed to have been on foot when they disappeared, including walking to or from a taxi rank, tube station, bus, or tram. The cars belonging to the other three had been found abandoned some distance away from their last known sighting. The first of the men to have disappeared was in 2005, five years before Charles Deighton. The most recent was only twelve months ago.

'I did a geographic profile,' Shah told her. 'They're all over the place. Furthest south is in Kent, furthest north in Newcastle.'

'And they're all Masons?'

'Every one of them.'

'Are there any geographic clusters?' she asked.

He pursed his lips.

'Not really. Not unless you count the fact that there are two more north of the Tees-Exe line than south of it.'

It did not fit any crime cluster pattern that Jo had seen before. Besides, the distances were so far apart that even if all of these were abductions, and they were all the work of one person, or a team of persons, all it meant was that the unsubs were mobile.

'Any patterns of any kind?'

'Only the parameters you gave me to work with.'

'And I'm assuming,' she said, 'that none of them would have appeared in the Violent Crime Linkage Analysis databases because there would have been no suspicion of violent crime having taken place?'

'Exactly. Missing persons don't automatically appear in ViCLAS. There has to be a pretty strong suspicion that there's been foul play. Otherwise the whole system would be gummed up with distractors.'

She shook her head.

'I find it difficult to believe that all seventeen were presumed to have just walked away without any prior indication that they were going to.'

'It happens all the time, Jo, especially with men, and particularly ones in this age range. As for reasons, you can take your pick: midlife crises, mental breakdown, depression, relationship break-up, or simply being fed up with the responsibilities that life has thrown at them.'

He handed her a printout. She was carrying it back to her desk when the computer chirped to tell her she had a Skype call. It was Harry Stone.

'I think I've cracked that cipher,' he said. 'Do you have your tablet handy?'

Her heart skipped a beat.

'Yes, Boss.'

'Good, I've got a web page I want you to bring up.'

It consisted of a series of images. Stone told her which one to click.

The screen of the tablet was filled with seven rows of shapes consisting in the main of one or more sides of a square, or complete or partial triangles.

'You're looking at The Royal Arch Cipher,' said Stone. 'Or the "ineffable characters" as they're known.'

Some of the shapes had a strategically placed dot. Beneath each symbol of the first two rows there was a corresponding letter of the alphabet. Beneath the next four rows numbers had replaced the letters. The final row used a combination of speech marks and symbols attributed to French Masonry, aided by members of the Jesuit Order.

'As for the symbol in your photographs,' he said. 'You'll find that it appears in both the first and second pair of rows.'

'I've found it,' she said.

'Then you can work it out for yourself. Depending on which row you're looking at, that symbol would stand for either a lower-case g or the number seven.'

Jo nodded.

'I can see that, Boss, but that still doesn't tell us what it means.'

Stone sat back in his chair.

'It suggests that at least one unsub is either a Mason, or has knowledge of this particular Masonic cipher.'

'That wouldn't be difficult,' said Shah, who had come over to see what was going on. 'How many clicks of the mouse did it take you?'

'Three,' said Stone. 'But you have to know what you're looking for. Look, I'm sorry I can't continue this. I have to go. Let me know where it takes you.'

He ended the call.

Jo stared at the list of names.

'Oh God,' she said.

'What is it?' asked Shah.

'What if it's not about the letter, but its alternate in the Masonic cipher, its numerical place within the alphabet?'

'Go on.'

'What if the perpetrator is numbering his victims?'

'In which case, your man Deighton could have been the seventh victim.'

They stared in silence at the list of names on the printout.

'Let's not get carried away,' she said. 'How many Freemasons are there in the UK?'

'May I?' said Shah pointing to her tablet.

Two clicks brought up the statistics from the United Grand Lodge of England.

'Two hundred and fifty thousand,' he said. 'But that only covers England and Wales.'

'These seventeen were all from England, weren't they?'

'Yes. That's interesting in itself.'

'And how many men in our age range were there in the last census?'

Three more clicks.

'Approximately twenty million.'

'So what percentage of that twenty million were Masons?'

He used the on-screen calculator. The result was 1.25 per cent.

'And what percentage of all of the Masons in the UK does our seventeen missing persons represent?'

The answer was 0.068 per cent.

'And how many men in our age range went missing in the past ten years?'

He shook his head.

127

'That's not the most relevant statistic, Jo. Two hundred and seventy thousand people go missing every year, but the majority turn up within the first forty-eight hours. You're only looking at around one per cent still missing a year after they disappeared. That's the really important figure.'

'Which is?'

'Between sixteen and twenty thousand.'

'So, taking the higher figure of twenty thousand, that's what, nought point one per cent of all males in our age range still missing after a year?'

He was impressed.

'That's right.'

'So our seventeen missing Masons is forty-six per cent less than we might expect, compared with the general population?'

She didn't know whether to feel relieved or disappointed.

'We have no idea how much more or less likely Masons are to go missing than non-Masons,' Shah pointed out. 'Nor do we know how many of the other MisPers were actually Masons, but not recorded as such. After all, it's not one of the required fields in a Missing Persons report.'

He was right, of course, Jo reflected. It wasn't as though being a Mason was something that would help to identify them, like a tattoo, or a scar. A MisPers' religion wasn't recorded so why should his membership of a private association end up on the form?

'Hang on,' she said. 'If the Missing Person report doesn't record the fact that someone is a Mason how come you've managed to identify these seventeen names?'

He beamed.

'Because I had the foresight to word-search the final data field on all of the forms.'

'Remind me?' she said.

He quoted it verbatim.

'"*What are the circumstances of this person going missing and where were they last seen?*"'

'And?'

'And all seventeen were last seen on their way to or from a Masonic meeting.'

'That can't be pure coincidence,' she said. 'And what about men who were Masons but went missing under other circumstances, like Deighton? That would go some way to explain the discrepancy in the statistics.'

'Don't forget,' he cautioned, 'we would expect a number of them to have disappeared without it having any sinister cause whatsoever. Maybe all of them.'

'I know,' she agreed, 'but seventeen, all on their way to or from a Lodge or a Chapter meeting – that has to be significant.'

'Plus the fact,' he said, 'that none of them turned up again. Mind you, some of them could be among the fifteen unidentified bodies that turn up every month. There are over a thousand corpses sitting in morgues around the UK that have never been identified.'

It was a sobering thought. All of those families waiting for news of a loved one, and all the time they had been lying in a freezer compartment in the mortuary, or had already been cremated, their fingerprints and dental records, where recoverable, archived together with their DNA and photo images.

'Thanks for this, Ram,' said Jo, standing up and taking her jacket from the back of the chair. 'It's a great piece of work.'

'What are you going to do?' he asked.

'Persuade Harry to issue a request that the United Grand Lodge of England ask all of their member organisations to report any missing persons from among their membership, and request that police forces in England and Wales red-flag any MisPers reports involving Masons.'

'You do realise that's going to spark a lot of media interest?' he said. 'It could also alert the unsub who's carrying out the abductions. Then all he'd do is go to ground, and keep a low profile until the heat dies down.'

'I'll get Harry to say that it is part of a national drive to improve our MisPers database.'

She started to walk towards her own desk.

'In which case, you'd better hope you're wrong,' he called after her. 'Because if there is a serial killer out there and another one does go missing, the Masons are going to want to know why you didn't tell them the truth. Forewarned is forearmed, isn't that what they say?'

Chapter 23

Harry Stone dealt with the police forces. Jo was left to email the United Grand Lodge, and call the Grand Secretary. He was surprisingly cooperative.

'Only too happy to help the NCA,' he said. 'If there's anything else we can do, just let me know.'

She had barely replaced the receiver when her desk phone rang.

'Ms Stuart?'

It was a pleasant voice. Jo thought she detected an African-Caribbean lilt.

'This is she,' she replied.

'It's Zephaniah, the Unit Administrator. We haven't met. I just transferred this morning from Ralli Quays. I've a call for you from Missing Persons.'

'Thank you,' said Jo. 'Please put them through.'

The line clicked.

'Investigator Stuart, how can I help you?' A male voice with a Home Counties accent. 'This is John Harold, Missing Persons Bureau. You had us put out a red flag alert?'

'That's correct. About an hour ago.'

'Well, I have a response for you.'

Jo's pulse quickened.

'When was this?'

'Unfortunately,' he said, 'the initial report was started a fort-night ago. But before the reporting officer was able to enter it on to our system he was taken ill. He only got back to work this morning and was wading through his backlog when he saw our round robin, brought the report to the top of the pile, put it on the system, and then gave us a call. Do you want me to email you his details, the contact details for the DS who's looking into the disappearance, and a copy of the report?'

'That would be brilliant,' she said.

'I'm doing that right now,' he told her.

She could hear his fingers moving rapidly over the keys.

'Incidentally,' he said. 'This is the second request from you guys about Masonic connections to missing persons. Is there something we should know?'

'It's not that we've been keeping anything from you,' she said. 'It's just that what we have so far is one confirmed case, everything else is pure conjecture.'

'That'll be the Deighton case then. The one Lancashire have down as a murder?'

'That's the one.'

'And you think that may have been something to do with him having been a Mason?'

She could see why he was working for the Bureau.

'That was a possible but unlikely line of enquiry until my col-league had a look at the stats in your database. Now we think it more likely than not.'

'How did you get on with those stats?'

'He found seventeen missing males matching the parameters I gave him.'

He whistled loudly enough for her to have to move the phone away from her ear.

'Bloody hell!' he said. 'That'll put the cat among the pigeons.'

'Which was why we didn't want to broadcast it too much until we were sure.'

'Don't worry,' he said. 'Your secret is safe with me. Mind you, if it turns out you're right, I'm afraid that this Bureau will have to become proactive in providing an explicit warning to Freemasons. It's a matter of public duty of care.'

'I'm relieved to hear it,' she said. 'I was worried that was something we'd have to do.'

'In the meantime,' he told her, 'I'll do a little digging at my end, see if I can turn up anything that might be helpful. Has that email come through yet?'

She checked her mailbox.

'I've got it. Was there just the one attachment?'

'That's it.'

'Thank you,' she said. 'I really appreciate it. I'll be in touch.'

The first thing that struck her was the photograph. Norbert Lawrence Welsh, born 17th May 1968, looked much older. Partly it was the receding hairline and the greying hair, but it was also the double-breasted worsted suit, tartan checked bow tie and solemn pose. She found it difficult to envisage the context in which the photograph had been taken, but whatever it was he was trying too hard to portray gravitas, while his dress sense suggested eccentricity.

He was described as five feet four inches tall, with a medium frame and weighing one hundred and twenty-seven pounds. That sounded distinctly underweight, which explained why the double-breasted suit was ill-fitting. He had a crescent-shaped scar at the base of the thumb on his left hand. His marital status was married, but separated.

He was last seen wearing a black overcoat over a black evening suit, white shirt, and black bow tie. He was carrying a black briefcase holding his Masonic regalia. According to his estranged wife, he would have been wearing a silver Seiko Premier Kinetic watch, and a single gold band wedding ring. Neither watch nor ring was personally inscribed but his spouse, using receipts retained for insurance purposes, had provided the serial numbers of the watch and the ring.

He was last seen at 8.30pm by fellow Masons, leaving a Masonic venue in Liverpool following a meeting of their Royal Arch Chapter. To the best of their knowledge, his intention had been to hail a cab to take him to the station, and from there to travel by train to Ormskirk where he lived on his own in a flat over a shop in the town centre.

Mr Welsh was known to have had his mobile phone with him because he had been observed making a call in the foyer of the Masonic Hall. His mobile phone number was recorded in the report.

Names, addresses and contact numbers of family members and friends were also recorded. There were no circumstances that might explain his disappearance, identify him as vulnerable, or increase the risk to his health and safety while missing.

He had regular, mutually agreed visitation rights to see his twelve-year-old daughter, and was due to do so on the Saturday morning following his last sighting. When he had failed to turn up, his wife had visited his flat, found it empty and reported him missing.

The officer who took the initial report had been scrupulous. There had been no recent changes to Mr Welsh's behaviour, and no physical medical conditions other than slightly raised blood pressure, as yet untreated. He had been treated for depression following his recent estrangement from his wife, but had recovered. There was no evidence that he had ever self-harmed, no indications of suicidal tendencies, no financial difficulties or problems at work, no drug or alcohol dependency, and no suspicion that he might have been abducted. In short, nothing other than his estrangement from his wife, that might explain why he had disappeared from the face of the Earth.

While Jo waited for it to print out, she sat back to reflect. Mr Welsh's business partner in their accountancy firm claimed that there was nothing in his manner at work to suggest that he was anything other than naturally upset by his marital problems. His wife claimed that he had accepted with equanimity her desire for a trial separation, on condition that he had regular contact with their daughter. Of course they only had the wife's word for it. There could be any number of reasons why a wife might want to cover up the real reason why her husband went missing. If he *was* actually missing, rather than in hiding with her assistance. Or dead.

Jo went to collect the printout, and brought it back to her desk. She read the email John Harold had sent, and copied down the contact details of the constable who had taken the initial report, as well as for the Detective Sergeant in Liverpool who was now dealing with the disappearance. She tried their phone numbers without success, and decided to send the DS an email briefly outlining her concerns and asking if they could meet up.

She opened the shared work folder she had created, wrote up the salient actions and conclusions from this morning's activity, and recorded the actions she proposed to take, and where she was hoping to go next. She saved it, and sent an email to Harry Stone to confirm his link to the shared folder. Then she repeated those details in the Operation Hound Policy File.

There was an email in her inbox from a Detective Sergeant Teresa Coppull. It was short and to the point.

Can't talk now, in court. Will be in the office – St Anne Street, Liverpool, L3 3HJ – this afternoon between 2pm and 5pm. Let me know if you can make it?

Jo sent a brief reply and gathered up her things. Before she left the office, she brought Ram Shah up to date.

'How long did you say he's been missing?' he asked.

'Fourteen days.'

'That's a shame,' he said. 'Still, it's a sight better than ten years. At least with this one they stand a chance of recovering CCTV footage. Do you know who's investigating his disappearance?'

'A Liverpool DS. I'm off to see her now. I need to convince her that it's a possible abduction, slash murder.'

'It won't be easy without a motive. Even harder without a body.'

'We still haven't found a motive for Deighton,' she reminded him. 'But that didn't stop him being murdered.'

She looked around the office.

'Have you seen our new administrator?'

'Dorsey?' he replied. 'I thought she was in here, unless she slipped out when I wasn't looking.'

'Looking for me?'

Jo turned towards the sound of the voice. The head of a woman of a similar age to herself peered around the side of one of the space dividers at the far end of the office. Her oval face, the colour of creamy coffee, was framed by long, jet-black braided hair. Her smile was broad and openhearted. She scooted her chair backwards, stood up as Jo approached, and held out a welcoming hand.

'I couldn't help overhearing,' she said. 'That's the trouble with these open-plan offices.'

Jo shook her hand.

'I don't think we'll be keeping any secrets from you,' she said. 'If my previous office manager was anything to go by, I think we'll be coming to you to find out what's going on. I'm Joanne Stuart, by the way. Jo for short. I'm also new.'

'Senior Investigator Stuart,' said Dorsey, 'formerly of GMP. Started two days ago. Leading on Operation Hound.' She smiled again. 'See, I'm getting to grips already.'

'You were already working for the NCA?' said Jo. 'That must help?'

'It means I have a reasonable understanding of the organisation, which does help, yes, but I was supporting a team within Organised Crime Command who are working with Customs and Excise and the Border Agency, so it's not exactly the same.'

'Why did you transfer to us?'

'Because I was asked to, because I thought it sounded interesting, because it's a promotion, *and* because it's only four stops on the Metro.' She laughed a deep, throaty laugh. 'And because it's close to the Lowry retail outlet mall.'

Jo felt an immediate connection with this confident, apparently open and happy woman.

'You live locally?'

'Chorlton. I'm a traitor. Originally Moss Side, but I moved upmarket. I haven't pulled out altogether – I'm a community volunteer helping with the police cadets.'

She caught Jo glancing surreptitiously at the office wall clock.

'Listen to me waffling on. You wanted me?'

'I thought I should let you know where I was going.'

'Always a good idea. So long as I have your contact numbers it's not a problem, assuming your phone is switched on. I had one guy who refused to put his phone on silent, or vibrate. Always switched it off till he wanted to make a call. Then he complained that nobody . . .'

She suddenly realised that Jo was itching to go.

'There I go again,' she said. 'Dizzy Dorsey Zephaniah.'

Her laugh followed Jo out of the office.

Chapter 24

The Liverpool St Anne Street nick was a forlorn concrete and glass building behind an equally miserable concrete wall topped with iron railings. A Union Jack at half-mast hung limp against a steel-grey sky.

Jo was shown to an office on the third floor. DS Coppull was in a cubicle at the far end. She was tall and thin, with a narrow oblong face, and mousey brown hair cut short. There were frown lines everywhere, and shadows beneath her eyes. She looked worn out, but her body was permanently on the move as though plugged into an electrical socket. She stood as Jo approached.

'I'm Teresa,' she announced in a broad Scouse accent. 'But everyone calls me Terry, if they know what's good for them.'

She pointed to a chair beside another desk.

'Drag that over here and park yourself.'

She waited until Jo was settled, and then stared at her intently.

'Well, well, well, NCA,' she said. The fingers of both hands drummed on the desktop. 'Haven't seen one of your lot before.'

'I hope I'm not a disappointment.'

Coppull shook her head.

'Not really, although I did have a vision of a clean-shaven young man with a crew cut, and the bulge of a shoulder holster beneath his shiny new suit.'

She folded her arms, and started to rock in her chair.

'So what's so special about my missing person that got you tear-arsing over here?'

When Jo had finished telling her, Coppull stopped rocking, sat up, and pulled her keyboard towards her.

'Not a lot to go on, have you?' she said, tapping away. 'One body and a number of MisPers that happen to be Masons, but on your own admission not enough of them to stand out as statistically significant.'

'It's also about the manner of their disappearance.'

'I get that. And the fact that there was no obvious reason why they might want to go off radar. However, in the case of my guy, it happens that there was.'

'His separation from his wife?' said Jo. 'But that . . .'

'Got to him a damn sight more than she realised.' Coppull was pointing to her monitor screen.

Jo moved her chair closer, and leaned in to read the text.

. . . revealed that he had had suicidal thoughts as a young man while at university, and that these had re-surfaced following his break-up with his wife. Clearly his wife's decision to seek a divorce had come as a serious blow, not least to his self-esteem. He claimed, however, that his strong attachment with his daughter, and his firm belief that he could persuade his wife to reconsider, would be sufficient to prevent him from acting on these thoughts. My current assessment is that he is probably correct in his judgement, and this suicidal ideation is an inevitable consequence of his current depression rather than their marital difficulties. He rated as Category Three on the Columbia Suicide Severity Rating Scale.

'Where's this from?' asked Jo. 'His doctor?'

'His therapist. The GP who was treating him for depression referred him for NHS-funded talking therapy. When we contacted the GP, he told us about the therapist, who only agreed to send us this limited response when we told him that Welsh was missing, and that we thought he might be in danger, a danger to himself or to others.'

'What made you think that?'

'I've got my own rating scale. If a bloke whose wife has just chucked him out, and who supposedly adores their daughter, suddenly goes off the radar without any explanation, in my book a simple risk assessment says assume the worst.'

'What does Category Three on the Columbia Scale mean?'

'It means active thoughts of suicide involving any kind of method, but without a plan, and without any intention to act on them.'

'But that still doesn't explain why he might decide to go missing.'

'It confirms that he was depressed and disturbed. Under those circumstances, anything is possible. Anyway, who's to know what it would take to progress from active thoughts to actions?'

Jo could tell that Coppull remained unconvinced that this could be abduction. If anything, her position was hardening.

'Did he take a taxi?' she asked. 'Did he catch that train to Ormskirk?'

Coppull pursed her lips.

'Negative to both. Unless it was an unlicensed taxi, in which case we'll never know. CCTV at the station confirms he was never there that evening.'

'What about his mobile phone?'

'Nothing since he made that call to his wife. Can't even get a physical trace for the phone.'

'Which call?'

'When he was leaving his Masonic meeting. She was out. He left a voice message saying he'd pick his daughter up in the morning.'

'There you go then,' said Jo. 'He's not going to make a call like that, and then decide to top himself.'

'He finished his message with, "*Tell her I love her.*" Sounded bloody miserable too. You can listen to it yourself if you don't believe me.'

Jo didn't know why Coppull was being so defensive.

'Don't you think it's suspicious his phone is no longer traceable?'

'Not if he didn't want to be traced. Only had to break up the SIM card, take out the battery, smash the phone on the kerb a few times and then drop them down three different grids.'

Jo was running out of questions.

'If he didn't hail a taxi, he could have been offered a lift, or been taken somewhere between the Masonic Hall and the station. Have you checked the CCTV?'

The Detective Sergeant sighed.

'It wasn't the Masonic Hall – that's used by the Liverpool Group. His Lodge is a different one. I've had a colleague go through the CCTV within the immediate vicinity. No positive sightings.'

She scooted her chair back, and stood up.

'You're welcome to have a look for yourself if you like?'

Jo was beginning to wonder why she had taken Coppull up on her offer. It was hot and claustrophobic in the box-shaped office to which she had been taken. There were two police officers in shirt-sleeves ploughing through tape after tape. There were dark sweat patches beneath their arms. Nobody spoke. The only sounds were sudden explosive sneezes from one of them, an occasional tap on a keyboard, and the opening and closing of disk drives.

After almost an hour, she was getting nowhere. Welsh's normal route to Moorfields Station was less than three hundred metres. Lime

Street Station was under half a mile away, but there was a myriad of potential routes he could have taken. Unfortunately, he would have emerged from his Lodge meeting into an area of dilapidated buildings and temporary car parks, randomly served by cameras.

The tapes had at least been stored in some semblance of order, and she had soon picked up Norbert Welsh leaving the building. He was carrying a black briefcase in his left hand. His right hand held a mobile phone to his ear. Having made his call, he placed his phone in his inside breast pocket and set off down the narrow street, little more than an alley, in a north-westerly direction. At the end of the street he turned right. A second tape from the camera on the rear of a club showed him crossing the car park. None of the subsequent footage picked him up at all.

She checked the immediate area again on Google Earth, selecting *Street Level*, and tracing possible routes. There were only two that made sense.

Continuing in a north-westerly direction would have led him to Moorfields, less than one hundred yards to the station where he would have been able to catch his train to Ormskirk. In that case, he should have been picked up by the camera on the office building on the other side of the road or, if he had made it as far as the station, on the numerous concourse cameras.

Crossing west towards Tithebarn Street, he would have had to avoid the obvious exits from the car park, and instead step over a low fence into the blind spot between the camera over the door of the Lion Pub, and the one twenty metres away on the wall of the former Exchange Station building that was focused on the bus shelter on the opposite side of the road.

It was inexplicable that he had not been captured on a single camera after having turned the corner into the car park. The only answer, of course, was to go and have a look for herself, but she was beginning to suspect that Norbert Welsh must either have voluntarily, or by force, got into a car or van in the car park, or one in a parking bay on Moorfields.

The door opened. DS Coppull stood on the threshold.

'I'm not staying,' she said. 'Just thought I'd check on how you were doing.'

Jo told her.

Coppull tapped the fingers of her left hand on the doorjamb.

'That was the conclusion we came to,' she said. 'We wondered if one of his fellow Masons hadn't offered him a lift.'

'You must have checked?'

''Course we did.' She sounded narked that Jo could have thought otherwise. 'They all said they hadn't. Maybe we were just unlucky with the CCTV. You know how it is. Some of them wipe the tapes. Some forget to change them when the memory's full. Some even forget to make sure they're switched on. We can only deal with what we've got.'

Jo pointed to the pile of disks.

'There's ample coverage of traffic up and down Moorfields and Tithebarn Street,' she said. 'It's continuous for the period before and after Welsh disappeared. If he was picked up, the vehicle must be here somewhere.'

'Good luck with that,' said Coppull.

She turned and closed the door behind her.

It would have been easy to be angry, but Jo understood that for DS Coppull this was not a murder enquiry. Nor did she believe that her missing person was the victim of a serial killer. If she spent this amount of time on every one of her missing persons, there would be no time left to deal with the serious crime that was uppermost in everyone's minds, not least the bean counters at Headquarters with their targets and completion rates.

Jo checked her watch, and sighed. She needed to let Zephaniah know, and then warn Abbie that she was going to be late home again. She had a good idea how that would be received.

It was gone six when Jo entered into the Police National Computer the details of vehicles she had identified in the area within five minutes of the time that Welsh had arrived in that CCTV dead zone. She had eliminated HGVs from her initial search on the basis that it was unlikely the perpetrator would use an HGV because of its size, distinctiveness, and limited access, or that Welsh would be inveigled into one. Similarly, it had already been established from on-board cameras that he had not boarded a bus. Another one hundred and sixty vehicles had passed so quickly down the relevant stretch of each road that she calculated they would not have had time to stop. That left seventeen vehicles. It took another half an hour to sift through the results, and come up with a checklist.

One of the vehicles had neither tax nor insurance. It had already been traced, the vehicle towed and destroyed. The owner was a twenty-one-year-old from Wallasey, disqualified from driving at the time. A second vehicle had false number plates. It had been stolen that morning in Birkenhead, and used the following day in a raid on a post office in Warrington. It was found burnt out on waste ground in Skelmersdale. Of the remaining fourteen, three were of particular interest.

All of them must either have been parked up in one of the bays on Moorfields, or have stopped momentarily and then set off again. Two of them were vans, which would have made concealment much easier in the case of Norbert Welsh's suspected abduction, and also the transportation of Charles Deighton to his final resting place in Chorley. Although, she reminded herself, it was perfectly possible that he could have been bundled into the trunk of a car, and still have left room for a spade.

The third was a black BMW X5 4x4. The registered keeper and owner was a Stanley Ford, forty-seven years of age, living in Southport. She had seen that name before, and recently. She sat back and closed her eyes. Nothing came, except a succession of CCTV images of number plates. The two detectives who had shared the suite with her were long gone. It could wait until morning. She packed her bag, and went in search of DS Coppull.

The room was empty. If there was a night detective, he or she was somewhere else in the building. Jo could not believe that Coppull had left without checking on her. She tore a sheet from the blank pad beside her telephone, scribbled a hasty note with the names and details of the owners of the three vehicles of interest. Then she left.

Chapter 25

Jo had just stepped out of the shower and was drying herself with a bath towel when she heard the door open to the apartment.

'Abbie?' she shouted.

The door to the wet room opened, and Abbie's head appeared around it.

'Hi,' she said. 'How are you this morning?'

It sounded perfunctory, rather than as if she was really interested.

'Tired,' Jo replied. She scrunched her hair with a smaller towel wrapped around her head like a turban. 'Despite having had eight hours' sleep.'

'You never sleep properly when I'm on nights,' said Abbie. 'Besides, you must have left bloody early yesterday morning?'

Here we go, thought Jo.

'I didn't want to wake you,' she said. 'You were fast asleep. I did leave a note.'

Whatever Abbie's response, it was lost in the sound of the door closing.

Jo dried her hair and dressed. When she emerged from their bedroom, Abbie was seated at the kitchen table in her nurse's uniform, three-quarters of the way through a bowl of cereal. A rack of toast stood beside the butter dish, and assorted jars of preserves and honey.

'I didn't know what you wanted,' she said. 'The kettle's boiled, and I can fix you a coffee or a tea as soon as I've finished this.'

'You stay there,' Jo told her. 'I'll get my own, and top yours up. What are you drinking?'

'Arpeggio. Lungo not espresso, and I used the frother not the stirrer for the milk.'

Jo made herself a mug of tea and poured a glass of cranberry juice. Then she took all three drinks to the table.

Abbie smeared honey on to a slice of buttered toast. 'Is that all you're having?' she said.

'I'm going to have some toast,' Jo replied, 'but I'm not really that hungry.'

Abbie frowned.

'That's not like you. What's the matter?'

'Nothing really, I just seem to have lost my appetite.'

There was an uneasy silence.

Abbie pushed her plate aside.

'This isn't about Saturday, is it?'

'Saturday?'

Jo was caught off balance. Then it dawned on her. The meeting with the donor. She had forgotten about it, or chosen to. 'Oh,' she said. 'The meeting with . . .'

'James,' Abbie reminded her.

'No, it's definitely not that.'

'You're looking forward to it?'

'What? Yes, of course I am.'

Abbie put her toast down on her plate.

'Only, if you're having second thoughts, I'd rather know now.'

'Abbie!' said Jo, a little more forcefully than she intended. 'I told you, it isn't that. I don't know what it is. I'm just not hungry, alright?' She picked up her mug and cradled it. 'It's no big deal.'

'What isn't? Not starving yourself, or meeting James?'

'For heaven's sake!'

Jo's hands shook. Tea slopped over the side of the mug on to her right hand. She slammed the mug down on the table, spilling yet more, and rushed to the sink where she turned on the tap, letting the ice-cold water cascade over the scalded flesh. She was annoyed with herself, embarrassed and confused. She had no idea why she felt as she did. Perhaps it was nerves because of the new job, or maybe Abbie was right. Perhaps she was more concerned about Saturday than she thought.

She heard Abbie come up behind her, and felt her arms encircle her waist. Abbie's head rested on Jo's back. She smelled of the eau de cologne she used when she finished her shifts, underscored by a hint of that familiar indefinable hospital smell.

'I'm sorry,' she said. 'I shouldn't be pressuring you.'

'It's me that should be sorry,' said Jo.

She turned off the tap, and shook the excess water from her hand. She spun around, kissed Abbie on her cheek and hugged her.

'I overreacted, Jo,' said Abbie.

'Me too, Abbs,' Jo replied.

That wasn't strictly true, Jo realised as she closed the door of the apartment, leaving Abbie to settle down for the second of her daytime sleeps.

She was dreading meeting this James. Turning up would set the wheels in motion. Turn Abbie's dream into reality. Jo had tried to pretend that all was well, but this relentless pressure to start a family had put far more strain on their relationship than either of them had realised until now. She felt guilty that she had not been honest with Abbie, or herself. Still, Abbie would soon be starting her new job, and then they would be able to live a normal life at last. No more passing like ships in the night or, come to that, in the morning. That was bound to make a difference. Wasn't it?

Chapter 26

'How did you get on with the Scousers?' asked a cheery Ram Shah.

'Some would consider that racist,' said Jo.

'They're not a race,' he retorted. 'They're a self-identifying tribe, and proud of it. Besides, they call us *Woollybacks*.'

'Us?'

'Everyone in the cotton towns east of Liverpool. Except for Wiganers.'

She smiled.

'I know, because they're . . .'

They said it in unison.

'*Pie-eaters!*'

'I thought I was the dizzy one?' said Dorsey Zephaniah as she walked between the desks towards them.

Jo pointed to the three large potted plants that had appeared overnight.

'Are those down to you?'

She beamed a smile.

'They sure are. And there's more on the way. They cheer the place up, don't you think? Plus, they gobble up all of the CO_2 we're pumping out and exchange it for oxygen. Double blessing!'

'I reckon you're the blessing, Zephaniah,' said Ram. 'She's magicked up a microwave,' he said, 'and a coffee machine of our very own.'

'Call me Dizzy, or Zeph,' she told them. 'Unless you're not happy with me, then you can call me whatever you please.' She turned to Jo. 'You had a call from a DS Coppull in Liverpool. She wanted you to ring her on her mobile as soon as you got in.' She handed Jo a note containing the number.

'Did she say anything else?' asked Jo.

'No. But she sounded like she got out of bed the wrong side. Right antsy.'

Jo nodded. That was probably DS Coppull's default setting.

'Those names, what did you expect me to do with them?'

Teresa Coppull sounded annoyed and stressed. In the background there were the sounds of heavy traffic, sirens, and people talking.

'I thought you might be interested in checking them out, Terry?' said Jo, as amiably as possible. 'At the very least, the drivers may have seen something even if they weren't involved themselves.'

Coppull's response sounded like a grunt, but it could just as easily have been a snort.

'*Interested*,' she said, 'does not put it at the top of my list of priorities. I'm stood here at the entrance to the Kingsway Tunnel, beside the splattered remains of a jumper who thought it would be a good idea to hurl himself into the windscreen of a juggernaut. He's managed to kill the driver, write off five vehicles and seriously injure seven other people in the process.'

'I'm sorry,' said Jo.

'Why? It's not your fault. But seeing as it was you that decided to check out those vehicles, Ma'am, why don't you do us both a favour, and do the follow-up too? When I can find a moment I'll certainly be interested in whatever you dig up.'

Before Jo could think of a suitable response, DS Coppull made it easy for her.

'Look,' she shouted, against the unmistakable churning drone of a helicopter landing, 'I'm going to have to go. The HEMS is here, and I've got a witness to speak to before they cart her off. Good luck, SI Stuart, and don't be a stranger.'

Jo replaced the phone in its cradle. She stood up and went over to Dorsey's desk.

'Dizzy,' she said. Zeph didn't feel right somehow. 'Do you know where Mr Stone is this morning?'

The admin officer nodded.

'He's in Risley. Caught the milk train, and arrived at Birchwood Park at eight oh two am. Do you want me to call him?'

'What's his diary looking like? I don't want to drag him out of an important meeting.'

Dorsey tapped one key, and pulled up his diary.

'He's talking to people from the forensics firm that share the building. He hasn't red-flagged it. In fact, he hasn't flagged it at all.'

'Red-flagged?'

Dorsey raised her eyebrows in a theatrical manner.

'It means of key importance. Do not disturb on pain of death!'

She leaned sideways, pulled out the bottom drawer of the desk, and flicked through the dividers.

'Here, I'll give you a list. You need to learn them even if you rarely use them.'

Jo stared at the list. It was like the one on her computer for marking emails. She doubted there would be many occasions when she would dare to red flag one of her own diary entries.

'In that case,' she said. 'I'd be grateful if you would call him. I'll be at my desk.'

'Never be sorry for contacting me,' Stone told her. 'Incidentally, well done for setting up that shared folder. I'm going to suggest it to the others. Now, what's on your mind?'

'I'm concerned, Boss, that I'm working with two senior investigating officers neither of whom are able to give it their full attention.'

'Able or willing?'

'A bit of each. Renton's in the middle of a child sex ring case. His deputy SIO is great but she's trying to hold the fort on a number of live cases. DS Coppull in Liverpool is not convinced there's any connection with her MisPer, and until there's a body I don't think she sees it as her priority.'

'Is this about the owners of those three vehicles you suggested should be checked out?'

'You read my notes?'

'On the train coming up.'

'She says she doesn't have the time to check them out. And to be fair, with what she's got on her plate, I don't really blame her.'

'But you don't think it's your job either?'

'I don't know, Boss. That's why I rang you.'

'Has she told you she's happy for you to go ahead?'

'Well, yes.'

'So what is it you're worried about, Jo?'

'Preserving the chain of evidence. What happens if I end up having to give evidence in her case, assuming there is one, and it goes to trial?'

'You've been talking to witnesses and suspects in the Deighton case. Were any of those under oath, and or accompanied by a signed statement?'

'No. Although I did record two of them.'

'That's fine. They still only count as hearsay, so it's unlikely they'd be used.'

'What about the CCTV evidence, and the Police National Computer searches?'

'That's different. The guidelines have changed. They'll be admissible as digitally retrieved factual information. As you know, the SIOs can either use them, or retrieve them for themselves.'

'I just wanted to be sure where I stood.'

'Lancashire sought our help as advisers,' he said. 'Consultants, if you prefer. Gathering evidence, and making a case is their responsibility. Seeking connections, with their approval, is what you're doing right now. That doesn't make you their dogsbody, even if it does feel like it. The minute you turn up hard evidence relating to a crime, you inform them. Then it's their responsibility to secure it.'

'Yes, Boss.'

'Good.' He paused. 'Look, Jo, as far as I'm concerned you've made a great start, and I have every confidence that you'll do what's right. Trust your instinct, and log everything, just as you have been doing. You'll be fine.'

'Thanks, Boss.'

'Was there anything else?'

She hesitated.

'Jo?' he said. 'Just spit it out.'

'Norbert Welsh,' she said. 'He's been missing for over a fortnight. If I'm right, and his disappearance is connected to Deighton's murder, what are the odds that he's still alive?'

It was Stone's turn to go quiet. Jo waited patiently.

'Andy Swift is better placed than me to answer that,' he said. 'But I don't remember anything in the post mortem report to indicated that Deighton had been starved?'

'If there had been, it would have shown up in the analysis of the bones. There wasn't.'

'So either they killed him shortly after he was taken, or they fed him while they were holding him. Given there was no ransom demand, I can't see why they would have bothered to do that.'

It was the conclusion Jo had come to. She had been hoping that she was wrong.

'According to your report, there's been no ransom demand for Norbert Welsh either?'

'If there had, it would have made DS Coppull take it seriously, and we'd have a reason to throw everything at it.'

'Don't beat yourself up, Jo,' he said. 'For all we know, Welsh is swanning around on a beach in the Costa del Sol. Now, was there anything else?'

She could tell from his voice that he was looking at his watch.

'No, Boss.'

'Got to go, Jo.'

'Thanks, Boss.'

'It's why I'm here.'

She replaced the phone, and walked resolutely to her desk. Maybe nobody else was taking it seriously, but she was damned if she'd join them.

Chapter 27

Twenty minutes later, Jo had the information that she needed. The owner of the first of the vans, the short wheelbase Transit, was one Donal Raines. His tax return gave his occupation as self-employed courier. He had a criminal record with four convictions. The first was for criminal damage at the age of seventeen years and three months. He had spray-painted graffiti on to the exterior walls of his former high school. That had earned him sixty hours of community service. A year later he was convicted of Common Assault, contrary to section 39 of the Criminal Justice Act 1988. He had fought, while under the influence of alcohol, with a landlord who was ejecting him from his premises. The injuries sustained by the landlord were superficial, and the level of alcohol in Raines's body was four times the legal drink drive limit. It was dealt with in the magistrates' court. Raines received a two hundred pound fine, thirty hours of community service, and six months on probation. He was warned that any repeat could result in a custodial sentence.

For the next nineteen years he had no further brushes with the law, other than two speeding offences that had earned him six points on his licence. Hardly surprising for a courier for whom speed was of the essence.

The owner of the second van, a custom long-wheelbase Transit, was a Lorna Driffield, aged thirty-nine. She had a juvenile conviction for shoplifting. At fifteen years of age she had been caught, along with four school friends, stealing T-shirts from a store. Given they pleaded guilty and it was a first offence, one of the newly established youth courts gave her a probation order that included all of them being banned from going together into the town centre for a period of six months. Nothing since then. She had a clean driving licence.

Her occupation was given as the sole trader and owner of the appropriately named Lorna's Garden Transformations. According to her website, *lornas-gardentransformations.co.uk*, she had been in business for over fifteen years. Flicking through the gallery of photos, Jo was impressed by the range and quality of her work.

That left the missing person's business partner, Stanley Ford. Ford was forty-seven years of age, and had no criminal record. Not so much as a few points on his driving licence. According to Companies House, Welsh and Ford Limited, Accountants, was formed in 1997. Turnover in the last set of company accounts was seven hundred and sixty thousand pounds.

Jo spent the next twenty minutes arranging interviews with Driffield and Ford. Raines had proved more problematic given that he was constantly on the move. Even his partner couldn't be sure when he'd be home, but had promised to get him to ring Jo as soon as she'd spoken to him. Jo packed her bag, and went over to Dorsey's workstation.

'I'm off,' she said. 'I've updated my diary on the shared drive, and I'll keep my phone on.'

Dorsey smiled.

'Perhaps you'd have a word with Mr Nailor. Show him how it's done?'

'Is he still working on Operation Gannet?'

The administrator nodded.

'As far as I know he is, but if he isn't I'll be the last to know. D'you realise I haven't even met him yet?'

Ram raised his head from his keyboard.

'You're in for a treat,' he said.

The administrator raised her eyebrows.

'What does that mean, Ma'am? I can never tell if he's being serious.'

'Neither can I,' Jo replied. 'You'll just have to make up your own mind when you finally come face to face. Incidentally, where is Mr Swift today? I could do with a word about the Liverpool case.'

'In London. Apparently it's a regular monthly catch up with his fellow crime behaviour profilers. He'll be back in the office tomorrow morning.'

As Jo drove under the barrier, she saw Nailor's BMW waiting to come in on the opposite side. She waved. He continued to stare blankly ahead through the windscreen, his forehead furrowed. As she pipped her horn, the barrier rose. He drove into the car park without so much as a sideways glance.

Jo had no idea if he had deliberately blanked her, or had been too wrapped up in his own thoughts. Either way, she was sorely missing the opportunity to bounce her thinking off a fellow detective, something that had been second nature in the Major Incident Team. Ram was clearly a brilliant intelligence analyst, and having a psychologist like Andy on tap was something DCI Caton would have given anything for. But it was not the same as exploring issues with another trained investigator, and she couldn't keep on bothering Harry Stone.

The hoot of a tram setting off from Harbour City shook Jo out of her reverie. She resolved to concentrate on her driving. There would be plenty more opportunities to probe the enigma that was Max Nailor.

Chapter 28

Three miles outside Ormskirk, Jo signalled right. The satnav led her to a stone-built barn conversion that bordered the single-track lane. A double garage had been integrated into the main building. A car-width gravel strip fronted the property. She parked on the gravel, and got out of the car.

The house stood on its own in what looked like acres of pasture and woodland. Immaculate drystone walls on either side formed the boundary where the land abutted the lane. She was trying to put a price on all this when the front door opened.

For a forty-seven-year-old, Stanley Ford had not worn well. It was, she decided, a combination of wispy comb-over hair the colour of a wet Manchester pavement, chicken jowls, and a girth almost as wide as his height.

'I saw you pull up,' he said.

His voice was disconcertingly high. She had to resist the temptation to cross him off her list of suspects. There was no template for a murderer, and certainly not for a serial killer. But she couldn't imagine him overpowering someone in order to abduct them, let alone carry Deighton's body all that way, dig the grave, and fill it in again. Of course, the two disappearances might not be connected.

His partner would not have expected foul play. Ford could have used a drug. He could have had an accomplice.

Ford had to back up down the hall, and into an alcove, so that she could squeeze past.

'That way,' he said, pointing towards an open door.

She stepped into a large open-plan lounge-diner with an ingle-nook fireplace complete with wood burner, and a high, vaulted ceiling with beams.

'I'm in here, Stanley!'

A female voice, horsey and commanding.

'Through there.' Ford pointed to another doorway.

An extension had been added to the rear of the property. Bifold doors, revealing green fields stretching away to high moors in the distance, had been fitted to the entire length of the kitchen-garden room. A tall, thin woman, with bright red dyed hair, leaned against a marble-topped island at the far end of the room.

'Are you it?' she asked.

'It?' said Jo.

Ford's voice trembled.

'This is Violet, my wife.'

'The National Crime Agency,' said Violet Ford. 'Are you it?'

'Not the whole of it,' Jo replied. She held up her ID card. 'I'm a Senior Investigator. One of a number.'

Mrs Ford snorted. Jo would not have been surprised if she had broken into a whinny.

Jo turned to the husband.

'Is there somewhere private we could go?'

The far from shrinking Violet slammed a hand on the marble.

'Private? I don't think so. There's nothing Stanley might say that he can't say in front of me.'

'It's alright, Vi . . .' Ford began.

'Alright?' said his wife. 'Is it hell alright. You're not going to be interrogated on your own. It's either me or our lawyer? Take your pick.'

'It's fine, Mr Ford,' said Jo. 'If you would like your wife to sit with you, I have no problem with that. In fact, it may save us time.'

The wife walked towards her. Her eyes narrowed as she eyed Jo with suspicion.

'Why is that?' she asked.

'Because I may have some questions that you would be better placed to answer than your husband.'

Violet Ford scowled.

'I can't imagine what they would be.'

Good, thought Jo. This wasn't the first alpha dominant woman she had come across. If Violet was true to form, attack would be her preferred form of defence. Snubbed, embarrassed or affronted, she was the kind of person who would seek vengeance. Instead of one potential suspect, Jo now had two.

'Perhaps, Mr Ford,' Jo began, 'we could begin with your relationship with Mr Welsh. Could you tell me a little about that?'

They were seated at the farmhouse-style kitchen table, Violet Ford to the right of her husband. Jo had a momentary mental picture of Stan Laurel and Oliver Hardy, except that in this case although the bodies matched, the personalities were reversed. Violet's Laurel was the bumptious confident one; Stanley's Oliver was the wimp.

'Isn't this a bit over the top?' interjected Violet Ford.

'I'm sorry?' said Jo.

'Involving the National Crime Agency in a simple disappearance. I assumed that you people only deal with serious crimes, like the FBI.'

Jo took a slow, deep breath.

'Firstly,' she said, 'I thought you would be relieved that we were taking seriously this sudden and inexplicable disappearance of your husband's partner? Secondly, if you don't allow me to conduct this interview without interruption, Mrs Ford, I will have no alternative but to ask your husband to accompany me for a formal interview at our offices, with a lawyer if he so chooses, but definitely without you.'

It was a calculated risk, but there was no way that his wife would want to miss out. She clearly despised her husband, and did not trust him to manage himself. More importantly, Violet's curiosity was palpable.

'There's no need to take that tone,' she replied. 'I was only asking.' She nudged her husband. 'Answer the question, Stanley.'

He seemed cowed, and confused.

'Sorry. What was the question?'

'Your relationship with Norbert Welsh. How you first met, formed the business, your relationship outside work?'

'Oh, right. Yes.'

He glanced nervously at his wife.

'Go on then,' she snapped. 'Tell her. It's not exactly *Mastermind* is it? More *Pointless*.'

'Mrs Ford,' Jo began.

She held her hands up in exaggerated surrender.

'Okay . . . okay.'

'Well, Mr Ford?'

'I was at school with Nobby. Ormskirk Grammar. Well, I say Grammar, but it went comprehensive five years before we started there.'

His wife sniffed her disapproval.

'We were in the same class right the way through. Even in the Sixth Form. We were best friends. We watched each other's backs.'

Jo nodded to show that she understood, even though she couldn't imagine Ford watching anybody's back.

'We even went to uni together, in Leeds. Did the same degree. Accounting and finance. Then he got a job with Coopers Lybrand, and I went to Price Waterhouse. The two of them merged in '98. The year before we left to set up our own company.'

He paused, shook his head, and then continued.

'PricewaterhouseCoopers was voted most prestigious accounting firm in the world six years running.'

He sounded wistful, regretful even. His wife confirmed it.

'No comparison with Welsh and Ford,' she said in a voice heavy with sarcasm.

Jo eased her chair back, and made a great play of clicking her biro closed, and reaching for her bag.

'Okay, I'm sorry,' said Violet Ford. 'I'll try, I promise.'

'Promise isn't good enough, Mrs Ford,' Jo told her. 'One more intervention like that, and I'll be inviting your husband to take that ride with me.'

'I told you, I'm sorry.'

Ford slammed the table with such violence that it took them both by surprise.

'I can't do this with you here,' he said. 'Get out!'

'Stanley!'

She gripped his arm. He tugged it free, and turned on her, his face crimson with fury.

'Get out!' he yelled. 'Get out! Get out! Get out!'

Violet Ford stood, thrusting her chair back so violently that it fell with a clatter on to the slate floor. She stormed from the room.

Jo was already reappraising her opinion of Stanley Ford.

Chapter 29

He ran cold water in the Belfast sink, splashed it over his face, took a small towel draped over the handle of the range cooker, and mopped his face dry. He folded the towel, and carefully replaced it before returning to his seat.

'I'm sorry,' he said. 'Sometimes she goes too far, and I just snap.'

'Are you alright to continue?'

He nodded.

'I'm fine.'

'You were telling me about your firm. Whose decision was it to form a partnership?'

'Nobby's, I think. It was something we talked about back at university. Violet is wrong. It wasn't about the money. It was about being our own bosses. Not chasing other people's targets. Being able to choose when we wanted to take time out for a round of golf.'

He pulled his handkerchief from his pocket, and mopped his face.

'Besides, we haven't done that badly so far as money is concerned.'

He looked out of the window at the fields beyond.

'We've got all this.'

He shook his head again.

'It's not enough for Violet though. She always wants more.'

'So, the firm has been doing well?'

'Coasting along, at a pace we were both happy with.'

'Were?'

'Are. Nobby and me. We're making as much as we need to keep the clients on board, and live comfortable lives.'

'Do you socialise outside of work?'

'We play golf two or three times a week. We're both members at a golf course just up the lane.'

He sat there in silence, looking dejected.

'The Masons?' she prompted.

He shifted uneasily, as did his eyes.

'Oh yes, the Masons. We applied together, twenty years ago. Nobby said that it wouldn't do our business any harm. Not,' he added hastily, 'that that is what Freemasonry is about.'

'No?'

'No!' he replied, more forcibly than seemed appropriate. 'In fact, using our connection as brothers to further our careers or business interests is actively frowned upon.'

'But don't you have to take an oath to support your fellow Masons and to keep their lawful secrets?'

'That's not the same,' he said. 'We support each other emotionally and spiritually. Or perhaps when someone falls upon hard times. But it certainly does not mean giving brothers preferential treatment over non-Masons.'

'Just camaraderie then?'

He frowned.

'And mutual support,' he said. 'For personal growth, spiritual development and charitable work, of course.'

'A bit like the Rotarians then?'

This time he did not rise to the bait.

'Notwithstanding all that camaraderie,' said Jo, 'is it possible Mr Welsh could have fallen foul of a fellow Mason? Made an enemy perhaps?'

He looked horrified.

'Absolutely not! It's unthinkable. He was popular with everyone. The entire Chapter was shocked and concerned when they heard he had disappeared.'

'And you?'

'Me?'

'What did you think had happened to Mr Welsh?'

'I was as surprised as everybody else. Even more surprised – I was his best friend. We were due to play golf together the following morning before he picked up his daughter.'

That 'was' again, she noted.

'But, as his best friend,' she said, 'surely you must have noticed how depressed he had been since he and his wife split up?'

'No.'

'You didn't notice?'

'Of course I noticed. I know what you're thinking, and you're wrong.'

'What am I thinking, Mr Ford?'

'That my partner wanted to disappear, because he intended to take his own life.'

'How can you be so sure that he didn't?'

'Because I spoke to him twice that day, at lunchtime, and again when I knew that I wouldn't be able to make the Chapter meeting. That was when he confirmed that he'd meet me on the links the following morning. He sounded absolutely fine. If anything, more upbeat than he'd been for some time.'

'Why weren't you able to make the Chapter meeting, Mr Ford?'

'Because my client that afternoon had just been informed that he was going to receive an impromptu VAT inspection on the

Monday morning. His record-keeping was a mess. I knew that it would take me the rest of the day to sort it, and I didn't want to sacrifice our golf date, or the rest of the weekend.'

His face clouded over.

'Violet doesn't like me working at the weekends.'

'What time did you finish working that day?'

'A quarter past eight. I remember because Violet rang me three times to ask when I would be home. I told her I would ring the second I was leaving. It was a quarter past eight.'

'And this client. He was in Liverpool?'

'Yes. How did you know?'

'And you travelled home by car?'

'Yes, but . . .'

'And where would your car have been around eight thirty that evening, Mr Ford?'

He had to think about it.

'Well, the first pay machine I tried in the car park was out of order, so I had to go down a couple of levels, and back up again, so I suppose I would have been leaving the city centre. Maybe just approaching the A59.'

'Would it surprise you to learn that your car was on Moorfields at exactly the time that we believe that Mr Welsh left the Chapter meeting and entered the car park abutting Moorfields, after which we have no further sightings of him?'

Ford paled. His mouth gaped open. His shock seemed genuine. She had no idea if that was due to her knowledge that he had been in the vicinity, or the realisation that he had been so close when his partner had disappeared.

'Norbert was there?' he said.

Norbert, not Nobby, she noticed.

'As were you.'

'I must have been,' he said.

He was still coming to terms with the magnitude of the coincidence. He ran his hand through what little was left of his hair.

'I did go that way. But I had no idea he would be there too.'

'You must have known what time his meeting was going to end? Why didn't you offer to give your friend a lift home?'

'Because I had no idea what time *I* would finish, and when I did all I could think of was to get home before she threw my dinner in the bin. Besides, I didn't know he'd come in on the train.'

'Was that not his normal practice?'

'It varied. It depended on whether or not he needed to use the car during the day.'

'How often was that likely?'

'Once or twice a week at most.'

That meant that anyone watching his movements might think, depending on which days they observed him, that he always used the train. It was just as likely that he had been targeted because he happened to be wearing a dinner suit, and carrying his Masonic case.

'So you didn't see him?' she said.

'No, I wish I had.'

'You drove straight home?'

'Yes, I told you I was already very late.'

'You arrived home at . . . ?'

'Just before a quarter to nine.'

'And your wife can confirm that?'

'She made a big deal out of pointing to the clock in the kitchen, and asking did I know what time it was.'

Jo looked at her list.

'One last question,' she said, 'for now.'

Ford lifted his head, and stared anxiously at her.

'Yes?'

'If Mr Welsh were to remain a missing person indefinitely or, in the worst-case scenario, it emerges that he's actually deceased, what happens to his share of the partnership?'

His brow furrowed.

'If either of us were to die, then the surviving widow will inherit fifty per cent of the company. But the surviving partner has the option to buy those shares following an independent valuation.'

'And would you exercise that option?'

'I thought you said one last question?'

'Think of it as a codicil.'

'I'm not a lawyer.'

'Then why are you behaving like one? Please answer the question.'

He frowned.

'I hope it never comes to it,' he said. 'And I've never thought about it. But if it did – yes, I probably would.'

For the first time in the entire interview, Jo had the distinct impression that he was lying. His body language, and the way in which his tone had changed, gave him away. The interesting thing was that it was over something so apparently insignificant and unnecessary that she had almost missed it. He had lied when he said, '*And I've never thought about it.*'

She closed her notebook and placed it in her bag.

'That's all for now,' she told him. 'Thank you for your time, Mr Ford.'

She pushed back her chair and stood up.

'You've been very helpful,' she told him. 'It's a difficult time for you. I hope that your partner turns up soon.'

'Not as much as I do,' he said. 'He's a good man, and a good friend. Nobby lives for his family.' He mopped his brow for the third time. 'His daughter must be distraught. I can't bear to think that something awful has happened to him.'

'If he contacts you,' she said, 'or you think of anything else, please immediately call either Detective Sergeant Coppull or myself.'

Ford was losing the battle with all his excess weight as he struggled to get up.

'I can see myself out,' said Jo.

Chapter 30

Jo closed the car door, and sat back. Violet Ford had corroborated the time that her husband had returned home on the evening of Welsh's disappearance. Her version was close enough without having been so exact as to call it into question. Jo took out her mobile, and switched the network connections back on. There were two messages waiting. One was a text, the other a new voice message. The text was from Dorsey Zephaniah.

DS Coppull has been trying to reach you. I suggest you call her ASAP. She was extremely UT!

Jo assumed that this stood for uptight. She rang her voicemail. The Liverpudlian detective sounded angry.

'This is DS Coppull! I've just had a call from Violet Ford. What the hell are you doing talking to them? I've already interviewed them. Ring me when you get this.'

Jo did exactly that. The call was answered immediately.

'I got your message, DS Coppull,' said Jo.

'And?'

'And I'm a bit confused, to be honest.'

'Confused! What's to be confused about?'

'I seem to remember you saying, "Why don't you do us both a favour, and do the follow up?"'

'For God's sake!' said Coppull. 'I was talking about the other two, obviously. Not Ford. I'd already spoken to him.'

'And when you spoke to him, did you know that he was right there at the time and place that his partner went off the radar?'

There was a telling pause.

'Not exactly.' For the first time she sounded defensive. 'But I did know he was in Liverpool, and what time he arrived home.'

'It would have been helpful to know that,' said Jo.

Coppull murmured something indistinct, and then found her voice.

'So, have you got anything new?'

'Not really. His story checks out, but only because the wife corroborates it.'

'And she's a proper pain in the arse,' said Coppull.

Jo laughed, the tension broken.

'He was hiding something to do with the business,' she said. 'Did you know that he has the option to buy his partner's shares if he's declared dead?'

'No. Is the business worth a lot? Or does he get the shares at a knock-down price?'

'Neither. But if there happened to be something dodgy about the business, it would be easier to cover it up if Welsh disappeared and Ford had sole ownership. Or perhaps someone wanted to buy the business and Welsh was against it. I don't know. I just think it might be worth following up.'

'There is no way we'll get a warrant to crawl all over the business on the basis of a missing person and a hunch.'

'You may not,' Jo replied. 'But I think you'll find that we can.'

'I take it you mean the NCA?'

'We can arrange a visit from Her Majesties Revenue and Customs to have a look at the company's record-keeping. There doesn't have to be a reason. If that proves interesting there would be a full-blooded inspection.'

'Mmm . . .' Coppull sounded unconvinced. 'I hope you weren't thinking of going after Welsh's wife next?' she said.

'I've no reason to,' said Jo. 'I assumed you'd spoken to her when she reported her husband missing.'

'I did. She's in the clear. She was at her parents' house with her daughter that evening and they stayed the night.'

'That leaves just the two Transit vans,' said Jo. 'I take it you're still happy for me to interview the owners?'

'Be my guest. It sounds like a long shot though. Welsh could just as easily have accepted a lift from a car. There must have been hundreds that time of night.'

Jo told her how she had eliminated all of the other vehicles on the three streets that evening.

'No wonder it took you so long,' said Coppull with grudging respect. 'Still, I suppose it's worth a shot.'

'I'll let you know how I get on,' said Jo.

'You do that,' Coppull replied. 'Be lucky.'

Chapter 31

Jo decided to surprise Donal Raines. Besides, it would save her having to pay an evening visit, and you could never tell with a courier what hours they might be expected to work. It took her one phone call to find out where he was heading next, and fifteen minutes to get there.

He was standing on the doorstep of a fine dining restaurant in Walkden, waiting for a parcel to be signed off. She parked in front of his van, got out, and waited by the passenger door with her ID at the ready. As he turned and saw her, he frowned. When he was within a couple of metres she raised her ID and flipped it open. The frown became a grimace.

'What have I done this time?' he said. 'Gone through a light on amber, or nudged a mile an hour over the limit?'

'Neither,' she said. 'I was just hoping that you could help with a case I'm working on.'

He glanced at his mobile device, and then at her. He looked really unhappy.

'How the hell did you find out where I was?'

He was even less happy when she told him.

'You what?' he exclaimed. 'You rang my employers? That's all I bloody need. What the hell are they supposed to think? You trying to get me fired or what?'

'Calm down,' she said. 'I told them you were a potential witness, and it was really important that I spoke to you. I assured them that we have no reason to suspect that you've done anything wrong.'

He scowled.

'Too bloody true.'

'This won't take long,' she said.

He checked his handheld tablet.

'It better not. I've got targets. I get paid according to how many deadlines I've met. I'm five minutes behind the next one already.'

'Blame me,' she said.

'And you think that'll work? Very funny.'

'Put it this way,' she said. 'The sooner you answer my questions, the sooner you'll be on your way.'

He folded his arms, and leaned against the side of the van.

'Get on with it then.'

'The Friday before last,' she said. 'Where would you have been at eight thirty pm?'

'The Friday before last?' His forehead furrowed. He consulted his tablet. 'I did my last drop in Birkenhead at seven twenty-seven pm. So I'd have been on my way home to Horwich. Why d'you wanna know?'

Jo felt a tingle of excitement. Horwich was four or five miles from the Deighton dump site.

'Your van was spotted on the cameras on Moorfields in Liverpool at eight twenty-nine that evening,' she told him. 'Can you explain why it took you over an hour to get there from Birkenhead, which I guess is less than a couple of miles? Even allowing for the tunnel, that's a long time.'

His smile was insolent.

'This makes a change. The cops normally do me for speeding, not for going too slow.'

'Please answer the question.'

The smile dissolved.

'First off, it's only one and a half miles. Secondly, because it was my last delivery I stopped for a brew and a sarnie at Ozzy's on the precinct on St Anne's Street. Give 'em a ring. They'll remember me. Just ask was Lanky Donal there. Anyway, what's this all about?'

'Do you know a Norbert Welsh?'

'No.'

'A Raymond Carter?'

'No.'

'Charles Deighton, perhaps?'

He sighed heavily.

'Again, no.'

'Did you see anything suspicious while you were driving down Moorfields?'

'Like what?'

'Like someone being bundled into a vehicle?'

He looked incredulous.

'What, like a hijack?'

'More like an abduction?'

'You're having a laugh?'

He stared at her to see if she was joking.

'No, I'm not,' she said.

His eyes widened. He seemed excited by the prospect that he might have been that close to something big. Then it dawned on him how dangerous becoming involved might be.

'What are we talking about? Rival drug gangs? Armed robbery? Kidnap for ransom?'

'Cast your mind back, Donal,' she said, hoping the use of his Christian name would keep him on side. 'Did you see or experience anything out of the ordinary when you were driving down Moorfields that Friday evening?'

He looked thoughtful.

'Now you come to mention it,' he said. 'I remember having to brake suddenly. The lorry in front of me stopped on a pin. I nearly went into the back of it.'

'Did you see why it stopped?'

'No. But the traffic was flowing okay just before, so maybe some pillock pulled out of one of the parking bays in front of it.'

'How long were you stopped?'

'I dunno. About forty seconds? Long enough for the cars behind me to start leaning on their horns.'

'Do you have a camera in your van?'

He shook his head.

'No way. It's as likely to prove me in the wrong as the other driver. The firm I work for want me to put one in though. I suppose I'll have to fit one eventually.'

'Did you notice anything about the lorry that might help identify it?'

He shrugged.

'Only that it was registered in Poland. The writing on the back was in Polish too.'

He straightened up and stared anxiously at his tablet.

'Can I go now?'

'Two last questions,' she said. 'Did you notice anyone on Moorfields that evening wearing a dinner suit, and carrying a small black briefcase?'

'A monkey suit? No. Next question.'

'Are you, or were you ever, a member of the Freemasons?'

Raines was still laughing as he drove away.

Chapter 32

Lorna's Garden Transformations, Dorsey informed her, were working on a garden in Worsley, less than three miles away. She'd spoken to the owner. Jo was expected. Despite a hiccup on the East Lancs Road because of the guided busway roadworks, it took her less than ten minutes to get there.

The house was down a metalled lane, lined with tall bare trees. Signs made it clear that this was a private road with no access for unauthorised vehicles. She had glimpses of several properties through the beech and horse chestnut trees, and beyond the identical high fences that surrounded them. It began to rain as she pulled up outside the electronic gate that guarded Edgerton Hall.

The speakerphone was too high for Jo to reach from inside the car, and she was forced to reach for her brand-new black-hooded cagoule with NCA emblazoned across the back in fifteen-centimetre-high white letters. Before she had time to walk to the speaker console, the gates began to open. She jumped back in the Audi, and set off.

The drive wound its way between perfectly manicured lawns strewn with leaves to a large Victorian mansion, its lower storey redbrick, above which everything was in the black-and-white Tudor Revival Style so prevalent around Worsley Village. The walls were rendered white, with black carved bargeboards, pegged timber joints, and quatrefoil panels.

A scruffy-looking man in a green pullover, green work pants and heavy-duty wellington boots, stood at the foot of the stone steps leading to the front door. Jo pulled up alongside him, and lowered the window. He leaned towards her and muttered something.

'I'm sorry,' she said. 'I didn't catch that?'

'Police?' he mumbled.

'That's correct,' she said. 'I'm Joanne Stuart from the National . . .'

He was already walking away towards the west end of the house. She decided to follow in the car. The drive curved around the side of the building all the way to the rear of the west wing. She pulled up beside a Range Rover, beyond which were parked a Porsche and a Transit van. Jo switched off the engine and got out.

Her guide set off across the lawn towards a tennis court surrounded by flower beds. Jo opened the trunk of the car, changed into her boots and followed him. He was over a hundred yards away now, turning right towards a half-size football pitch.

Suddenly the man disappeared from sight. It was only when she was closer that she realised that the lawn fell steeply away. In the long, broad hollow below was a pitch-and-putt golf course. To the east lay something like a sports pavilion to which her guide was heading. In front of the pavilion knelt a woman, putting the final touches to a large semicircle of Yorkstone flags. Jo started gingerly down the slope.

Chapter 33

Lorna Driffield knelt with her back towards Jo. She had a short length of bent copper piping in her right hand that she was drawing along the mortar between the flags to create a bevelled finish. Her unkempt dark hair, cropped short, barely covered the nape of her neck. Leather pads fastened with elastic covered both knees. She wore a green short-sleeved T-shirt, and matching dark-green trousers tucked into ankle-high work boots. Jo waited for her to finish.

Driffield sat back on her haunches and studied her work. Then, in a sudden and deceptively graceful movement, she sprang to her feet and turned to face Jo. Weathered by the sun and wind, her face and arms were nut-brown. Her biceps strained against the sleeves of her T-shirt, and her forearms were tautly muscled. Her build reminded Jo of a female professional wrestler – muscular yet athletic, with a low centre of gravity and feet planted firmly on the ground. Driffield's brow and jaw were a little too prominent and her face too square for her to be considered pretty. She looked much older than her thirty-nine years. Her gaze struck Jo as mildly inquisitive rather than apprehensive.

'National Crime Agency,' she said. 'What is that? Police? Spooks?'

Her voice was lighter than Jo had expected and her tone neutral.

'Police,' Jo told her. 'Except that unlike the regional forces we have a national and international reach, especially with respect to serious and organised crime.'

The corners of Lorna Driffield's lips twitched with the hint of a smile, and the pupils of her blue-grey eyes dilated.

'Wow!' she said. 'Serious *and* organised. If you're talking about garden landscapes, you've come to the right place. But crime?' She shook her head slowly, and looked over to her colleague. 'What do you think, Shaye? Or have you been moonlighting with a drugs cartel behind my back?'

Jo turned and saw him clearly for the first time. He was a head taller than her, broad-shouldered and muscular. His skin, like Driffield's, was creased and weathered but much paler, as though he spent too much time in the dark. There was something about his face that made her skin creep.

His shrug was noncommittal. He pointed to the flags behind her, and held out his hand. Driffield handed him the copper pipe. He took it, and without a word, stepped past her, knelt down, and began to work on the few remaining flags. His boss watched him for a moment, and then turned to face Jo.

'Seriously though,' she said. 'What's this all about?'

Jo looked around.

'Is there somewhere we could go to discuss this?' she asked. 'It'll probably take ten minutes or so. You may want to sit down.'

'I've been on my knees for the past hour,' Driffield replied. 'I need to stretch my legs. Let's walk for a bit? We can always sit down over there when I've loosened up.'

She pointed to the pavilion behind her. Jo could see a pair of benches on a balcony above the steps.

'That's fine,' she said.

They set off side by side towards the golf course.

'Guy who owns this is a premiership footballer,' Driffield told her. 'Household name, which I can't divulge of course.' She smiled thinly. 'It's in my contract. He's got everything. An indoor swimming pool, the tennis courts, that pitch-and-putt, a football range where he practises free kicks with his kids, a games room and this croquet lawn. Now he wants a traditional rose garden and a lake for coy carp. I'll be working on those in the autumn, but right now the priority is this patio for his hog roast parties.'

'It must be a lucrative contract?' said Jo.

'It is, but I've had bigger.'

She stopped suddenly and turned to face Jo.

'Hang on. You're not here about *him*, are you?'

'Him?'

'The footballer, the guy who owns all this. What is it? Match-fixing, money laundering, under-the-counter payments? I wouldn't know anything about any of that.'

'Your contract's safe,' said Jo. 'It has nothing to do with your client. I'm here about a missing person.'

Driffield set off walking again.

'Missing person? Sounds intriguing. Is it someone I know?'

'That's what I'm here to find out. We're routinely interviewing everyone who was in the vicinity where this person was known to have been before he disappeared.'

'Routinely. So what you're saying is that I might be an unwitting witness?'

Jo was regretting having agreed to go for a walk. She would much have preferred to be able to see Lorna Driffield head on as she responded to her questions. As it was, all she had to go on was her face in profile, the words themselves, and the tone of her voice. None of which was proving helpful one way or the other.

'That's correct,' she said.

'So, which vicinity exactly are you interested in?'

Jo stopped, forcing the other woman to do the same. It also meant that Driffield had to turn to face her.

'Moorfields in Liverpool, the Friday before last, at approximately eight thirty pm.'

Driffield pursed her lips and thought about it.

'Moorfields. Is that the one by Moorfields Station?'

'That's right.'

'The Friday before last, at half past eight?'

'Yes.'

Her brow furrowed. Then she remembered.

'Thursday and Friday, the week before last, I was running a course on hard landscaping for the Green Angels at the Festival Gardens in Liverpool. Shaye did most of the labour, I did the commentary.'

'Green Angels?'

'It's a range of courses funded by the Big Lottery for people who want to help out with community projects. I was invited to run a couple of courses because of some work we did last year for the regeneration of the Festival Gardens.'

'What time did the course finish?'

'Half five.'

'And you set off back home at . . . ?'

'Eightish?'

'So what were you doing in between finishing the course and leaving for home?'

'We went for something to eat. It was pointless getting stuck in the rush-hour traffic so we nipped down to the Pump House at Albert Dock. It's only a couple of miles. I wanted to go to Smugglers Cove, but it would have been too much for Shaye.'

She noted the confusion on Jo's face.

'Have you ever been to Smugglers Cove?'

'No.'

'It's just like you'd expect, a cross between the inside of a pirate ship and a cellar. Lots of wooden panels, beams and tables, low-slung lanterns, and bucketfuls of rum. Far too much stimulation for Shaye.'

'I don't follow?'

'He's on the autistic spectrum.'

'Oh,' said Jo. 'I understand.'

'Do you? Most people don't.'

'I have no personal experience of autism,' Jo told her. 'But as a police officer I do. It's something we need to be trained to understand, and respond to appropriately. Ignorance can lead to all sorts of unfortunate outcomes.'

'I bet,' said Driffield. 'Anyway, I had haddock and chips, and Shaye had the Gloucester Old Spot Sausages and mash. We were sitting outside, so when we'd finished, we watched the comings and goings on the quays for a while and then when I thought the traffic had calmed down we set off.'

'And your route home took you down Moorfields?'

'The satnav did. Maybe it was avoiding congestion. I don't know Liverpool that well, only around the Albert Dock. So I was happy to do as I was told.'

'Did you stop on Moorfields at all?'

'Stop?' she said. 'How do you mean?'

'Stop. Pull in to the side of the road? Park up perhaps? Get stuck in a traffic jam?'

Driffield's forehead furrowed again. She folded her arms, and stared at the sky as though playing it back on a wide screen. Then she shrugged her shoulders.

'To be honest, I don't remember. But I'm sure I didn't park up. I'd have remembered that. After all, I'd have to have had a reason, wouldn't I?'

Jo noted the two tells, and logged them for later.

184

'Did you notice anyone on Moorfields that evening wearing a dinner suit and carrying a small black briefcase?'

Driffield shook her head.

'Why would I? I'd have been busy watching the satnav and the cars in front of me.'

'I would still like you to try and remember,' Jo told her. 'It's important.'

Driffield sighed and closed her eyes. Twenty seconds passed. She opened her eyes and shrugged.

'Sorry. It's not like anything dramatic happened that my brain might have hung on to. I can't even visualise the street, just the station.'

'Don't worry,' said Jo. 'If anything does come back, you can always ring me. So, you went straight home from Liverpool?'

'Yes.'

'And home is where?'

'Hobson Moor, near Hollingworth.'

'That's a long way from Liverpool.'

'It's a long way from most places. I go where the work takes me, and I can be on a motorway within fifteen minutes on a good day.'

'What time did you arrive home?'

The eyebrows rose.

'There you go again,' Driffield said. 'What difference does it make what time I got home?'

'Humour me,' said Jo. 'It's all about elimination. It's something we have to do.'

Driffield shrugged.

'Quarter past nine. Maybe nearer half past.'

'That's some going.'

'What, you're going to do me for speeding?'

'You didn't have to drop Shaye off first?'

'Shaye lives at the farm too. He has no family to speak of. The farm is where I run my business from and store my tools. There's a small nursery for especially hardy plants. It suits us both. And before you go jumping to conclusions, he has his own cottage.'

'Can anybody confirm what time you arrived back at the farm?'

'Shaye can.'

'Nobody else?'

Driffield shook her head, weary of these pointless questions.

'There is nobody else. Can we go back now?'

She sounded irritated.

They began to retrace their steps.

'I wonder,' Jo said. 'Do you keep a record that would show where you were working on any particular day?'

Driffield stopped and stared at her. For the first time, her gaze was full of suspicion.

'Of course I do. But why would you want to know? What the hell has it got to do with this bloke going missing in Liverpool? One minute I'm a routine witness, the next it feels like I'm the prime suspect.'

'I don't remember mentioning that it was a man,' said Jo, watching her closely.

Driffield's smile was contemptuous.

'How many women do you know who wear a dinner suit and carry a black briefcase?'

Jo smiled back.

'Touché,' she said.

By the time they reached the patio, Shaye Tamsey had disappeared, as had the bucket of mortar and the copper pipe. The patio looked perfect, and pristine.

'He should be happy with that,' Jo observed. 'Your footballer.'

'I bloody well hope so,' Driffield replied. 'Because I'm going to have to tell him that he'll have to wait a couple of weeks for the next phase. I had to leave another job halfway through to do this one. One more day here and then we're off. They don't like having to wait for anything, people with more money than they know what to do with.'

'I don't suppose they do.'

There was an uneasy silence.

'If it's Shaye you're waiting for,' said Driffield, 'he'll be round the back of the pavilion cleaning the tools and the bucket. You're welcome to have a word on your own, but he'll only tell you what I've told you. If you're lucky that is. He's not big on talk.'

Tamsey corroborated, in monosyllables, everything that Driffield had told her. His facial expressions and body language were impossible to read. Jo went to have a final word with his boss.

'That work record you promised me,' she said. 'If I were to send you some dates, could you let me know your movements on those days?'

Driffield raised her eyebrows.

'I didn't promise you anything, officer. I only told you that I kept a record. However, since I have nothing to hide, I'll be happy to oblige. Just send me over the dates you're interested in and I'll be sure to let you have them. You'll find my email address on my website.' She smiled. 'I'm sure you've already checked that out.'

Jo refused to rise to the bait.

'Thank you,' she said. 'Just one more thing. Do you know any Masons?'

Driffield looked surprised.

'My business includes hard landscaping. That includes the installation of statues, and rocks of various shapes and sizes. Sometimes there are inscriptions. Even memorials. So of course I know some masons.'

There was not the faintest trace of sarcasm or artifice.

'I was referring to Freemasons,' Jo said.

'Freemasons? No, I don't think I do. Although I'm not sure I'd know one if I saw one.' Driffield's lips formed a wry smile. 'But from what I've heard, as a police officer, you must know quite a few?'

Jo stepped on to the driveway at the back of the house, and walked around the front of the Transit van to the side furthest from her Audi. Along the width of the side-loading door was stencilled a logo, the name '*Lorna's Garden Transformations*', a mobile phone number and the website address. On rounding the rear of the van, she discovered the same logo, phone number and website address stencilled on to the rear of the vehicle. She wiped the fingers of her right hand across the surface. They left a series of white streaks in a thin film of red dust that had flown in on the wind from the Sahara.

The van had not been cleaned for a few days at least, but it was evident that the stencil had been there for much longer. This was not the van that had been recorded by the cameras on Moorfields the day that Norbert Welsh had gone missing.

She walked to her car, disarmed the alarm, changed into her shoes, and started the engine. She sat there listening to the engine purr. Did it matter that Lorna's Garden Transformations had more than one van? It was not as though Driffield had tried to hide the fact. She would have known that she was driving the other van on the day in question, and they had traced it to her. So what if she owned more than one? On the other hand, for all that their conversation had revealed nothing concrete, there had been a number of unconscious signals, verbal and physical, that set alarm bells ringing.

Jo sighed. Tintinnabulation was unlikely to impress DS Coppull, let alone DI Renton. She backed up and set off towards the entrance gates.

Chapter 34

It was gone five when Jo arrived back at the Quays. Zephaniah and Shah had already left for the day. The only person at his desk was Andy Swift, his head buried in a weighty academic tome. It was only when Jo stood beside him that he registered her presence. He put the book down on the desk, removed his spectacles and let them hang down from the chain around his neck.

'Hello, stranger,' he said. 'How's it going?'

Jo slumped on to the chair opposite, and placed her bag on the desk behind her. Swift scooted his chair around until he was facing her.

'To be honest, I'm a bit knackered,' she said. 'I hadn't realised how much driving this job would entail.'

'You've swapped a manor fifteen miles long by three miles wide, for the whole of the North of England,' he said. 'How did you get on today? Weren't you following up on potential witnesses to the Liverpool disappearance?'

He saw her surprise.

'I'm not checking up on you, Jo – Dorsey told me where you were.' He laughed. 'Actually, she told me where everyone was. I think she likes to make sure that we're all connected.'

'I know what you mean,' said Jo. 'I really like her.'

'Right,' he said, 'tell me about your witnesses.'

He listened intently, without interruption, until she had finished.

'If I've understood correctly,' he said, 'all three have admitted to being in the immediate area when your missing person disappeared. None of them remember having seen your missing person, nor anyone dressed in a dinner suit and carrying a black briefcase. One of them – Raines?' He waited for her to nod. 'Says that he remembers having to stop because he thinks another vehicle pulled out into the traffic in front of him. Raines and your garden landscaper . . . ?'

'Lorna Driffield.'

'. . . Driffield, do not have an obvious motive, but they both move around a lot, unlike the victim's partner . . .'

'Ford.'

'Who is the only one who appears to have anything approaching a motive. He is also the only one who has any acknowledged connection with Freemasonry and with your missing person?'

'Correct.'

'All three of them have legitimate reasons for having been in the area at that time. You do have one person – a Mr Carter – with a possible motive in relation to the Chorley victim.'

'Charles Deighton.'

'But you have not yet been able to establish a direct connection between Charles Deighton and the latest missing person, or any of the three people you interviewed today?'

She shook her head.

'No.'

'You have nothing that would meet the Crown Prosecution Service's evidential test but, based solely on the manner in which your witnesses responded to your questions, you wouldn't rule out

Carter for the Chorley case, or Ford and Driffield in connection with the Liverpool case?'

'That's about the size of it,' she said.

Andy scratched the back of his neck, and then folded his arms.

'What exactly was it,' he said, 'about the way in which Driffield responded that set those alarm bells ringing?'

Jo had been so impressed by the clarity of Andy Swift's summary, and depressed by how little progress she had made so far, that she was worried that this was going to sound pathetic.

'You know how it is,' she said. 'It's just an impression I got.'

'There's nothing wrong with feelings, and impressions, Jo. Millions of years of evolution have helped to hone man's ability to interpret facial movements, gestures and body language. Animals are still better at it than we are. Their senses are not distracted by language. What they see and smell is what really helps them to decide whether to fight or flee. We wouldn't describe that as a hunch, it's much more visceral than that. That's why we call it a gut feeling. So, what was your gut telling you?'

'That there were times when she was trying to avoid having to answer the question, and that on at least one occasion she was lying. Why would she do that?'

Swift shrugged.

'Because she has reasons not to like the police? Because she likes to play games? Because she does have something to hide, but it has nothing whatsoever to do with your investigation?'

Jo had interviewed enough people to know that there were plenty of reasons why the innocent might want, or need, to lie.

'Possibly all three of those,' she said. 'But it was more than that.'

'What kind of tells did you pick up?'

'The usual, straight out of the manual. Deviation, obfuscation, deflection, far too much detail in some of her responses, defensive posture at salient moments. Answering a question with a question.

When I asked if she'd stopped at all on the street where Welsh disappeared, she even said, "*To be honest, I don't remember.*"'

Swift chuckled.

'In other words, I *do* remember but I'm not telling you.'

'Why would she do that if there was nothing sinister about it? Raines admitted to stopping, and was able to account for it.'

'Unless he was also lying, but more convincingly?'

'I know, but I got the impression that he was telling the truth.'

'But you haven't ruled him out?'

'Not yet.'

'Was there anything else about Driffield?'

'When I asked did she know any Masons, she pretended to assume that I was talking about stone masons.'

He raised his eyebrows.

'She was joking, right?'

'No, just thinking on her feet. And when I told her I meant Freemasons, she actually said, "*No, I don't think I do.*"'

Swift laughed.

'She definitely hasn't read the manual. That one is right up there with "*to be honest*".'

Jo reached for her bag and stood up.

'It still doesn't amount to anything though, does it?'

'It's enough to make you want to take a closer look at her.'

'I will. Not least because she certainly has the means.'

'In that?'

'She's a garden landscaper. If anyone knows how to dig a hole and bury a body, she does. And she lives on a farm up on the moors above Oldham. Where better to hide someone for a few days?'

Swift put his hands on the arms of the chair and stood up.

'In which case, why wouldn't she bury her victim up there on the moors, like Brady and Hindley did? Much less chance of it ever being discovered.'

'Bugger,' she said. 'Why didn't I think of that?'

'Because subconsciously you already knew the reason why she might not want to use the moors.'

Jo searched his face for a clue.

'Because it's too close to home?'

He shook his head.

'Try again.'

She looked blank.

'Remember the Deighton crime scene, Jo?' he said. 'What was odd about it? Apart from the fact that he had been buried alive.'

'The cat,' she said. 'The planks.' Her eyes lit up. 'That carving on the tree. The unsub had gone to a lot of trouble to make sure that the grave wasn't discovered, or if it was, that hopefully the body was not. And yet he, or she, had marked the spot.' She stared at him. 'Why would the unsub do that, Andy? As a sick joke? As a record of his achievement? Either way it's not something you could do on moorland where it would disappear in no time.'

'There are two other possibilities that occur to me,' said Swift. 'Firstly, it's not uncommon for some serial killers to deliberately taunt the police with ingenious clues. You know that. Sometimes they're trying to show off, to flaunt their superiority. Sometimes they actually want, or more accurately need, to be caught.'

She nodded. Like the Bojangles perpetrator in her first investigation with DCI Caton.

'Secondly,' he continued. 'I'm not convinced that the Birkacre site was the intended deposition site. Like you, I think the crime scene has the hallmarks of a hastily constructed solution when something went wrong. You said it yourself, Jo. Someone thinking on their feet.'

An annoying voice came out of nowhere.

'*Ring ring ring, ring, ringaling . . .*' A chorus joined in, louder, higher and more persistent. '*Ring ring ring, ring, ringaling . . .*'

Swift grimaced, reached behind him and seized his mobile phone.

'*The Minions* ringtone,' he said. 'My nine-year-old downloaded it when I wasn't looking.'

He checked the screen.

'It's Rachel, my wife. I'll have to take it.'

'It's fine,' said Jo. 'And thanks.'

She picked up her bag, and walked over to her own desk. It was time to ring DS Coppull, on the off-chance that she hadn't left for the weekend. She didn't want her complaining that she'd been kept out of the loop.

Coppull was still there.

'SI Stuart,' she said. 'I'd forgotten about you.'

Why did I bother? Jo wondered.

'Only because it's been a bloody awful day,' the Liverpool detective explained. 'We've had an armed robbery on a supermarket and a drugs-related shooting.'

She sounded overwhelmed. There was a brief pause as Coppull recalled their previous conversation. 'You were going to follow up on those registration numbers?'

Jo repeated everything she had shared with Andy Swift, ending up with the recommendation that Driffield and her employee should be placed under surveillance, while she, Jo, investigated their backgrounds and contacts.

There was a hollow laugh at the other end.

'Good luck with that,' said Coppull. 'Even if I was prepared to request it based on the flimsy evidence, no, let's be honest, *hunch* you've got, there's no chance my Boss would take it up the line. Even if he did, it would never be approved. We simply don't have the resources. I thought that's what you lot were for?'

Jo's heart sank. She knew that the DS was right. She'd have received the same response if she'd been back with the Greater Manchester Force.

'I understand,' she said. 'I'll try my Boss.'

'What if he says no?'

'I'll start with the background checks on both of them, and Ford. If that turns up something more substantial, I'll try again.'

Coppull sighed.

'For what it's worth,' said the detective sergeant, 'I'll see if I can get one of my DCs to take another look at Ford and the wife. From what you've told me, I'd say she had as much of a motive as he did. If there was any funny business, and I'm not saying I've bought into that, I'd fancy those two before the gardener or the courier fella.'

'That would be really helpful.'

'It's my case,' said Coppull. 'Least I can do.'

Andy Swift paused by Jo's desk. He had a helmet in one hand, and his backpack in the other. She placed her hand over the mouthpiece.

'Been given my marching orders,' he said. 'I'm off. I suggest you do the same.'

'I will,' she promised. 'See you tomorrow.'

'Don't go burning the midnight oil,' he said as he headed for the doors.

'Hello? You still there?'

Jo removed her hand.

'Sorry, Terry,' she said. 'That was a colleague letting me know that he was going home.'

'Which is precisely what I intend to do,' Coppull replied. 'I'm not hanging round here when I'm going to have to come in on Saturday and Sunday. Two weekends in the month and I have to end up with the one that's stacking up like the lorries either side of the Channel Tunnel.'

'I'll give you a ring tomorrow,' Jo told her.

That provoked a throaty laugh.

'Make that a text. The way I feel right now there's every chance I'll be taking a nap in the stationery cupboard. Ta-ra.'

Jo checked the time. Quarter to six. If she hurried, she'd see Abbie before she left for the hospital. Just one more night, and then there would be no more shift work to contend with. No passing like ships in the night. She entered her password into the computer, brought up the shared drive, typed in her report and sent Harry Stone a message alert so that he would know it was there. Then she logged off, sent the computer to sleep, grabbed her bag and ran towards the exit.

Chapter 35

Alex Trott stepped out into the cold wind funnelling down the narrow street, and shivered. He placed his briefcase on the pavement and turned up the collar of his overcoat. He stooped to retrieve his case, turned left, and set off towards the main road where he would hail a taxi. It was a routine to which he had become accustomed over the five years in which he had been a member of the Lodge. This was a route that he could follow blindfolded.

His mind was on his forthcoming installation to the Chapter of the Royal Arch Mason. There were so many things to remember, and he was determined to put up a good show in front of the brethren. He had been learning it by rote, never mind that the instructions were repeated by the principal officers. Hardly surprising then that he failed to notice the figure standing in the unlit doorway two doors down.

Like an athlete using mental imagery to rehearse the steps of his discipline, Alex pictured Zerubbabel asking if he wished to be admitted to the mysteries of the secret degree. He verbalised his own response. Heard the invitation to advance towards the sacred shrine where those mysteries were deposited. Counted out each of the seven steps it would take to reach them. Saw himself stop and bow after the third, the fifth and the seventh step as he came closer to the mysterious name of the True and Living God Most High. Now he visualised his arrival at the crown of the vaulted chamber. First he must move two of the Arch or Keystones of the vault.

Alex stopped, placing the briefcase containing his Masonic regalia on the floor. Unaware that he was being watched, he raised his left hand level with his shoulder. He could almost feel the crowbar being placed diagonally across his palm. He raised his right hand, and imagined it being grasped firmly by the Principal Sojourner, and guided to grasp the crow at its highest point. Now he mimed the act of levering the crow beneath each of the Keystones in turn to deftly wrench them free and open the vault.

In his mind's eye, he saw Zerubbabel step forward to speak.

'Let the Candidate be duly lowered into the vault.'

Smiling to himself, Alex picked up his case and carried on walking.

The blow struck him at the base of his neck on the side closest to his right shoulder. The briefcase fell from his slack fingers, and his legs gave way. Strong hands grabbed his left shoulder and the right-hand sleeve of his coat, preventing him from pitching forward on to the ground.

In a pain-induced haze, Alex was dimly aware of an arm wrapping around his back, and another grasping his right arm and pulling it across his assailant's back. His legs trailed helplessly as he was dragged along the pavement. Suddenly he felt himself free, and falling again. His head struck the side of the kerb, and there was darkness.

Chapter 36

Andy Swift was already at his desk. Ram Shah was over by the coffee machine.

'Hi, Jo,' he said. 'What's your poison?'

'I'll have a double shot skinny latte, please,' she told him.

'In which case, you'll have to wait for Dorsey. I only know how to press and go.'

'I'll have the next closest then,' she said. 'Just so long as it doesn't have the word fat in the title.'

Swift was on the phone, so Jo went straight to her desk and woke up the computer. While she waited, she checked her phone for messages. There were none.

'Here you go,' said Ram, carefully placing her coffee on the Stockport County FC coaster she'd positioned well away from her keyboard.

He perched on the edge of her desk, and pointed to the coaster.

'The Hatters,' he said. 'Supporting the underdog?'

'A friend was on their books for two years, until he realised he wasn't going to make it. He sends me one of these every year. I think he must have a stash hidden away somewhere.'

Ram grinned.

'Better that than heroin.'

'I still follow them,' she told him. 'They drew with Manchester United in the summer.'

'Pre-season friendly doesn't count.'

She began to open up her emails.

'I thought I'd left the football banter behind when I joined the NCA.'

He chuckled.

'What were you expecting, polo and croquet, Proust and Chopin?'

One of the emails was from Harry Stone.

'I'm sorry,' she said. 'I need to deal with this.'

'No problem, you know where to find me.'

She smiled absent-mindedly, and opened the message.

You've been busy. I'm afraid I have to agree with DS Coppull. In relation to Driffield, you don't have enough to justify additional resources at this stage, or a warrant to search her premises. But I can tell from your report that you already know that. This does not mean that I'm discounting your instincts, far from it. Go with the plan you've outlined. At least Coppull has agreed to take her missing person case a lot more seriously. That gives you less to worry about. I'm tied up today, as is Ian Stannard, the Director of Operations, but if there's anything really urgent you can always contact Deputy Director Simon Levi. I've kept him in the loop as far as you're concerned. He has way more influence than I do.

    Stone

Simon Levi was the last person with whom she wanted to converse. Whenever Levi and DCI Caton's paths had crossed, her former boss had left Levi angry and resentful. The NCA man had not struck her as being someone who easily forgave or forgot. It was probably enough for her to have been part of Caton's team for Levi to give her a hard time. That had crossed her mind when she agreed to take the job, long before she realised how high up the organisation Levi had risen in just two years.

The remaining emails were quickly dispensed with. She created a new document, entered the bare details that she had on Lorna Driffield and Shaye Tamsey, together with the web address of Lorna's Garden Transformations. She printed a copy and took it over to Ram Shah's desk.

He rubbed his hands.

'What treasures have you got for me?'

She handed him the sheet of A4.

'I thought it was the other way round? I give you lots of random pieces of debris, and you turn them into treasure.'

'That's just it,' he said. 'One man's trash is another man's gold.' He placed the sheet on the desk and looked up at her. 'What is it you most enjoy about being an investigator, Jo?'

'I'm not sure I follow?'

'Hunting the bad guy? Catching the bad guy? Taking him out of circulation so he can't do it again? Bringing some kind of justice or resolution for the victim?'

'All of those.'

He shook his head.

'That's cheating. You can only pick one. The clue is in the word "*most*".'

Her brow furrowed.

'I'll make it easy,' he said. 'Is it the process or the product that you most enjoy? The hunt or the kill?'

'You can't have one without the other.'

'Actually you can. We call them cold cases.'

'Okay,' she said. 'The kill gives me the most satisfaction; the hunt gives me the most enjoyment.'

'Me too,' he said. 'That's why I switched from forensic psychology to become an intelligence officer and data analyst.'

He turned his attention to the sheet she had given him.

'When d'you need this by?'

'As soon as?'

He smiled.

'Good, because that's exactly when it'll be ready.'

Jo spent the next two hours going over the Charles Deighton and Norbert Lawrence Welsh case notes. She was unable to find any connection between them other than the fact that they were Masons.

She then turned her attention to the other seventeen names the MisPers search had produced. Any one of them could provide the key that she felt sure would unlock the mystery, but where to start? And could it wait until she had exhausted her investigation of Lorna Driffield? And why the hell weren't DI Renton and DS Charnock following up on her list of missing Masons? After all, they were the ones who had a body, and a bona fide murder. What more did they need?

She pushed back her chair, stood up and stretched. Perhaps another coffee would help.

'Going somewhere?'

Ram stood there with a sheaf of papers in his hand, and a grin from ear to ear.

'I was just going to fix myself a drink,' she said.

He held out the papers.

'You start on these, and I'll see if I can get Dorsey to bring us both one. Let me guess, a double shot skinny latte?'

Before Jo had a chance to reply, her phone rang. She placed the papers on her desk, and picked up.

'Joanne Stuart, National Crime Agency.'

'This is DS Marsh, Mike Marsh, Leeds CID.'

He sounded too young to be a detective sergeant, and distinctly wary.

'What can I do for you, Mike?'

'It's more what I can do for you,' he replied. 'I was told to ring this number.'

'What's it about?'

'We're investigating a suspected street robbery,' he said. 'Last night in Leeds city centre. A couple found this guy unconscious in the gutter. At first they assumed he was drunk. Then they saw blood on his forehead and dialled 999.'

'Go on,' she said, her mind racing ahead.

'By the time he got to hospital he was conscious, but suffering from concussion and loss of memory. He was admitted for observation.'

'What made you think it was a mugging?'

'First off, the medics found a bruise on his neck consistent with him having been struck from behind. Secondly, his wife insisted he had a briefcase with him. The thing is, it was handed in the following morning. Apparently it had been in the street all the time, only the couple that found him had missed it.'

Jo felt the familiar tingle of excitement.

'When he was found, he was on his way home from a Freemasons' meeting?' she said.

There was a pause at the other end.

'That's why I was told to ring you,' he said. 'How did you know?'

'It's a long story. All you need to know is that what you thought was a street robbery is almost certainly an attempted abduction.'

He must have placed his hand over the mouthpiece because she heard a muffled exclamation, and what she assumed was him sharing the news with someone else in the office. When he came back on, he sounded confused.

'Are you sure, Ma'am?' he said.

'Ninety per cent,' she replied. 'And it's SI Stuart, not Ma'am. Where is he now, your victim?'

'Leeds General,' he said.

She was already on her feet.

'I'm coming right over. Whatever you do, Detective Sergeant, don't let them discharge him before I get there.'

Jo sped past the boundary stone between Lancashire and Yorkshire, high up on the Pennines. Forbidding cliffs of millstone grit towered above her. The hands-free told her there was a call. It was Stone.

'I got your message,' he said. 'This is a game changer, Jo.'

'That's what I thought.'

'Where are you now?'

'On the M62, approaching Huddersfield. I should be in Leeds in twenty minutes.'

'Right, this is what you do. If it's kosher, then you can tell them that the NCA are now responsible for coordinating the investigation into suspected abductors of members of the Freemasons, across at least three separate police forces. That means you, Jo. I'll draft in some additional support for the team, but we'll have to use the front-line resources of each individual force.'

Jo's head was spinning. In a heartbeat, the investigation had spiralled into something far more daunting.

'Frontline resources?' she said.

'Forensics, Tactical Aid, Armed Response. Given time and a specific planned operation, we do have some of our own NCA people. Until then, you'll have to negotiate with the locals.'

She had slowed down and moved into the inside lane to take the call. A monster HGV suddenly applied its air-assisted brakes, causing her to do the same.

'Shit!' she exclaimed, her heart in her mouth.

'It's not that bad,' said Stone, his tone betraying surprise.

'It's not that, Boss,' she said. 'This lorry in front stopped on a sixpence, and I thought the one behind was going to plough into the back of me.'

'My fault,' he said. 'I should have got you to ring me back when you arrived. You'd better get off the phone. Don't worry. I'll arrange everything our end to smooth your path. Speak later, Jo.'

'Bye, Boss.'

She checked her mirrors, pulled across into the fast lane and put her foot down.

Chapter 37

DS Marsh was waiting for her at the Infirmary.

'He's not happy,' he said. 'He wanted to discharge himself, and frankly there was nothing I, or the hospital, could do to stop him. We could hardly section him under the Mental Health Act. Fortunately, I managed to persuade his wife to talk him round.'

'Well done,' she said. 'Where is he?'

'He's in one of the rooms they use to talk to relatives. You know, when it's bad news. His wife and kids are with him.'

'Show me,' she said.

Alex Trott looked in better shape than Jo had expected. He had five dissolvable sutures on a wound on his forehead, and a surgical collar around his neck. Two young girls sat on either arm of his chair, each of them holding one of his hands. His wife sat opposite them on the edge of her chair. They all stared at her expectantly.

'Hello, I'm Joanne Stuart,' she said. 'I'm a Senior Investigator with the National Crime Agency. Thank you for agreeing to wait, Mr Trott.'

He frowned, and then winced at the pain it caused.

'I didn't have much choice, did I?'

'National Crime Agency?' said his wife, wide-eyed. She turned to her husband. 'What's going on, Alex? What's this all about? I thought it was a mugging?'

'That's what I'm hoping to find out,' said Jo. 'Your husband is not in any trouble, Mrs Trott, far from it. He's a victim, one of a number we have reason to believe. We need to catch his assailant as quickly as possible.'

'Too true you do,' said the husband.

'I won't keep you long,' Jo told them. 'I just have a few questions, and then I'm sure it'll be fine for you all to go home.'

Mrs Trott stared at DS Marsh.

'I thought you said it wasn't safe for Alex to leave?'

'We'll know one way or the other, when Mr Trott has answered my questions,' Jo told her. She glanced at the children, and noted the concern on their little faces.

'Don't worry,' she said. 'You'll have your daddy back home with you in no time.'

'But what if it isn't safe?' their mother asked.

'Then we'll take appropriate precautions, and your husband will still be able to leave with you.' She held up her hand to indicate that she had not finished. 'Now, I suggest that you go down to the cafeteria with your daughters, and leave Alex and I to get this over with as quickly as possible.'

Mrs Trott was about to protest but her husband beat her to it.

'It's alright, Jen,' he said. 'The sooner we get this sorted, the sooner we can get out of here.'

'Come on, girls,' she said. 'Give Daddy a kiss.'

As soon as the door had closed, Jo sat down on the chair the wife had vacated. DS Marsh pulled up a chair alongside her, and prepared to take notes.

'How's your memory of what happened, Alex?' asked Jo. 'Has it come back?'

He would have shaken his head but the surgical collar made that impossible.

'Not really. I remember the Lodge meeting, and leaving the building. I have this vague recollection of a blow on the side of my neck, but I could be imagining that. But that's all. I'm sorry.'

'No need to be sorry,' she said. 'Do you remember any sounds, any noises?'

'No.'

'Any lights flashing. You know, like a torch or headlights?'

He pulled a face.

'Only the ones in my head when I came round.'

'Do you always take the same route home from Lodge meetings?'

'Invariably,' he said. 'Unless I haven't had a drink. Then I use my car.'

'Did you have your wallet and mobile phone with you last night?'

He looked surprised.

'Of course I did. I had about fifty pounds in my wallet, and both of my credit cards.'

'And nothing was stolen?'

'No.' He held up his left wrist. 'And I still have the watch that Jen bought me for my thirtieth. It's worth over a grand.'

'Okay,' she said. 'Now, I'm going to show you some photographs. I want you to tell me if you know, or recognise, any of these people?'

She went over and sat on the arm of his chair, holding the screen of her tablet in front of him so that he did not have to turn his head. The first two images were mugshots of Lorna Driffield and Donal Raines. They were taken when they were much younger, but it was all she had. The others were of Shaye Tamsey, Stanley Ford and Ray Carter, all obtained from the Passport Office. The final two were photos of Charles Deighton and Norbert Welsh, taken from the case files.

'No,' he said. 'I don't know any of them.'

Jo closed the app, opened a document containing a list of the seventeen missing Masons, and showed it to him.

'Do you recognise any of these names?'

He took his time over it.

'No,' he said. 'Who are they?'

'I'm sorry, I can't tell you that.'

She returned to her seat.

'You must have thought about this, Alex, but is there anybody who may have a grudge against you?'

He appeared puzzled.

'Like who?'

'I don't know – someone you may have upset?'

'Actually, I haven't thought about it,' he said. 'Because it's so absurd, it didn't even occur to me.'

Jo turned to the DS beside her.

'Mike, do you have any questions?'

He thought about it.

'There is one,' he said. 'You remember leaving the Lodge meeting. Do you recall if there was anyone leaving at the same time? Is it possible that someone could have followed you out of the building?'

'No, I don't recall if anyone left at the same time as me. And yes, of course it's possible that someone might have followed me into the street, but if they did I wasn't aware of it. But there's CCTV in the foyer so it would be easy to find out.'

'In that case,' said Jo, 'I'm pretty sure that this was not a street robbery, and nor were you targeted personally because of who you are.'

'Then why the hell was I attacked?'

'Because you're a Mason.'

He looked confused, and then incredulous.

'You mean like a hate crime? Like people attack gays and goths?'

209

'Something like that,' she told him. 'But I think it's more than that.'

'Like what?'

Jo shook her head.

'I don't know, Alex. That's what I'm trying to find out.'

———

DS Marsh took her to the place where Trott had been found lying in the gutter. They retraced his steps to the door of the Masonic Lodge.

'I can see how someone might have been waiting for him, hidden in a doorway,' she said. 'There's hardly any street lighting here, and no cameras until you're on to the main road.'

'That's what we thought,' said Marsh. 'Incidentally, you said "*waiting for him*". I got the impression from what you said to Trott that you thought it could have been any one of them. That he was just unlucky?'

'It was a figure of speech,' she said. 'I think he was unlucky. Only in the end, he was a damn sight luckier than the ones that didn't get away.'

They walked down to the end of the street, to the main road.

'If I'm right, this is where the assailant's vehicle would have been waiting,' she said. 'Have you had any luck with the details of those vans that I sent you?'

He shook his head.

'I've got two DCs going through the CCTV footage. We've got nothing so far, so I'm going to widen the search area.'

They were both silent for a moment, then he said, 'How d'you know they haven't used a different vehicle?'

'I don't.'

He sighed.

'You know what that means? Hours and hours of CCTV analysis, logging vehicles and owners, trying to get close-ups of drivers and their passengers. And all the time we're fishing in the dark.'

He turned to look at her.

'Are you sure about this? That it's really an attempted abduction?'

'I'm sure,' she said. 'Only not just abduction. Like I told you, we're talking attempted murder. It's not the first, and unless we stop them it won't be the last.'

He shuffled his feet.

'The thing is . . .' he said.

Jo sensed this was going to be an apology.

'My boss says he hasn't heard anything from the NCA about you taking over this investigation.'

'Coordinating,' she said, 'not taking over.'

'My boss isn't sure of the distinction,' he replied. 'Anyway, he's willing to give it another twenty-four hours of my time, but if he hasn't heard anything by then, the odds are he's going to tell me to scale it down.'

Ten minutes later Jo was back on the motorway. There had been no point in hanging around, particularly since there was still confusion over who was in charge of what. She tried Harry Stone's number several times, but each time it went to voicemail.

The Trotts were a really lovely family, she reflected. How many other families like that had lost their husband and father, just because he was a Mason? How many more might still do so if she failed to identify and stop the perpetrators? Follow your gut instinct, Andy Swift had said. She knew exactly where that was leading her.

Chapter 38

They kept her waiting for five minutes at the gates to Edgerton Hall while they checked her credentials with the National Crime Agency. They wouldn't even accept the number she had given them to ring. Finally, the gates slid open.

Shaye Tamsey was marking out an area of lawn with an aerosol spray. There was no sign of Lorna Driffield. He didn't look up as she approached, and she was forced to walk along beside him.

'Do you remember me, Shaye?'

''Course I do. You're police. Sue Hart.'

'Stuart,' she said. 'Joanne Stuart. I'm with the National Crime Agency.'

'If you say so.'

'Is your boss around?'

'Boss?'

He shook the can violently, sprayed a yellow mist into the air, and then carried on marking the ground.

'Lorna. Lorna Driffield.'

'No.'

'Where is she, Shaye?'

'Abbott's,' he muttered.

'Abbott's. Where is that?'

He was back at the starting point. He pressed the nozzle one final time, and then stood up to admire his handiwork. An almost perfect octagon enclosed what she estimated to be about a quarter of an acre.

'Abbott's,' she repeated. 'Can you please tell me what and where it is, Shaye?'

He turned and stared at her, as though seeing her for the first time. This close to him, Jo suddenly realised what it was about his face that had unnerved her. His eyes were small and widely set. The bridge of his nose was flat, and the groove between his nose and upper lip was missing. His upper lip was so thin that it barely registered. Last, but not least, his head was far too small for his tall, muscular body.

'Builders' merchant, Swinton.'

He made it sound as though even a fool would know who Abbott's were.

'What's Lorna doing there?'

'Gravel,' he said. 'She's getting gravel.'

Tiring of the conversation, he turned and began to walk towards the pavilion.

She hurried after him.

'How long ago did she leave?'

He shrugged.

'Fifteen minutes.'

Jo looked at her watch. Swinton was less than a mile and a half away. At this time of day, she could do it in five minutes or so.

'Where were you last night at eleven thirty pm, Shaye?' she asked.

He stopped suddenly, and stared down at her.

'With Lorna.'

'Yes, but where?'

'At home.'

'Doing what?'

His face was expressionless, but his hands balled into fists the size of grapefruits.

'None of your business,' he said.

Lorna Driffield was standing at the end of the builders' yard talking to one of the staff. As before, she was decked out in green. She seemed surprised to see the NCA officer walking towards her. Jo hoped that meant that she had not heard from Tamsey so they would not have been able to get their stories straight. Driffield excused herself, and came to meet her.

'This is getting silly,' she said. 'What do you want now?'

'I need to know where you were last night, Lorna, at eleven thirty pm. Purely for purposes of elimination.'

Driffield raised her eyebrows.

'What are you hoping to eliminate me from exactly?'

'Please,' said Jo, 'just answer the question.'

Driffield thrust her hands into her trouser pockets. The muscles on her arms were as pronounced as those of Shaye Tamsey.

'Show and tell,' she replied. 'You answer mine, I'll answer yours.'

'An incident,' Jo told her.

'Where was it this time?'

Jo shook her head.

'It's your turn.'

Driffield laughed.

'You've got me there. Remind me, when was this incident?'

'Last night, at eleven thirty pm.'

She smiled.

'That's easy. I was home all night, from about six pm onwards.'

'Were you alone?'

This time Driffield grinned.

'Your turn.'

This game, Jo decided, was all about avoidance, distraction, and winning time to construct an alternative narrative. Just like the first time, only more so.

'Right,' she said. 'I've had enough. We can continue this in an interview room if you prefer. Either in Manchester, or at the nearest police station.'

Driffield folded her arms.

'No, I was not alone. Tamsey was also there.'

'In his cottage?'

Notwithstanding the deadpan expression, Jo could tell that she was working out the implications before she replied.

'No, he was in mine. We were discussing our work pattern for the next two weeks.'

Jo was uncertain about the first part, about him being there, but the extra detail about their work pattern was definitely a lie.

'How many vehicles do you have?'

Driffield had clearly not been expecting that. She shuffled her feet, and pretended to count them up in her head before she answered. Even when she did respond, her reply was evasive.

'It depends on what you're asking?' she said. 'We've got a Land Rover, a Transit, an old tractor we use on the farm, and a four-wheel quad bike.'

'I'll need the registration number for the Land Rover,' Jo told her.

Driffield pointed past Jo.

'Help yourself. It's the only one in the car park.'

'You were going to send me details of your work record,' Jo said.

'So I was. Sorry about that.'

'So when can I expect them?'

'I'll email them tonight, when I get home.'

'Thank you,' Jo said. 'That will be all for now.'

She turned and started to walk back towards the car park.

'I tell a lie,' Driffield shouted after her. 'We've also got two mountain bikes and a wheelbarrow.'

Chapter 39

Ram had placed a set of notes on her desk. Jo picked them up. The first sheet was headed *The Driffield Family*.

Lorna Driffield's mother, Nancy Clayton, was seventeen years of age when she gave birth to Lorna. The father was twenty-seven years old. A brother, Bradley, was born two years after Lorna in 1978, and a sister, Marina, eighteen months later. All three had their father's surname although the parents were never married. She stared at the father's name: Sidney Spencer Driffield.

Ram arrived with their coffees, and pulled up a chair from the adjoining workstation.

'Where are you up to?' he asked.

She pointed to the father's name.

'Just started.'

'He was an insurance salesman,' Ram told her. 'The kids had his name on their birth certificates. Him and Nancy were still living together at that address in Fallowfield according to the 1981 census. However, the father doesn't appear in the 1991 census. His National Insurance record has him working two hundred miles away in Billericay. He died five years later in 1996.'

He leaned forward, flicked over the page, and pointed halfway down the other side.

'There you go,' he said. 'The death certificate states "... *multiple organ failure following collision with a motor vehicle.*" The coroner recorded a narrative verdict that "*Mr Driffield had been walking along the High Street from The Railway public house in Billericay towards the London Road roundabout when he was struck by a BMW 4 Series Coupé, which is thought to have been travelling in excess of sixty mph.*" The driver of the BMW failed to stop.'

'I wonder if the driver was a Freemason?' she said.

'We'll never know because they never caught him. Mind you, call me stereotypical, but I can't see a Mason driving a BMW 4 Series Coupé, let alone doing twice the speed limit in a built-up area, can you?'

'You *are* being stereotypical,' she said. 'But I take your point.'

'What does that make me?' he asked. 'A Masonist?'

'A clever dick?'

He laughed.

'You're not the first person to call me that.'

His face was a picture of innocence.

Jo turned back to the bottom of the first page and read on. Nancy Clayton's work history was that of a frequent changer. Supermarket checkout operator, high street laundry operative, barmaid, tan studio receptionist and manager, Swedish sauna receptionist.

'I checked on that Swedish sauna,' Ram said. 'It was busted several times, and the owners arrested. Query running a brothel, query supplying Class A drugs. Clayton was never arrested, and the owners were never actually charged with any offence. Her final job was on a supermarket checkout. You could say she'd come full circle.'

'Final?' said Jo.

He flicked over the page again.

'She died twelve years ago – fourth June 2003, aged forty-four – cirrhosis of the liver.'

'Was she an alcoholic?'

'I don't have that information. But then only ten per cent of heavy drinkers ends up with cirrhosis.'

'If there was any foundation to those sauna raids, it could have been Hepatitis C from needle-sharing?'

'Or any number of other causes,' he said. 'Hepatitis B and D, non-alcoholic steatohepatitis from diabetes, high blood pressure, high cholesterol, Budd-Chiari syndrome, genetic disorders, auto-immune disease, pancreatic cancer.'

'Enough,' she said. 'You're making me feel ill listening to you.'

'I'm just saying,' he said, 'there's no point in hypothesising.'

Ram turned the sheet over.

'Even more interesting is the fact that Bradley Driffield, Lorna's brother, died one year to the day after their mother died.'

'How did he die?'

'The death certificate has it down as "Misadventure: Equivocal Death Analysis".'

'What are they saying, manslaughter or suicide? Manslaughter or homicide? Homicide or suicide?'

'None of those.'

'Okay. Suicide or Accident?'

'Bingo.'

'I should have opted for that first,' Jo said. 'That's what most coroners go for if there's any doubt. It's a way of sparing the family's feelings.'

'And getting the life insurance policy paid out.'

She speed-read the next paragraph.

'Why was there no psychological autopsy?'

'You know how it was back then,' he said. 'Nobody liked talking about auto-erotic asphyxiation, but if it was a toss-up between that or suicide, most coroners preferred to hedge their bets. In any case, neither of the sisters were prepared to give evidence as to his state of mind.'

'Weren't prepared to, or weren't in a position to?'

'As far as I've been able to ascertain, it was the former. They'd both had contact with him in the weeks prior to his death, although not in the five days preceding it.'

'And there was no one else who could attest to his state of mind?'

'Only the GP, who wittered on about "depressive episodes", without climbing off the fence.'

'What d'you think?' she asked.

He picked up his mug.

'On pages four and five, you'll find the crime scene evidence given before the coroner, and a summary of the pathologist's report.'

Jo took a sip of her coffee, and turned to page four. She began with the pathologist's evidence.

The precise cause of death was asphyxiation resulting from the sudden loss of oxygen to the brain, and a build-up of carbon dioxide. The mechanism was hanging. This was therefore, death by hanging. The carotid arteries on either side of the neck were compressed by a tension in excess of eleven kilograms on the belt, resulting in a combination of asphyxia and venous congestion – the most common form of death by hanging.

When asked by the coroner if the constriction might have been intended to have an auto-erotic rather than a fatal effect, the pathologist agreed that the build-up of carbon dioxide could equally have induced feelings of lightheadedness, giddiness and pleasure, which would have intensified masturbatory sensations. '*However,*' she added, '*it was impossible for me to ascertain from the post-mortem evidence whether that was or was not the intention.*'

Obviously, thought Jo. *Not unless you were psychic.* She turned to the crime scene evidence hoping the answer would lie there.

Bradley Driffield had been discovered by his landlord in the one-bedroom flat that he rented over a convenience store in Tameside. The landlord had come to collect his rent, and became suspicious because of the amount of junk mail spilling out of the mailbox.

Bradley was discovered in the shower. He was hanging from a belt that looped around his neck and had been secured to the shower bracket. His body was slumped forward, neither fully suspended, nor on his knees. He was wearing a pair of boxer shorts. The landlord had to use his keys to enter the flat. All of the windows were locked. There were no signs of forced entry, nor of any disturbance to the property. Bradley's bedcovers were turned back to one side as though he had just got up. Jo looked up at Ram.

'I don't see anything equivocal about this,' she said. 'He's not naked. There's no erotic paraphernalia. No pornographic material. No drugs. Correct me if I'm wrong, but I thought that in most cases of auto-erotic asphyxia, the victims were found kneeling because that gave them more control. Not hanging like this.'

'I'm inclined to agree,' said Ram. 'It didn't strike me he was a gasper.'

She shuddered.

'That's a horrible term.'

'It's onomatopoeic. It simply describes what they do.' He shrugged. 'Not all of it, obviously. That would be . . .'

Jo raised her hand.

'Please, spare me the fine details.'

He grinned.

'I'm assuming,' he said. 'That the coroner went for misadventure because there was no suicide note, and he didn't have sufficient evidence of the victim's state of mind.'

'I get that,' she said. 'But I still don't buy it. He was what, twenty-four? That's the optimal age for young male suicide.'

Ram nodded.

'And you'll buy it even less when you read his police record.'

'He had a record?'

'Animal abuse, arson and assault.'

She had the distinct impression that Ram delighted in drip-feeding all this information, rather than letting her read it for herself.

'You're enjoying this,' she said.

'I love watching the expressions on your face. It gives me clues as to how your mind is working.'

'When you find out,' she said, 'will you let me know?'

She skipped through the next two pages until she found the details. Bradley first came to the attention of the authorities aged seven. He had been observed on numerous occasions pelting a neighbour's cat with stones from the garden. When the cat was found dead one morning, hanging from a chain-link fence round the woods where the neighbourhood kids used to play, he was the obvious suspect. He denied it, and because of his age no action was taken.

Jo looked up. Ram had logged on to the computer behind him and was typing away.

'This cat incident,' she said. 'How did you find out? There wouldn't have been any kind of formal record.'

He swivelled to face her.

'Him and his mother were probably given a rollicking by the local bobby. But it was flagged up the next time he came to their attention. He was ten, still below the age of criminal responsibility, which before the '98 Act was thirteen years of age. But it was so serious they had to involve Social Services. The cat business came up in the case conference. That's how I found out. Of course, if he'd still been alive I'd have needed a warrant.'

What kind of serious offence, she wondered? The answer was in the plural. The first, and by far the most serious, was arson. In 1994, he was arrested on suspicion of having set fire to two wood and asbestos garages, and attempting to start a fire at the secondary school that he attended. He appeared before a Youth Court, was found guilty in relation to the garages, but not the latter offence. Jo got the impression that had it been in Scotland, the verdict would have been 'not proven'.

Bradley was too young for a custodial sentence, and was ordered to attend a youth treatment centre. Jo was curious to know what that meant. Rather than bother Ram again, she entered the details into the search engine.

It turned out to be a unit run by the Department of Health for disturbed young people for whom other custodial options were considered inappropriate. The one to which Bradley had been sent had closed down in 2002.

There were no details regarding his time there, but whatever treatment he had received did not seem to have been entirely successful. Aged sixteen, he was arrested for assaulting a forty-six-year-old male, occasioning actual bodily harm. The charges were dropped when the victim withdrew his complaint. His police record ended at that point. Ram had summarised Bradley's work record.

Aged sixteen and a half, he was working for a small insurance company in Hyde, a job he held on to for the next three years. She was impressed that he had kept this job for so long, but from there on it had all gone downhill.

In the remaining three years of his life, he was on the dole for two of them, interspersed with three short periods of employment in a fast-food outlet, a cold-call centre, and stacking supermarket shelves. At the time of his death he was unemployed.

Jo sat back and picked up her mug. The coffee was cold but she downed it anyway.

'D'you see what I meant?' asked Ram.

She turned her chair to face his.

'If he was still alive today,' she said, 'he'd be top of my list. Of the thirteen most common characteristics of serial killers, I counted six dead certs and two possibles.'

'I get the dead certs,' he said. 'Unstable family life, abandoned by his father, sadistic cruelty to an animal, arson, time in an institution, trouble holding on to jobs. What are your possibles?'

'That he was intelligent, otherwise how would he have got that job with the insurance firm? And secondly, that he was unhappy at school, and underachieved there.'

He nodded grimly.

'Trying to burn it down would support your hypothesis. Which only leaves bed-wetting, hating his parents, obsessive sexual deviancy and suicidal ideation. The last of which I think you can safely add to the list.'

'Given that he died before any of the men on my list went missing,' she said. 'I don't know that any of that is going to help me, unless either of his sisters followed a similar pattern?'

'I don't know about the youngest, Marina,' he said. 'But I can tell you that she's still alive, and she doesn't have a police record.'

'What about Lorna?'

He levered himself out of his chair, picked up his mug and reached across for hers.

'It's all there,' he said, nodding at the papers on her desk. 'I'll go and fix us another cup. Same again?'

Chapter 40

Harry Stone had still not replied to Jo's emails, texts or voice messages. Without confirmed authority, she knew that it was going to be impossible to accelerate the hunt for the perpetrators, let alone coordinate resources across so many forces. She decided to ask Zephaniah if she knew what was happening with Harry.

'Sorry,' she said. 'I was told not to say anything except that Mr Stone was unavailable.' She lowered her voice. 'But between you and me, I gather it's a domestic crisis involving his daughter.'

Jo gritted her teeth.

'In which case,' she said, 'please ask Mr Simon Levi to ring me. Tell him it's in connection with Operation Hound and it's a matter of urgency.'

Back at her desk she sent Levi an email as a backup, and then turned her attention to the rest of Ram's report.

The section on Lorna Driffield was thin in comparison with that on her brother. She had one juvenile conviction for shoplifting at the age of fifteen, which had resulted in a referral order that led to her working as a volunteer at a community farm. Ram had added an observation of his own.

*I'm assuming that this would not have been a first offence other-
wise she would have been unlikely to receive a referral order. I'm guess-
ing that she had already been given a reprimand, followed by a final
warning for a second offence, the breach of which would have merited
such a sentence. I'll try to get hold of a record of the court proceedings,
but it's notoriously difficult in the case of a juvenile.'*

Jo was beginning to realise that if anyone could, it would be Ram.

The next entry showed Lorna studying Horticulture and
Landscaping at the Northenden campus of what was then City
College. She left with a BTEC Extended Certificate and began
working for one of the region's best known garden centres. Five
years later, she left to set up Lorna's Garden Transformations.

'Here you go.'

Ram handed Jo her mug, and sat down opposite her.

'It looks as though that referral order they gave her turned out
to be a lucky break,' Jo observed.

She blew across the surface of the coffee, and took a mouthful.

'God, this is awful!'

'Sorry,' he said. 'Dizzy was down in the mailroom. I should
have waited till she came back.' He reached for her mug. 'I'll ditch
it and ask her to fix you a new one.'

'It's alright,' she told him. 'I'll manage. So, what I'm wondering
is where did she get the money to set up her own business just five
years after leaving college? There's no way her mother could have
helped her.'

'I wondered that too,' he told her. 'It's one of the things I've
been following up on while you've been reading.'

'And?'

'And it turns out that her mother must still have had her facul-
ties back in 1996.'

'Why 1996?'

'That was when the father was killed. He may not have kept up the maintenance payments, but he certainly made up for it when he decided to walk home drunk that night.'

'Compensation?' she guessed.

'Exactly. Nancy Clayton made an application to the Motor Insurers Bureau under the Untraced Drivers' Agreements. She was awarded a hundred thousand pounds between her and the children. It would have been more but their lawyers argued that although they should have been his dependents, strictly speaking, since he wasn't paying maintenance they were not dependent on him, and had therefore not suffered a material loss.'

'When did the children get the money?'

'When they reached their twenty-first birthday.'

'That might go some way to explain Bradley's erratic employment history,' she observed. 'He wouldn't have had that much incentive to work.'

'And when the money ran out, maybe that's why he topped himself.'

'It doesn't seem to have done the mother much good either. Not if it went on booze.'

'But Lorna must have had an iron will,' he pointed out. 'To have waited until she'd gained the knowledge, skills, and the experience before she decided to set out on her own.'

Jo turned the page. 'That just leaves Shaye Tamsey.'

'Let me save you having to read it,' he said. 'He was born June 1978, to a twenty-three-year-old single mother, with four other children, and three different father's names on the birth certificates. Shaye was abandoned at eighteen months, into the care of Social Services.'

'Abandoned, or taken into care?'

'Abandoned. He was left on the doorstep of her local GP surgery. She made no attempt to hide his identity. The social workers tried to persuade her she could cope, but it was obvious she couldn't, didn't want to, and wasn't going to. There were multiple failed attempts at foster care with a view to adoption.'

'He had problems?'

'Suspected foetal alcohol spectrum disorder.'

'Poor kid.'

Jo had seen more than enough examples of the cruel legacy of a pregnant woman's heavy drinking. She had heard estimates that as many as two in every thousand live births in the Western world carried FASD. That went some way to explaining educational underachievement, alcoholism and petty crime.

'You can say that again,' said Ram.

'Now that you've told me,' she said. 'I could see it in his face, I just didn't recognise it.'

'You're not alone. It wasn't till he started school that they had him properly assessed. At first they thought he might be on the autistic spectrum, Asperger's to be precise. But the diagnosis was never confirmed.'

'What were his particular problems?' she asked.

'Poor short-term memory, communication difficulties, introversion, egocentricity. He had a lot of difficulty understanding the consequences of his actions. He also found it difficult to distinguish between fiction and reality.'

'Hyperactivity?'

'Only as much as he had a very short concentration span.'

'Any police record?'

'No. He was probably saved by the fact that he never mixed with the kind of people who were likely to get him into trouble.'

'When did he leave the care system?'

'At seventeen, he was given a one-bedroom council flat, sent to college, and then found an apprenticeship.'

'Let me guess. At a garden centre?'

'Very good,' he said. 'The gardener at his last care home got him involved. Tamsey was at college at the same time as Lorna, but he was doing a Level One RHS certificate. They must have met at the garden centre.'

Ram sat back and folded his arms. There was just a hint of self-congratulation.

'Is that everything?' said Jo.

He pretended to look hurt.

'Is my best not good enough?'

'You've done a great job,' she told him. 'There is one other thing you could do for me?'

'Anything.' He smiled broadly. 'Given that's what I'm being paid for.'

She smiled back.

'In which case, remind me not to be so effusive with my gratitude in future.'

'What is it you want?'

'Can you find out where the sister, Marina, is living right now? She may be the only person left who can tell me about Lorna and Bradley.'

'Miracles I do at once,' he said. 'The impossible will take a little longer.'

Jo spent the rest of the morning trawling through the details of the remainder of the seventeen missing Freemasons. The problem that she faced was that each of them had been treated as an isolated disappearance. Had there been any suspicion of foul play, a major investigation would have been launched. As it was, the details were sketchy. No motives had been established. The steps taken by the relevant missing persons team had been perfunctory. She decided to bring Andy Swift up to speed.

'I can see where you're coming from, Jo,' he said. 'I told you yesterday to trust your instincts, and everything Ram has uncovered about Driffield and her brother only strengthens your argument. I think you and I should put a behavioural profile together. I'll get started. In the meantime, why don't you see what you can find out about the sister? What was her name?'

'Marina. Ram's already on the case.'

'In that case,' he said. 'I was going to stretch my legs, and grab a sandwich. Why don't you join me?'

Jo checked the clock. It was 12.45.

'That's a great idea,' she said.

She logged out and jumped to her feet. As they passed Ram's desk, he slid his chair back and held out a sheet of A4.

'You might want to check this out,' he said.

'What is it?'

'Marina Driffield's current address. Not only that, but her present whereabouts.'

She turned to Andy Swift.

'I'm sorry,' she said.

'I know,' he replied. 'You're going to take a rain check. I'd do the same.'

Jo was already reading Ram's notes.

'Ram, this is brilliant,' she said. 'How did you track her down?'

'Her last known address was in Clayton. A bedsit rental paid for through housing benefit. She was unemployed, theoretically job-seeking.'

'Theoretically?'

'Her last employer was a firm of office cleaners. I spoke to them. She was sacked because she'd become totally unreliable. They said she had a drink problem and was constantly late for work.

Sometimes she'd miss her shift completely and claim she was sick. Then she had her housing benefit suspended.'

'Why was that?'

'She was under investigation for suspected benefit fraud.'

'Working in the shadow economy?'

'You could say that. They believed she was on the game.'

'What happened?'

'She didn't wait for the outcome of the investigation, she just upped and left. I guessed she'd stay fairly close to home, either sleeping rough, in a squat somewhere or in a brothel. I contacted the police, and Riverside.'

The No Second Night Out Service. Jo knew of them from her time in GMP. Anyone could report online or by phone a rough sleeper or someone begging. In the case of the former, they would make contact and offer emergency accommodation, with the promise of a more permanent solution. In the case of a beggar, the police would deal with it and point the person to the most appropriate service to help them and hopefully get them off the streets.

'They got her a detox and rehab referral to the Turnkey Service,' he added.

He indicated the sheet of paper in her hand.

'That's where she's at right now.'

'Residential?'

'She's coming up to her third week.'

'Three weeks? That sounds like more than just alcohol?'

He shrugged.

'I didn't ask. But if you want to interview her, you'll have to make the approach yourself. It could be tricky. After all, it's not as though she's committed a crime or is even a suspect in an on-going investigation.'

He was right. Recovery from addiction was a long, slow and sensitive process. The last thing they would want was one of their clients being knocked off track by an interview with an NCA investigator. And it wouldn't just be that client that was affected. There would be others in the facility who had reason to be suspicious of the police.

'I'll give them a ring,' she said. 'See if I can arrange a visit.'

'Good luck,' he said.

⁓

Jo got through first time. Emelia Cox, the nurse therapist and service manager, was extremely cagey.

'So you're hoping that Marina may be able to provide some background information in relation to an on-going investigation?'

'That's correct,' Jo replied.

'She's not a suspect?'

'No.'

'In which case, I'll have to insist that Marina is given the opportunity to decide for herself if she's prepared to speak with you.'

'I understand.'

'How soon do you need to see her?'

'Ideally, today.'

There was a pregnant pause. A sigh. The sound of fingers on a keyboard.

'It may be possible. Marina has a slot between a group-work session and a one-to-one key worker session. Ring again in fifteen minutes. I'll have an answer for you by then.'

Chapter 41

'Marina was referred to us two and a half weeks ago,' explained Cox as she led the way down a long corridor. 'She's one of a number of our clients who are homeless and lead chaotic lifestyles.'

'I take it that in her case it includes multiple substance abuse?' said Jo.

The manager stopped walking and looked keenly at her.

'What makes you say that?'

'I'm aware that Marina had a problem with alcohol abuse, but that alone would not require such an extended detoxification programme, or would it?'

'You're right, it wouldn't.'

'Look,' said Jo. 'I'm not prying. I don't need to know what she's been taking, but it would be helpful to have some understanding of the situation she's been in and her current state of mind, if only so that I can assess the reliability of the information she may give me.'

'Do you have any experience of substance misuse and detoxification?'

'Only second-hand but plenty of that. I've been involved in referring offenders to your service. I've also seen for myself the work of a rehabilitation centre.'

She noted the sudden arching of the woman's eyebrows, and regretted that last piece of information. It would not be helpful, she realised, to admit that she had done so in an undercover capacity.

'Really?' said Cox.

'Really.'

When it was obvious that Jo was not going to explain, Cox pursed her lips and started walking down the corridor. They reached a door at the far end. She paused, her hand on the handle.

'Marina has asked her key worker, Marvin, to sit in on your interview. I take it you have no objection?'

'Certainly not,' Jo replied. 'Although I may be asking some quite sensitive and personal questions. There's no knowing what Marina may divulge.'

Cox's smile was of the annoyingly tolerant sort one might form at a child's question.

'The whole basis for a psychosocial intervention is to surface those sorts of things. I doubt there's anything she would have to say that Marvin hasn't heard before or won't hear again, but then, of course, with your experience you would know that.'

Jo could have kicked herself. Cox would have known that what she was really concerned about was that Marina might not open up completely with someone else there.

'Of course,' she said. 'I just thought I ought to check.'

Cox nodded.

'Marina has made excellent progress with us. She's leaving for Denton House next week to embark on her rehabilitation phase. We have high hopes that she will achieve a really successful resettlement into employment and independent living. We wouldn't want anything to put that in jeopardy.'

'Neither would I,' Jo assured her.

'Good. One more thing. We don't allow the use of mobile phones for the residents. And we ask all visitors to please switch theirs off before they enter.'

'Mine already is,' Jo assured her.

The room was larger than she had expected. The light-blue walls held posters containing positive exhortations to support the patients' recovery, together with some of their own paintings. On a long table, beside bottles and tubes of paint, stood jars full of paintbrushes.

Marina Driffield was sitting beside her key worker on a black leather sofa framed by greenery in a courtyard garden visible through the plate-glass window. She looked small and sad beside Marvin, a mixed-race male with a strong lived-in face framed by long curly hair. There was very little resemblance between Marina and her sister Lorna. She looked nervously at Jo as Emelia Cox made the introductions.

Jo pulled up a chair so that she faced the sofa, a comfortable and discreet distance away.

'Marvin and Marina have just had a tea break,' said Emelia, 'but I'd be happy to get you something?'

'No thanks,' Jo told her. 'I'm fine.'

'In that case, I'll leave you to it. Marvin will bring you back to reception when you've finished.' She checked her watch. 'Remember, Marina, you have your next session in forty minutes.'

Jo knew that the reminder had been given for her benefit, not Marina's.

Marina Driffield folded her arms, appeared to recognise the impression that would make, unfolded them and placed her hands, one on top of the other, in her lap. She eyed Jo nervously.

'Thank you for agreeing to talk with me,' said Jo, trying to put her at her ease. 'Is it alright if I call you Marina?'

Driffield glanced at her key worker. Marvin's nod was almost imperceptible. *God*, thought Jo, *I hope it isn't going to be one of those.* She might just as well have asked for her lawyer.

'Marina, you don't have to check with me,' said Marvin in a calm and measured voice that was both authoritative and non-judgemental. 'You know that?'

She nodded.

'Yes. I'm sorry.'

'And you don't have to . . .'

'Apologise,' she said, pointing to one of the posters on the wall.

He laughed and she joined in.

That's better, thought Jo.

'Just pretend that I'm not here, Marina,' he said. 'You too, Jo.'

'Thank you,' Jo replied, noting the way in which he had cleverly used her first name rather than her professional role. Everything designed to put them both at ease.

'Before I begin,' said Jo. 'Would it be okay for me to record our conversation, Marina, or would you prefer me to make notes?'

For the first time, Marina Driffield looked anxious, and Jo feared her key worker was about to intervene.

'On second thoughts,' she said. 'Why don't I just make a few notes. Nothing formal. Just to jog my memory.'

Marina nodded and visibly relaxed. Jo took out her notebook and balanced it on her knee.

'I would like to start by asking you about your brother,' she said. 'Is that okay?'

'Bradley?'

There was no flicker of surprise in her eyes. It was as though she had been expecting this.

'That's right.'

'What do you want to know?'

Jo had rehearsed this next part on the way over. She had intended to work up to it slowly, but given the limited time available, and Marina's apparent readiness, she decided to go for it.

'Why do you think he committed suicide?'

Jo expected the key worker to object, but he seemed eager to hear the reply.

'They never actually said that he took his own life,' Marina replied. 'They said it could have been an accident.'

There was something about her tone that told Jo his sister had never believed that.

'What do *you* think, Marina?' she said. 'Could Bradley have committed suicide?'

There was no change in her expression or demeanour, other than her hands changing places in her lap, but Jo could tell that she was struggling to arrive at a major decision. When she answered, it came with a sense of relief.

'Yes,' she said. 'He could. In fact, I'm certain that he did.'

'How can you be so certain?'

'Because Bradley and me were close. Closer than anyone else I've ever known. We both knew what each other was thinking. It was like we were twins.'

She paused. There was no way that Jo was going to break that silence other than with an encouraging nod.

Marina turned to her key worker.

'I knew that Bradley would kill himself one day. It was only a matter of when.'

She turned back to Jo.

'He had good reason.'

Jo counted to three.

'Would you like to tell us about it?' she said.

There was something in Marina's eyes and in the tone of her voice that told Jo that it would be best to let the narrative flow uninterrupted. Marina had a pressing need to share her story, like a dam that had been waiting to burst.

Jo put her biro down, closed her notebook, and waited for her to begin.

Chapter 42

'If the photographs are anything to go by, our mother must have been beautiful when our father first met her.'

Marina's voice cracked a little. She paused and took a deep breath. When she began again, her head was bowed but she had found her rhythm and her voice was strong.

'I can see why she fell under his spell. He was ten years older than her, and a flashy dresser despite his job. Charming too, according to Lorna, although I was too young to see any of that. He wasn't a heavy drinker, but he liked going to the pub of an evening, mainly because he had an eye for the ladies. Our mother was more of a home bird, besides she had the three of us to look after, and if she wasn't going to keep an eye on the pennies, who was? He quickly bored of our mother when we came along. He told her it was like being tied down by four children, not three.'

She raised her head.

'I suppose you're wondering how I know all this if he left when I was only three? Well, I heard it often enough from our mother. Years later. Mainly when she was drunk.'

She turned to her key worker.

'Like me, I suppose? History repeating itself.'

He smiled. She switched her attention back to Jo.

'Our mother started drinking shortly after our father left. Not long after that, she began to bring men home. We were told to call them uncle. It was very confusing for someone my age. We had more uncles than any other family in the street.'

Her smile was ironic.

'At first it was a novelty. Most of them would start off by bringing presents for the three of us. To keep us occupied and out of the way, I suppose. But it never lasted long. Nor did they. Apart from one.'

That last was said with barely controlled anger.

'Some of them would beat her up. I'd hear her crying in her room at night, or find her sitting on the stairs with her knees tucked under her chin, cradling her legs, and sobbing her heart out. I can still see the bruises, and the cut lips, from the times when she'd say she'd walked into a door. Lorna began to threaten them that she would call the police. She even did once. Not that the police ever came.'

Jo wasn't sure if there was an accusing tone in Marina's voice, or a gleam in her eyes, but she felt a twinge of collegiate guilt. It had only been in the past few years that domestic violence had begun to be taken seriously by the justice system.

'They stopped coming,' Marina continued, 'and things were better for a while. I was about seven, I think. Our mother got a new job as a manager in a tanning studio. She stopped drinking. She used to take the three of us to the park or to the cinema, then for a Big Mac as a treat.'

She smiled to herself.

'It was the one time in our lives I remember us being happy. Feeling like a proper family.'

Suddenly it was as though a shadow had passed across her face. She bowed her head again, took a deep breath and looked up.

'Then Uncle Ralph arrived. I found out much later on that her boss at the studio had introduced them. A sort of blind date.'

She shook her head.

'Blind being the operative word. He was tall, dark and good-looking in a smarmy sort of way. I always thought he resembled our father in a photo stuffed in a drawer in the front room. He was a good bit older than her too. Lorna was coming up to eleven. Bradley was nine. I was seven and a half. The first couple of months were fine. He behaved like I imagine a stepfather should. He took the trouble to play with us, especially Brad. I can still see him kicking a football in the yard, hear them laughing and the sound of the ball thudding against the gate. He came on our outings together as a family. He brought us presents, but only on our birthdays, and at Christmas. Our mother adored him. Me, I always thought there was something creepy about him.'

She stopped as though she had suddenly run out of steam. Her key worker placed a hand on the seat of the sofa between the two of them.

'Are you okay, Marina?'

She nodded.

'Would you like a drink of water?'

'Yes, please.'

Jo sneaked a look at her watch. Twenty minutes had passed, and they had only just reached the heart of this narrative. On the other hand, Marvin's intervention had been both timely and sensitive. It was obvious that Marina's mouth was drying up. Jo only hoped that her story had not.

'How about you, Jo?' Marvin called across from the water dispenser.

'Yes, please,' she replied.

She knew from experience that it helped to mirror someone volunteering a difficult account. Marvin handed them their water, and sat down. Marina took a sip, and then another. She cradled the plastic cup in her hands and smiled at her key worker.

'Thanks,' she said, for a second time.

He smiled back.

'You're welcome, Marina.'

She turned to face Jo.

'Where was I?'

'Uncle Ralph,' Jo prompted. 'You always thought there was something creepy about him?'

Marina nodded.

'I can't say what it was exactly. It was just a feeling I had. But once he'd got his feet under the table, it became more obvious. He still tried to be nice to Lorna and me, but looking back it was clear his heart wasn't in it. He was just going through the motions.' She paused, and her voice trembled. 'It was Bradley he was interested in.'

She lifted her tumbler and took another sip.

From the moment that Marina had mentioned Uncle Ralph, Jo had seen this coming but for some reason she had painted herself another scenario. The girls abused. The brother racked with guilt. Either way, here was a motive. All it needed was a connection.

'I think I remember the first time,' Marina continued. 'But I can't be certain because it became a pattern that went on for years. It was a Saturday. Our mother worked on Saturdays, he didn't. It was the school holidays, and the cinema had a summer season of kids' films. He said he and Bradley were going to stay home and play football – did Lorna and me want to go to the pictures? We jumped at it.'

She paused. Her expression betrayed the fact that she was mentally beating herself up.

'Of course we did. He gave us money for popcorn and a Coke. What child's going to turn that down?'

She looked at Jo, seeking some kind of understanding. Jo nodded, and then felt compelled to reply.

'You weren't to know,' she said. 'You were only seven years old.'

'It was *Benji the Hunted*,' Marina said. 'The main film. There are two reasons I remember that. It was the first film I ever saw where we went on our own, Lorna and me.'

She stopped and didn't seem able to continue. One of her hands began to tremble. She squeezed it hard with the other one, took a deep breath and turned to look at her key worker. There was that look of confusion on her face again.

'The other reason, Marina?' he said gently.

She nodded, exhaled, breathed in again and continued.

'Have you seen it?' she asked, looking directly at Jo. '*Benji the Hunted*?'

'No, I'm afraid I haven't.'

'It's about a dog, Benji, only he's a mutt really. Nothing special, not your Lassie or your Scooby Doo. But he's a hero. He's lost in the woods on a mountainside. He comes across four cougar cubs whose mum has been killed by hunters. He rescues them. Feeds them. But the bravest thing he does is to protect them from predators. There's this bear, and a timber wolf.'

For the first time, tears began to well up.

'He's this tiny scruffy mutt and he saves them from this bloody great wolf. Why couldn't we do that?'

It was a question that Marina had been asking herself over and over again for almost a quarter of a century. Tears poured down her cheeks. She bowed her head, and tried to wipe them away with the back of her hands.

Jo reached for her bag, searching for a handkerchief. Marvin beat her to it. From down by the side of the sofa he picked up a man-size box of tissues. He pulled two out and handed them to Marina, offering a fresh tissue in exchange for the sodden ones a minute or so later. It seemed like a routine they had practised many times before. Marina held the clean tissue tight as she folded her hands in her lap again.

'Bears and timber wolves,' said Marvin. 'Those are the kind of predators that a child would recognise without anyone having to explain about them. The kind you're talking about, an adult would have trouble spotting. You were only seven, Marina.'

She sniffed. When she replied, Jo could barely make out what she had murmured.

'I wasn't always seven.'

Chapter 43

'Are you saying that you found out, that you knew?' her key worker asked.

She shook her head.

'No, I didn't. Not till much later.'

She turned to address Jo.

'You know I said me and Bradley were close, like twins?'

Jo nodded.

'Well, that was only true before Ralph arrived on the scene. After that, nobody knew what Brad was thinking. He changed.'

'In what ways?'

'He started having nightmares. He wet his bed. He even soiled his trousers at school a few times. He'd get angry at the smallest things. And he became really secretive.'

'In what way?'

'He'd never discuss anything with any of us, not even me. He'd spend most of his time in his bedroom. Rarely went out playing with the lads who used to be his mates.' She paused. 'He ran away twice but he always came back. He had nowhere else to go. Then he started getting into trouble.'

She watched Jo carefully.

'But I suppose you already know about that?'

'Yes,' Jo admitted. 'I do.'

Marina's shoulders slumped. She looked wretched.

'Looking back, all the signs were there, only I didn't know what to look for. Ralph was into photography. He had one of those Instamatic cameras, and another really expensive one with a flash and different lenses. He was always taking photographs of us. In the garden, on the Red Rec.' She saw the confusion on Jo's face. 'The recreation ground up the road from us. It was made of red shale. He took pictures of us in our undies when he was putting us to bed. And he was always wrestling us, even when we didn't want him to. Especially Brad.'

She took another sip.

'Then Ralph started bringing male friends back. There were a few that were regulars, but sometimes there were different ones. Usually they'd be gone before Lorna and me got back home, but sometimes we'd pass them on the doorstep, or see them getting into their cars. He told us it was a card school. What were we to know? Our mother didn't seem to notice either. I'm not sure if she simply chose not to. I think she was terrified of losing Uncle Ralph. He was the only person who showed her affection. He was generous to her, and to us. Now I think she must have found out, and that was when she started to drink heavily again.'

'Did Lorna find out?' Jo asked, conscious that time was flying.

Marina nodded.

'About a year after we went to see that *Benji* film. Our mother was working late. I remember there was this godawful row between the two of them, Lorna and Ralph. She was screaming, calling him all sorts of names. He kept trying to put his hand over her mouth and telling her to calm down. She said she was going to tell our mother. Then he totally lost it. He grabbed her, dragged her kicking and screaming down the hall, kicked the mat aside, opened the trapdoor to the dungeon and pushed her inside.'

Her eyes began to well again. She dabbed at them with the tissue.

'I can still see her little hands scrabbling to hold on to the sides. She'd stopped screaming. She was pleading with him now.

'*"Please, Uncle Ralph! Please. No! I won't tell. I promise. Please!"*

'He just stamped on her fingers till she let go, gave one last shove, and slammed the lid shut. Then he made us go to our rooms. I just lay on my bed listening to Lorna's muffled cries. Then I couldn't hear her any more.'

She dabbed her eyes again and wiped her nose. Marvin handed her another tissue, and took the spent one.

Jo checked the time. There were less than ten minutes left.

'What exactly was this dungeon, Marina?' she asked.

'That's what we kids called it.' She'd composed herself a little now. 'It wasn't a cellar or anything like that. Just a hole less than two metres square, with a wooden ladder, a bare floor, and sheets of corrugated iron on the walls, like you see on garage roofs. A man who lived there in the 1950s was obsessed with the Russians dropping atomic bombs, so he dug down under the floorboards to make a bomb shelter. We weren't allowed down there. Mum said it wasn't safe.'

She took another mouthful of water.

'Growing up, we're all frightened of something, aren't we? I was frightened of spiders. Bradley was frightened of bees and wasps because he was stung when he was little. Lorna was always frightened of the dark. It started when our father left. She couldn't go to sleep unless there was a light on, either on the landing or in her room. What that bastard did to her, it must have been her worst nightmare. I don't know what time he let her out, but it'll have been before our mother got home. After that, Lorna never spoke about it to us, and she never spoke to him. But she can't have told our mother either, because we'd have known. I think it was because of Lorna that he never brought any men home after that. But he started taking Bradley out with him, and we stayed home. When they got back, Bradley would go straight to his room. He didn't even speak to us.'

'You can't blame Lorna,' said Marvin. 'She must have been terrified.'

Marina turned to look at him. She shook her head.

'I don't. It's *him* I blame. He was a monster.'

'Was?' said Jo, only too aware that time was running out. 'What happened to him?'

'God knows. I hope he's dead and rotting in hell. He left one day, when I'd just turned ten, and never came back. I think Lorna had something to do with it, because she came home from school one afternoon all on edge, like she was waiting for something to happen. When he came in from work, she told him she needed to speak to him in private. He was as shocked as we were. Anyway, they went out into the yard. I watched through the kitchen window. She said something, and he went pale. Then he grabbed her arm, but she wrenched it free. She stood her ground, pointing her finger in his face. I couldn't hear her shouting, but I could tell she must have been. She was threatening him. He spat on the ground by her feet, turned, and came back inside. He packed his things and left without a word.'

'Did you ask Lorna what happened?' said Jo.

'All she said was "*He's going, and good riddance.*" The next day a policeman came round. He spoke to our mother and then he left. We never saw him again. That's when our mother's drinking took off.'

Marvin made a point of looking at his watch.

'Two minutes,' he said.

'You mentioned that you and Bradley became close again, after Ralph had left,' said Jo. 'Is that when he told you what had been going on?'

'I suppose so, but not immediately. It was a few years later. I found him on his bed, crying his eyes out. I asked what was the matter. He'd been arrested by the police for starting fires, and was going to have to go to court. I tried to comfort him. That's when he opened up. No details. Just that Uncle Ralph had made him do things. Not just with him, but with all those other men who came to the house. He said it made him feel dirty. That it was all his own fault.'

She turned to her key worker.

'It was horrible, seeing him hurting like that. Blaming himself for what that bastard had done to him.'

She looked at Jo. There were tears in her eyes.

'He said that some of the other boys at school were going out with girls. They were all obsessed with sex. Always bragging and bigging it up. Poor Brad was scared of girls. I suppose he was intimidated by them. He couldn't join in any of the banter. It worried him that he didn't know what normal sex was.'

She shook her head again.

'The only person he could talk to about it was his twelve-year-old sister. What did I know?'

'I'm sure you helped him far more than you realised,' said Marvin.

'I hope so,' she replied.

'How did it affect him later on?' asked Jo.

The key worker flashed her a look of concern, but Marina took it in her stride.

'It ruined his life,' she said. 'He was in trouble with the police over and over again. It was like he was trying to get back at the world, and punishing himself into the bargain. He started out with a good job, and then it was all downhill. I don't think he ever managed to form a meaningful relationship with women, or with men for that matter.'

Marvin heaved himself up from the sofa.

'That's it, I'm afraid,' he said.

'Can I ask one last question, Marina?' said Jo, making it seem like an afterthought.

'Was Uncle Ralph a member of the Masons?'

Her brow furrowed.

'What, the one on Oxford Road? The Masons Arms?'

'I meant the Freemasons. Was he a member of a Masonic Lodge?'

She shook her head.

'I've no idea. I wouldn't have known, would I? Besides, I thought they were a secret society?'

'Do you remember his surname?' Jo asked.

She shook her head.

'I'm sorry, I don't remember hearing anyone use it. He was always Uncle Ralph to us.'

'Do you remember any letters coming to the house addressed to him?'

'No, I'm sorry.'

Jo was tempted to ask if any of those men who called at the house wore dinner suits, or carried briefcases. The key worker made the decision for her.

'That's definitely it,' he said. 'I think both Marina and I are going to need a break. And I'm afraid that there are people queueing to use this room.'

He walked to the door, and waited for Jo and Marina to join him.

'I really appreciate you agreeing to see me, Marina,' Jo told her. 'I realise that it was hard for you. But believe me, you have been really helpful.'

'In a way,' Marina replied. 'It was good to get it all out. I think I've been needing to do that ever since Bradley's funeral.'

'I only hope it helps with your recovery,' said Jo, instantly wondering if it had been the right thing to say. Once again, Marina Driffield surprised her by smiling.

'So do I,' she said.

Marvin opened the door and let them exit first. There was a queue outside of seven or so men and women talking amiably to each other. Several greeted Marina, others eyed Jo with mild interest.

'I'll walk you down to reception,' the key worker told her. He turned to Marina. 'I'll see you in the lounge, in ten.'

'Okay,' she said. 'Bye, Jo.'

'Goodbye,' said Jo, watching as Marina turned left and headed towards the garden.

Marvin led her through several fire doors and out into the reception area. They stood on the step outside to say their goodbyes.

'Will it help with her recovery?' asked Jo.

'That depends.'

'On what?'

'On what happens next. On whether or not you'll be coming back.'

'She's not a suspect.'

He raised his eyebrows.

'I didn't think she was.'

He glanced over his shoulder to make sure that the door had closed behind them.

'Look, you never told us why you really wanted to speak with her, and don't worry, I don't need to know. But you and I both know that you persuaded her to open Pandora's box in there. Whatever's going on, that box can never be closed again. To answer your question – yes, I do think it will have aided her recovery. But I also think that you'll be back. Even if you're not, I have a hunch that this won't be the end of the pain for her.'

Jo suspected that he was right.

'I'll do my best to minimise the effect of any fallout,' she said.

He nodded.

'I hope you will. Marina will be moving to one of our rehab houses next week. It's a safe environment where she can prepare for independent living once again. If you can leave it for at least a couple of weeks, she's likely to be in a stronger frame of mind by then.'

Jo held out her hand.

'Thank you again,' she said. 'It's important work you do here, repairing and rebuilding people. There should be a place like this in every prison.'

He shook her hand.

'They do most of it by themselves,' he said.

Chapter 44

Jo was stuck in the middle of the Friday evening exodus from the city, made worse by Metrolink improvement work, and the overhaul of Victoria Station. She was less than a mile from the office when Ram Shah called.

'Those background checks on Carter and Kantrell,' he said. 'I came up with a couple of very interesting coincidences concerning your Mr Kantrell.'

'Go on.'

'It turns out he must have been a member of another Lodge before he joined Charles Deighton's.'

'How do you know?'

'I came across a photo of him presenting a set of computers last year to a special school on behalf of his Lodge. It was in the Manchester Evening News, and on the Lodge website. They both came up when I googled his name. The blurb said he'd been a Freemason for twenty-five years. He's only been at his current Lodge for the past fifteen.'

'And the second one?'

'He lives less than a quarter of a mile away from what was the Driffield family home. Has done all his life. He still lives with his mother. Odds on, he knew them.'

'Ram, you're a bloody genius,' she said. 'Do me a favour. See if Kantrell is still at work. If he is, tell him to stay there until I arrive. Tell him, if he doesn't, I'll follow him home and embarrass him in front of his mother.'

'The Driffields?' Kantrell said. 'I don't understand. What have the Driffields got to do with Charles Deighton?'

He was sweating even more profusely than the first time she had seen him.

'Just answer the question, Mr Kantrell,' said Jo. 'How do you know the Driffields?'

'How *did* I know them?' he corrected her. 'I haven't seen any of them in years. Decades for that matter.'

He mopped his brow.

'We all went to the same primary school. But we went to different high schools. After that, I only saw them from time to time in the neighbourhood. I heard they'd all left the area after their mother died.'

She believed him.

'You were a member of another Masonic Lodge before you joined your current one, weren't you, Mr Kantrell?'

The way in which his expression transformed took her completely by surprise. Where there had been anxiety, there was now fear.

'Weren't you?' she repeated.

'I d-don't want to talk about it,' he stuttered.

'Why not?'

He tried to mop his brow again, but his handkerchief was now soaking wet.

'Because I've spent the last fifteen years trying to put it out of my mind.'

'And why was that?'

'Because it scares me to even think about it.'

'If you believe that sharing with me something that happened at that Lodge might incriminate you, then I'm going to have to caution you,' she said.

'No,' he said. 'It's not that. It's not that at all.'

'Then what is it?'

'I left because I was ashamed, and frightened.' His eyes were those of a child appealing for help. 'I'm still frightened of them,' he said. 'Even now.'

'Who are you frightened of, Karl?' she asked. 'Who?'

She had to strain to hear his reply.

'The Shrine of Belos,' he said.

She had made them both a cup of coffee in his office kitchen, and brought him some sheets of kitchen roll to dry his face. Kantrell had recovered some of his composure, and now seemed desperate to get it off his chest.

'It started out as a normal Masonic Lodge, but then we got a new Worshipful Master, and it began to change. He started a new Chapter and called it the Shrine of Belos. Only certain members of the Lodge were invited to apply. They moved to new premises, just for the Chapter. After about a year, I was approached and asked if I would like to join.'

'And you said yes?'

He nodded.

'I was flattered, and curious. And I'm ashamed to admit it but I got the impression that joining would help my business to take off.'

'Did it?'

He looked sheepish.

'I wasn't a member long enough to find out.'

'Tell me about the Chapter,' she said.

He had a drink, and then wiped his face on a sheet of the kitchen roll.

'When I got to the Chapter house, I was taken into a small room by two of the Brethren. They were already dressed in black hooded capes. I was told to strip off, and then given an apron to tie around my waist. It was just like my Lodge apron except that it was black, with a white pentagram on it. There was a male goat's head in the centre of the pentagram. I was given a cloak like theirs to put on.'

He shook his head.

'I knew then it wasn't for me.'

'So why did you stay?'

'Because I was frightened of what they might do.'

'What happened next, Karl?'

His voice deepened and trembled as he spoke.

'I was led into a larger room. I don't know how large because it was in darkness, except for the light from a single black candle in the centre of a pentacle chalked on the floor. A group of about a dozen men stood in a circle around the pentacle. They wore identical cloaks, and their hoods were up. The two guides removed my cloak. I was given a piece of paper, told to enter the pentacle, and pick up the candle.'

He faltered. Jo prompted him.

'What happened then, Karl?'

'I had to use the candle to read the oath of installation. I was instructed to turn to each of the five points of the pentacle, renouncing YAHWEH as I did so, and acknowledging Belos as the one true Master of the Universe.'

He fell silent again. His left hand began to shake, and he had to place his right hand over it to keep it still. She decided to let him take his time.

'Then one of the guides came forward and grasped my left hand, holding it palm upwards. The other one took a knife from his sleeve, and passed it across my palm. I hardly felt anything but a line of blood appeared, and began to pool.'

He looked up at Jo as though in shock.

'I had to sign my name to that oath in my own blood. They took the paper and burnt it in a clay bowl in the middle of the pentacle. Then they told me if I ever broke that oath, or betrayed their secret mysteries, I would die a horrible death and burn forever in hell.'

He fell silent again.

'What happened then?'

'They took me back to the anteroom, put plasters on my hand, and told me to get dressed. Then I was taken to another room where there was a bar and a table covered with a superb buffet. It was surreal. Just like a proper post-installation meal. I had some drinks and something to eat, and then I got out of there. I never went back.'

'Were there no recriminations?'

'I got veiled threats, and I was sent to Coventry by some of the Lodge members. So I left the Lodge and moved away. Later I joined the one I'm in now, with Raymond.'

'And the Shrine of Belos? Is it still going?'

He shook his head.

'About six months after I left, the Provincial Grand Master declared them a rogue organisation, and the United Grand Lodge of England expelled them.'

'What happened after that?'

'I don't know. They continued to meet though. There were all sorts of rumours about satanic goings-on. That's why the Province set up an investigation.'

'Goings-on?'

He blushed.

'Underage sex, orgies, animal sacrifices – that kind of thing.'

'And the police never became involved?'

'They already were.'

'What do you mean?'

'I understood that at least two of the members were in the police. One was quite high up. A superintendent, I think.'

'What was his name?'

'I don't know. In any case, they only used their Christian names in the Chapter.'

Jo didn't believe him, but she could see that there was no way that he was going to tell her.

'One name you'll definitely remember,' she said. 'The name of the founder of the Chapter. You told me he was the Grand Master of your Lodge.'

For a moment she thought he was going to pretend he had forgotten. Then he surprised her.

'Bates,' he said. 'His name was Ralph Bates.'

Jo fought to hide her elation.

'There is one more thing that you can do for me, Karl,' she said. 'You can meet me tomorrow morning, and show me the former Chapter House of the Shrine of Belos.'

'I'll take you there,' he said, 'but I'm not going inside.'

———

Later, when Jo told her that she would have to go out first thing in the morning, Abbie was surprisingly relaxed about it.

'It's just as well that James has had to change the time we're meeting up,' she said. 'It's now at one thirty. We can't afford to be late, because he's booked on the three thirty-five pm back to Euston.'

Chapter 45

The next morning there was a text on Jo's phone from Karl Kantrell.

Mum had a fall last night. Had to take her to A&E. Will be with you as soon as possible. Sorry.

Jo rang the mobile number he had given her.

'Where are you up to?' she asked.

'Mum's on the assessment ward. With it being the weekend, there was no one in a position to decide if they should admit her, or send her home. She's waiting to be seen by the consultant. The staff nurse reckons they'll definitely keep her in for a couple more days. I should know shortly. Then I can come straight over.'

Jo decided to pass the time by going to have a look at the house the Driffields had occupied before their mother died.

It was a neat little terraced house that had obviously been bought up by a buy-to-let investor. It had a new roof and gutters, pointed brickwork, new windows and a new front door.

On the spur of the moment, she decided to knock on the door. A barefoot young woman in jogging bottoms and a sweatshirt responded. Jo showed her ID, and asked if she could come in for a moment.

'It's a historical case,' she said. 'Nothing to worry about. Could you spare a couple of minutes?'

''Course,' said the young woman. 'Come in. I'm Mel, by the way.'

'Do you own this place, Mel?' Jo asked as soon as she was through the door.

'No chance. I rent it together with two other girls. We were at uni together, and we decided to do this while we all save a bit of cash. They're still in bed.'

'Well, I'm not going to disturb them,' said Jo. 'I just wondered if I could have a look at your cellar?'

'Cellar? We haven't got a cellar. Wish we had. We could do with one for all our junk.'

Jo looked down at the floor. Whoever had refurbished the house had replaced the floorboards with woodblock flooring. So much for just lifting the carpet, and finding a trapdoor.

'I know this is going to sound odd,' she said. 'But would you mind if I did a bit of knocking on your hallway floor?'

Mel laughed.

'What are you looking for – stolen goods? A cannabis farm?'

Jo knelt down, and began to knock with the knuckles of her right hand on the boards as she shuffled along. She was met by dull thuds, until she drew level with the door into the lounge. Right there, in the centre of the floor, she was rewarded with a sound that reminded her of knocking on a hollow tree. She tapped away until she had identified a perimeter approximately two feet square.

She sat back on her haunches. The new boards had been laid over the original floorboards, including the trapdoor that Marina had described.

Mel put a hand to her mouth.

'Oh God!' she exclaimed. 'Please don't tell me there's a body down there?'

Jo got to her feet, and brushed the knees of her jeans.

'I doubt it,' she said. 'We can always check with ground-penetrating radar, but I doubt that will be necessary. If it is, I'll let you know, Mel. In the meantime, don't let it give you any sleepless nights.'

Jo rang Kantrell's mobile again.

'Sorry,' he said. 'They've admitted her. I'm just settling her in. I should be with you in about fifteen minutes.'

'Make sure you are,' she told him. 'Or your mother won't be the only one being admitted.'

Chapter 46

Jo followed Kantrell's BMW up the winding road towards the top of the wooded hill. He signalled left, and turned off on to a private road. On the side of the wall at the entrance to the drive was a blue slate on which she could just make out the name, Brock House.

She followed him between beech trees that crowded in on either side, their bare branches stark against the grey sky. His brake lights came on, and he stopped. She switched off the engine, and went to join him.

Kantrell stood by a rusty iron gate that hung between two low brick walls. Beyond the gate was a drive, overgrown with knee-high weeds and grass, in front of what must have once been an impressive Victorian mansion. The windows were boarded, the walls blackened by smoke. There were gaping holes in the roof where a combination of fire and vandals had dislodged the tiles. The remains of fire service tape hung limp across the sheets of plywood that had replaced the door. The burnt-out skeleton of a Rover saloon poked through a heap of weeds and charred wood.

'Come on,' said Jo. 'Help me shift this gate.'

'I'm not going inside,' he told her.

'I'm not asking you to,' she said. 'Just grab hold of this gate, and lift.'

Together they managed to heave it open wide enough for her to squeeze through. She went back to her car, opened the trunk, and took out a long-handled torch and the tyre lever.

'You stay here,' she told him. 'And listen out in case I need you.'

'I'm not . . .'

'Going inside,' she said. 'I know. You've told me. But I may need you to ring for help.'

'You'll be lucky,' he replied. 'There's no signal up here.'

'Well, if I do need you to make a call, you can get in that car, and drive to somewhere where there *is* a signal. Alright?'

'Alright.'

'Good. Now I'm going in.'

My God, she thought as she squeezed through the gap. *I sound like the Navy Seals when they took out Osama Bin Laden.*

At the side of the house she found a ground-floor window where the plywood board had already been levered away, leaving a gap wide enough for her to climb inside. Jo used her torch to dislodge the few remaining shards of glass from the frame, and hauled herself into the room.

It was immediately evident that this part of the building had been gutted by the fire. The walls were blackened, the ceiling had caved in, and the room above was open to the sky. Between the mounds of plaster, charred floorboards were a trap for the unwary. Gingerly, Jo made her way to the skeleton of a door hanging drunkenly on its hinges.

She found herself in a passageway with doors on either side. Keeping as close to the walls as possible, she edged forward, inspecting the rooms in turn. Finally, she came to the hallway.

Her torch picked out the heaped remains of a crystal chandelier on the floor that sent shafts of rainbow light whirling around the hall. A broad central staircase divided left and right at the landing. Half of the stair treads had gone, as had all of the balusters, and both of the handrails. There was, Jo realised, no way of reaching the upstairs rooms.

She picked her way around the debris and entered a room to the right. It was a large room, more or less intact. Wooden tables, chairs, and a large dresser had been placed along the edges of the walls without windows. There was a raised platform at the far end. The smoke-damaged ceiling was intact. Paintings hung on all of the walls, except where they had fallen to the floor. Some appeared to be portraits of men in what she assumed was Masonic regalia. Others were of symbols, some of which she recognised from the Masonic Temple she had visited.

She picked up the painting on the floor beside the door, and blew off the fine layer of ash. Staring back at her was an eye, enclosed in a golden triangle, surrounded by the rays of the sun, above a pair of conjoined hands enclosed within a pair of compasses and an open divider. What was it Wakeman had called it? The Eye of Providence, or the All-Seeing Eye of God. She laid it down on one of the tables.

What the hell are you doing here? she asked herself. What are you hoping to find? Jo went back into the hall and tried the two rooms on the far side. The first was a mirror image of the one that she had just exited. The other room was tiny, and had a row of metal pegs along one wall. Was this the room in which Kantrell had been asked to disrobe? She stepped back into the hall, and swung her torch around one final time. Her heart skipped a beat as it lighted upon a tiny door built into the side of the stairs.

The door was locked. Jo made short work of it with the tyre lever. A set of smooth stone steps led down into a cellar. In the absence of a handrail, she leaned her weight against the wall as she edged down one step at a time, brushing cobwebs from her face.

The cellar ran the width of the house, and was half as long. It was cold, damp, and evil-smelling. Jo shivered. The first pass of her torch told her that the cellar was empty. There were steel rings bolted into two of the walls. Two more rings were fastened two feet apart in the centre of the vaulted brick roof. She shone the torch on the floor.

Directly beneath the rings, a pentacle had been carved into the stone floor. At each of the five points of the star, within a circle, a letter had been inscribed. The letters spelt out BELOS. Jo shivered again. She had to fight off the images threatening to crowd her brain. She feared that if she began to allow herself to imagine the sorts of things that may have happened here, she would never sleep again.

The cellar door slammed. Jo jumped, and the torch clattered to the floor and went out. She scrabbled around until she found it, pressed the button and was rewarded with a reassuring beam of light. Grasping the torch in her left hand, and the tyre lever in the other, she climbed the steps, counted silently to three, and threw her shoulder against the door. She fell in a heap on the hall floor, rolled to her left, sprang to her feet, legs hip-width apart, knees slightly bent, tyre lever raised. She scanned the hall with her torch.

The hallway was empty. The only sounds were her laboured breathing, and doors creaking in the draught from the open window.

Chapter 47

Jo was on the road back into town when her hands-free came to life. She had five missed calls, all from Abbie. She looked at the digital clock. It was twenty past two. She was already fifty minutes late for the meeting. She beat the steering wheel with her fist.

'Shit! Shit! Shit!'

She selected redial. There was no response, not even a voicemail.

'*This number is unobtainable,*' she was told. '*Please try again later.*'

The most recent missed call had a message attached.

Abbie sounded both tearful and angry.

'How could you?' she sobbed. 'How the fuck could you do this to me? How the fuck could you do it to *us*?'

Jo selected redial again, and put her foot down.

Two suitcases stood in the hall. Jo squeezed past them and hurried into the lounge. Abbie emerged from the bedroom wearing a coat and carrying a handbag.

'Abbie, I'm so sorry,' Jo began.

'Save it,' said Abbie. 'I've got the message.'

Her calm demeanour was ten times scarier than her anger had been.

'Abbie,' Jo pleaded. 'You've got to hear me out. I messed up. And when you called to remind me, I didn't get them because my phone didn't have a signal. I didn't deliberately miss the meeting.'

Abbie stared at her. Her gaze was hard and cold.

'Are you sure about that?' she said. 'You do know that your alarm doesn't need a signal?'

She pushed past Jo and headed for the hallway. Jo followed her.

'Where are you going, Abbs?' she asked.

Abbie slipped her handbag over her shoulder, and stretched forward to open the door.

'What do you care?'

Jo placed her hand on Abbie's shoulder.

'Of course I care.'

'To my sister's. It will give us both a chance to decide what it is we really want out of this relationship.'

'I already know what I want,' said Jo.

Abbie shook her head.

'Well, I don't, not any more.'

She bent, picked up the suitcases and walked out of the apartment and on to the mezzanine.

'Please don't do this, Abbie,' Jo called after her. 'Please don't go!'

⌣

Jo sat on the sofa with her head in her hands. She wasn't sure exactly how she felt. She was stunned, and devastated, but there was something else. Was Abbie right? Had she deliberately missed the interview? After all, she had felt railroaded into the decision to go down that path. Why couldn't Abbie be satisfied with the life they had? And it wasn't as though she had kept her concerns hidden from Abbie. You either had maternal instincts, or you didn't. And who in their right mind would want the responsibility of raising a child in a world full of paedophiles, sex traffickers and serial killers?

She found a spaghetti bolognese microwaveable meal for two in the chiller, and ate that accompanied with a bottle of Chianti. She began to flick through the latest edition of *Marie Claire*, and then remembered that it was the @Work Live section of the magazine that had prompted Abbie to seek her career change with a view to becoming a mother.

Jo scrolled through Netflix but couldn't find anything she could bear to watch. Finally, she gave in, found the number for the duty inspector at Leeds Central, and asked if there had been progress with the hunt for Alex Trott's abductors. There had not. There was, however, a list of vehicle registration numbers they would be tracing in the morning.

Jo prowled the flat like a caged animal before finally deciding to do some research on the Internet. Within minutes she was hooked.

Belos was the Greek name for Baal. Baal was reputed to have defeated death, a feat that was repeated every year when he came back from the underworld to make the earth fertile in spring. According to the Old Testament, the Canaanites swung between devotion to Baal and allegiance to Yahweh. A battle between good and evil. Ultimately it was Yahweh who won. Over the years Baal became associated with Paganism and Satanism; Yahweh with the Jewish faith and, among others, Freemasonry.

The deeper Jo dug, the more disturbing it became. Much of what she read about the more extreme devotees was consistent with paedophilia, involving both sexes. There were even recent claims in the US that a shadowy organisation known as the Illuminati practised child sacrifice. She knew that virtually all of the claims amounted to unsubstantiated conspiracy theory, but couldn't help thinking of the accusations by victims of historical child abuse that were being investigated across the United Kingdom. What she knew for certain from her contacts in the Child Exploitation and Online Protection Team, was that there was a Dark Web in which children and adults were killed for the sole purpose of making and distributing snuff movies.

It was gone midnight when she typed *Rogue Masonic Organisations* into the search engine – it brought her 155,000 results. She selected the most recent and verifiable accounts. There was the well-documented *Propaganda Due* Masonic Lodge, or P2, that had been implicated in the collapse of Banco Ambrosiano and the murder, among others, of God's Banker, Roberto Calvi, found hanging from Blackfriars Bridge in 1982.

Another story that caught her eye was a newspaper report as recent as June 2015 about a Lodge that had been formed by past and present British Intelligence employees. There was absolutely no suggestion that the Lodge itself had behaved improperly, but it was unfortunate that one of its Worshipful Masters, now dead, had previously been convicted of child sex abuse offences, and had been the membership secretary of the Paedophile Information Exchange and a friend of Jimmy Savile.

And so it went on. At ten past two she gave up, and went to bed. She was unable to sleep. Her brain was full of words and images that spun around like a Rubik's cube. When her eyes finally closed, dawn was breaking and her dreams were filled with disturbing images.

Chapter 48

'You look terrible, Jo.'

'Thanks, Ram.' Jo dropped her bag on her desk. 'That's all I needed.'

'Bad night?'

'You could say that. I overslept.'

'Let me get you a coffee,' he said. 'Least I can do.'

She fired up her computer.

Levi had still not replied. Nor had Harry Stone. Looking around the office she could tell that the extra resources Stone had promised hadn't arrived. Andy Swift came over to her desk and pulled up a chair. He had removed his cycling vest. There was a black-and-white print of Count Dracula on the front of his T-shirt.

'Are you alright?' he asked.

'I didn't sleep too well, that's all.'

Shah's arrival with a mug of coffee saved her from further probing.

'D'you want one, Andy?' asked Shah.

Swift raised a drink bottle containing a liquid the colour of a blood orange.

'Carrot and tomato,' he said.

Shah grinned.

'Matches the T-shirt.'

'The one and only Christopher Lee,' Swift told him. 'And before you ask – yes, I am an aficionado. Get over it.'

He turned back to Jo.

'How did you get on with Kantrell?'

She told them.

'Appropriate name, Brock House,' said Shah.

'What do you mean?' she asked.

'Badgers live underground and come out to hunt at night. Sounds about right for those nutters. Paganism, Satanism, that's pure Dennis Wheatley. The fantasy of sad, horny old men who have never grown up.'

'That doesn't make them any less scary or dangerous,' Andy Swift pointed out. 'It gives credence to the story that Marina Driffield told you, Jo. If that house is where Ralph Bates took Bradley Driffield, it would certainly provide Lorna with a motive.'

'Means and motive,' observed Shah. 'Now all we need is to establish the opportunity, and place her at the scene.'

'According to DS Coppull, Lorna Driffield isn't the only one with a motive for the disappearance of Norbert Welsh,' she told them. She turned her screen so they could all view it, and opened the email attachment.

Hi Jo,

You were right to persuade me to take another look at this. My lad's come up with another motive for the wife. Mrs Welsh may have been estranged but, when he's eventually either found dead or declared dead, she still stands to land not only his share of the firm but also, get this, a life insurance payout to the tune of £300,000 plus the mortgage is paid off, and any inheritance tax liability is covered. That's a cool three-quarters of a million in total. On Monday we're going to have a look at

phone records, and see what we can dig up in relation to her contacts.
Watch this space!

'It looks as though DS Coppull hasn't read the email I sent her about the failed abduction in Leeds, or if she has, she can't have seen the connection.'

'This may help,' said Andy Swift, placing a slim file on her desk. 'While you've been gadding around, I've worked up a crime behavioural profile for our unsub based on the Deighton murder, and the Leeds abduction. I think you'll find it interesting.'

Dorsey Zephaniah interrupted before Jo had a chance to open the file.

'Mr Levi for you, Ma'am,' she said. 'Where do you want to take it?'

———

'No, Mr Stone hasn't spoken to me, and no, I haven't had time to read your reports on the shared drive,' he told her. 'From what I can gather, you don't even have circumstantial evidence in relation to this Driffield woman. All you have is a possible motive, and the fact that she digs for a living. The rest consists of supposition and conspiracy theory.'

Jo found it difficult to disagree.

'I've just established motive,' she said. 'If I had more resources . . .'

'But you don't, and you won't be getting any until you come up with something a damn sight more substantial. As for my trying to convince the Chief Constables of three different forces to allow you to take over their investigations . . .'

'Coordinate,' she said.

'Take over,' he insisted. 'Well, that's not going to happen until you're in a position to name your unsub, and have sufficient evidence for an arrest warrant. You're with the National Crime Agency now, Ms Stuart, not the Greater Manchester Police Force.'

Thanks for nothing, she thought as she handed the phone back to Zephaniah.

Chapter 49

Jo finished reading the profile that Andy Swift had constructed. It fitted almost exactly with her own impressions of Lorna Driffield and Shaye Tamsey, and what she knew of their backgrounds. It was still not enough.

Ram waved her over.

'I've been searching on the net for this Ralph Bates,' he said. 'There are dozens of them but none that fit what little we know about him.'

'Nothing at all?'

'Apart from some historical references to him as Worshipful Master of that Lodge.'

'What about a birth certificate, National Health number, National Insurance number, tax reference?'

He shook his head.

'None of those.'

'So Ralph Bates was a pseudonym?'

'Looks like it.'

'What about the Belos Chapter?'

'Nothing on that either.'

She was running out of questions. Desperation was setting in.

'Brock House?'

'I've just started on that.'

'Jo!'

It was Zephaniah. She was pointing to her monitor.

'I bet you're glad you're not still with GMP. Did you ever come across this guy?'

Jo went to see, and Ram Shah followed her.

'What guy?' she asked.

'This guy, Mr Hadfield.'

There was a head-and-shoulders shot of him in uniform.

'Martin Hadfield?' Jo replied. 'Of course I know him. He's Assistant Chief Constable Crime. What about him?'

'What about him indeed?' said the administrator. 'That's what GMP would like to know. He's gone missing. It's only been ten hours but they've put out an all-ports warning so they must be worried. See for yourself.'

It was an alert on the Police National Computer, all of which were automatically picked up by the Agency.

'He's not a Mason, is he?' asked Ram.

It didn't sound like one of his usual jokes. Jo's heart began to race, and her fingers tingled, as she pressed the zoom keys.

All-ports warning, all-ports warning. Urgent observations are requested in relation to the following missing person. Assistant Chief Constable Martin Hadfield of Greater Manchester Police. Last seen yesterday, Sunday 22nd November 2015, on foot at 10.17pm on Albert Bridge Street, Manchester, wearing a black dinner suit, white shirt, and black bow tie, his current whereabouts are unknown. Any sighting should immediately be reported, and action taken to ensure that he is safe.

'Oh my God!' she said.

'He's not, is he?' said Ram.

'I don't know,' she said. 'But it looks like it.'

She turned and hurried to her desk, banging her left thigh against a chair as she did so.

'Shit!'

As she stopped to rub it, Andy Swift caught up with her.

'Slow down, Jo,' he said. 'It could just be a coincidence.'

She pulled out her chair, sat down, and brought her computer to life.

'He was wearing a dinner suit,' she said. 'And that last sighting, Albert Bridge Street? That's where the Central Manchester Masonic Hall is. It's been let to restaurants and bars, but Lodges still meet there.'

'Perhaps he'd been in one of the restaurants?' said Swift. He didn't sound convinced. He pulled up a chair beside her.

As she waited for the software to load, Jo took her mobile phone from her jacket pocket, and speed-dialled Caton. It went to voicemail. She flicked through her contacts, and tried Gordon instead. His number was busy.

'Shit, shit, shit!'

She found another number. The Force Major Incident Team office manager. This time it was answered.

'Is that you, DI Stuart? Or should I say Agent?'

'Ged,' said Jo. 'Thank God I've got you. I've heard about Mr Hadfield. I tried Mr Caton, but he's on voicemail.'

'DCI Caton's on annual leave in Scotland with his wife and their daughter. You'll be lucky to reach anyone – they're all in a flap over ACC Hadfield. It's terribly worrying.'

'I'm calling about his disappearance,' Jo told her. 'I may be able to help. Who's in charge?'

'Detective Chief Superintendent Gates is the senior investigating officer but you won't be able to speak with her – she's in with the Chief Constable and the rest of the Command Team.'

'Is Gordon there?'

There was a pause.

'Yes, Jo, but he's on his mobile at the moment.'

Jo took a deep breath.

'Ged, this is really serious. I think I may know what happened to Mr Hadfield. Can you get Gordon's attention? I have to speak to him.'

'Give me a minute,' said Ged.

Jo placed her hand over the handset, and turned to Andy Swift.

'Gordon is a DI in my old team,' she explained. 'He'll take me seriously.'

'Jo, is that you?'

Beneath her hand, his muffled voice sounded even gruffer than she remembered. She flicked her phone on to speaker for Andy's benefit.

'Gordon, thank God,' she said. 'I heard about Hadfield. I think I can help.'

'I can't imagine how, Jo,' he said. 'It's got us all baffled.'

'Is Martin Hadfield a Mason?' she asked.

'A Mason? What's that got to do with it?'

'Is he, or isn't he, a Mason?'

The urgency in her voice was unmistakable.

'Yes,' he said. 'He is. But I don't see . . .'

'Had he been to a Masonic meeting last night before he disappeared?'

'Yes. He'd just left.'

She could hear his mind working overtime.

'What's going on, Jo?'

'I'm involved in supporting three investigations in the north-west, all involving the unexplained disappearance of Freemasons. One of them is a murder.'

'Christ!' said Gordon. 'Please tell me you're joking?'

'We sent out a bulletin asking to be informed immediately of any missing persons reports involving Masons. I'm surprised this wasn't flagged up.'

'It's only been ten hours, Jo. It won't have been entered on to the system as a MisPer yet. It's only because it's him that there's an all-ports been issued.'

'Tell me what happened,' she said.

'His wife rang 101 at midnight last night. She said her husband should have been home by eleven. He wasn't answering his phone. She contacted the friends he'd been with. They told her he said he was going straight home. The wally who took her call told her not to worry, and someone would call first thing in the morning if he still hadn't turned up. She dug out her husband's address book and rang the Chief Constable. He sent a duty inspector round. When Hadfield was still missing this morning, and didn't turn up for a scheduled meeting with the Command Team, the shit hit the fan. Helen Gates is Gold Command.'

'They've already operationalised it?'

'Fortunately, the duty inspector did all the right things. Put a trace on his phone. Asked for an examination of the city centre cameras. We already know where he went missing.'

'How?'

'He was captured by cameras on Bridge Street waving to his mates before he set off down St Mary's Parsonage. Then we've got footage from the Lowry Hotel of him coming off the Trinity Bridge, and heading for the short cut through the Clowes Street car park on his way to Victoria Station.'

It wasn't a route Jo would have taken at that time of night, however well lit.

'Only trouble is,' Gordon was saying, 'he never reappeared on Chapel Street.'

'What about the car park cameras?'

'The only two that were functioning were on the back of the car park, and the towpath. They show him entering the car park, and starting to cross it. The two covering the other half and the entrance were out of action. It's too early to tell if they'd been tampered with.'

'And his mobile phone? Did they manage to trace it?'

Gordon grunted.

'A TAG team smashed down the door of a semi in Burnage half an hour ago. Gave the owners a hell of a shock. Their eighteen-year-old son had it on his bedside locker. Said he found it at about half ten last night on the pavement near the Crown and Kettle on Oldham Road. We're assuming it was thrown out of the ambulance window.'

'Ambulance window?'

'There's this dodgy-looking vehicle that was on Bridge Street the same time as Hadfield. We have a shot of it waiting at the traffic lights as he headed down St Mary's Parsonage. Only it didn't move off when the lights went to green the first time. It waited till the second time, then indicated right, and followed him slowly until he turned off on to the Lowry Bridge. Then it headed off towards St Mary's Gate. Next thing, we have it going west on Chapel Street and then, ten minutes later, heading east towards Victoria.'

'They marked him on Bridge Street,' she said. 'Then when they knew where he was headed, drove round to the car park to wait for him.'

'Looks like it.'

'What did you mean by dodgy?'

'It's a Land Rover Defender 110. The armed forces used to use them as ambulances, so did mountain rescue, coastguard, cave rescue, people like that. This one has yellow stripes down the side, and the word "Ambulance" prominently displayed on the front, back and sides.'

'How d'you know it's not a real one?'

'The plates are cloned. They're also for a 1990s registration but this model went out of production in 1986. What's more, the ambulance stencil on the bonnet is the right way round. That means it can't be read in a car mirror. Bit of a giveaway.'

He must have turned his head away because she barely heard him say, '*Tell 'em I'll be with them in two minutes. No! Just tell them.*'

'Sorry about that, Jo,' he said. 'I'm going to have to go.'

'Wait! You have to hear this, and so does Helen Gates.'

'You've got one minute.'

She gave him the guts of it.

'So,' he said. 'You have one suspect with a theoretical motive? You have another with possible means and motive, and a theoretical opportunity for one of the disappearances? But you have no hard evidence for either of them.'

'It's reasonable grounds for suspicion,' she said. 'Come on, Gordon – if they were in the street you'd have no hesitation in searching them.'

'The thing is, Jo,' he said, 'we already have a suspect. Someone Martin Hadfield put away for twelve years for armed robbery when he was Head of the Serious and Organised Crime Unit. This guy, Jenson Gatley, threatened to get his own back at the trial, and he repeated those threats in prison a month ago. He was released last Monday, and missed his second probation appointment. We don't know where he is.'

'Gordon, you're not listening. There is a pattern here. Gates has got to pursue both lines of enquiry. If she's right, Martin Hadfield is already dead. If I'm right, he may still have a chance.'

There was a moment's silence while he thought about it.

'Send me what you've got,' he said. 'I'll do my best to persuade her. Now I've really got to go. We're on the midday news.'

'Thanks, Gordon,' she said, but he'd already gone.

'What d'you think?' said Andy Swift, who'd been listening in with Ram Shah. 'Will they take it seriously?'

Jo had already begun the process of sending her latest report across as an encrypted attachment to both Gordon's and Helen Gates's mailboxes.

'God knows,' she said. 'But I can't sit around here waiting to find out.'

'What are you going to do?'

She swivelled her chair and stood up.

'I'm going up to Driffield's farm. It's the only thing I can do.' She shrugged on her jacket. 'Can you let Harry Stone and Simon Levi know, and see if one of them will approve an alert going out to all forces for both of Driffield's vans? The registrations are in my report in the shared folder, so is the address for Lorna's Garden Transformations. Tell them I also need a warrant to search her premises. I'll need uniformed backup to assist me in executing it.'

She picked up her bag.

Swift stood up. 'What about the Land Rover DI Holmes mentioned?' he asked.

'GMP will already have an alert out for that. I'm sorry, Andy, I've got to go.'

She hurried towards the door.

'I think you should wait for backup,' he called after her.

'They'll want the whys and wherefores, and a bloody risk assessment,' she shouted back. 'There isn't time for that.'

The door slammed shut behind her.

Chapter 50

'*Make a U-turn as soon as possible.*'

Jo swore. Stopped the Audi, and got out. She shivered. The temperature had dropped dramatically. Menacing black storm clouds were gathering from the north, painting the high moors blue, and the treetops emerald-green in the valley below. She crossed the road, and climbed a ladder stile set into a drystone wall.

There was a cluster of farm buildings in the valley. The roofs of the hangar-like barns glistened silvery blue in the changing light. To her left, the ground fell sharply away to the mass of trees that she assumed was Swallows Wood. Beyond that lay an expanse of steel-grey water whose regular sides identified it as a reservoir. The nearest farm, a mile away on the far side of the reservoir, looked to be inaccessible from this side of the moor. The fields around it were dotted white with flocks of sheep. Where the hell was the farm where Lorna Driffield ran her business?

She got back into the car, cancelled the satnav, and set off. Another half a mile brought her to a sign on the left for Holgate Farm. She decided to pull in. If nothing else, she might find someone who could give her directions. A Range Rover blocked her way. The ruddy-faced male driver stared angrily down at her.

Jo got out of the car, and approached warily. He lowered his window.

'Move your car,' he demanded. 'This is private property. I'm in a hurry.'

'I'm sorry,' said Jo. 'I'm lost. I wondered if you could tell me how to find Lorna's Garden Transformations?'

'Never heard of it,' he barked. 'Now bugger off out the road!'

Jo reached into her inside pocket, produced her warrant card and held it up.

'This is an urgent police matter,' she said. 'I believe there is a former farm near here, from which a woman and man operate a land-scaping business.'

He squinted down at her ID and then spat into the driveway beside her.

'Them buggers,' he muttered. 'Bloody incomers! Keep themselves to themselves, do nowt for the countryside or the community.'

His arm snaked out of the window forcing her to step back to avoid being struck. His hand curved around the windscreen, index finger pointing left along the road behind her.

'Keep going. When you can't go any further, you've arrived. Now shift your bloody car!'

The window rose silently and his foot revved the engine. Jo backed on to the road and watched as the Land Rover hurtled out of the drive, swung around the front of her bonnet, missing it by centimetres, and sped off in the direction from which she had come.

Less than a mile later, the road turned into a grass and gravel-covered lane, wide enough for a tractor and a combine harvester. It soon became a rutted farm track, which ended abruptly with a five-barred gate secured with a padlock and chain. Jo pulled over to the side so as not to block the gate, and switched off the engine. She set her phone to silent, and sent a speed-dial text to Andy Swift saying that she had arrived. Then she put it back in her pocket and got out of the car.

Chapter 51

The clouds had bunched into the ominous anvil shape that foretells a violent thunderstorm. Jo strapped on her regulation Kevlar vest from the trunk of the car and pulled her NCA cagoule over her head.

Now dressed for the elements, she lifted the floor mat to reveal a solid, black and silver security case, anchored by a thick steel cable to the floor. Unlocking the tumblers, she took out a set of handcuffs and an expandable baton and clipped them to her belt. Finally, she selected a Maglite torch, and a can of incapacitant spray with its own clip-on holder. Two hollow spaces that should have held a Glock 17 pistol and a Taser were a reminder that she had still to complete her NCA refresher weapons training, not that she would have had the time to seek their release and sign them out.

As she locked the Audi, the heavens opened. Jo pulled down her hood and walked over to the gate. The padlock and the chain were both in good condition. She climbed over the gate and, in an attempt to avoid the rapidly forming pools of water, straddled the ruts as she walked the hundred or so metres to the buildings.

The first of these was a large two-storey stone farmhouse with a wooden porch. Ochre walls and uniform tiles suggested a recent restoration. Alongside, but not attached, stood a row of three terraced cottages that may once have belonged to farmworkers. The first two appeared derelict. Slates were missing from the roof, while moss and lichen grew up the walls. The door of one hung lopsided. In place of glass, blue plastic sheeting had been nailed to the rotting window frames. It resembled the torn piece of sheeting found beneath the remains of Charles Deighton.

The roof of the third cottage had recently been restored. The door and windows had been newly painted industrial red. Hadn't Lorna Driffield said Tamsey lived in his own cottage? Further down the track was a large aluminium barn with a corrugated roof, opposite four stables. Beyond the buildings, just visible through the curtain of rain, was a field full of polytunnels. There was no sign of a vehicle, nor of life.

Jo made straight for the farmhouse, pressing her back against the side wall as much to shelter from the rain as to avoid discovery. She inched her way to the first ground-floor window, and peered in. Despite the windows on both sides it was dark inside. She could just make out a kitchen table, a white Belfast sink, and a range cooker. She ducked beneath the window, and made her way around to the rear. The first of the windows was above the sink. The second window was double width, and almost floor to ceiling.

Inside this room were a leather sofa, two armchairs, and a television. On the facing wall, a pile of logs in a scuttle stood beside an unlit wood burner. Jo stood up, and carried on to the furthest corner of the building. Twin forks of lightning lit up all the buildings around her. Jo instinctively ducked into a squat. A clap of thunder burst overhead, echoing in the hills and rolling down into the valley below.

She took a deep breath, and sprinted across the open ground to the rear of the first of the terraced cottages. The yard was uneven, and strewn with bricks, cans and broken tiles. A cascade of water drenched her from head to foot. She stepped back, banging her calf against something hard and sharp. Cursing silently, she looked up at the roof. A piece of plastic guttering had failed under the pressure of the rain.

The pain in her leg was searing. She switched on her torch, and rolled up her left trouser leg to reveal a diagonal crimson slash across her calf. A small trickle of blood ran down towards her ankle. She rolled her trouser down again, and turned to discover that she had backed into a pile of stone flags. She manoeuvred one of the flags over to the cottage, angled it up against the wall, and used it as a step to reach the window. Tearing back a piece of plastic sheet from the frame, she directed the beam of the torch into the room. It was empty.

She placed her good leg on top of the flag, tested that it would take her weight, and then hauled herself up and over the window ledge and into the room.

Jo lay there, listening for any sound other than that of her heart thumping in her chest. Then she made her way from room to room until she was certain that the cottage was clear.

She retraced her steps, dragged the flag to the remaining cottage, and repeated the process. This former dwelling was also clear. That left the renovated cottage.

Closed shutters covered the ground-floor windows, blinds those on the upper storey. As far as she could tell, no lights were on. A careful reconnoitre of the three exposed sides of the cottage told her that there was no way in, other than a forced entry.

Jo sat on the flags with her back against the wall, listening to the rumble of thunder as the storm moved slowly southwards. Water poured from the cowl of her hood on to her nose, mirroring the rivulets flowing down the hillside, and out into the farmyard behind her. The wind had whipped up, and her fingers were freezing cold. She hauled herself to her feet, and hobbled around the corner and out into the open.

Now there were choices. Go back and tackle the farmhouse, or try the barn or the stables. She opted for the barn.

The two huge steel bolts were securely padlocked. Jo made her way around the side hoping to find another door. A foot above her head was a small square window covered with a protective wire mesh. She turned and swung her torch through a hundred and eighty degrees in a vain attempt to penetrate the gloom, and the rain.

Another bolt of lightning struck somewhere close at hand, lighting her up like a rabbit in headlights. When she opened her eyes an image of the farmyard, as clear as day, lingered on her retina. In the thirty seconds that it took to fade, she could see a wheelbarrow leaning against one of the stable doors. A rumble of thunder told her that the epicentre of the storm was now fifteen miles away. Shaking the rain from the peak of her cap, Jo bowed her head, and sloshed towards the stables through the water streaming over the cobblestones.

She found the wheelbarrow, wheeled it to the barn, and set it upside down beneath the window. Placing a tentative foot on the upturned base, she grasped the mesh with her left hand, and hauled herself up, holding the torch in her right hand. Slowly she quartered the barn with the beam, left to right, and then up and down as though walking a crime scene. There were free-standing shelving units holding tools of various sizes, a tractor and the bonnet of a van. It was a white Transit. She was unable to see the number plate, but felt sure this was the one that had been caught on the Moorfields CCTV the day that Norbert Welsh had disappeared.

Jo carried on with her search. There were stacks of sacks, some full, others neatly folded, two bikes, a cement mixer, and various pieces of building equipment whose use evaded her. Then she made a discovery that made her heart leap. Her foot slipped on the wet metal, and it went from under her, yanking her shoulder as she clung desperately to the wire mesh. The wire bit deep into her fingers. She managed to regain her footing and haul herself back up.

It was an old white Land Rover that had excited her. It matched the description Gordon had given her of the one that the cameras had spotted stalking Martin Hadfield. There were, however, none of the distinctive markings that had identified that vehicle as an ambulance.

There was one area beneath this window, running two-thirds of the length of the barn, that was out of her vision, and there were blind spots behind the vans. Jo's gut feeling was that if Hadfield was in this barn at all, he had to be in that Land Rover.

She climbed carefully down from her vantage point, sat on the wheelbarrow, and trailed her wounded hand in the water pooling by her feet. It hurt like hell, but she was more concerned with her own stupidity. She should have called for backup, and waited for it to arrive. They would have been here by now with a number of officers and full equipment to search this place from top to bottom.

She pulled her phone from her pocket, hunched over to keep off the rain, and speed-dialled. There was no signal. Not just from her network, but from any of them. She cursed again. Of course there wasn't. She was sitting in the middle of a thunderstorm, high up on the moors, surrounded by farm buildings. For all she knew, the nearest communications mast had been struck by a thunderbolt.

Jo hauled herself to her feet. She had to find a way into that barn. The rain had eased to a steady drizzle. Patches of light between the clouds lifted the gloom. Her forlorn hope was that she might find something in one of the stables with which to force the locks on the doors of the barn, a fork perhaps.

She walked to the nearest of the stables, found the latch for the upper swing door, and pulled it open. Leaning on the lower stable door she shone her torch across the concrete floor and up the walls. It was a standing stall, one and a half metres wide and two and a half metres long. The walls were stone, the roof supported by wooden beams and rafters. There was a window in the wall adjoining the next stable with a grill instead of glass so that the horses could see each other. The stable was bare.

She pushed the swing door to, and tried the second stable. This one was identical, except that there were garden implements propped neatly against the walls. Forks and spades of various sizes, a rake, a set of hoes, two sledgehammers and others that she didn't recognise. She found the bolt for the lower stable door, opened it and went inside.

One of the hammers had a steel head with a heavy flat surface at one end tapering to a narrow hook-like spike at the other. She seized it by its rubber-covered handle, wincing as it chafed her bruised fingers, and hefted it on to her shoulder. She was surprised by how well balanced it was.

She closed the stable door, turned towards the barn and froze. Something was wrong. There was a noise that hadn't been there before. She strained to hear it above the howling of the wind, but it had gone. She wondered if it was a figment of her nervous imagination. All she could hear now was the drumming of the rain on the roofs, the flutter of plastic sheeting and a shutter banging to and fro.

She was about to start towards the barn when something made her turn and shine her torch on the last of the three stables. Shiny new padlocks secured the bolts to both the upper and lower stable doors.

Jo limped over to the stable, inserted the hook side of the hammer into the hoop of the padlock on the lower door, and attempted to snap the lock. She could tell it was hopeless. Next she turned her attention to the bolt itself. This time she leaned on the shaft with her entire body weight and the clasp snapped with a wrenching sound. As it came away, she fell to her knees.

Jo stood up, tried to yank the door open, then realised that the upper door was holding it firmly in place. She attacked the clasp on the upper door. Seconds later, the doors swung open. She shone her torch into the stable.

Her heart raced and adrenalin coursed through her body. She almost dropped the torch as she fought to control her breathing.

Chapter 52

A body lay slumped against the back wall of the stable, its head covered with a black balaclava. Broad tape covered the eyes and mouth. The feet and torso were trussed with rope that passed behind the back, and snaked up the wall to where it had been secured around a beam.

She threw down the hammer and ripped the tape from the face.

Martin Hadfield gasped as he filled his lungs with air, his eyes full of fear.

Jo shone the beam on to her own face.

'It's alright, Sir. It's me, DI Stuart.'

It took a moment for his eyes to adjust and his brain to accept what he was seeing.

'Thank God,' he croaked. 'Get me out of here.'

'That's what I intend to do.' She pulled the balaclava from his head. 'Best that you keep your voice down while I untie this rope.'

She swung the torch beam across his body and up the rope to the point where it was secured. Without a knife, she would have to climb up there and untie it. Quartering the room with the torchlight, the beam settled on an aluminium ladder propped up in a corner.

Jo hooked the torch in her belt and picked up the ladder, bringing it over to the back wall. She propped it up beside him, and mounted the rungs. Her left hand was still painful. Her injured leg felt heavy, and the trouser was sticking where blood had congealed.

'You're dripping all over me,' Hadfield complained.

'Keep your voice down,' she said. 'This won't take long.'

She had to stand on the topmost rung to reach up to the beam. Holding the rope with her left hand, she shone the torch on the knot. The free end had been looped twice around itself, and then pulled under and through at the top to form a timber hitch. Jo's fingers tugged desperately at the topmost loop, her fingernails ripping as she scrabbled to pull the tail through the taut rope.

'See if you can stand?' she said. 'I need you to take your weight off the rope.'

She heard Hadfield's feet scrambling against the concrete floor. He groaned as he inched his back up the wall behind him.

'That's better,' she said, pulling the tail through the first loop, and then the second.

'Look out!' he shouted. 'Behind you!'

Jo turned her head, lost her footing as the ladder tipped, and fell to the floor. Heedless of the pain in her back, she rolled instinctively to one side and raised the Maglite that was still in her left hand.

Framed in the doorway, his face impassive in the beam of her torch, stood Shaye Tamsey. In his hands he held the pick that she had so carelessly discarded. Beside her, Hadfield cursed.

Steadying the beam on Tamsey's face, Jo used her other hand to lever herself to her feet.

'It's me, Shaye,' she said. 'SI Stuart. Police. Put that down.'

He shielded his face with his arm, but showed no sign of responding to her command. Jo switched off the torch, and dropped it. In a single movement she wheeled, and winced with pain as she grasped the ladder with both hands.

Tamsey, his eyes attempting to adjust to the sudden darkness, raised the pick and stepped into the room. She aimed the ladder at his chest, and charged across the damp concrete floor. At the last moment, her left foot slipped, the leg gave way, and she fell backwards. Her momentum carried the ladder forwards, the steeper angle that her slip had imparted sending the topmost rung directly beneath his chin. Tamsey fell backwards into the yard, his head slamming on to the cobblestones.

Jo scrambled to her feet, wrestled her baton from her belt, and limped after him. She kept the baton raised as she approached. His eyes were closed. The water between the cobbles by his head was stained with blood.

She knelt beside him, placed her baton on the ground, and checked that he was still alive. His breathing was shallow but steady, and there was a faint pulse in his neck. She lifted his head, and shone her torch on the back of his skull. The cut looked superficial, but you could never tell with head injuries. Jo did not want to risk worsening his injuries by turning him over. She handcuffed his hands together in front of him, then stood up and checked her phone.

There was still no signal. Above the wind, she heard the noise of a diesel engine and the intermittent sound of a car alarm. She looked back towards the gate. Another bank of jet-black clouds had arrived, obliterating what remained of the winter sun low in the western sky, accentuating dipped headlight beams as they darted from side to side down the farm track. She could tell from the height of the vehicle that this was not a car. There were no flashing blue lights, no sirens. This was not the cavalry coming to the rescue.

Chapter 53

Jo placed her baton in its holster and limped back into the stable.

'Well done, Stuart,' said Hadfield. 'Now you can untie me.'

'I'm sorry,' she said, bending to retrieve the tapes. 'I haven't time.'

He tried to push himself away from the wall.

'What the hell are you talking about?'

'Sorry about this.' She slapped the first tape across his mouth. 'His accomplice is coming. You'll be safer if she thinks you're out of it.'

His eyes stared wildly back at her. Jo covered them with the second piece of tape, pushed him firmly into a seated position against the wall, and then threw the loose end of the rope so that it looped over the beam where it had been secured. It was not exactly as she had found him, but it would have to do.

'Don't move,' she said. 'And you'll be fine. I'll be back as soon as I can.'

She switched off her torch, clipped it on to her belt, and slipped out of the barn, closing the doors behind her.

Tamsey was on his knees, and attempting to get up. The vehicle was through the gate and approaching the first of the farm buildings. Once it rounded the corner, the headlights would light up the farmyard and expose both her and Tamsey. Jo gritted her teeth, and jogged across the yard to the end wall of the cottages, backing into the shadows.

The cold had all but numbed her hands and legs, dulling the pain. She heard the vehicle slow as it reached the farmhouse, its beams of light lighting the farmyard. Tamsey was on all fours, attempting to rise. Now he was on his feet, although barely able to stand. He put his hands to his face and staggered as the vehicle accelerated through the puddles of water spraying muck and water as it came. When it drew level with Jo, she saw that it was a dark-coloured Mitsubishi pickup – another vehicle that Driffield had failed to disclose.

The vehicle stopped in front of Tamsey and he placed his hands on the bonnet to support himself. A light came on in the cab as the driver's door was opened and Lorna Driffield climbed down, going quickly to his aid. Jo could see them talking but was unable to hear a word. Tamsey pointed towards the stable in which Hadfield lay. Driffield moved away from the Mitsubishi and began to turn through 360 degrees.

Jo stepped back, and flattened herself against the wall, confident that she was out of sight. When she peered out again, Tamsey was upright and unsupported. Driffield was back in the cab, reaching across to the glove compartment. She straightened up, got out and began to walk towards the stable. In her hand, she had a lighted torch. Jo placed her hand on her baton and braced herself to race across the yard.

Driffield had almost reached the stable. Jo estimated the distance she would have to cover. Twenty paces. Yelling all the way. Two of them, one hopefully more injured than her. She had the element of surprise. They, on the other hand, would be desperate. Jo tightened her grip and began to ease the baton from its holster as

Driffield reached out, opened the upper door and directed her torch inside to where Hadfield lay.

Jo took a deep breath and was about to step out from the shadows when Driffield closed the door, and turned around. Jo flattened herself against the wall and listened to the sound of Driffield's footsteps on the cobbles. She counted nine paces and then heard murmured voices. Edging her way to the corner of the cottage, she risked a peep.

Driffield was walking to the back of the pickup. She reached over the side and removed what looked like a spade, and a heavy narrow bar of some kind. She walked to the front of the Mitsubishi and handed Tamsey the spade. He was surprisingly steady on his feet now and hefted it with ease, despite the handcuffs. To prove his readiness, he swung it several times from right to left and back again. Apparently satisfied, Driffield reached into the cab and switched off the headlights, plunging the yard into darkness. Jo could barely make out the shapes of her pursuers but she could tell from the sound of their footsteps that they were coming for her.

Now she knew that Hadfield was no longer their primary target, Jo's plan was to get back to the car and use the radio to call for backup.

Not daring to use her torch, she retraced her steps in the gloom, relying on memory to avoid the bricks, the cans, and the broken slates and guttering. Several times she caught something with her foot, and made a noise that caused her to stop, hold her breath, and listen to see if they heard. All she could hear was the sound of the windows rattling in the freezing wind that whistled between the buildings.

Jo stepped out into the open ground beyond the farmhouse, and was surprised that there was no one waiting for her. She jogged the hundred yards back to her car, desperate to put as much distance between herself and them, to give her time to make the call. The gate was open. The clouds had gone, and the Audi was bathed in the soft golden glow of sunset. It was listing on the passenger side. The front and rear offside tyres had been slashed.

Jo went to open the door and saw that the driver's window had been smashed. She shone her torch inside. The radio had been wrenched from its housing and lay on the passenger seat. Jo had a sick feeling in the pit of her stomach. She straightened up, and checked her mobile phone. There was still no signal. Her text to Andy Swift was shown as undelivered.

A sixth sense told her to turn around. Walking up the track towards her, silhouetted against a blood-red sky, were Lorna Driffield and Shaye Tamsey.

Chapter 54

Jo climbed into the driver's seat. There was no way that she could reverse back to the road with the car in this state. Even if she did, she had no hope of outrunning the pickup. She switched on the engine. To her relief, the engine fired up. She locked the door, and switched the lights on full beam. Releasing the handbrake, she slipped into first and set off. Accelerating through the gears, she was up to fifteen miles per hour as she approached them. The steering was completely unpredictable, the Audi lurching from side to side across the ruts as she fought to control it. She feared that the offside suspension would fail and the car would dig into the mud and stall.

Blinded by the headlights, Driffield stepped back against the fence and raised the iron bar in both hands. Tamsey stood to the left of the track, his spade held high above his head. As the car drew level, he hammered the spade against the windscreen. The nearside wing spun him backwards. Glass shattered inside the screen's laminated pocket. As Jo pushed herself back into her seat, Driffield thrust the bar through the broken side window missing her by millimetres. The window frame flung the bar sideways and back out again, as the car careered on.

Jo's heart pounded. She could barely see the track ahead. Torn strips of rubber slapped against the wheel arches. The steering wheel fought her every move. Suddenly she was rattling along the cobbled section and the dark bulk of the farmhouse loomed to her left. She slowed as the car approached the pickup, and steered towards the passenger side.

Jo braked, climbed out and looked back towards the farmhouse. There was no sign of her pursuers. She hurried around to the Mitsubishi driver's door, yanked it open, and climbed in. She pressed the starter button. Nothing happened. *No key present* appeared on the head-up display. She searched the overhead glasses compartment, and the glove box. Then she climbed out, and ran her frozen fingers under each wheel arch in turn. There was no sign of a spare key.

Jo leaned against the back of the Mitsubishi, slowed her breathing, and regained her composure. Her intention had been to bundle Hadfield into the pickup without bothering to untie his hands and feet, leave the farm, and call for help. There was no plan B.

She stared towards the farmhouse. Driffield and Tamsey had rounded the corner, and were walking confidently towards her. She turned and shone her torch in the back of the pickup. There was a half a ton of gravel, but no more implements. She ran the five strides to the second of the stables, and wrenched the doors open. The fork was still leaning against the wall. She grabbed it, and stepped back into the yard.

They were now twenty metres away, five metres apart. Tamsey was moving around the right-hand side of the pickup, Driffield around the left, in a classic pincer movement. Jo backed away until there was open ground, in front and behind her. She would face them on her terms.

It had started to rain again, and her frozen hands were slipping on the steel jacket around the shaft of the fork. Grant's words echoed in her brain.

'*Rule one, avoid violence at all costs. Rule two, you have to be prepared to do whatever it takes to stay alive. Rule three, you will never, ever win a defensive fight . . .*'

The two of them rounded the Mitsubishi. Tamsey's left side had dropped and he was limping.

'Lorna Driffield, Shaye Tamsey,' she shouted. 'Stand still. Don't make this any worse than it already is.'

Neither of them responded. The gap was closing.

'My colleagues know that I'm here. You will only make it worse for yourselves.'

They kept coming.

They were less than five metres away.

'. . . *Rule four, get in first and finish it fast.*'

Jo took a deep breath, and darted towards Shaye. As he raised the spade above his right shoulder, she exhaled a growling shout.

'Eiii!'

Shaye hesitated for a fraction of a second. Long enough for Jo to thrust the prongs of the fork at the point where the shaft met the blade, and wrench it from his hands. As his body lurched to the right, she slammed the arch of her foot against the side of his left knee.

As he collapsed, she whirled to face the threat from Lorna Driffield. Jo's fork was lying out of reach, entangled with the spade. Jo pulled her baton from its holster and snapped it open.

Lorna Driffield had not moved. She smiled at Jo, and then placed the iron crowbar on the ground beside her.

'Officer,' she shouted, more loudly than seemed necessary. 'I'm sorry, I didn't recognise you.' Then she shook her head, and pointed to where Tamsey was lying on the wet cobbles. 'I assume you're here for Shaye? What the hell has he done now?'

Above the sound of Driffield's voice echoing around the farmyard, and the rain hammering on the corrugated iron roof of the
barn, Jo heard the familiar wail of sirens.

'Lorna Driffield,' she said. 'I'm arresting you for criminal damage, assault on a police officer, and the suspected abduction and
false imprisonment of one Martin Hadfield. You do not have to
say anything, but it may harm your defence if you fail to mention,
when questioned, something that you later rely on in court, anything you do say may be given in evidence. Do you understand?'

Driffield smiled thinly.

'Not really,' she said.

Headlights blazing, a patrol car and a Tactical Aid Group van
led a procession into the farmyard. Max Nailor climbed out of the
passenger seat of the patrol car and hurried over towards them.

'Are you alright, Jo?' he asked.

She wiped the rain from her forehead with the back of her
hands.

'I'm fine.'

'You don't look it.'

'How did you know where to come?' she asked.

'Andy Swift filled me in on your conversation. Zephaniah gave
me the postcode from the report on your shared drive. Ram went
one stage better, and pinned this place down using Google Earth.
It's called teamwork.'

He pointed to Shaye Tamsey, who was prone on the floor.

'How is he?'

'He'll live. I hope.'

'Are you sure you're okay?' he asked.

'It's nothing that won't keep.'

She pointed to the third stable door.

'Assistant Chief Constable Martin Hadfield is in there. Can you
get someone to untie him?'

'I'll see to it,' said an inspector with the Tactical Aid Unit.

'And we could do with a secure ambulance and a paramedic,' she told him.

'Will do,' he replied. 'In the meantime we've got a medic with us.'

Nailor turned to look at Lorna Driffield. She was leaning, arms folded, against the bonnet of the Mitsubishi, watching the proceedings with simulated surprise.

'What about her?'

'I've arrested her for criminal damage, assault on a police officer, suspected abduction and false imprisonment. Now it's his turn.'

Nailor turned back towards Jo and lowered his voice to a whisper.

'What about murder, or attempted murder?'

She shook her head.

'We don't have enough evidence for that. Once the PACE clock starts ticking, I can only ask for so many extensions, then they'll have to go before the courts. If they're remanded for these offences, then we can question them while they're on remand without the constraints of the custody clock.'

'What if they're not remanded?'

Jo shook her head.

'I don't even want to think about that.'

'I'm waiting for the search warrant you asked for,' he told her.

'I don't need it,' she said. 'My search was on the grounds that I reasonably believed a life to be in danger. Once I've cautioned Tamsey, we can search all of these premises for evidence linked to the arrests.'

The inspector and one of his sergeants emerged from the stable supporting ACC Hadfield between them. He looked dreadful, but was trying hard to maintain his dignity. He nodded towards Jo.

'Well done, Inspector,' he said.

They watched the three of them walk slowly towards the Tactical Aid van.

'*Well done?*' said Nailor. 'A thank you wouldn't have gone amiss. And Inspector? Why not, Jo – he knows your name.'

'Believe me,' said Jo. 'That "*Well done*" is a miracle in itself, and the last time we met, he insisted on reminding me that I was an *Acting* Inspector.'

Chapter 55

'I'm sorry, Jo,' said Gordon Holmes. 'That was a complete waste of time.'

It was gone midnight, and she had spent the last fifteen minutes in the observation room watching, as he and Helen Gates attempted to interview Shaye Tamsey in the faint hope of eliciting an admission of guilt.

'I don't think I've ever heard so many "*No Comments*",' she agreed.

'So much for hoping he'd implicate Driffield,' said Holmes. 'Getting him to admit his own role would have been a start.'

He chuckled.

'What?' she asked.

'There is a silver lining,' he told her.

'Go on?'

'At least he hasn't claimed he's a victim of police brutality, and told us he wants you charged with assault.'

Jo returned to the empty apartment, stripped off her wet, filthy clothes, had a warm shower, re-dressed her calf and hand, washed down two paracetamol with a hot chocolate, and slipped between the warm Egyptian cotton sheets that she and Abbie had chosen together. She was exhausted. Without Abbie beside her, she tossed and turned through a fitful night's sleep until the alarm rudely woke her at 6.30am. She changed into her NCA hoodie and jogging bottoms, and set off for the Quays.

The rest of the team were waiting for her, cradling cups of coffee and eating pastries.

'Are they going to let you sit in on the Driffield interview?' asked Andy Swift.

'No,' she told him. 'But I'll be able to watch and listen in the observation room, and make suggestions in their earpieces.'

'That's insane,' said Ram Shah. 'You're the only one who actually met her. You've researched her background and spoken to her sister. And you were the arresting officer.'

'But until Harry sorts the respective roles of the NCA, it's going to be GMP's investigation. After all, Hadfield is their man. Besides, this allows me to concentrate on proving a link with the Deighton murder and all of the other missing Masons.'

'Jo's right.'

Max Nailor had shaved the stubble from his face, and for the first time looked alert and attentive.

'Until it is officially ratified as an NCA operation,' he continued, 'we have no procedural role in an investigation unless invited to take part.'

'They should have offered,' said Ram.

'I agree,' Max replied. 'How are you, Jo?'

'I'm fine, thanks to you,' she said.

'Nothing to do with me, you had it all under control.'

'Only because you arrived with the backup.'

He grinned.

'I was supposed to be keeping an eye on you. As a mentor,' he added hastily, 'not checking up on you.' He frowned. 'I've been neglecting you. I owe you an apology.'

She smiled.

'You're forgiven.'

'Get a room, you two,' said Ram.

All three of them stared at him.

'What?' he said.

Jo began to laugh, and the others joined in.

'Changing the topic,' said Andy Swift. 'How is Jo going to convince her former Detective Chief Superintendent that Lorna Driffield may be a serial killer?'

'That won't be easy,' said Nailor, perching on the edge of the desk. 'When did GMP last have a female serial killer? Other than Myra Hindley?'

'Not in my time,' Jo admitted. 'They thought they had one over the Stepping Hill poisonings. He turned out to be a male nurse.'

'The problem with female serial killers,' said Andy Swift, 'is that we know a lot less about them. What we do know is that they're much less likely to seek or attract attention. Their goals are usually material gain, or a highly personal cause linked to love or loathing that takes the form of revenge. Then there are the Munchausen's syndrome "Angels of Death". Female sexual predators who go on to kill are rare.'

'So rare,' said Jo, 'that it has yet to be established that any female serial killer apart from Jane Toppan had a primary sexual motivation. But what they do have in common with men is a need to act out revenge and take control of their victims, which would definitely fit in Lorna Driffield's case.'

'True,' said Swift.

'But her sister didn't know the identity of the men who were involved,' Shah pointed out, 'nor of a possible link with Freemasonry.'

'That doesn't mean that Lorna might not have,' said Jo. 'She was the oldest of the siblings. Her brother's death triggered her to do something about it.'

'That's all very well,' said Shah. 'But how are we going to prove it?'

Jo reached for her hoodie and stood up.

'I think the answer lies out at that farm,' she said.

Chapter 56

Jo donned her Tyvek suit, showed her warrant card to the duty loggist, and walked slowly past the gate and down the lane. The pain in her leg, all but dissipated, had been replaced by another in her hip.

Floodlights had been erected by the open doors of the barn, and the stable where Hadfield had been held. Blue-suited Scenes of Crime officers crawled on their hands and knees across the floor of the barn conducting a fingertip search. All of the lights were on in the farmhouse, and in the terraced cottage where she assumed that Tamsey slept. A line of other SOCOs emerged from the door of the farmhouse, carrying boxes of evidence over to one of the vans parked on the cobbles. Jo's former colleague Jack Benson, clipboard in hand, stood on the doorstep directing operations. He beamed as he spotted her.

'What are you doing here? Last I heard you should be in hospital.'

'The other guy came off worse.'

'Seriously though,' he said. 'Are you okay?'

'I'm fine,' she replied for what seemed like the umpteenth time. 'Have you found anything yet?'

He shook his head.

'It's early days, Jo. The barn and the stables were sluiced with chemicals used to clean dressed stone. All of the vehicles appear to have received the same treatment. We did find traces of adhesive on the Land Rover consistent with it having had transfers stuck to on the front, sides and back, but there's no sign of those transfers, nor the false number plates. I've had the van and the Land Rover flatbed lifted and towed away for detailed forensic examination.'

'If there are any bodies out here,' she said. 'They're going to be in cesspits, or buried in open ground.'

'Tactical aid are already conducting an initial search,' he said. 'If authorised, there'll be aerial and ground surveys for signs of disturbance. The trouble is, up here on the moors they could be anywhere.'

'Can you do me a favour, Jack?' she asked.

'What?'

'I need to have a look at their business records.'

'You'll have to be quick,' he said. 'And remember, you can look, but you can't touch.'

Upstairs, they were busy dismantling the computer and filling boxes with documents.

'Did you come across a calendar?' she asked a SOCO.

'On that pile over there,' he said. 'It was too big for these boxes. We're waiting for the A2 art folders.'

Jo pulled a pair of neoprene gloves from her jacket pocket, and picked it up. There were vague references to current projects, but no addresses.

'What about job records?' she asked.

He shook his head.

'Sorry, Ma'am. I guess they'll all be on the computers. The digital forensic techies have already taken them away for analysis.'

'There's some paperwork over there,' said a female SOCO. 'Loads of names and addresses.'

On top of two sealed evidence boxes Jo found a pile of computer printouts in files, waiting to be boxed up. She leafed through them. Halfway down the pile, she found exactly what she'd been hoping for. There were two files containing projects completed during 2013 and 2014 respectively, and a third headed *Current Projects 2015*.

'Is there a photocopier anywhere?' she asked.

'Next door,' said the female SOCO.

It took Jo ten minutes to copy everything she needed, and return the originals to their place on the pile.

'Find anything useful?' asked Benson as she exited the farmhouse.

She held up the wad of paper.

'I hope so.'

He frowned.

'It's alright,' she said. 'I copied them.'

'I'll still need to record what you've taken from the premises,' he said. 'Protocol.'

Forty minutes later, Jo pulled up outside an Edwardian detached house on the outskirts of Alderley Edge. It didn't come close in size or grandeur to the footballers' mansions that abounded here, but was probably worth well over a million simply by association.

An angry man in his late fifties answered the doorbell.

'Did you not see the sign in the window?'

The sign read, *NO Cold Callers, Hawkers, Sales Persons, Utility Companies, Charity Collectors or Religious Bodies. Official callers should have their identification ready. Thank You!*

Jo flipped her ID wallet open, and held it for him to read. She took comfort in the rapid change in his expression.

'Police?' he said. 'To what do we owe this pleasure?'

'I'm sorry to trouble you, sir,' she said. 'But I wonder if you could show me your back garden?'

High hedges ran down both sides. At the far end, there were views over open fields beyond a low fence punctuated by three oak trees. In borders backed by shrubs and apple trees, late-flowering perennials added rich splashes of colour. She could see a greenhouse, a shed and a very smart summerhouse. What really interested her was the gaping hole in front of the conservatory.

'What's going on here?' she said.

'That's exactly what I asked.' He pointed to the stack of flag-stones, the concrete mixer, and the pile of grit-stone. 'We came back from a holiday in France a couple of days early, and found it like this. I thought it was only a matter of laying a new patio. We didn't expect a bloody great hole.'

'What did the landscaper have to say?'

'She was surprised to see us. I asked her what was going on. She said she'd come across some unstable soil, and had to excavate it to create a solid area on which to lay the sub-base before she could pour the concrete, and lay the bedding course. She was due back this after-noon to fill it in. I was beginning to wonder where she was.'

Jo's phone rang.

'You'll have to excuse me,' she said. She waited until he'd moved out of earshot. It was Gordon Holmes.

'Where are you?' he asked. 'We're just about to question Driffield.'

'I'm in Alderley Edge, at the site of Driffield's current landscape project. It'll take me the best part of forty minutes to get back.'

'I wouldn't rush,' he said. 'With what we've got so far, I doubt this interview will tell us much apart from establish some facts that we can later use against her. Assuming we can get her beyond *No Comment*, we'll see if we can get her to dig a little hole, and then keep digging.'

Chapter 57

By the time Jo arrived back at Central Park, the preliminary interview with Lorna Driffield had ended.

'You should have been here,' he told her. 'She put on an Oscar-winning performance. If I didn't trust your judgement, I'd have said she was telling the truth.'

Jo's heart sank.

'Which was what exactly?'

'Same as when you arrested her, and again in the custody suite. Horror that Hadfield should have been found at the farm. Surprise and disappointment that Tamsey could have let her down after all she has done for him.'

'So she's admitting *his* guilt?'

He rubbed his chin.

'Accepting, not admitting. She's obviously decided to cut Shaye adrift.'

'That's a hell of a risk. When he finds out that she's dumped him, he could decide to tell us everything.'

'You'd think so, wouldn't you? Trouble is, he *has* found out. DCS Gates decided to go and tell him straight after we finished with Driffield.'

'And?'

'Have you ever seen Shaye Tamsey smile?'

'No.'

'Well, that's what he did. Just before he said "*No Comment*".'

'He's got a martyr complex,' she said. 'He's going to take the blame.'

'If you ask me, he's obsessed with her. Thinks he owes her even more than she thinks he does. My guess is she groomed him from the start. I'd be surprised if there wasn't a sexual element to it.'

Jo knew he was right. Here was a younger, vulnerable, impressionable young man, with low self-esteem and limited intellect, sexually inexperienced and starved of love. Along comes an older, highly intelligent, driven and manipulative woman offering him everything he's never had and always wanted. Of course he was going to take the blame.

'It doesn't help that Hadfield never saw or heard his attackers.' Holmes reflected.

'Not even once?'

'Nope. He thinks he was hit on the back of the head, and sedated as well. He's got partial retrograde amnesia. Doesn't remember anything after leaving his Lodge meeting. Neither of them ever spoke.'

'Did he smell anything distinctive? Perfume?'

She knew she was clutching at straws. Gordon laughed.

'Only BO and halitosis. You've met Driffield.'

'Tamsey doesn't have the intelligence to plan something like this,' she said. 'How could he possibly have disguised the Land Rover as an ambulance, gone to Manchester, mugged and abducted Mr Hadfield, brought him back and hidden him in that stable without Driffield having known about it?'

'That's what we'll be asking her next, but you can bet she's already concocted a plausible story. If she does, Jo, I'm warning you, Helen Gates is minded to charge Tamsey and let Driffield go on bail. The CPS advice is that without more evidence, or a statement from Tamsey implicating Driffield, there's not sufficient evidence to charge Driffield. She claims she didn't recognise you or your car. She assumed you were an intruder. Furthermore, there's currently only sufficient evidence to charge Tamsey with criminal damage, kidnapping and false imprisonment, contrary to common law.'

Jo was almost speechless.

'How long would he get for that?' she asked.

'How long is a piece of string? Look at the mitigating factors: there's only one victim,' he held up a warning hand to forestall her objection, 'that we can prove. Hadfield cannot be classified as vulnerable: he was freed within twenty-four hours, and his treatment, although unpleasant and degrading, could have been a lot worse – no ransom was involved and no specific threats were made.'

'They were going to bury him alive!'

'An unsubstantiated allegation. All in all, without a proven motive, but taking into account who Hadfield is, I'd say twelve years to life. He could be out after six.'

'What about possession of an offensive weapon with intent to cause harm?'

'Couple of problems there. First off, it was not in a public place. Secondly, you didn't have a search warrant. Maybe he believed you were an intruder? Maybe he was as surprised to find Hadfield there as you were?'

'He did know who I was. I showed him my warrant card when I went to talk to Driffield.'

He dismissed that with a wave of his hand.

'It was dark, pouring with rain. I'm surprised his brief hasn't cited you for breaking and entering, and causing actual bodily harm.'

He adopted the tone of prosecution barrister.

'Did you identify yourself as a police officer, and warn him to drop the pick before you launched yourself at him with that ladder?

Would you consider your action to have constituted reasonable force, given that according to your own account he hadn't uttered a specific threat or made a threatening move?'

'*No Comment*,' she said. 'Look, Gordon, you have to apply for a custody extension, for both of them. You've got to give me time to tie them in to Deighton's murder and the other disappearances.'

'Tamsey's not a problem,' he replied. 'What I haven't told you is that we already have his fingerprints on the padlocks and the tape he used to cover Hadfield's eyes and mouth.'

'Not hers?'

He shook his head.

'No, she's been careful. Either that or she's telling the truth. Maybe she really didn't know.'

'Of course she knew. I just need more time to prove it.'

'Gates has agreed to use her discretionary powers to extend Tamsey's detention for another twelve hours. Then he'll be charged regardless of what's happening with his boss. I'll try to persuade her to extend Driffield's detention for another twelve hours. After that, unless you or Forensics come up with something, she's going to walk.'

'On police bail?'

'Obviously,' he said. 'We're not that stupid. What are you going to do now, Jo?'

'I've got their job records for the past two and a half years. I'm going to check them against the dates that our suspected victims disappeared. If I get any matches, I'm going to go and see what I can find.'

He sighed.

'It sounds like a long shot.'

'Right now,' she said, 'it's all I've got.'

Ram was the only one left in the office. Once she'd brought him up to speed, he immediately volunteered to compare the worksheets and the MisPers list.

Jo decided to contact DI Renton and DS Coppull. The last thing she needed was for them to see it on the news, and wonder why she hadn't let them know what was happening.

Renton had already gone home. DS Coppull was still at her desk.

'Nice one!' she said when Jo had finished. 'It's a bloody good job you found him before they buried him. Mind, if it'd been my boss I'd have been tempted to bugger off, and leave them to it.'

Her laugh transformed into a chesty cough.

'How did you get on with Norbert Welsh's wife and the life insurance?' Jo asked.

Coppull cleared her throat.

'There's nothing in her phone records or her emails that would suggest collusion. We'll keep digging. Speaking of which, let me know what you turn up tomorrow.'

'I will,' said Jo.

'Good,' said the Liverpool detective. 'And for the record, I think what you've achieved so far is little short of amazing.'

Jo put the phone down, and leaned back in her chair. Her hip still ached, the bandage around her hand was beginning to chafe, and she felt exhausted. And she still hadn't heard from Abbie. She let her head loll against the headrest, and closed her eyes.

'Jo?'

She opened one eye. Shah was standing beside her with a look of concern on his face.

'Thank God,' he said. 'I thought we'd lost you.'

Jo opened the other eye and smiled at him.

'You should be so lucky.'

He held up a sheet of A4.

'As matter of fact, I have been.'

She pushed herself upright.

'How many did you get?'

'Seven!' he exclaimed, beaming from ear to ear. 'We've got seven matches.'

Jo didn't know whether to laugh or cry.

The nearest location was a house in Bolton where Lorna's Garden Transformations had begun work in August 2014, and finished in the last week of October. One of the missing persons on Jo's list had vanished on October the fifth. Justin Pollock had last been seen in the town centre, on his way home from a Lodge meeting.

Tempted as she was to rush straight there, Jo knew that it made sense to wait till morning. It would be too dark to see anything. Besides, she was mentally, physically and emotionally exhausted. Even though the custody clock was ticking, it was not as though Driffield or Tamsey were going anywhere. And whatever discoveries waited for her, sadly, they were unlikely to include the living.

Chapter 58

The address was up a winding tree-lined road on a private estate that bordered a golf course. Remote-controlled electric gates guarded the driveway. Jo stopped and got out of her replacement car. State-of-the-art CCTV cameras followed her every move. A metal plaque informed visitors that the property enjoyed police monitoring of both the CCTV and alarm systems.

She pressed the intercom button.

'Yes?'

The disembodied voice was male, the tone authoritative.

'Senior Investigator Joanne Stuart, National Crime Agency, by appointment,' she said.

'You're nice and early, I like that,' said the voice, a shade more welcoming. 'You can park in front of the Range Rover.'

Not any old Range Rover. This was a customised, brilliant white, LUMMA limited edition, with personalised plates. Gordon Holmes would have been able to tell her its value to within a pound. Well over a hundred and fifty grand was her guess.

Terence Tucker waited for her between the imposing pillars at the entrance to his house. In his late fifties, he had the trim yet solid frame of a middleweight boxer, and the confidence to match.

The manner in which he appraised her, and the sharp intelligence behind his eyes, shouted wily self-made man. His weathered complexion hinted at foreign holidays and hours spent on the golf course behind his house. He smiled. Two rows of teeth, as dazzling as the Range Rover, lit up the porch.

'Terence Tucker,' he said. 'Call me Terry.'

'Joanne Stuart,' she said, shaking his hand. 'I'm happy to answer to SI Stuart, or plain Jo.'

'Certainly not plain,' he quipped, as he led her inside the house.

Twice the total area of her apartment, the hallway boasted a wrought-iron, double-winged staircase with marble steps. The overall effect was enhanced by chandeliers, ornate mirrors and original paintings on the walls.

'Come on through to the kitchen,' he said, heading for an open doorway. 'I hope you drink coffee?'

Black marble topped the gleaming cabinets. Chandeliers competed with recessed downlighters. Full-height, bi-fold doors framed a beautiful garden. Jo sat down on one of the red plastic designer chairs.

'Here you are,' he said, pouring her a coffee. 'Help yourself to milk and sugar.'

He sat down opposite her, poured himself a cup and sipped it.

'So,' he said, 'the National Crime Agency. To what do I owe this pleasure?'

'It's quite a delicate matter, Mr Tucker,' she began.

'Terry,' he said. 'And don't worry about me, security is my business. I work hand in glove with your lot, not to mention the regional agencies, the prison service, the security services. Discretion is my byword. Has to be. I assumed that was why you wanted to meet with me?'

'Actually, no.'

He put his cup down and folded his arms.

'Now I'm intrigued. If it's not about work, what is it about?'

'It's in connection with a series of suspected abductions, and at least one murder.'

'Abductions I specialise in,' he said. 'But not murder, not yet anyway.'

'I understand you had your garden redesigned and landscaped last autumn?' she said.

His brow furrowed.

'That's right.'

'Lorna's Garden Transformations?'

'Also correct. Bloody good job she made of it. I'll show you if you like?'

'That's what I was hoping,' she told him.

He led her out through the bi-fold doors on to a raised terrace of Yorkstone flags with a sandstone retaining wall that ran the length of the rear of the property. The garden was as stunning as the house. Steps led down to a stone bridge that crossed a pond. Lawns bordered by bushes and mature trees stretched away to the northern boundary, where she glimpsed between the trees the rolling fairways of the neighbouring golf course. There was a rotating wood and glass dining pod, a newly planted orchard, and a knot garden with a rose bed at its centre.

'Not so shabby, is it?' said Tucker.

'It's stunning,' she told him. 'How much of this were Lorna's Garden Transformations responsible for?'

'This terrace, the steps, the bridge, the orchard and the rose garden. Why, what are you looking for?'

'I'm not sure,' she said. 'I hope I'll know it when I see it.'

Tucker looked at his Breitling watch.

'I've got a meeting with the Assistant Chief Constable of Lancashire in Hutton at eleven. I'll need to leave by quarter past ten at the latest. You're welcome to wander round on your own till then. Give me a shout if you need anything.'

Where the hell do I start, she wondered. She looked at her watch. It was already half past eight. Imagine this as a crime scene, she told herself. What would you do? Take it one section at a time. Quarter it, return to areas you think most likely to yield a result, and then fingertip search them, twice.

She began in the western corner of the house, slowly pacing the terrace west to east, and then south to north, head down, looking for anything out of the ordinary. Out of the corner of her eye, she was aware of Tucker watching her through a lounge window. Having finished the terrace, she examined the steps, the bridge and the knot garden. Finally, she inspected every tree in the orchard.

Jo approached the bridge with the intention of searching the terrace for a second time. As she reached the foot of the steps, her attention wandered to the statuary. A pair of wolves stood guard, on the left a she-wolf, on the right a male. Something urged her to examine them more closely. On the second time of circling the she-wolf, she noticed markings in the centre of the slab of stone beneath its feet. Jo knelt to take a closer look. She blew from between the grooves fine grains of sand carried in on the wind. Within a perfect square, someone had carved what looked like a pick, a spade and a vertical rod. She had a vague recollection of having seen this image somewhere before.

She used her mobile phone to take a picture. Then she sat back on her heels, attached the image to a text, and sent it.

'Found something?'

Terence Tucker was walking across the terrace towards her. He started down the steps, a worried look on his face.

'Do you know what this is?' she asked, indicating the carving.

He squatted down beside her, then smiled with relief.

'It's just their trademark. Lorna's Garden Transformations. She asked if I minded if she had it carved on there. It was fine by me. When someone does a job as good as this, it's only fair they get to sign it.'

'Who picked these statues?' she asked.

'It was Lorna's suggestion. I was happy to go along with it. I've always seen myself as a bit of a wolf.'

Her phone rang.

'Do you mind if I take this?' she asked.

Tucker stood up.

'Feel free.'

'You've got ten minutes left,' he called out as he wandered across the bridge and on to the lawn.

She put the phone to her ear.

'Jo? It's Ram. I got your text.'

'Can you see if you can find out what it means?' she asked.

'I can do better than that.' She heard the smile in his voice. 'Here's Harry Stone.'

'Jo, it's Harry. How are you?'

'I keep telling everyone I'm fine,' she said. 'But I get the impression they don't believe me.'

'That was a bloody stupid thing you did,' he said. 'Going up to that farm on your own.'

'I know . . .'

He cut her off.

'Bloody impressive though. We can talk about it when you get back. The thing is, I know what it is you've got there.'

She tried to mask her excitement.

'Go on?'

'The pick, the spade and the crow.'

'Crow?'

'As in crow bar. Those are the tools of a Royal Arch Mason.'

She would have punched the air had Tucker not been watching. 'I knew it!' she said. 'They were among the symbols I saw on the walls of the Lodge that Charles Deighton attended.'

'I know what you're thinking, Jo,' he said. 'But it could take a lot of persuasion to get a warrant. It'll be quicker if you can persuade the owner to agree to a search.'

She turned to check where Tucker was. He was standing on the lawn, arms folded, staring back at her. She could tell from the look on his face that he was way ahead of her.

'Leave it with me, Harry,' she said. 'I'll ring you back.'

As she put the phone back in her pocket, he strode across the bridge towards her.

'No!' he said. 'I'm not having you smash all this up. No way!'

'Calm down, Terry,' she said. 'Nobody's talking about smashing anything up.'

Not yet, she thought.

'Oh no? What was all that on the phone then? I saw the look on your face. It was like you'd won the bloody lottery.'

'Let's go inside, and talk about it,' she said. 'You may have to postpone your meeting with the Assistant Chief Constable of Lancashire I'm afraid, but when you tell him why, I think you'll find he'll be pleasantly surprised.'

~

'You're telling me you won't do anything until you're sure there's something down there?'

Tucker had calmed down. It took a stiff brandy for him, and lot of gentle insistent persuasion on her part, but Jo felt she was getting there.

'The science has come a long way,' she told him. 'We'll do everything we can to avoid disturbing anything we don't absolutely need to.'

He poured himself another brandy.

'Now you're sounding like a politician. I think I prefer it when you tell it like it is.'

'Anything that is disturbed will be reinstated,' she told him.

He slumped on the sofa.

'I can't believe it. Not of her. Now that Shaye, I could believe it of him. Real oddball he was. But not her.'

'You weren't here when the work was done?'

He shook his head.

'I was in the Caribbean with my girlfriend. Driffield said it would be best to do it while I was away. There'd be a lot of toing and froing, skips in the drive, noise, a lot of mess. It made sense. I'd planned to go away then anyway.'

'You agreed the design before you left?'

'I insisted on seeing the detail. I like to stay on top of everything. It's how I got to be where I am now.'

'We can apply for a warrant if you'd prefer?'

He gave her a knowing smile.

'Like a magistrate is going to turn down a request from the National Crime Agency? I don't think so. I've always cooperated with the law. That's why they've given me so many contracts. Besides, if I do it your way, it's on the condition you do everything in your power to minimise the publicity. I don't want the media crawling all over this place.'

'With those electronic gates and all that surveillance equipment, I'm sure you'll be fine.'

'You're joking. Unless you do something about it, there'll be helicopters and drones overhead, and paparazzi with zoom lenses on the fairways.'

'I promise we'll do everything we can,' she said, crossing her fingers.

Chapter 59

'This is Doctor Hendricks,' the crime scene manager told Jo. 'From the School of Chemical Engineering and Analytical Science at Manchester University. As soon as you told me we were talking about stone slabs laid over concrete, I knew a cadaver dog was out of the question. The same with ground-penetrating radar. Doctor Hendricks is keen to try out a new method developed in the States. I'll let him explain.'

Tall, thin and surprisingly young, Hendricks was excited by the prospect.

'The beauty of this method,' he said. 'Is that it is highly sensitive, specific to the matter in hand and hardly intrusive at all.'

'How intrusive is *hardly at all*?' asked a sceptical Terence Tucker.

'All it requires,' Hendricks replied, 'is a small hole drilled through the flagstone, the setting bed, and the concrete beneath.'

He held up a length of narrow gauge plastic.

'This tube is then inserted into the hole, and any gases detected are fed into this colorimeter.'

He pointed to a white cabinet by his side, the size of a small fridge.

'Bodily tissues break down as a body decomposes. As they do so, they release compounds containing nitrogen into pockets of air in the surrounding soil. When these compounds react with another compound called ninhydrin, they cause it to change colour. If the resultant colour happens to be a bluish-purple, then we can know for certain that a decomposing corpse is present.'

'Bloody hell!' Tucker exclaimed, imagining how many holes they might have to drill across the whole of his pristine patio.

'Of course we may not need to drill a hole at all at this point,' said Hendricks.

He pointed at the set of flagstones that ran from the foot of the steps to the start of the bridge.

'We could dig a small trench in the ground at the side, and then drill the hole beneath the floating concrete platform.'

'How small?'

'Thirty centimetres by one point eight metres. It depends on the thickness of the concrete.'

'You'd better get on with it then,' Tucker said grudgingly.

They reassembled thirty minutes later at the foot of the steps.

'We had to go down one and a half metres,' said the crime scene manager. 'I've never seen foundations like it. Not for flagstones.'

They watched as the scientist supervised the drilling of three boreholes, sideways into the soil, at half-metre intervals. Then Hendricks passed the tube to the technician crouching in the trench.

'Let's start with the one closest to the steps,' he said.

When the tube had been inserted as far as it would go, he asked for it to be retracted a centimetre or so.

'Right,' he said, crouching down in front of the colorimeter. 'Let's see what we've got.'

He opened the door revealing several black flasks, and a square panel showing rows of numbers.

'One of these flasks contains an amino acid, which has already been heated. I now insert the tube into this aperture.'

He fiddled around with the tube until he was satisfied, and then sat back on his heels. Jo craned forward, not quite sure what she was looking at. The numbers on the last line in the panel began to change. They finally came to rest at 501.

Hendricks shook his head.

'Promising,' he said. 'But inconclusive.'

He left the tube in the aperture and, turned to his colleague in the trench below.

'Try the middle one, Jane.'

His assistant withdrew the tube from the first of the holes, and inserted it into the second of the three.

Jo watched with bated breath as the numbers began to flicker. They began at 560, and fluctuated for a second or two, before settling at 590. Even from behind his back, she could tell that Hendricks was smiling.

'Five hundred and ninety nanometers,' he said. 'If we could see the colour of the liquid in that flask it would be a beautiful violet-blue.'

He turned to look up at them. Despite the triumph in his eyes, his tone was sombre.

'Ladies and gentlemen,' he said. 'You have yourselves a corpse.'

Chapter 60

It was gone midnight. An autumnal chill had replaced the heat of the day. Floodlights cast shadows on the canvas tent as ghostlike figures bent to their ghoulish task. Harry Stone had come out to join her.

'How does it feel to be vindicated?' he asked.

'More bitter than sweet,' she told him. 'It was the only way that we were going to nail them both. But think about all of the families and friends of those other missing persons still hoping that their loved ones are out there somewhere.'

'You've ended the uncertainty,' he reminded her. 'Given them the opportunity to grieve, and move on.'

Jo sighed.

'There's no way that all of these men could have been involved in the abuse of her brother. There's no evidence that they knew each other. They're geographically scattered. Two of them would have been barely out of primary school.'

The crime scene manager emerged from the tent, and wiped the back of a gloved hand across his hooded forehead.

'Ma'am, Sir,' he said. 'You'd best put your masks on.'

The blackened body lay on its back in a state of partial decomposition. The wrists were bound, the arms bent back on the chest. It appeared to be naked, except for something that lay across the pubis and genitals. Jo saw flashes of blue and gold in the harsh lights.

She heard Stone swear under his breath.

'It's a Masonic apron,' he said. 'Poor beggar would have had it in his briefcase when he was taken.'

'It's the same as Deighton,' she said. 'Except for the apron. That's an escalation of the ritual. That and the pick, the spade and the crow.'

'Speaking of which,' said the crime scene manager. 'My guys found something else while you were up at the house.'

He led them out of the tent, and around the side. He stopped by the statue of the male wolf. He called to one of his colleagues.

'Ben, can I borrow your torch?'

He aimed the beam at the underside of the wolf, in the centre of its belly. Incised into the stone, this mark was less distinct than the carving on the she-wolf. It looked like an inverted capital letter V.

Beside her, Jo felt Harry stiffen.

'It's the same sort of thing as the one on that tree at the Deighton crime scene, isn't it?' she said. 'Part of the cipher?'

He nodded.

'I'm afraid it is.'

She hardly dared ask.

'How bad is it?'

'It depends. If it's the Royal Arch cipher, then it stands for a lower case w.'

Jo's stomach knotted. She stood up. There was a bitter taste at the back of her throat.

'The twenty-third letter of the alphabet,' she whispered. 'Twenty-three. God help them.'

'We don't know that for certain,' said Stone. 'It could just be braggadocio.'

'You don't really believe that, Boss,' she said. 'When she can snatch people like Mr Hadfield from the street. Bury them under people's noses. What need would she have to exaggerate?'

She turned to the crime scene manager.

'That apron, can you rush the forensics tests? I'm especially interested in DNA, hair, foreign fibres, anything like that.'

'I'll do my best,' he said.

Chapter 61

The gruesome discovery ensured that both suspects were held without charge for the full ninety-six hours that the law permitted. With so many suspected murders, and two corpses already found, the NCA's role had finally been agreed. Jo would lead on the interviews, and take responsibility for charging both of them.

She had spent several hours with Andy Swift preparing the interview strategy based on his psychological profile of Lorna Driffield. With twenty-four hours left on the clock, Jo was ready. They went for Tamsey first.

Confronted with the evidence of his DNA on Hadfield's blindfold, balaclava, the ropes he used to tie him up, and the traces of his DNA on the binding around the victim's wrists in Tucker's garden, Tamsey immediately claimed sole responsibility.

'She had nothing to do with it,' he said. 'It was me. Everything was.'

'Why the Masonic apron, Shaye?' asked Jo.

He looked at his solicitor and then at her.

'Because he had it with him when I took him.'

'Tell me about the symbols carved into the stone plinth where you buried your victim?' she said. 'And in some of the gardens you worked on, that we're still checking?'

'What about them?'

'A pick, a spade and a crow. Why those?'

He shrugged.

'Why not?'

'Who chose them, Shaye?'

He shrugged again, and looked away.

She took two photographs from the folder, and laid them on the table in front of him. They were of the ciphers from the Deighton and Bolton crime scenes.

'Can you tell me what these symbols mean, Shaye?'

He stared at them, looked directly at her, held her gaze for a second or two, folded his arms, lowered his head and closed his eyes. In that brief moment, Jo knew that he had realised that no matter what he said, he would not be able to save his employer, lover, and partner in crime.

Lorna Driffield looked up as the two detectives entered the room. She smiled thinly at Jo as she and Gordon sat down.

'I wondered when you'd turn up.'

Jo addressed the solicitor.

'Is your client ready for us to begin, Mr Mayhew?'

'Certainly,' he replied. 'She would like to begin by reiterating her complete—'

Jo interrupted.

'Your client will have the opportunity to make any statement she wishes at the end of this interview. Until then, my colleague and I will be asking all of the questions.'

Gordon Holmes immediately launched into the formal procedure. When he had finished, Jo placed her elbows on the table and leaned forward.

'I have to remind you, Lorna,' she said, 'that you are still under arrest on suspicion of the abduction and false imprisonment of Martin Alexander Hadfield, and that this was extended at nine am this morning to the murder of a person whose remains have been discovered, but who has yet to be identified, as well as the suspected murder of Charles Deighton in Chorley in the County of Lancashire, among others yet to be specified. Your solicitor, as part of our pre-interview disclosure, has been informed of the circumstances surrounding your arrest and detention, and the purposes of this interview. Do you understand?'

'I'm sure it will all become clear,' Driffield said.

'I very much hope so,' Jo replied.

She nodded to Gordon Holmes, and opened the folder on the table in front of them.

'Perhaps we could begin,' said Holmes, 'by you telling us about a job that you did for a Mr Terence Tucker at his house in Bolton?'

'You don't have to answer that, Lorna,' Mayhew told her.

'I think I do,' said Driffield. 'After all, I have nothing to hide.' She smiled as though what she had just said amused her. 'It was quite a challenge. One of my most impressive achievements, I like to think.' She smiled again. 'Terry was very happy with it.'

'Terry?' said Holmes.

'Mr Tucker,' said Driffield.

'I doubt he's happy with it now,' said Holmes.

It was typical of Gordon, thought Jo. He had to make the odd quip. He couldn't help himself. Sometimes it had the desired effect of rattling the suspect. On this occasion it had the opposite effect.

'I'll be happy to restore it to its original condition at the taxpayer's expense,' Driffield responded. 'Isn't that what happens when the police damage someone's property?'

Jo selected the first of the photographs from the file, and placed it on the table facing Driffield.

'Tell us about the wolves,' she said.

Driffield's eyebrows arched.

'Striking, aren't they?'

'What are they supposed to represent, Lorna?'

Driffield began to smile. Her lips drew back to reveal a little of the gums, and her eyes dilated. Jo thought it a conscious effort rather than an instinctive response. Driffield was playing with them.

'What do *you* think?' Driffield asked.

'I don't know, Lorna. Why don't you tell us?'

'Because that would be too easy.'

'This isn't a game,' said Holmes.

Driffield switched her gaze to him.

'Isn't it?'

'So this is a game in which people get killed?' he retorted. 'Is that what you're saying?'

'I didn't say that. This is a game in which you try to put words into my mouth, and my role is to resist.' She turned to Jo. 'Isn't that right, Senior Investigator Stuart?'

She had, Jo reflected, all of the characteristics of an intelligent and accomplished liar. She was not only deflecting their questions, but also attempting to take the initiative by ending every response with a question of her own. With all of the evidence they now had, there was no point in taking this slowly. It was time to go for the jugular. She selected another photograph.

'You chose to use a pick, a spade and a crow as your signature on the plinth supporting the she-wolf at Mr Tucker's house.'

Driffield folded her arms, and sat back.

'Is that a question?'

'No it isn't,' Jo replied. 'It's an observation. We have already discovered the same inscription in two more gardens that you designed, one on a flagstone and another on a plinth.'

'Both of which were Shaye Tamsey's work,' said Driffield, flagging up the direction of her defence.

Jo shook her head.

'The owners have confirmed that you specifically asked if you could leave your mark in this way.'

Driffield shrugged.

'So?'

'Would you care to tell us the origin of those three symbols placed together in that way?'

Her solicitor leaned in towards her.

'You don't have to answer that.'

'I don't see why not,' Driffield replied. 'Seeing as how it's perfectly innocent.' She searched the faces of the officers opposite. 'And they already know. The pick, the spade and the crow are the tools of the Master Mason.'

'The Royal Arch Mason,' said Jo. 'To be precise.'

'There you go then,' said Driffield. 'Our stonework, Shaye's and mine, is traditionally carried out by masons. What more appropriate mark should we choose?'

Jo placed a third photograph on the table alongside the others. Mayhew craned forward to see. She saw him wince.

'Can you tell us what this is?' Jo asked.

Driffield pretended to scrutinise it. Then sat back, and shrugged.

'It looks like a corpse,' she said, with a fair attempt at a shiver. 'It's horrible.' She turned to look at her solicitor. 'How could he do that? *Why* would he do that?'

'I was referring to this,' said Jo, indicating the apron with the tip of her biro.

Once again, Driffield leaned forward, shrugged, and sat back in her chair.

'Don't know. You tell me.'

'This is the apron traditionally worn by a Mason during Royal Arch rituals,' said Gordon Holmes.

Driffield shrugged.

'If you say so, I've never seen it before.'

The two detectives looked at each other, and smiled.

'It's funny you should say that,' said Jo.

Slowly and deliberately, she took two sheets of A4 paper, and laid them down on the table side by side.

'These are DNA results,' she said. 'Comparing samples taken from the apron found beneath your landscaping in Mr Tucker's garden, with those from the oral swabs taken from your employee Shaye Tamsey and yourself.'

The first sheet contained four vertical columns of short bars in various shades of black and grey. The second contained a table with five headings: STR Locus, Crime Scene Evidence Sample, Suspect A, Suspect B, and Suspect B's Genotype Frequency for each STR. Under each heading was a set of numbers. It was obvious, even to the untrained eye, that on both of the sheets the data for the crime scene evidence, and that for Suspect B, were identical.

Despite herself, Lorna Driffield found it impossible not to study the evidence in front of her. Jo noted, with a frisson of excitement, the moment that her eyes dilated and her shoulders drooped.

'As you can see, Lorna,' Jo said, 'there is an incontrovertible match between DNA retrieved from that apron, and one of the suspects.'

'The chances of such a match are put at one in one point five billion,' said Gordon Holmes.

'Which of the two of you, Lorna, is Suspect B, would you say?' said Jo.

Driffield had slumped in her seat. There was no smart retort and, although her lips were moving, no impertinent question on the tip of her tongue. She appeared to be singing to herself. Jo leaned forward in the hope of hearing what it was.

The words were indistinct, but she detected the unpleasant musty odour that she had noticed on many suspects in the past. It was the stench of defeat.

Chapter 62

'What do you think?' asked Gordon Holmes. 'Will she play, or will she fold?'

Mayhew had asked for a break so that he could consult with his client. They had no objection. Driffield was dead in the water, whatever happened. Andy Swift had left the observation room and joined them.

'Fold,' said Jo. 'The more she'd convinced herself that she could hold out, that Tamsey would take the blame, and that there was nothing other than circumstantial evidence to connect her to these crimes, the harder this will have hit. And, no matter what justification *she* thought she had for murdering all these men, deep down she must know that it was wrong. Suppressing that level of guilt for so long is like trying to plug a volcano. Sooner or later it has to burst.'

Andy rubbed his chin with a vengeance.

'Unless she's a real psycho, an Ian Brady type,' he said. 'Then she won't be capable of guilt. I think she's a borderline psychopath. Shaye Tamsey is a conundrum.'

'He's stayed loyal to Driffield,' said Gordon. 'He was never going to give her up. She's a cold and manipulative cow.'

'A she-wolf,' said Jo. 'A predator.'

Holmes opened the door of the observation room, and stood back to let Jo enter. They were met with universal approval.

'Well done,' said Helen Gates. 'All that's left now is to give her the opportunity to explain herself. We have the means, the opportunity, and forensic evidence that she was involved. The icing on the cake will be to have her confess and admit her motivation.'

'If Mayhew lets her,' said the woman from the Crown Prosecution Service.

Gates shook her head.

'My hunch is that she'll want to explain herself, either because she needs to or because, in some sick way, she believes that it will be accepted as mitigation when it comes to sentencing.'

'She might actually be proud of what she's done, and want to boast about it, like Dahmer, Ramirez, and Ted Bundy,' suggested DI Renton. He had come down from Lancashire in the hope that Driffield would make his life easier by admitting the Deighton killing.

'I don't believe she's that kind of killer.' Andy Swift spoke softly, and with authority. 'And I would advise against any interview strategy that went down that route.'

He turned to Jo and Gordon.

'Just before you switched off the tapes, did either of you notice something odd about her?'

'The singing, and that rocking signing thing she did?' said Holmes. 'Like they do in loony bins?'

'Psychiatric hospitals,' said Helen Gates, in a rebuke that was lost on Gordon.

'I couldn't make out what she was singing though,' said Jo.

'Me neither,' said Gordon.

'Then you may want to look at this,' he told them. 'We've had it slowed down and amplified.'

The technician pressed the play button. On the screen, in slow motion, they could see Gordon reaching across to stop the tapes,

Jo replacing the photographs in her folder, Mayhew staring at his client, and Lorna Driffield rocking almost imperceptibly as her lips moved. The words, indistinct in the room were now discernible. She was singing 'Falling to pieces', over and over again.

'We googled it,' said Helen Gates, nodding to the technician. He stopped the recording, turned to another screen, clicked History at the top of the screen, and selected a saved link. A video began to play. They saw a naked woman morph into a lone wolf pursued by hunters across a bleak, snow-covered landscape. There was a haunting song, and an insistent beat.

'It's called "She Wolf" by David Guetta,' Andy Swift told them as they watched with uneasy fascination.

'The video was released in September 2012,' said Swift. 'She must have seen it and cast herself as the she-wolf, and her victims as the deer referred to in the song. Except that right now, she's reverted to seeing herself as the victim, and you two as the hunters.'

'What I don't understand,' said Holmes, 'is why she went after Mr Hadfield when she must have known that SI Stuart suspected her?'

'I don't think she realised that he was a police officer, let alone an assistant chief constable,' said Jo. 'All of the abductions had the hallmark of opportunism. All they had to do was find the nearest Masonic Lodge to their latest project. Check when the meetings ended. Pick one off when the time was right and the opportunity presented itself.'

'Time was right?' said Renton.

'When they had a hole prepared, and the householder away. Mr Hadfield's abduction was probably intended as a diversion. Except that the householder in Alderley Edge came home early and blew her plans out of the water. Otherwise he would have disappeared just like the others.'

'I bet that's what happened with Charles Deighton,' said DI Renton. 'They had to improvise, and that was the best they could come up with.'

'We'll know for sure,' said Jo. 'Once we've found the garden they were working on at the time.'

There was a knock on the door. The custody sergeant walked in.

'Mr Mayhew says they're ready for you.'

Chapter 63

'I suspected that something bad was going on.'

Lorna Driffield seemed to have shrunk into herself. The sense of physical power and overweening confidence had melted away. When she spoke, it was like a reflective monologue, rather than an explanation.

'I was too young to know about sexual abuse. I just knew that Bradley had changed. He started having nightmares. He wet the bed, soiled his pants. I was the one who had to clear it up. Mum was too wasted to care. Brad stopped mixing at school. He became a loner. Used to be a chatterbox, now he was secretive.'

Her hands became fists. She took a deep breath.

'One night after he brought Bradley home, I challenged him.'

'Lorna,' Jo's tone was empathetic, 'I'm sorry to interrupt, but when you say *he,* can you remind us who you are referring to?'

Driffield looked confused. Surely they knew?

'For the tape,' Jo said.

Driffield followed Jo's pointing finger.

'The Beast!' she said, spitting out the words. '*Uncle* Ralph: the Beast.'

'Ralph Bates?' Jo prompted.

She nodded.

'For the tape, please, Lorna.'

She locked eyes with Jo. There was no anger or challenge in them, only unfathomable sadness.

'Ralph Bates,' she said.

It seemed for a moment that she lost the thread of her narrative.

'You challenged Bates?' said Jo.

Lorna nodded.

'I asked what was going on that was making Brad so miserable. He grabbed my arm and twisted it up my back. Then he marched me to where the trapdoor was, and dragged back the carpet with his heel. I knew what he was going to do. I was terrified. I started kicking back at him. I tried to bite his hand but he grabbed my hair and yanked my head back. Then he opened the trap and pushed me in. I tried to get out but he stamped on my fingers, then he slammed the door shut and locked me in.'

Suddenly she began to shake. Her face was unnaturally pale. She seemed unable to get her breath. Jo began to rise from her seat, and Driffield's solicitor reached out towards his client. Her eyes rolled upwards as she fell sideways into his open arms.

⌣

'It was a vasovagal faint,' the police surgeon told them a few minutes later. 'Not uncommon. It's caused by stress, heat, dehydration, confined spaces. She's suffered on and off with them since her teens. It's all there in her medical record.'

'Is it okay to continue the interview?' Jo asked.

'Absolutely. Only I'd make sure she has plenty of water, and leave the door slightly ajar.'

⌣

'I stayed out of his way after that,' Driffield said, continuing. 'I did try to raise it with our mum but it was a waste of time. The sun shone out of his arse as far as she was concerned, yet at the same time she was terrified of him.'

She looked at Jo.

'That's what control is all about, isn't it?'

Jo wondered if Lorna was referring to her own hold over Shay Tamsey and her victims, or to Bates's hold over her mother.

'By the time I was about to start high school, I was tougher, more streetwise. I'd figured out what was going on. I waited till Brad and I were alone in the house, and got it out of him.'

She paused for a sip of water. Put her plastic cup down and carried on.

'I waited for the Beast to come home, then I confronted him. I told him I'd been to the police and they were coming for him.'

'Had you?' asked Gordon Holmes. 'Been to the police?'

Jo nudged him, but Driffield had not been fazed by the interruption.

'No,' she replied. 'But he didn't hang around to find out. He just brushed past me, got his things from Mum's room, put them in a case and left. As soon as he'd gone, I went down to the police station and made a statement.'

'What did they do, Lorna?' Jo asked.

'They came round in the morning and spoke to our mother. They wanted to know if there was any truth in it.'

She grimaced.

'What was she going to do? Admit that she'd turned a blind eye to the abuse of her son, or that she'd been too weak, and too off her head to stop it?'

'So she refused to corroborate your statement?'

Lorna shrugged.

'I suppose so. I don't know. I wasn't allowed in the room.'

'What about Bradley? Didn't they believe him?'

'They didn't even question him.' Her expression was scornful, her voice full of contempt. 'Why do you think there are all these historical inquiries into child abuse? Nobody listened to us then, just like they don't listen to victims of rape now.'

Neither Jo nor Gordon had a reply to that.

'How did you know that Ralph Bates was a member of the Freemasons?' Jo asked.

Driffield was surprised by the change in direction. She had another drink, and wiped her mouth with the back of her hand. When she replied, she seemed more alert and composed, and her expression had hardened.

'Sometimes he would arrive to take Bradley out wearing a black overcoat over a dress suit, and carrying a black case. When he brought Bradley back, he'd leave it on the table in the hall. One day, while he was upstairs, I took a peek inside. There was a pair of white gloves, an apron, a diary, and a badge with his name on it. *Ralph.*'

She turned to her solicitor.

'Those gloves represent the fact that all members of a Lodge are equal, and the work they do together is pure in thought and deed.'

She turned back to face the police officers.

'Like the work they did together at Brock House.'

'Did you follow him there, Lorna?' Jo asked.

She shook her head.

'So how did you know about it?'

'Bradley told me. After it burned down.'

'Did Bradley burn it down?'

Driffield slowly shook her head.

'I don't know.'

She turned to her solicitor again.

'I don't wish to answer any more questions,' she said.

'That's your prerogative,' he replied.

Driffield looked at Jo. Her expression was resolute.

'No Comment,' she said.

Chapter 64

'What if she pleads insanity?' asked Gordon Holmes. 'I mean, who in their right mind would do what they did?'

'Lorna Driffield, for one,' Jo told him as they reached the door to the debriefing room. 'You heard what Mayhew said. She's refused to go down that route. She regards herself as righteously vengeful. Those murders took place over more than ten years. They were carefully targeted, planned and executed. They were carried out in cold blood. She stood there staring into the eyes of her innocent victims, feeding off their terror as Tamsey shovelled the soil on top. But that doesn't mean that she's insane.'

She opened the door.

They were met with smiles and nods of approval, but no applause. It didn't seem appropriate.

'The CPS say you can go ahead and charge her,' said Harry Stone who had joined the others to observe the interview.

'With ACC Hadfield's abduction, the murder of Charles Deighton and the yet to be identified remains in Bolton?' Jo guessed.

'And with the abduction and murder of Norbert Welsh,' said DS Coppull.

'Norbert Welsh?'

'They've located his corpse,' Coppull told her. 'Under the patio at a house in Worsley.'

It felt as though a cold hand had clutched Jo's heart.

'Oh no,' she said. 'Please don't tell me it was . . .'

Her words stuck in her throat.

Coppull finished the sentence for her.

'Edgerton House? I'm afraid so.'

'Don't beat yourself up, Jo,' Harry told her. 'You weren't to know, and even if you did it would have been too late to save him.'

Jo was remembering the smile on Driffield's face, as she put the finishing touches to his burial chamber. She had been standing on top of Welsh's grave as she spoke with his murderer. It was yet another memory that would haunt her. Worse still, she would have to recount it all from the witness box in front of his widow.

'I thought you said she felt guilty?' said Detective Chief Superintendent Gates. 'There wasn't much sign of that.'

'About what happened to Bradley.' Jo replied. 'About not having been able to prevent the abuse, and then not having been able to stop him taking his own life.'

'Not for killing all those men?'

'No. I get the impression she's relieved that it's finally over, but that's all.'

'She falls into the category of a Power and Control Killer,' said Andy Swift. 'When she began to abduct and kill those men, she will have felt an overwhelming rush, a sense of omnipotence. It would have helped to relieve the anxiety and stress that she was feeling. It will also have reversed the sense of powerlessness that lay behind her guilt. It's no surprise that it became an obsession.'

'The revenge paradox,' said Jo, recalling their conversation when she had first started investigating the murder of Charles Deighton. 'Taking revenge rarely leads to closure. It's like picking the top off a scab and revealing the wound beneath.'

The psychologist nodded.

'It became an addiction for her. The more she killed, the more emotionally numb she became, and the more detached from normal life. Spiritually dead if you like.'

'What I don't understand,' said DI Renton, 'is why she picked at random on apparently innocent Masons?'

'Scenes of crime officers,' said Gates, 'found a small library of books and articles at the farmhouse about alleged involvement of renegade Masons in ritual child abuse.'

'It's the first I've heard of this?' said Coppull.

'That,' said Jo, 'is because most of the allegations originated in the States, and in Australia. There's a strong Christian element behind most of the allegations, which is ironic when you think about it. The Mormons come in for criticism too. But, as the historic abuse investigations over here deepen, I suppose it's inevitable that among the rich and famous and powerful who are being implicated, there will have been some Freemasons. Like the Christian churches, it's not about the institution – it's about individual members who have their own evil agenda. Their own perverted desires. When Driffield failed to track Bates down, she unleashed her retribution on the first Mason she came across who matched his profile. After that it escalated.'

'If she *did* fail to track him down,' said Ram Shah.

They turned to look at him.

'Ask yourself why he never resurfaced,' he said. 'It's like he was a ghost. Maybe he was the first? Maybe he was one of the others?'

'We'll never know, unless she tells us,' said Jo.

Gordon Holmes shook his head.

'I wouldn't hold your breath,' he said.

Chapter 65

It was late when Jo closed the door and switched off the alarm.

'Abbie?'

Her voice echoed around the empty apartment. She went through to the lounge, dropped her bag on the floor by the sofa, and went into the open-plan kitchen.

It was their practice to leave messages for each other under the magnets on the fridge door. There was only one message, two days old.

Don't forget this afternoon! 1.30pm prompt.

She crumpled it in her hand, and dropped it in the pedal bin.

Then she walked over to the phone and checked for voice messages. There were none. For the first time in over six years, she had no one with whom to share her success, let alone her worries or her failures.

Jo sat on the sofa, and took out her mobile phone. She had seven Facebook notifications, and three invitations to play *Candy Crush*. There were also invitations to claim her PPIs and change her bank passwords, and several genuine emails. One was from head office in Pimlico informing her that she'd been booked on to the next NCA firearms training course at the SAS Killing House. There were no replies to the score of texts she had sent to Abbie.

She put the phone down, rested her head on the sofa and stared at the ceiling. Outside on the city streets, the nightlife would be moving towards a crescendo that would last until the early hours. Here she sat with an emptiness in the pit of her stomach that was beyond hunger, and all of the aches and pains resurfacing that adrenalin and anti-inflammatories had held at bay. *If this is loneliness*, she thought, *it stinks*. One thing was certain – weary as she was, sleep would not come easily.

Jo stood up, slipped off her jacket, and dropped it on top of her bag. She walked to the fridge, and found a half bottle of Sauvignon Blanc with a cork rammed into the neck. She took a glass from the cupboard, and filled it to the brim. Then she returned to the sofa, placed the bottle and the glass on the coffee table, and reached for the TV remote.

Her phone rang. It was Max Nailor.

'Are you alright, Jo?' he asked.

'I'm fine,' she lied.

'Only you didn't come back to the Holiday Inn for that celebratory drink. We were wondering where you were?'

'I just didn't feel like it,' she said.

'I understand.'

It sounded as though he really did. A comfortable silence settled between them like a bridge.

'I could bring a bottle over if you'd like to talk?' he said. 'Maybe pick up a takeaway? You must be starving? I know I am.'

Jo thought about it. Tomorrow really was another day. Perhaps Abbie would return her calls. Maybe even want to meet up. Perhaps they could work it out? In the meantime, there was at least one person who cared. And Max was really making an effort.

It would be silly to knock him back, especially since they were supposed to be partners.

'I'd like that,' she said.

'Brilliant!' he replied. 'Chinese, Indian, pizza?'

'Surprise me,' she said.

Acknowledgements

I wish to acknowledge the following whose specialist knowledge and technical advice has been invaluable: former GMP Officers – Chief Superintendent Brian Roe and Gordon Ritchie; former Scotland Yard Senior Forensic Science SOCO and Visiting Lecturer at Thames Valley University, Anthony Wood; Barbara and Carlton Catterall and Stephen 'Wally' Walsh, for Secret Services rendered.

My special thanks go to everyone at Amazon Publishing UK, and their Thomas & Mercer imprint team. In particular, Emilie Marneur for coaxing me over to the dark side after six years of total freedom; my editor, Jane Snelgrove, for leading me through the process with great wisdom and sensitivity; editor Jenny Parrott, and copy editor Monica Byles for their ability to get inside my head, their meticulous attention to detail, and their brilliant advice.

And finally, to anyone who has read my previous crime novels, without whom this series would not have been born.

Bill Rogers
August 2016

About the Author

Photo: Paul Whur, 2015

Bill Rogers has written ten earlier crime fiction novels featuring DCI Tom Caton and his team, set in and around Manchester. The first of these, *The Cleansing*, was shortlisted for the Long Barn Books Debut Novel Award, and was awarded the e-Publishing Consortium Writers Award 2011. *The Pick, The Spade and The Crow* is the first in a spin-off series featuring SI Joanne Stuart, on secondment to the Behavioural Sciences Unit at the National Crime Agency, located in Salford Quay, Manchester. Formerly a teacher and schools inspector, Bill has four generations of Metropolitan Police behind him. He is married with two adult children and lives near Manchester.